IN TH
of the
Serpent

CAROLE CARGAL REEVES

CAPSTONE FICTION

WATERFORD, VIRGINIA

To Corrie
I would love
to see you again.
You were always
one of my sweethearts.
Carole Reeves
2007

In the Eyes of the Serpent

Published in the U.S. by:
Capstone Publishing Group LLC
P.O. Box 8
Waterford, VA 20197

Visit Capstone Fiction at
www.capstonefiction.com

Cover design by David LaPlaca/debest design co.
Cover image, starburst © iStockphoto.com/Graeme Purdy
Cover image, serpent © iStockphoto.com/Aleksandar Velasevic

ISBN: 978-1-60290-043-1

To my loving husband, Bill,
who never stopped believing in me,
and to the three greatest children
in the world—
Mark, Marion, and Jonathan.

Acknowledgments

I have many people to thank:

First, a special thanks to Ramona Tucker and Jeff Nesbit, two wonderful people at Capstone Publishing Group, who were willing to take a chance on an unknown writer.

To Nancy Irish, my longtime and faithful friend, who encouraged and prayed for me.

To all those kind friends and loved ones who read my manuscript and provided suggestions, especially Hal Schell, Mark Reeves, Dick Briggs, and my sister, Jane Dickinson.

A special thanks goes to my husband, Bill, who overlooked late dinners and never tired of talking me through difficult passages.

An especial thanks to my parents, Wyatt and Helen Cargal, who are now with the Lord. Without their encouragement to strive for the stars and to be all that God has called me to be, I would have given up long ago.

And, above all, to a loving, fantastic God who hears our prayers and makes the unimaginable a reality.

The Nephilim were on the earth in those days—
and also afterward—
when the sons of God went to the daughters of men
and had children by them.
They were the heroes of old, men of renown.
Genesis 6:4

PROLOGUE

Out of the mists of time, humankind emerged and multiplied upon the face of the tiny blue planet, farming the land, fishing the waters, and building great cities.

The oral traditions of the Old Ones claimed life had begun where the four rivers flowed—the Pison, the Gihon, the Hiddehel, and the Euphrates. Over the centuries many of the people forgot not only the Old Ones who had taught them but also the Old Ways themselves. Only the Stargazers continued to believe in Yah-Adon, the Great Light, the One who had hung the luminaries in the dark firmament. It was He, they said, who had emblazoned a message across the heavens, a story written in the stars, promising a mighty warrior king who would one day free the people from the powers of evil threatening to engulf their world.

Unknown to them, Yah-Adon was already engaged in a great conflict with the spirits of darkness, entities led by Abaddon, the Destroyer, who desired the destruction of humankind. For many years these demonic beings had remained inactive, withdrawing to a remote corner of the universe until once again they were ready to marshal their dark forces to attack man, the work of Yah-Adon, their ancient nemesis. The time had arrived.

One

Time: Two hundred years prior to the Great Flood
Place: Land west of the Fertile Crescent

Utriel hesitated at the edge of the lake. An uneasiness gnawed at the edge of her consciousness. She glanced toward the bank where she had dropped her tunic. It lay as she had left it, lingering patches of early morning mist still hovering above the surface of the water. She tilted her head and listened before wading into the chilling water, shivering as it lapped around her young, strong legs. With each step the soft mud oozed between her toes and swirled darkly about her feet.

Again, she paused and scanned the bank.

"Jirad!" she shouted. "Is that you?"

Was her twin trying to frighten her? It would be just like him. He did not want her coming to the lake by herself. "You are no longer a child," he admonished. "It's not safe to roam the countryside. I know my friends. Just because our father is a tribal elder gives you no protection."

Such a worrier! The morning was beautiful, not a day to worry or wear a frown.

She waded farther into the cool water and inhaled the strong, spicy fragrances emanating from the huge clusters of white, red, and yellow lilies undulating in the water, their flat, green leaves floating on the surface.

She loosened her hair, letting the thick, chestnut strands tumble about her shoulders. She stood motionless until the ripples cleared and the image of a girl barely beyond childhood stared back. Dark lashes brushed smooth, high-boned cheeks, and large, hazel eyes peered from a face considered beautiful by many in Gibara-boni in spite of the stubborn squareness to her jaw.

She placed her index finger on the tip of her nose and wiggled it, wondering if she would like it better turned up instead of its straight, sculptured line. She grimaced and splashed the surface, sending a spray high into the air. Each tiny droplet caught the morning light and fell like minuscule suns upon her upturned face. She cupped her hands and filled them, raising her arms to watch the sparkling liquid trickle down her sun-darkened skin. She drew in a breath, preparing to plunge beneath the surface.

The skin prickled on the back of her neck; her muscles tensed. Not a sound was emanating from the forest, not even the trill of a bird or the scurrying of an animal among the trees and bushes. Her eyes scoured the rocky shoreline. White seed puffs drifted in the still air, several catching in her sun-burnished hair. She saw nothing, yet an inner sense warned her. Something was out there, something that did not want to be seen.

She clasped her hands over her nakedness and sank into the water. Tilting her head, she listened for a snapping twig or a rustling branch, but her heart drummed within her head, obscuring all outside noise.

Seized by an uncontrollable panic, she spun in the water, first one way, then another, straining to see the unseen. It could not be her imagination for the unnatural silence in the forest was real. She drew in her breath and struggled toward shore, her arms still clutched across her chest.

At the edge of the bank, her foot slipped in the soft mud. She caught herself, then scrambled to her feet, grabbed her clothes, and fled into the thicket, running like a gazelle with the scent of an unseen enemy fresh in its nostrils. Her hair flew about her head, a hawthorn branch whipped across her face. She stumbled and crashed to her knees, her long strands of hair tangling in its thorns. With a high-pitched whimper, she yanked at her hair with both hands, ripping it from its snare. Her sense of direction momentarily skewed, she paused, her eyes wide with fright, then fled through the underbrush, oblivious to the torn flesh or the warm blood running down her leg.

Utriel did not stop until she reached the edge of the clearing. Once there, she gasped and pressed her hands against the pain piercing her side. She turned toward the lake expecting to see her pursuer crashing through the brush. All was still, only the leaves shifting in the morning breeze. She whispered a prayer of thanks and bent over, hands on knees, to catch her breath.

Visible through the trees were the low, sprawling, baked-brick buildings of her father's compound outside the fortified walls of Gibaraboni. Several of his women were scurrying around open fires as they prepared food to break the night's fast, the mingled aromas of thick, roasted yams and hot, baked bread heavy in the air.

She wiped her face with her tunic, then yanked it over her head. She dashed unseen across the open ground, running between the buildings, her lean body dodging a pack of rangy, yellow-brown dogs scavenging through garbage tossed from the surrounding houses.

When she reached the main house where she lived with Bithra, her father's chief wife, she stopped, suddenly conscious of her appearance. She leaned against the side of the building and took a deep breath before tiptoeing to a large jar standing by the door. She dipped her hands into its cool water and rubbed her burning face, wincing as the water stung the cut on her cheek. Only then did she see the streaks of dried blood and dirt on her knees and legs. She dabbed at the cuts, taking care not to restart the bleeding.

Voices drifted through the doorway. She stepped closer and listened, catching the high, strident tones of Bithra and the occasional low rumble of her father. She glanced over her shoulder, then smoothed her disheveled hair with both hands and picked up the clay jar.

The woman raised her head as Utriel entered the room. Obed lay sprawled on a dark fur by the eating mat. His barrel chest shook as he coughed loudly, wiping the back of his hand across his grizzled beard.

His once dark hair strained at its binding, loose strands springing like newly carded wool around his large, square face.

Her brother stood, feet splayed and hands on hips. He spoke no word, but his eyes signaled a warning. He was a replica of his sister, only more angular. His chiseled features were coarser, but he had the same hazel eyes and long, brown lashes, the same dark, reddish-brown hair, his barely touching his shoulders. A sparse beard covered his chin.

"Where have you been?" demanded Bithra, her small, close-set eyes flashed in her round face. "I was ready to send Jirad to look for you. Have you no care that you are needed to prepare the meal?" She stirred the thick porridge several times with a flat, wooden spatula, and shook her head. "I don't know what to do with you. Your mind always seems to be wandering outside of your body." She turned to her husband. "Obed, if you don't speak to the girl about her behavior, no man will want her for a wife."

Her father brandished an understanding look at his daughter but frowned when he saw her flushed and sweating face. "Where have you been?" He broke off a chunk of white cheese from a slab lying on the mat before him, tossed the piece into his mouth and chewed, his eyes studying hers.

Utriel bit her lower lip while picking up a flat loaf of hot, dark bread and began pulling it apart. "I've been to the lake."

"By yourself?" bellowed Jirad.

"Don't shout!" She brushed back a strand of hair. "I was careful."

"Something happened, didn't it?"

"I'm all right. I can take care of myself."

"Then how did you get the scratches on your face? And why are you so red?"

"I was running." She flinched inwardly, already wishing she had not lied. She added, "I knew Bithra would need me."

Obed shrugged and chuckled, exposing a large gap between his two front teeth. "Leave her alone," he mumbled. "She'll talk when she wants. She's stubborn like me."

Jirad removed a robe of finely woven brown wool before dropping onto the furs and rugs surrounding heavy, clay bowls filled with steaming lentils. "At least," he said, suppressing a grin, "she did place a full jar of water at the door."

Utriel blushed with shame and kept her eyes on the food she was serving. No doubt he had filled the jar and left it beside the entrance. He had always protected her, even as a child. He was the thoughtful one, the deliberate one, the peacemaker who dispelled many squabbles she had thoughtlessly created among their peers. "After all," he would tell her, "I came into this world first," to which she invariably added, "But never forget, I was hanging onto your foot."

"Enough," Bithra chided petulantly. "The food grows cold. Let's eat before the day is gone."

Utriel puckered her face and stuck out her tongue behind the woman's back. Jirad stifled a laugh, but Obed roared.

"Eat your food," snapped Bithra, sopping a large piece of bread in her remaining broth.

Utriel picked at the spicy legumes. "I'm not hungry."

"Watch your mouth, girl," ordered Obed. He ran the back of his large, callused hand across his lips and beard, then wiped it down the front of his chest.

Food was the farthest thing from Utriel's mind. She wanted to share her frightening experience with Jirad, but the apprehension that he would scold her again for going to the lake alone or, even worse, call her fears foolish kept her silent. They had always had such fun together. Only recently, at Bithra's insistence, had she stopped wrestling with him. While growing up they had been equals. Now that they had stepped into adulthood, she felt unsure of herself, and she could not bear the thought of possible ridicule from her twin, although she ached to tell him.

No, the time was not right. Perhaps, though, the old holy woman Ganah would know what had frightened her and made the forest silent.

When the meal was over, Bithra gathered the bowls. "Utriel, throw the scraps to the dogs. And don't leave before you've finished your chores."

Conscious of the older woman's eyes upon her, the girl kept her own averted as she hurried about her tasks. Although Bithra had raised the two children, Utriel had never felt close to her, for she was either angry or impatient, and her face always wore a scowl. The two children had learned that life was more pleasant when out of her presence and had spent most of their young days roaming the countryside or playing at the lake.

During that time, the beautiful and precocious little girl had caught the eye of Ganah, the ancient Ulah-rah of the Sethites. The old woman had no children of her own, and she found great joy and amusement in the lonely child. A strong bond quickly formed between the two with Utriel spending long hours sitting at the prophetess' feet to learn the stories and traditions of her people.

As soon as Utriel finished helping Bithra, she wiped her hands on her skirt. "I'm going to Ganah's," she said.

"Why do you spend so much time with her?" asked the woman. "She has outlived her usefulness."

"How can you say such a thing?"

"Because it is true. Few pay any heed to what the old crone says."

Utriel stared incredulously at her father's wife. "She is the voice of Yah-Adon," she said, and the sacred keeper of the Old Ways. But more than that . . . she is my friend and teacher."

The older woman shook her head in exasperation and waved her hands. "Go, then. Go see your holy woman."

Utriel grabbed a scrap of cheese and ran from the room, knocking over one of the smaller children playing by the entrance.

Bithra walked to the doorway and watched the girl dart between the buildings. She sighed and rubbed her chest.

Utriel ran, weaving her way among the low brick houses scattered outside the thick, stone walls of Gibara-boni. Many times she had uttered prayers of thanks to Yah-Adon that her father's ancestor, leader of one of the four tribes, had long ago chosen not to seek safety within the walls. He had understood the necessity of those who farmed, also remaining outside the town, to defend it from the tribes of barbarous plainsmen that periodically raided and pillaged the land. Never could she imagine herself living within the confines of the walls, amid the dirt and the noise.

When she reached the gate, the town was alive with activity. Already townspeople and animals trampled the narrow ways, turning them into dust. Ass and goat dung littered the streets, adding to the already pungent smells within the walls. Dark-faced old men displayed their wares stacked within open wooden stalls, each merchant hawking his own in a loud, strident voice. Chattering women drifted through doorways, some with deep baskets piled high with flat loaves of dark bread or fresh fruit from the orchards, others with dirty-faced children clinging to their skirts.

Utriel ran through the crowded streets, dodging the stalls and milling people. She ignored the lewd gestures of two young men and turned a deaf ear to their vulgar calls. If she told Obed of their disrespect, heads would be cracked before evening.

Unaware of the beauty blossoming in her slender body, she could never have imagined how her angular face stirred the passions of men, both young and old. Or the allure of her wide, generous lips that alternated between laughter and an unconscious hint of petulance. Or the tempting curves of her long, shapely legs.

Utriel paused outside Ganah's house long enough to catch her breath. Although the house was modest in size, hundreds of colored tiles outlined every doorway, even the small, slit-like windows. Time had dulled the reds, blues, and yellows, but the skill and beauty of the workmanship was still evident. Each intricate, painted tile—sprawling trees, delicate flowers, twining serpents, and exquisitely formed figures of animals and humans—depicted stories told by the old woman.

Ganah, Ulah-rah of the Stargazers, as they were derisively called by surrounding tribes, had been dedicated to Yah-Adon since she was a young girl, but to Utriel she was much more.

A mountainous figure stood by the entrance to the house, his eyes mere slits nearly buried in a fleshy face, massive arms crossed over a huge stomach. Eliah the Tumulac stood guard night and day before the Ulah-rah's house. At the sight of the young woman, he nodded and shifted his mammoth bulk to one side.

The door to the dwelling was made of dark, ancient wood. Marks from an obsidian edge patterned its surface, but age had produced a rich patina. Heavy hinges of bronze and thick leather, replaced many times over the decades, secured it in place. Utriel lifted the latch and pushed the door. "Ganah," she called. She did not step into the room, for custom prohibited a person from entering another's house unless invited. Again she called, "Ganah? Are you resting?"

"Enter, child," a husky voice replied. "I hoped you would come."

Utriel stepped inside, blinking as her eyes adjusted to the dim light filtering through the small openings in the walls.

Reclining on a pallet, among an array of furs and brightly dyed cloths, lay an old woman, thin and frail, her skin like tanned leather. Long, steel-gray hair hung loosely around a lined face that, in spite of its age, still evidenced a former fierce beauty. She looked to be at least three hundred years old. She was, however, well over seven.

"Come here, my child," motioned the Ulah-rah, her faded, blue-gray eyes squinting in the dim light. She shifted several cushions covered in shades of blue and ochre.

Utriel sank to the floor and placed her hands in Ganah's wrinkled ones, their skin like transparent parchment. She pressed her face against them, feeling their cool dryness.

Ganah gazed at the young woman by her side. She whispered, as if to herself, "You are very precious to me, little one. I pray every day for Yah-Adon to pass the staff to you. You are my daughter as truly as if I had birthed you. Although the Old Ways have always forbidden children to the Ulah-rahs, Yah-Adon has filled my emptiness with you."

"I am not worthy of such honor." Utriel lifted her distraught face. "It is enough to be allowed in the presence of the Ulah-rah. I am content just to sit at your feet."

Ganah shook her head, her eyes troubled. She placed her hands on each side of the girl's face, gently rubbing her cheeks with the tips of her long fingers. "Enough of my rambling, child. I see that your face is troubled."

Her sentences tumbling over one another, Utriel recounted her terrifying experience at the lake. When she finished, she whispered, "Could I have imagined it?"

Ganah lay with her eyes closed, the only sign of life the slow rising and falling of her chest.

Unsure if the Ulah-rah were awake or asleep, Utriel sat quietly by her side. It was unthinkable to disturb her. At last when she feared the old woman had forgotten her presence, Ganah spoke, her voice so low that Utriel had to bend close to the woman's mouth. "No, you did not imagine it."

Utriel exhaled sharply at her voice.

Ganah's words remained low but harsh. "That which I have feared the most is happening."

A knot tightened in Utriel's stomach.

"It is the Destroyer—the Evil One. He and his dark forces have returned once again to our world. I have felt their presence for many cycles of the moon, but I prayed fervently that I was wrong."

"How can you know such things?" asked Utriel, her eyes narrowing.

The Ulah-rah shook her head and rubbed her forehead with one hand. "The visions are back. I thought Yah-Adon had chosen no longer to use me, but even as I speak, He is showing me things once again."

"How—what do you mean?"

The furrows deepened across Ganah's brow. "He shows me images, pictures, within my head. "Even now," she moaned, "He is taking me back through the long passage of time into an earlier world, back into the veiled, shadowy beginning of humankind, back to the time when He spoke the world and all upon it into being."

Great drops of perspiration bathed the old woman's face. "I see images of the ancient past, scenes of a battle waged eons ago, visions of a conflict that raged across the universe, desolating all it touched. I see flaming swords wielded by the hands of mighty warriors as they lift up high golden shields. I hear the Dark One hurl shouts of defiance toward the majesty of Yah-Adon Himself." Her breathing grew deep and labored and her voice hoarse. "I hear the hiss of rustling wings and the howls of fury. I see the legions of defeated dark gods retreating into a far corner of the universe, like spiders withdrawing into a hidden recess, waiting for the moment to seize their unsuspecting prey.

"Yah-Adon," she implored, shaking her head, "to see the past, though, is not enough. Tear away the gray veil covering the future, or I can do nothing. I must see what lies ahead."

A tremor shook her body, her eyes snapped open, wide and unseeing.

"Ganah," cried Utriel as she scrambled to her knees and cradled the Ulah-rah in her arms. "Have I caused this?"

The old woman's eyes fluttered, struggling to focus on the girl. She grasped her hand. "No." Her chest heaved. "You have done nothing. I am just too old."

Utriel winced as the woman's hand squeezed her own. "Should I get Paniel?" she asked. "I saw her outside making bread by the ovens."

The Ulah-rah shook her head but did not open her eyes. "Don't leave. Sit with me for a moment."

Utriel huddled beside her, watching with frightened eyes and smoothing the gray hair from the weathered face.

Gradually, Ganah's breathing slackened. "Ah, child, it has been many years since the Placer of Stars has given me visions. I am sorry to have frightened you so." She patted the girl's hand, then sighed and pursed her thin lips. "I must do something now for you."

Utriel tilted her head to one side.

"I must pray for you, for I fear you are in danger."

Utriel put her arm around Ganah's waist and pulled her forward while she rearranged the furs behind her thin back. She could feel the old woman's bones though the soft layers of cloth covering her body.

The prophetess placed her hand on Utriel's head and lifted her eyes. "Oh great and holy Yah-Adon," she entreated, "Creator of everything, extend your hand upon this child and guide her through the coming days."

She paused as a tremor shook her body. "Protect her," she whispered, "and help her to see through the guise of evil."

A cold draft of air swept over Utriel, and she shivered, rubbing her hands over her arms.

Ganah lay back against the furs. "To be a seer is a great gift, my child, but the power is beyond my control. I have not had a vision for many cycles of the moon. But—" she sighed—"not seeing has been a blessing. For to be able to see the future, but be powerless to change it, weighs heavily upon my spirit."

She placed her hands on her thin chest. "I pray that Yah-Adon will soon release me from this body and take me to the land of shadows."

"No, Ganah!" cried Utriel. "You can't leave me! Not now!"

The old woman patted her hand. "My dear, you are the only reason that I choose to remain. But," she said, her lips trembling, "I am so tired."

"I'll take care of you. I'll stay with you. Bithra won't care."

"No, impetuous one." She brushed a tear from the girl's cheek. "You've been here far too long. Soon Bithra will be wondering where you are."

"I don't care. You're more of a mother to me than she could ever be."

"Child, child. You know that I love you, but you must respect Obed and your family."

"Then I'll send Paniel to let them know where I am."

A movement in the doorway, blocking the light from the sun, caught Utriel's eye.

The Tumulac filled the entrance. He peered anxiously into the room, his heavy-lidded, brooding eyes missing nothing.

"I'm not leaving your mistress until I know she's all right."

He nodded and backed from the doorway.

"Wait!"

He turned his broad head.

"Tell Paniel to make some broth and bring it to me?"

He lumbered from the room.

Ganah patted the young woman's hand. "Remember, my dear, flies are attracted to honey, never to sour wine. So it must be with your words."

Utriel lowered her eyes.

She fed Ganah, then stayed beside her until she was resting. When at last she rose to leave, she kissed the weathered cheek and whispered, "I love you."

The sun was slipping behind the mist-covered mountains that nearly surrounded Gibara-boni, and darkness was spreading across the valley.

In the stillness of the approaching night, Ganah stared into the deepening shadows. "Why, Yah-Adon?" she whispered. "Why do you refuse to take me? I am a useless old woman who has outlived her time. Choose a new Ulah-rah, someone who can guide the people with power and authority. Pass the El-cumah to one who can call your people back to the Old Ways." She sighed. "I am too tired to try any longer, for they are a rebellious lot."

Her hand trembled as she rubbed her eyes to erase the images crowding her mind. "No! Don't show me any more!" she pleaded. "I don't want to be part of your plan. There is nothing I can do. The evil is too strong."

She flung back the coverlet spread over her legs and rose from the mat. She groaned and beat her clenched fists on her chest. "What can one old woman do against such monstrous evil? Use someone who is young, someone strong, someone who can be a formidable opponent. Use Utriel. I have taught her well."

She crossed to the narrow openings in the wall and gazed at the night sky. "For centuries I have done your will. I have searched the heavens to read the Mazzaroth,* the pictures you set in the sky at the beginning of time. They are a constant reminder of your power and might and that you have not forgotten us. But more cycles of the moon have passed than I can recall. Now, a dark apathy eats its way into our hearts like a voracious cankerworm. Our minds have become dull, and many no longer care."

A falling star streaked across the heavens, then another, and another. She studied the narrow bit of sky for a moment, then began pacing the perimeter of the room in slow, monotonous circles, her mind listening and weighing each thought. Once she mumbled, her mouth barely moving, "I don't want to know that the enemy is on the move."

*Constellations (Job 38:32)

She closed her eyes, squeezing them to blot out the images, as well as the voice inside her head. "I can't do it," she cried, pressing her hands to her temples. Great sobs welled up from her chest, and hot tears dropped from her ancient cheeks.

Night had wrapped its inky cloak over the countryside when the Tumulac stepped inside his mistress's doorway, treading lightly to her side in spite of his size. He set a flat crucible of oil beside her pallet, its tiny flame casting a pale glow over the face of the aging holy woman.

She lifted her red-rimmed eyes to the large, gentle face nearly concealed in the shadows. "Thank you, dear friend, but there is nothing you can do for me. I must be alone for now."

He backed from the room.

At last, late into the night, long after the tears had dried on her cheeks, Ganah ceased struggling with the One who had called her ages before to guard the El-cumah, the staff so lovingly carved for the first woman by her mate and whose inscriptions had been dictated by Yah-Adon Himself. It had been the duty of each succeeding Ulah-rah to preserve the staff and to retell the glorious story written in the stars, a story that promised a Mighty Warrior, a Deliverer, and a King who would one day free them from the dark powers of Abaddon and his legions.

"Yah-Adon." Ganah sighed. "I can fight you no longer. I'll do what you ask even though I know it may cost me dearly." She continued, softer than the fanning of an insect's wings, "And of that I have no doubt."

The adversary was called by many names . . . the Destroyer, the Shadow Walker, the Deceiver, the Bent One, the Corrupter, the Serpent . . . Abaddon. It mattered not which name he used, for he and his dark dominions, fueled by their consuming hatred, had only one goal—to destroy man, the creation of Yah-Adon.

When little more than a child, Ganah's life had been forever altered the night Anah, one of her father's four wives, had shaken her awake. "Dress quickly!" the woman had urged. "You must hurry to a gathering of the virgins."

Frightened, the young girl pulled on a short, woven tunic and with trembling fingers and Anah's help fastened a girdle of black-and-white goat's skin around her narrow waist. She followed the woman to the center of the village, where a ceremonial fire blazed on a large, raised stone altar.

Flames leaped toward the night sky, sending grotesque shadows gyrating wildly among the people. Dark, nightmarish patterns flitted over the faces of the young, unmarried women huddled in a terrified group before the fire. Ganah, shivering in the night air, had felt her fear give way to a tingling excitement.

The older women wailed with low, mournful cries, their eyes closed and their bodies swaying in the night. The men waited in the background. At last the Gomana, their leader, stepped from the shadows. A hush descended over the assembly as he raised his arms high in the air. In his hands was the El-cumah.

Understanding then flared within Ganah, for the staff never left the presence of the Ulah-rah as long as she was alive. It could mean only one thing: Yah-Adon had taken her to the land of shadows, and a new prophetess was to be chosen. The young girl began to tremble, and her heart raced wildly, beating in cadence to the frenzied wailing of the women whose eerie cries once again crescendoed into the night.

Suddenly, the Gomana's voice roared above the din. "Tonight Yah-Adon, Creator and Great Light, has taken our Ulah-rah back to the land beyond the shadows from whence she came. She brought many of you into this world, saw you win battles, have children, and grow old. Now, her life has come to an end. A new guardian of the El-cumah must be chosen."

He lifted the rod high into the air, threw back his head, and shouted into the starry blackness of the night, "Yah-Adon, we call on you for help. You have already chosen your servant. You called her name from her mother's womb. Now we ask you to show us your choice through the power of the El-cumah."

The people stirred in the darkness, a few voices murmuring, "Show us . . . . Show us."

Abruptly, all noise ceased. The Gomana swung away from the people and advanced toward the terrified, young women. He held the staff aloft, stretching it forth above each frightened head.

The blood pounding in Ganah's head had cast everything into a dull, throbbing redness. The Gomana stood before her with the staff in his hand. Without a word he held it above her head, his eyes searching her face in the flickering red light, both hands gripping the heavy rod.

Excited cries rose in the crowd, and terror appeared on his face. His hands and arms began to tremble, the tremors increasing in intensity. His body convulsed violently, his feet held to the hard ground by an unseen force.

As the crowd watched in terrified awe, the staff began to glow like a hot ember fanned by a bellows. Bursting into a magnificent blaze of light, it flared brighter and brighter until, finally, exploding into a blinding, blue-white brilliance.

A surge of power shot through Ganah's body. A cry arose from deep within, erupting into a piercing scream. The new Ulah-rah crumpled amid the light and flames.

Two

Craggy prominences, petrified behemothic sentinels, stood guard over Gibara-boni. The town lay at the bottom of a broad, flat valley protected on three sides by towering mountains, their peaks shrouded in heavy, blue-gray mist. Rough-barked pines mantled the granitic skeleton and dug their relentless roots into the hard, rocky terrain, clinging to rugged cliffs and boulders that overlooked fertile fields below.

The Stargazers had discovered the valley centuries before while fleeing the fierce, nomadic tribes that were ravaging the land. After finding the shielded sanctuary, they offered thanks for their new home, built a memorial from the gray stones scattered over the valley floor and dedicated it to the One who had guided their steps. Then they cleared the ground and planted seeds brought with them in their flight.

The plants sprang forth and flourished in abundance under life-giving rays, which filtered through a belt of water vapor that enveloped the earth, protecting it from the ravages of a burning sun. The weather and temperature remained constant. Rain was not known in this pristine, virgin world, for the land was watered both from moisture in the air and beneath the ground.

The people cleared no more land than they needed. The rest they left in the forest they called the Shinar, or Place of Peace. Its trees, like ancient monoliths, towered above the earth, their foliage-laden branches interlocked, forming a dense, variegated canopy.

For generations, the Stargazers had depended upon the Shinar to provide much of their food. They gathered fruits and nuts from its vast variety of trees as well as succulent berries and wild yams that grew in the rich soil of the forest floor. They ground wild roots and blended their powders with berries and beetles to make a wide range of brilliant dyes for coloring yarns and skins. They prepared life-saving poultices, ointments, and potions from the forest's hidden roots of the licorice, gentian, and angelica.

Lately, however, stories were related in hushed breaths around fires in the dark of night or whispered behind cupped hands. They told of those who had wandered into the forest's depths never to be seen again. Strange, unearthly cries were said to echo from its shadows, and monstrous, hairy shapes were described lurking among the trees. Now, only the foolhardy ventured beyond the safety of its shaded periphery.

A stream, originating high above the valley, cascaded over sharp, rocky crags to crash into the riverbed below where it expended its energy like a wild beast until at last, broken and tamed, it meandered docilely into a large, placid lake at the far end of the valley. The darkness of the forest accentuated the neolithic beauty of the lake. Cormorants, gulls, long-legged herons with daggerlike beaks, and black-and-white terns darted along the shore to pick morsels from the mud while an occasional osprey glided above the water in search of fish.

Over the years Gibara-boni had grown into a thriving community, a successful caravan stop along two trade routes. Long ago, most of the people had forsaken the agricultural life, choosing instead to move within the protective boundaries of the town walls where they had become merchants, craftsmen, or traders. Those individuals who remained outside grew hard and conditioned from farming the land. They developed skills in drawing the bow, wielding the war axe and throwing the spear. Before long, they became the watchmen and protectors of the people.

Utriel sat by the bread stone in front of her father's house as she prepared the flat loaves for the day's meal. She sprinkled a handful of flour over the soft pliable mass, folded it, and began working and kneading the dough into a proper consistency. With the tranquil passing of the weeks and no repetition of the terrifying experience at the lake, she had pushed the incident into a remote corner of her mind.

As she worked, beads of perspiration from the heat of the open oven dotted her upper lip. She brushed at a wisp of hair tickling the side of her face, her thumb leaving a floury smudge on her cheek. She checked the position of the sun and smiled. For a change, Bithra would be proud of her, since she would have the bread finished in time for the noon meal. Then a frown settled on her brow—no matter how hard she tried she never pleased that woman. Utriel pounded the dough with her fist. No matter what Bithra said, she did try. At least she had in the beginning.

With a cry, she ducked as a shadow hovered above her head. She threw up her arms to shield her face. A shrill cry rent the air, and fluttering wings beat against her ear.

She burst into laughter. "Piava!" She clapped her hands in childlike fashion. "You frightened me! Where have you been?"

A hawk hung, suspended in the sky, hovering on a current of air. It glided in a wide arc, extended its talons, and lighted on a limb stretching above the bread stone.

"Oh, Piava," cried Utriel, her face glowing with excitement. "My beautiful Piava. I've missed you so."

The bird cocked its delicate, sculpted head and shifted from one sharp-taloned foot to the other, all the while staring unblinkingly at the young woman. It stretched long, pointed wings, never taking its eyes from her, before folding them against its sleek body.

Utriel rose to run her fingers over the downy breast. The bird shifted from one foot to the other, the loose feathers on its thighs lifting in the breeze.

"Wait here!" the girl cried. She ran into the house, emerging minutes later with a heavy piece of leather wrapped around her forearm. "Here," she coaxed, holding out her swathed arm. "Come and rest on me." The bird hopped onto the girl's arm, gripping the leather with its talons.

Utriel had found Piava after the beginning of her first monthly flow. That morning she had awakened, frightened and disturbed by the thought that her childhood had ended. The squeals and laughter of children playing in the compound only increased her agitation, for she did not want to grow up. She wanted her life to stay as it had always been. She wanted to run in the forests with her brother, to compete for being the swiftest or the most cunning.

As she dressed in the early light, she had heard Bithra and Obed's other wives preparing to card and spin the recently sheared wool. Without a sound she left her room and entered the eating chamber where she cached several chunks of bread and goat cheese in the girdle around her waist. She knew Bithra would be angry if she didn't help with the work, but she could not face the winks and knowing nods of the women as they made comments about her official arrival into their ranks. Soon enough she would be one of them, but for now she desired to hold on to the freedom of childhood for one more day.

She slipped from the house and raced across the open ground into the shadows of the forest. Since she knew well the stories told of strange encounters and disappearances within the Shinar, she stayed near the edge where she could still see the men working in the fields. She was brave, but she was not foolhardy.

No sooner had she settled herself on a moss-covered log and pulled the food from her girdle than piercing cries and the frantic drumming of wings shattered the serenity of the scene. She shielded her eyes from the mottled light streaming through the leaves and scanned the sky for the cause of the ear-splitting clamor. High above her head, two hawks, shrieking with rage, plummeted again and again into the lofty branches.

Peering into the trees, she spotted the object of their attacks—a deadly, black mamba slithering toward a teetering fledgling perched precariously on the edge of a large nest. The crazed parents screamed and dived in a frenzied effort to distract the lethal predator whose sole attention was focused on its next meal.

Utriel watched as the snake poised to strike. One of the hawks plunged again, this time striking the fledgling with its wing. Down it tumbled from its hazardous perch, a screeching mass of feathers and talons as it fluttered its immature wings. With a flurry of down it disappeared into the midst of a large clump of maidenhair.

Utriel ran to the quivering plants and pulled back the fronds. The tiny hawk arched its wings and hissed as if to attack. She reached among the feathery ferns, making sure to grab the fledging from behind. It would certainly die if left on the forest floor, an enticing meal for yet another predator. She struggled to hold the recalcitrant bird in her hands and to keep her fingers away from its sharp beak. Its piercing cries rang through the forest. "Don't be afraid," she murmured. "I'll take care of you. Nothing will harm you. You'll be my beautiful Piava!"

She had kept the hawk and raised it, tethering it outside the house. Finally, at Jirad's insistence when it was fully grown, she released its bonds, tears streaming down her cheeks. Now, the hawk had returned.

Utriel gazed at the bird perched on her arm. "I wish you could tell me where you've been," she murmured. "Oh," she whispered, running her finger over its breast, "if only I could go with you. What fun it would be to run away, to leave the valley and travel to far places." A dreamy expression settled on her face. "I've even heard of a land beyond the great sea, a place called Itu-lantu, where people live in glistening, white dwellings perched high on the sides of great cliffs. It is said they sail long, slender ships that skim swiftly over the waves like birds."

The hawk cocked its head and stared as if it understood. Then it blinked, stretched its wings and leaped, lifting itself into the air, circling as it searched for a current. Finding one, it rose higher and higher into the sky. Utriel gazed after the graceful bird until it became a tiny speck, at last vanishing into the distance.

She sighed, placed both hands on her hips, and stretched. She brushed at another strand of hair. As she walked back to the large bread stone, she drew in her breath. Striding toward her was a lean but muscular, dark-haired man. She smiled when their eyes met, but she quickly lowered her head lest he see the flush rising to her face. "You look thirsty, Noah. Would you like some water?"

"Yes," he said, his dark eyes absorbing her beauty.

Still feeling the heat in her face, she wiped her hands on her skirt and hurried to the jar. She dipped her hand into the water and touched her cheeks and lips, grateful for its coolness. She filled a heavy clay cup and returned to the waiting man. "Here, Noah," she said, holding out the cup, her hand brushing his. Nearly as tall as he, she looked easily into his eyes.

Thick, coarse, brown curls framed his darkly tanned features. His nose, although long and straight, did not dominate his face. Utriel loved the way the corners of his eyes crinkled and one side of his wide, thin mouth curled higher than the other when he smiled. And his teeth! So white and perfect! A gold circlet pierced his right ear, sending tiny sparks of light from its surface. Although nearly twice as old as she, he possessed a tenderness she did not sense in the other men of Gibara-boni, and he stirred her heart. Since falling in love with Noah, her earlier fears of womanhood had almost vanished.

She knew the single women in town longed for him to notice them, for she had seen their brazen glances and the sensuous sway of their hips when in his presence. She had feared he would be tempted since many of the younger men outside the walls were drawn to the townswomen. They were so different from Utriel and her friends. Even young girls inside the town painted their lips and eyes, hung beads in their ears and combed oil through their hair to arrange it more easily in large loops and twists about their heads.

Yet, to her delight, as the weeks passed, Utriel realized that Noah showed no interest in them. She no longer doubted that she was his choice. Now it remained only for him to speak to Obed.

She watched him drink the cool water. Drops clung to his thick, dark mustache. He ran his hand across his mouth before handing her the cup.

She loved him, but she also knew Ganah desired to pass the El-cumah to her. Since falling in love, Utriel found herself torn between the desire to serve Yah-Adon and the longing to be Noah's wife and to bear his children. She believed in Yah-Adon, but He seemed so remote from her life. She did not want to disappoint the old holy woman who had patiently taught her the Old Ways in preparation for the task, but she could not rid her mind of this strong yet gentle man. Besides, what if Yah-Adon chose another? In spite of her desire to please Ganah, she found herself each day breathing a prayer that tomorrow would be the one when Noah would speak to her father.

She sat on the ground and laid fresh dough onto the worn bread stone.

Noah squatted beside her, resting on his haunches. "I have something for you." In his hand was a box of acacia wood, carved with a fine, interlacing design and rubbed with oil to a smooth, warm glow.

"Oh," she cried, "it's beautiful. Did you make it?"

"Yes, but open it," he urged.

"There's something inside?"

He smiled.

She raised the ornate lid, laid it on the ground, and lifted its revealed treasure with her fingers, her eyes glowing with delight. In her hand lay an arm bracelet made from strips of dark leather woven and braided into a fine, delicate band. In the center, encased within the decorative weaving, was a dark green, opaque stone. Milky white lines swirled over its polished surface.

She held it to her chest. "I can't accept this. Obed would never allow it."

"Utriel," said Noah, "I'm going to speak to Obed before the moon wanes. I am going to ask for you. Do you object?"

Once again she felt the blood rushing to her face and dared not look up. She should first speak to Ganah for wisdom and direction before she answered, but she heard herself whisper without hesitation, "No. I do not object."

"Then accept this as my pledge to you. Wear it where no one will see it until I have talked to your father."

"But . . ."

"Please," he said, closing his hands over hers. He lifted them and pressed her fingertips lightly to his lips. Then he rose without another word and hurried from the compound.

Noah strode toward the field where he had left his brothers. His slender body was well developed from long hours of tireless work in the fields. His robe hung from one shoulder, revealing a torso the color of pecan shells. Dark, curly hair covered his chest and abdomen. Leather sandals laced around the ankles of his muscular legs.

His reverie was broken by loud, strident voices. He paused and listened. Cursing and shouting drifted through the trees, coming from the direction where he had left his brothers. His hand touched the finely honed bronze knife strapped at his waist. He began running through the thicket dividing the farmland from the dwellings. He leaped over fallen trees and shielded his face from low-hanging branches.

As he broke through the trees, he nearly collided with the large group of men who had gathered from neighboring fields. They were shouting, urging on eight men—three of them his brothers, Ephran, Haniah and Uzzah—now barely recognizable from the blood and dirt caked on their bodies. He winced at the loud crack of bone upon bone. Haniah staggered backwards, another gash opening over his already bloody eye. Ephran ducked, parrying a blow with his forearm.

Two men had Uzzah's arms pinned behind his back while a third punched him in the face and gut. His lower lip had split, swollen and grotesque. Blood streamed from a broken nose. With every blow a loud grunt escaped his mouth, and he sagged lower in the men's arms.

"Stop!" screamed Noah, charging through the ring of onlookers. Clasping both hands together as he ran, he swung his arms like a club, slamming them across the back of the one beating his brother. The man collapsed, crumpling to the ground. Startled, the others dropped

Uzzah's arms. He fell forward, sprawling limply across his attacker, his blood soaking the unconscious man's back.

"Have you lost your minds?" Noah yelled, staring at the men in unbelief. "You are our friends. Why are you fighting my brothers?"

Gerah and Lemiel glared back, their eyes red-rimmed with anger, spittle matted in their dark beards.

"Stay out of this, Noah," yelled Lemiel, struggling to stay on his feet. "It's not your fight. This is between your brothers and us."

"We were only having a good time," gasped Haniah. "We didn't force her."

Lemiel screamed and lunged forward, fist in the air.

Noah threw out his leg, sending him sprawling across the ground. "What's happening here?" he demanded.

Gerah cursed and spat blood onto the ground. "Your brothers have defiled our sister. They got her drunk and forced themselves on her. What man will want her now? She's good only for the dung heap. Who'll take her into his house when she has a big belly? Our father'll never receive a decent price for her. She's useless. We demand payment for our father's loss."

Uzzah groaned and tried to sit up. He rubbed his hand across his face, smearing the blood dripping onto his chest. "We pay nothing," he mumbled. "She's been used. She gives herself freely to every man in town. Collect from *them*—maybe that'll satisfy your father."

"Liar," screamed Gerah, grabbing Uzzah's long hair in his fist and yanking his head backward.

As Noah's fist struck Gerah with lightning speed, knocking him to the ground, a spear whistled through the air, embedding itself with a thud in the earth beside the fallen man.

"Enough," roared an angry voice. "What's the meaning of this?" Obed and Jirad strode forward, Jirad with a spear grasped in one hand. "We fight our enemies, not each other," shouted Obed. He pushed himself between the glaring men. He yanked his weapon from the ground and faced them. "If you must kill each other, be sure it is over something worthwhile."

Gerah nodded in agreement, but the anger in his voice was not to be quieted. "Uzzah, Haniah, and Ephran have defiled our sister. We ask only repayment for our father's loss, but they refuse."

"She's a whore," shouted Ephran as he lunged for Gerah. "We'll pay nothing."

As swift as an eagle's flight, Obed swung his arm backward, catching Ephran in the chest and knocking him to the ground. "Do you want to settle this in front of the whole assembly, or shall we do it here among ourselves? Would you bring dishonor on your father because of a woman?"

Gerah glared at Obed.

"Uzzah," said Obed, pointing his spear at Gerah and his brothers. "Give them ten sheep for their father and tell him to buy his daughter a husband. Now, all of you go before I lose my temper."

The men mumbled among themselves, but they had no desire to take on Obed and Jirad.

Finally Gerah spat at Uzzah's feet. "We'll go, but be sure the sheep are in our fold by noon tomorrow."

The five men stalked sullenly from the field.

Ephran grabbed Uzzah's hand and pulled him to his feet. "You are a mess. Lemiel almost gave you a new face. In fact," he laughed, "it looks better than your old one."

Uzzah grimaced a contorted grin with his bloodied and swollen lips, his nose already spreading across his face.

"Well, it was worth it," sneered Haniah.

Noah stared at his brothers in disbelief. What was happening to them? A sickness seemed to be spreading over the land, infecting even those he loved with its stench of corruption.

Ephran's eyes narrowed. "What's the matter, little brother? It was only Leah. She barely has a woman's shape." He guffawed. "We just gave her a little practice."

"Don't you realize what you have done?" Noah asked, swallowing hard to stop the bile rising in his throat.

"We did only what any man would do," said Uzzah, feeling his front teeth with a blood-smeared finger. "If she didn't want it, she shouldn't have taunted us. She brought it on herself."

"Don't you care what they will do to her? Now she can no longer stay in her father's house. You have acted dishonorably."

"Dishonorably?" sneered Haniah. The big man spit a mouthful of blood on the ground. "You talk like a woman."

"No, I talk as our father taught us."

Ephran laughed. "Who cares about the Old Ways. Those days are gone. Now, if a man wants something, he must take it. It is the strong who will survive."

"Enough," growled Haniah. "Come. Help us get Uzzah home."

Noah slung his brother's arm over his shoulder and started across the field. These men were his brothers, his own flesh and blood. How could they have done such an act? They had always been a rough lot, but now they were like strangers.

Three

Noah swung his scythe in a harsh, downward arc. The ache in his shoulders and arms felt good. For the last two days he had struggled with anger toward his brothers. When he tried talking to them, they laughed and joked about the incident. Now, he paused, grasping the scythe firmly in his hands as he looked at the three men working beside him. Finally, he shook his head. "The three of you disgust me!"

"Enough!" yelled Ephran, raising his fist and anger in his eyes. "We will speak of it no more, little brother."

Noah flung his scythe to the ground and stalked from the field. He had to get away from them, to think and to let his anger lessen. He headed toward the grove.

The ancient, sacred place was now a tangle of vines and trees. Someone had attempted to clear the overgrowth of weeds from the stone altar built centuries before by members of his tribe, but brown lichens and creeping vines were relentless in the pursuit to repossess what had once been theirs. When he was a child, his mother had taken him to the grove while his father and brothers were laboring in the fields. She had held him on her lap and repeated to him the old stories and mysteries she had learned when young. She taught him to talk to Yah-Adon, the Placer of Stars, and to listen for his voice.

Noah had learned well. He had learned that often the words of Yah-Adon were as quiet as the rustling of leaves in the evening breeze, or as delicate as the whirring of insect wings brushing against his skin. He listened to Him at night when he lay in the silence of his room, and he sometimes heard Him as he labored in the field.

He had never lost his belief in Yah-Adon although most of the townsmen over the years had stopped coming to the sacred grove. Once it had echoed with the cries of animals sacrificed to their Holy One on the ancient stone slab worn smooth by age and stained with blood and smoke from many generations of burnt offerings. Now, few men in Gibara-boni believed any longer in the Old Ways, and fathers seldom taught their sons the old stories. Since tradition, however, depicted the Placer of Stars as a wrathful deity, some thought it wise not to reject Him completely. Some, out of habit, continued to bring their offerings to lay on the altar at harvest or birthing time.

Noah squinted into the sun, checking its position. Already it had begun its descent. He muttered a curse under his breath and hoped none of his brothers had begun looking for him. They would ridicule him if they knew he had come to the grove, and that was the last thing he needed.

He rose to his feet and stretched his tingling legs, gently shaking them to restore circulation. He had been on his knees for some time. Although he had heard no voice while in the grove, at least his anger had subsided.

A dove cooed from the limb of a large elm directly above his head. Shielding his eyes from a shaft of light piercing the canopy of leaves, he watched the bird descend from the branch onto the weathered stone. It rested uncertainly for a moment, then flew to his shoulder. Its beak stroked his cheek and gently pecked at the lobe of his ear, all the while chucking to him. A warmness swelled in his heart. He turned his head and slowly raised his hand. With a whir of wings, the bird flew into the air, disappearing among the trees.

Noah rubbed the side of his face as he surveyed the branches surrounding him. He shook his head and smiled, then headed toward the fields, sprinting easily over the large rocks nearly hidden among the underbrush.

As he rounded a thicket of trees, his heart leaped. Before him, seated on a large rock, was Utriel, her knees drawn up to her chin, her attention on a flock of quietly grazing sheep.

At his approach, she looked up.

His breath quickened.

He was afraid she would lower her head again, but she stopped, then lifted her chin and stared directly into his eyes.

Yes, he thought, *I must speak quickly to Obed and request her for my wife.*

Four

"Caravan!" shouted a watchman from the town wall. "Caravan coming!"

The sun was overhead the following day as excitement mounted in Gibara-boni. Men, women, and children ran through the narrow streets toward the massive wooden gate so as not to miss the arrival of the dust-covered traders. In the fields, men gathered up their implements and stopped their work for the day. Children laughed and waved to travel-weary merchants who shouted curses at their braying asses and prodded with long, pointed sticks a line of stoic camels. The animals, laden with enormous bundles and oversized clay jars lashed to carriage saddles, lumbered toward the city walls.

Swarthy drivers halted the caravan outside the stone barricade to begin unloading their tired animals. Boys, thin and wiry, led the camels by their halters to watering troughs near the town wells while others pitched an array of travel-worn, goat-hair tents. Macaques brought from distant lands chittered and squawked and yanked at ropes tied around their necks. The traders threw colorful mats and blankets over the trampled ground to display exotic and mysterious wares, traded or stolen, along the route.

Crowds were gathering around the foul-smelling entourage. Little children scampered about the legs of skittish, half-wild asses. With squeals and giggles the youngsters darted out of spitting range of the long-legged, one-humped camels that shifted their weight on broad-toed feet. The animals chewed their cuds and watched the pests through long lashes, shielding eyes sunk in their heads. Several calves nuzzled their mothers in a vain attempt to suckle.

Among the most sought-after items in the caravan was salt brought from the northern country, somewhere beyond the mountains. The traders also displayed delicately carved stone figures and a thin, blue-glazed pottery made by the skilled craftsmen of Itu-lantu, so different from the thick clayware formed by the Stargazers; jewelry from Enoch, fashioned of exquisite, polished stones and gems; mirrors of burnished bronze; exotic spices: cinnamon, calamus, cassia, and myrtle; and great vats of rich, green olive oil.

Young townswomen pushed and shoved, eager to be the first to see what new baubles they could find to dangle around their necks or fasten in their oiled and twisted hair. Matrons examined finely woven cloths, marveling at the intricate designs. The clamoring voices filling the air signaled that the bargaining had already begun.

As the orange-gold rays of light slipped behind the dusky hills, trading began to cease for the day. Some of the townsmen returned to their houses while others carried to the clearing bulging skins full of sharp, red wine and large vats of souri, a dark and heavy beer. A roaring fire already flamed against the evening sky. The revelry would continue far into the night as the men drank and listened to tales gathered by the traders along their circuitous routes.

With a little coaxing from the townsmen, a merchant swaggered to one of the tents and returned leading nine women, naked and dirty, their hands and feet secured to a tether. The pitiful collection shivering in the night air huddled in the flickering light of the flames. Three were terrified girls, barely out of childhood; the others, sad-faced women resigned to their fate. With a few moments of haggling, each disappeared into the darkness with her purchaser.

As the night grew old, the laughter and noise diminished. Some of the men had passed out, their unconscious bodies sprawled over the clearing. Others sat around the fire, swapping gossip and news.

"Oudabi," shouted the caravan's leader, a large, rough-looking man with dark-red curls matted over his head and chin. He was calling to a comrade sitting across from him engrossed in dislodging food from several back teeth. "Oudabi, tell everyone about the giants we've seen."

"Giants?" questioned Obed, his words slurring as he lifted a near-empty wineskin.

A townsman chuckled and sneered, "Were they as big as mountains?"

"It is no jest," retorted Oudabi, spitting the dislodged fragments of food onto the ground. "If you had seen them, you would not laugh. They were twice the size of an average man. I stood beside them, and I felt as a grasshopper."

"Where did you see these . . . giants, Oudabi?" Obed demanded, belching loudly.

"In a village at least twenty risings of the sun from here. I had taken some men and camels with me to look for the sparkling stones I was told were there. I did not find the stones, but I did find something that drove fear into my heart like a spear."

Several men snickered, but most were now listening, their eyes on the speaker.

Oudabi leaned forward, his arms resting on his knees. "In that village were two young men barely out of boyhood. Yet they towered above even the largest man in my group." He lowered his voice as if afraid to be heard. "Such fierceness in their faces and darkness in their eyes, a darkness the likes I have never before seen."

"Who were the men who could father such children?" asked a voice from the darkness.

Oudabi spoke slowly, "No one would say. . . . The mothers had died in childbirth, leaving the babies to be raised by women in the village."

"Why didn't they just kill the monsters and be done with it?"

A murmur ran through the group.

"That I cannot say, but while I was there, I heard of others like them who have been seen in neighboring towns."

"What did they look like?"

"Ah-h-h," interjected the red-bearded leader. "Each bore a red mark, like a coiled snake, on his shoulder. But it was their eyes—like stones, cold, blue, and lifeless. Even the villagers were afraid." The dying flames cast shifting shadows across the faces of the listeners.

"There is more," said Oudabi, his voice an ominous whisper. "There were no old men in the village." He tapped his finger to his nose. "Only young ones, strong and virile, but their women—their women were haggard, like plums left out too long in the sun." His voice fell even lower. "There was great evil in that place. We did not stay."

No one spoke. Only the forlorn mating cries of tiny tree frogs broke the stillness.

"Ha," Obed roared at last. "It must be the goats' milk they drink." At that some of the men chuckled, relieved to break the tension. "Here," he said, slinging several full wineskins into the air. "Have another drink. Are we children to be afraid of the dark?"

Deep within the Shinar, the dark, moist ground trembled and split. Subterranean pressures convulsed the mantle beneath the earth and heaved it upward. Steam exploded from Stygian depths, spewing noxious, sulfurous fumes high into the dark night air. The floor of the forest shuddered in travail, like a woman giving birth. The gash widened, inflamed, red and ugly, belching gaseous flames and vapor from the glowing interior of the earth's core. Ripples of shimmering heat danced above the fiery fissure, twisting and writhing into a nebulous, perverted shape—a mockery of man, more animal than human—bent and grotesque.

The form wavered, solidifying. The figure shifted, steadying itself on two sharp, cloven hooves. Strong, hairy thighs quivered as the form struggled to maintain its massive upper torso. In the red glow, powerful but misshapen arms lifted hands to a contorted visage, all the while clenching and unclenching long, knotted fingers.

The abomination staggered to a nearby tree, its hooves sinking into the earth. Groaning, it wrapped its arms around the trunk to maintain balance for the final metamorphosis. Its body convulsed as bones snapped and shifted, while muscles stretched and tore in realignment on new points of insertion and origin along newly formed bones. At last, with heaving chest it stumbled backward, unaccustomed to the long, muscular legs on which it now stood but finding it easier to stand erect with feet rather than hooves.

The transformation complete, the counterfeit trembled. Long, thick hair, the color of sun-ripened wheat, framed strong, chiseled features and shone palely in the red glow. The creature threw back its now resplendent head, lifted its chest and roared in exaltation. As fumes and smoke spiraled from the crevasse, it raised one massive fist high above its head and screamed into the darkness, "I, Asmodeus, come in the name of Abaddon, Lord of the Abyss. Our legions are taking human shape all over the land. By the time we finish our master's bidding, humankind will be so tainted and corrupted that even you, Yah-Adon, will blot it from the face of this earth."

The magnificent face twisted into unmitigated hatred as the creature bellowed into the heavens, "Yah-Adon, you will never win, no matter what your plan. When we are finished, even you won't want these pitiful pieces of humanity." The creature's visage grew dark with rage. "This time we won't fail."

Once again insidious laughter, cold, hard, and cruel, resounded through the darkness. "We have waited eons to destroy your work, and now the time is right. A dullness has fallen on the people. Their hearts have become hard, and their ears can no longer hear your voice. They think only of their bellies and their loins. They have forgotten you. Do you hear me?" screamed Asmodeus. "They have forgotten both you and your promises."

Anger and pride swelled within the fiend. Clenching its enormous fists, it stood like a mighty colossus, its head lifted to the sky. "Once I was a creature of glory and magnificence! I, with my master, wore holy garments encrusted with precious stones. We stood before you, wise and beautiful!"

The handsome face contorted in agony as the titanic body writhed in remembered anguish. Slowly, a twisted smile formed, and its eyes glowed in the darkness.

"How simple it is to twist and corrupt this insignificant clutter of human garbage. And now," it bellowed, "your miserable, paltry creatures, those images of yourself, will belong to us forever. Just as the serpent grovels in the dirt and dung, so these people will sink until they can never rise again. We will grind them under our feet. We may not be able to assault you, Old Enemy, but we will utterly destroy these creatures that you love. Even the ravens will not pick at their carcasses."

The entity lifted its arms to the dark sky and vented a millennium of hatred in one final, long cry that rose, swelling and receding, as it reverberated in the night air.

Five

Bithra wound newly dyed yarn onto a large wooden spindle with the automatic motions of one long accustomed to the task. She had placed a loom beneath the spreading branches of an ancient oak since the light was poor within the building. Now, she watched Utriel out of the corner of her eye, shaking her head at the girl's attempts to weave the bright, colored threads into an intricate pattern.

"So—you are actually weaving today?" puzzled the bewildered woman. "Are you sick?" She cocked an eyebrow. "I don't understand! The last few days you've done everything I've asked, even volunteering to take the ashes from the oven."

A secret smile played around Utriel's lips.

Bithra continued shaking her head. "Sooner or later I suppose I'll know what is going on. At least you aren't roaming the forest or daydreaming by the lake." As she watched the girl, her eyes softened. "I can hardly believe you have grown up so fast."

The unexpected tenderness in the woman's voice caused Utriel to glance up from her work.

"Keep your eyes on what you're doing," snapped Bithra. "You're getting careless with the strands. Don't let them get tangled!"

The girl bent over the loom, trying to undo a hopelessly knotted strand. Since Noah had said he was going to ask Obed for permission to take her to the marriage bed, she could think of nothing else. Whenever she shut her eyes, his handsome face appeared, and she could feel the pressure of his strong arms around her. Even the guilt she experienced over disappointing Ganah could not suppress her excitement.

"Here," said Bithra, laying down the spindle, "let me do that.

You're making a mess. I don't think you'll ever—"

Both women stopped and listened. Voices, loud and excited, were coming from the other side of the grove.

"Can you see anything?" asked Bithra, rising to her feet.

Utriel shook her head and listened, straining to make out the words. She squinted and shielded her eyes from the bright sun.

The voices were growing louder. "Get Obed! Hurry!"

Bithra dropped the spindle and turned toward Utriel.

With a sinking feeling in her chest, Utriel began running, tucking the hem of her skirt in the girdle around her waist as she raced across the field.

The voices grew louder with each step.

She halted, her breath catching in her throat. Emerging into the sunlight from the copse of trees was the most magnificent figure she had ever seen. Morning rays glistened upon long flaxen hair that tumbled about the man's shoulders. He was a full head taller than any of the others crowding around him, and his broad shoulders strained under a deerskin jerkin which reached the middle of thighs the size of tree trunks. Rabbit skins, bound to his legs with leather strips, covered well-developed calves, and deerskin boots shod his feet.

Bithra's hand flew to her mouth to stifle a scream. In the stranger's arms, carried as if a child, was a torn and bloodied body.

Utriel felt disoriented and confused.

"Stop!" shouted a familiar voice.

She spun around.

Her father was running toward them across the field, his strong legs covering the ground in great strides. Gitel and Benu, two older sons, raced close behind.

When Obed reached the man's side and saw his bloodied burden, he bellowed, "No-o-o! Not Jirad!" His reddened face contorted in agony.

"It was a lion!"

"He was mauled by a lioness!"

"With cubs!" Several villagers hollered at the same time.

"Give him to me!" cried Obed, lifting his son from the man's arms. He spun around, searching the crowd. Spotting Bithra, his voice rasping with emotion, he shouted, "Take Utriel and hurry to the house. Prepare a pallet."

The woman grabbed Utriel's arm, pulling her toward the compound. The girl stumbled, not comprehending what was happening.

"Come!" ordered Bethra.

"Follow me!" barked Obed. Then he turned, his jaw set like stone.

When the men reached the house, Bithra was already placing furs and cloths over a woven straw mat. With great care Obed lowered Jirad to the pallet.

The woman had regained her composure and now had command of the situation. "Utriel, fill the basin with water. And hurry!"

The young woman left, returning almost immediately with a wide bowl, water sloshing over the sides and tears streaming down her cheeks. As she set the basin beside the pallet, a strangled noise escaped her throat. Deep scratches ran across his right cheek, dangerously close to his eye, and ugly gouges laced his right arm and shoulder, the flesh torn and ragged. She stepped aside to give Bithra more light to clean the ugly wounds.

The woman knelt beside Jirad, her mouth a grim line. "I have seen injuries like these before," she said. "It is not good."

"Be still, woman," snapped Obed, "and tend the boy's wounds."

Jirad's eyes were closed, his breathing labored and uneven. He had passed out from the pain and loss of blood, his face already the color of ivory.

Bithra gently cleaned the raw flesh with water and strong wine.As she worked, excited murmuring arose from the crowd gathered outside the house.

Ganah, carrying a covered basket, entered the room. Although frail, there was no stoop to her shoulders. She carried herself tall and straight as she walked to the woman's side and touched her shoulder.

Bithra laid down the cloth she was using to clean Jirad's wounds and rose. She bowed slightly and stepped back, a scowl on her face.

The prophetess knelt beside the injured young man and placed the basket on the floor. She examined the wounds. "You have done well, Bithra."

Utriel searched the faces of the two women. She let out her breath when she saw the frown slowly dissolving from Bithra's face.

Ganah opened the basket and withdrew a single long, dark strand of hair taken from the tail of a wild plains horse. With an effort she steadied her hand and carefully inserted the strand through the eye of a slender, curved needle made from finely polished bone. Then, pushing it through the torn skin, she pulled the edges of the jagged wounds together, sewing them with tiny, even stitches as if she were making a new wineskin.

When she had closed all the wounds and tied off the hair, cutting it with the blade of a razor-sharp obsidian knife, the prophetess poured a mixture of oil and wine onto the injuries and wrapped them with wide strips of clean linen.

She lifted an alabaster vial from the basket. She placed her hand behind Jirad's head and lifted it—enough to force the opening of the vial between his lips. A stream of dark amber liquid trickled down the side of his face. She repeated the procedure. This time his lips parted slightly, allowing some of the fluid to seep into his mouth. When the vial was empty, she lowered his head to the soft furs and rose stiffly to her feet.

"Will he be all right?" Obed asked, his voice husky and his brimming eyes red-rimmed.

"He will live," she murmured.

Utriel lifted her tear-streaked face to the prophetess. "How can you be so sure?"

Ganah touched the young woman's cheek but said nothing, then made her way slowly through the crowd as it parted before her.

"Wait," Obed called.

Ganah paused.

"Will he truly live, old woman?" Obed asked as he struggled to calm his voice.

"Do you think I am too old to hear the voice of Yah-Adon?" she asked.

Obed shook his head and bowed, not willing to offend her, but continued, "You have not used your skills for many moons. Why are you doing so now?"

Ganah straightened her back, drawing herself to her full height, her eyes blazing with an authority thought lost.

A murmur ran through the crowd.

"The Presence!" cried an old woman, pulling her headscarf over her face. "It is Yah-Adon's Presence!"

"Your son will live, Obed," said Ganah, her voice strong and deep. "Yah-Adon wills it."

Before Obed could respond, she departed through the crowd.

Obed walked uncertainly to the side of his son.

"Father," said Utriel, placing her hand on his arm. "Believe what she says."

Obed sighed deeply as he left the room. He stood outside the door, his hands on his hips and stared at the ground. "Go back to your work," he said to the crowd. "There is nothing here you can do."

"He will live, Father?" asked Gitel, glancing at Benu from the corner of his eye.

"I don't know," muttered Obed. "Go now, and leave me alone."

With a frown and a tilt of his head, Gitel gestured to Benu. The two men, whispering to each other, sauntered from the area.

When the last straggler had left, Obed walked to the stranger who had been leaning against the trunk of the large oak.

Utriel stood in the doorway wiping tears from her cheek with the heel of her hand. How could this have happened? Jirad would never have taken a chance with a wild animal, particularly a lioness with cubs. He was too careful.

She sniffled and wiped her eyes again as she watched Obed and the man through her tears. Again, her breath caught in her throat at the sight of the handsome stranger. Obed was one of the largest men in Gibara-boni, yet he seemed dwarfed by the man. She knew her father would not approve of being spied upon, but she could not take her eyes off the blond giant.

She strained to hear their faint voices. "Tell me what happened to my son," her father said as he massaged his forehead with his fingers.

"I am called Bel," said the stranger, his voice deep and mesmerizing.

Utriel shivered in spite of the absence of any breeze.

"I come from a place far beyond the mountains. I travel the land teaching men to make weapons, the finest ever seen."

Utriel could not believe the color of the man's hair, like ripened wheat in the fields ready for harvesting. Even his brows and lashes glistened in the sunlight against his sun-bronzed skin.

"My wanderings," continued the stranger, "had brought me within a short distance from here when I heard the roar of a lion and screams for help. I found your son struggling with a ferocious lioness, her cubs huddled under a nearby boulder. I speared the beast but not before she had severely mauled him."

Without warning he glanced in Utriel's direction. She gasped and involuntarily drew her arms to her breasts. She tried to draw back, but it was too late. She felt light-headed and grasped the doorway as the room began to spin.

"Utriel!" hollered Obed. "Bring our guest some wine. He's tired and has traveled a long way." He gripped the man's arm with great emotion. "I am greatly indebted to you, for you have saved my son's life. If you will stay, it would give me great pleasure to honor you with a celebration tomorrow. I will invite friends and neighbors, for because of you, my son is alive."

The man smiled and bowed his head.

That evening Obed stared into the darkness of his sleeping room. Kadrah, one of his younger wives, lay on her side, snoring softly. In the moonlight filtering through the openings in the wall, he looked at his huge hands, turning them back and forth. He ran a finger over every scar, callus and line. His hands had served him well during his sixty-eight years. Even as a boy he had worked hard, and with approaching manhood he had rejoiced in the strength of his body. He was proud that he never found a task he could not complete. It pleased him to force his body to its limits, pushing himself until he felt a burning in every muscle.

He threw a spear farther and with greater accuracy than any man in Gibara-boni, and he could hit a flying bird with ease. He was an excellent tracker and a legendary archer, always bringing back to his family more skins than they could use. His extraordinary skills had made him an unchallenged leader in the tribe.

Obed, the firstborn son of Hamon's favorite wife, had been his father's constant companion. As a boy he had learned well, becoming a hard man like his father and developing a reputation among the tribes as a leader who protected his own with ferocity and brutality. No man who challenged him had lived long enough to boast of it. He lived life to its fullest, tasting every pleasure within his reach. Temperance and moderation were unknown to him. Yet he had a weakness—his love for Utriel and Jirad.

"Mira," he groaned in the stillness of the night. "You were the only wife I ever loved. You left me too soon. The others are no more to me than my animals." He sighed. "Now, Utriel and Jirad are all I have left of you."

When Mira died in childbirth, he gave the twins to Bithra because her womb was barren. She had been glad to care for the twins since a married woman without children was a thing of scorn.

As the children grew, he discovered that his heart was strangely warmed whenever he sat in the evening shade and watched them play. He felt great pride in Jirad, who grew taller and stronger than any of his other sons, and in Utriel, who looked more like her mother with each day. Often he winced when he saw Mira's look of defiance mirrored in her daughter's eyes, but he had found Mira's boldness intoxicating even though that was not a trait most Sethites desired in a wife.

Before Mira, he had never loved anyone, but then, the men in his village did not consider love when choosing a wife. Wives were taken for what they could provide, either possessions or power, and for the children they would bear. He had selected each of his wives for a specific reason—but never for love. Bethuel's father had promised him a hundred and fifty sheep. Taking Kadrah into his house had cemented strong ties between their two villages. Bithra had great skill in dying and weaving, and Gadriel knew how to prepare beautiful skins. But only Mira had captured his heart.

Now, as Obed lay in the darkness, he thought of his exotic, graceful Mira. Usually, he did not permit himself such luxury, but tonight he wanted to let her memory wash over him....

He and several of his companions had stopped at a spring to fill their waterskins. They had been tracking a wounded leopard, crazed and dangerous, that had killed sheep and goats in the area. The men had been on its trail for many days and were tired and thirsty.

Several young women from a nearby village were filling large, earthen jars from the spring when one of the girls spotted the weary hunters and whispered a warning to the others. All became quiet and timidly lowered their eyes—all except Mira, who stood defiant, feet apart, staring at the men as they approached. She was unusually tall although little more than a child and had not yet acquired the softness of a woman's body. Long, chestnut hair, its red hues reflecting the brilliance of the sun, fell about her shoulders, and large hazel eyes stared at the hunters. She kept one hand on her water jar, the other on her waist.

As Obed drew near, she asked boldly, "Do you want a drink?"

"Yes, pretty child," he replied, smiling at her impertinence, yet captivated by her beauty.

Mira dipped a gourd into her vessel and placed it into his hands. She did not draw back when dirt from his fingers rubbed off on her own, nor did she lower her eyes as he drank in long, gulping swallows. Then, she picked up her jar, rested it on her shoulder and strolled toward the village in the distance.

He vowed then that he would have her. He neither knew nor cared what she could give him. He knew only that he wanted her.

Obed had thought it would be a simple matter to obtain the

beautiful girl for his wife. Several weeks later, he drove fifty of his finest sheep into her village and brought bundles of colorful wool dyed by his wives. He had expected to return to Gibara-boni the next day with his prize. Instead, he left the village shortly after entering it, full of anger and lust.

What did he care that she was a godchild, promised from birth to Kalesh, the serpent-headed god of her people. Or that she was a sacred virgin, undefiled by any man and set aside until she could be given to their god on the high-feast day of her thirteenth year.

Obed did not worship Kalesh, nor did he fear him. In his own way, he honored only Yah-Adon, the God of his fathers, and he no longer truly believed even in Him.

But Obed was not a man to be denied. A plan had already begun forming in his mind. "Go back to Gibara-boni," he commanded his men. "Take the sheep and donkeys with you."

"What do you intend to do?"

"I will not return without the girl," he vowed.

After his men left, he hid in a secluded thicket of dense underbrush and trees where he could see anyone entering or leaving the village. Toward evening his vigilance was rewarded—Mira walking to the spring, balancing a large jar. And—she was alone. He slipped silently through the underbrush to the isolated grove surrounding the cold, bubbling water. There he waited.

When the girl approached, she paused, set her jar on a large rock and knelt by the edge of the spring. She held her hand in the running water and patted her face with the cool water.

Obed pushed aside the drooping branches of a locust tree and stepped out of the shadows.

She raised up, startled. An involuntary gasp escaped her mouth. In the twilight it was impossible to tell if she was afraid, but she did not run or cry an alarm. Obed wished she would struggle, for it would increase the excitement.

Without a word he lifted her in his arms, knocking the earthen jar to the ground where it shattered into jagged pieces. He could feel her heart racing beneath her thin tunic, but still she uttered no sound nor did she struggle as he bore her into the darkness of the forest.

When the first rays of sun filtered through the trees, loud shouts startled Obed from a deep sleep. Mira lay by his side, her head on his shoulder.

He roused the girl. "Quickly!" he commanded, tossing her his tunic, "Cover yourself." With his spear clutched in one hand, he pulled her to her feet, drawing her after him as he strode toward the approaching voices.

When the villagers saw them emerging from the trees, they yelled excitedly for Kamul, the girl's father, who hurried forward, followed by several armed men at his heels. Five priests of Kalesh, robed in bright scarlet, waved their hands wildly in the air, necklaces of bones and beads bouncing on their chests and the sun glistening off their shaved heads. They shouted angrily and pulled at their long, braided beards.

Kamul halted when he saw the burly man walking toward him with Mira's hand grasped in his own. Blood rushing to the old man's face distended the veins on his neck as he screamed, "You have desecrated my daughter! How dare you bring dishonor upon my name! I shall have you both killed!"

"You have the right," Obed replied, "but my name is known to you. I am Obed, a leader of the Sethites. If you value your lives, leave us alone. No man has stood before me and lived. But if you are lucky enough to kill me, my men will sweep down upon your village like locusts. Nothing will be left alive, not even your animals. Why be foolish, old one? I want only this girl. Is she worth a whole village?"

"You are the fool," Kamul hissed. "She belongs to the god Kalesh. She must be given to him at the rising of the New Moon. Do you think I have kept her a virgin to let you have her? She is to be his bride, not yours."

"Think about it, old man," warned Obed. "Your village or the girl!"

Kamul's face was purple and his eyes ready to explode from his face as he glared at the infidel before him. In a rage, he turned to the priests, conferring heatedly with them, spittle flying from his mouth. Finally, he turned back to Obed. "Give me the girl, and we will allow you to leave with your life. But Kalesh must be satisfied."

"No," Mira cried, clinging desperately to Obed. "You mustn't leave me here to be sacrificed. Take me with you. I promise to serve you and bear many children."

Obed put his arm around her and drew her close. "Surely, Kamul, you do not want to sacrifice a blemished gift to your serpent god. Even one such as he would be offended. My seed is now within the girl. Let me have her. She can be of no use now to you or your god."

Again the old man huddled with the priests while Obed watched, his spear poised.

Once again Kamul confronted his taunter, a cunning look in his eyes. "You have won, Obed. Take her. She is not worth losing our lives, but I call down the curse and wrath of Kalesh upon both of you—and upon your descendents. Now, go, and never let your shadow darken this land again."

Kamul signaled to his men, then headed toward the village, never once glancing back....

Obed shifted on his pallet. Outside he heard the menacing growls of dogs fighting for scraps of food. He stretched and rubbed a soreness in his arm from a recent wound. His hand touched Kadrah's bare hip as she lay curled beside him. Heat flared within his loins. He rolled over and shook her roughly. "Wake up, woman," he muttered. "I need you."

Noah tossed restlessly in the last hours of night. He had thrown off his cover in his sleep, his hands now clenched at his sides. Perspiration ran from his body, drenching his pallet. He flung his head from side to side. "Utriel . . . Utriel," he moaned.

In his dream she stood waist deep in water so clear that even the stones lying on the bottom flashed like gems in the sunlight. She laughed and lifted her arms, sending sparkling droplets of water spraying high into the air. Unseen by her undulated an enormous serpent, its sinuous body scarcely rippling the surface.

Noah opened his mouth to warn her, his lips struggling to form words, but his voice refused to issue from his throat. He wanted to run to her, but his legs remained rooted to the ground. Helpless, he watched the reptile approach its unsuspecting quarry. It lifted its huge, flat head and began coiling its glistening body slowly around the one he loved. "Run!" his mind screamed with such vehemence he feared his skull would burst. In horror he saw Utriel serenely watch the glistening body encircle her. Then, with a cry of delight, she flung her arms around the immense, spiraling body and embraced its loathsomeness.

"No!" screamed Noah, bolting upright. His body trembled as he ran his hands over his face, trying to obliterate the hideous dream. He shook his head to clear his senses, but the vision refused to leave. He scrambled to his feet and stumbled to a water jar in the corner of the room. He filled a hollow gourd, then shuffled outside. His hand shaking, he poured the contents over his head, welcoming the coldness as it drenched his hair and shoulders and ran down his back.

"What does it mean?" Noah cried in the stillness of the night. The gourd slipped from his grasp, and he buried his head in his hands. "Utriel," he groaned. "The very thought of you brings a tightness to my throat. I've loved you from the first moment I saw your sweet beauty."

He heard the melancholy hooting of an owl in the darkness and shivered. Tomorrow, as soon as Obed's celebration was over, he would ask him for his daughter.

Six

Long before daylight Obed's wives began preparations for the festivities. After stoking the fires in three shoulder-high brick ovens, they kneaded the dough they would soon bake into flat, round loaves of dark, nutty bread.

Kadrah started the younger children sorting through piles of vegetables while others were sent out with baskets to collect apples, pears, pomegranates, berries, and nuts. Several older girls ground spices, purchased from the recent caravan, to flavor a variety of tasty dishes. They bent low over their work, trying to stifle giggles of anticipation at the thought of the number of eligible young men soon to be in their midst.

Early that morning Bithra roused Utriel. "Hurry!" she urged. "Get dressed! We have much to do."

Utriel opened her eyes and—remembered. "Jirad!" Immediately awake, she asked, "How is he?"

She had stayed beside him late into the night until Bithra had finally made her leave. "Go to your room," the woman had sighed. "There is nothing further you can do here. You need your rest, for tomorrow you will be greatly needed."

Deep circles now ringed Bithra's eyes, making them darker than usual. "I fixed a pallet for myself in his room to be near if he needed me."

"Is he still in great pain?"

Bithra pursed her lips. "I'm not sure. Get dressed, and you can see for yourself." The older woman left the room, shaking her head and muttering under her breath.

Utriel threw back a soft, wool coverlet and stood up, her lissome body a pale shadow in the early light of the room. She shivered. A sudden chill touched her, like a cold hand caressing her shoulder and brushing languidly over her breasts.

"Bithra!" she called hoarsely. No sooner had she called than she heard the woman's strident voice issuing orders outside the house.

She scanned the sparsely furnished room. Someone was here! In the dim light she could see that she was alone, yet, a presence lingered as if unseen eyes peered from the shadows.

"Not again!" she whimpered. A cold sweat covered her face and hands. She wiped her palms down the sides of her legs, then knotted her hands into fists and muttered through clenched teeth, "No . . . one . . . is . . . here."

An unseen hand touched her bare thigh. "Uh!" she cried, whirling around. She grabbed the coverlet, hugging it to her chest, and backed against the wall. Her breath came in short, rapid gasps as she huddled against the cool bricks. She waited, her heart pounding. "Nothing . . . is . . . here," she repeated over and over.

Gradually, as the panic lessened and her body relaxed, she began to feel foolish. "I'm acting like Old Katel who has to be watched every moment."

Still glancing around the room, she dipped her hands into a basin of water she had poured the night before and splashed her skin. She had listened too long to Ganah. She must not give in to the fear. She loved the Ulah-rah dearly, but she would not accept the idea that evil spirits were stalking her. Nevertheless, she scanned the room once more. Realizing she was holding her breath, she exhaled, pulled on a pale blue shift and ran into the sunlight.

She hurried barefoot across the hard-packed earth to where Jirad was sleeping. She had to see him before she began the preparations. No matter how cross Bithra could be, Utriel knew the woman was doing everything possible for him. She vowed to be kinder to her. Her heart pounded at the thought of how close she had come to losing her twin. She couldn't imagine life without him. They were so different in many ways, yet there was a bond between them that seemed to join not only their hearts but also their souls.

She slipped into his room, careful not to wake him. She knew

Bithra had given him wine laced with an herb to make him sleep, but she was unsure how long it lasted. She knelt beside him and tenderly brushed back the dark curls from his forehead. His beard was coming in thicker. It made him look older.

He moaned in his sleep, his finely chiseled mouth twisting in pain.

"Sleep, brother," she crooned, "and grow strong."

In the dim light she bent closer to view his wounds. The bandages were gone! She had not noticed when she entered the room. Surely the shadows must be playing tricks on her. She looked again, drawing in her breath sharply. No wonder Bithra seemed disturbed. The deep claw marks on the side of Jirad's face were already closed, and the edges of the torn flesh on his shoulder and arm had begun knitting together. Where only yesterday the wounds had been gaping tears of raw flesh, now the skin was tender and pink. Gingerly, she touched the side of his face with her fingertips, tracing the marks down his cheek. Ganah possessed marvelous healing elixirs and ointments, but never had Utriel seen anything like this.

She took hold of Jirad's hand, wrapping hers around his long, strong fingers. Suddenly, she cried out. Excruciating pain radiated through her body, pulsating in her face and right shoulder like claws ripping into her flesh. A violent spasm rent her body. She collapsed to the floor, her hand wrenching free as she fell.

She gasped and scrambled to her feet, rubbing her shoulder, her eyes wide with fright.

Jirad lay undisturbed, oblivious to what had occurred.

She backed slowly from the room, never taking her eyes off the sleeping man. Once outside the door, she leaned her head against the wall and closed her eyes. "Dear God," she whispered, "what is happening?"

"There you are," called a cheerful voice. Bethuel beckoned for her. "Bithra said to help me prepare the bread."

"Bethuel," she said, "I—"

"Hurry," chided the woman. "The rest of us have been working since dawn." She turned and rushed back to the ovens.

Utriel, holding her bruised shoulder, peered in at Jirad once more. He was still sleeping. Rubbing her shoulder, she joined the women and children in their frantic preparations.

In the shadowed room, a distraught expression twisted the sleeping man's face. "Help me!" he moaned. While preparations for the feast continued on the other side of the wall, strange and frightening images tormented his dreams. Claws—confusion—unable to move—cold, cruel, maniacal laughter—pain—blood—fear!

Later that day Obed would honor the man who had risked his life to save his son. He would bestow the greatest gift one man could offer another—the ancient and sacred ritual of cutting a blood covenant.

A breeze stirred the heavily leaved boughs of the trees surrounding the dwellings. Birds warbled in the afternoon sun, and bright, diffuse light filtered warmly through the perpetual layer of moisture in the sky.

As Obed's friends and neighbors began gathering, the festivities were marred only by the occasional whispered questions: "Why is Obed entering covenant with a man he doesn't know?" and "What if Jirad dies?" They were concerned since the cutting of a blood covenant created a bond closer than that between milk brothers, men from the same mother. However, the Sethites were not a people to ignore an occasion for celebrating, and Obed's feasts were well-known for their abundance of food and drink.

Colorful mats, striping the ground at one end of the compound, were covered with large tureens of bubbling stews, platters of polished hickory piled with various roasted tubers and yams, baskets of sweet fruit, breads, cheeses, and pots of honey.

Obed placed Bel on his right, the place of honor. Next to him on his left were his five sons and numerous close friends. Gitel and Benu sat beside each other—the former's face dark and sullen, the latter's blank but smiling. After a long series of toasts with the dark-red wine, the meal finally commenced.

As fast as the platters were emptied, the women replenished them. Already wine flowed freely. Spicy and pungent aromas, along with raucous shouts and laughter, filled the air, promising a long night of revelry. Children ran in and out of the houses, hiding behind water jars, snatching food from platters, and enjoying freedom from the usual constraints of adult supervision.

As the evening progressed, a solemnity gradually descended upon the people, and a sense of anticipation filled the air.

After his guests had eaten and drunk their fill, Obed, weaving slightly as he walked, invited them to assemble around a rise in the middle of a clearing at the edge of the compound. He lifted his arms high into the air, a signal for all attention to be directed toward him.

Utriel remained in the doorway of Jirad's room. From there she could see the ceremony and still be near her brother. She had been tending him while at the same time trying to keep the ever-depleting platters filled.

She watched her father. It had been a long evening with many people to feed, and her legs felt tired and heavy. She yawned, covering her mouth with her hand.

Obed turned to Bel, who stood to one side, solitary and aloof, and motioned for the man to join him in the clearing.

The setting sun behind the stranger formed a gold corona around his long, flaxen hair. "Oh, great Yah-Adon," Utriel muttered, "the man looks like a god!"

The flirting glances and inviting looks of young girls and marriageable women directed toward him had not gone unnoticed. Utriel knew what they were thinking, for the same thoughts plagued her own mind. Even now her face grew red. Unconsciously, her hand went to her throat, drawing her bodice tightly to her chest.

"Friend, come," shouted Obed, motioning again to his honored guest. A newly killed bull lay on the ground. The men had formed a large ring around the dead animal but stepped aside as Bel strode to the clearing.

Obed's friends had taken great care in preparing the young sacrificial bull. They had split the animal down the middle—from the head to the tail—the two halves separated by no more than a man's height. Blood still drained from the body, soaking into the soft earth, staining the grass in dark, sticky pools.

Obed and Bel stood side by side between the bloody halves as flies buzzed lazily around their newly found treasure.

With the setting sun behind them, framing them in its glow, the two men paced the blood-soaked ground from the head to the tail of the bull. Then they turned their backs to each other and walked around the carcass, continuing until they met once again in the center of the halves.

"To all who are present," Obed bellowed, "I—"

"Stop!" demanded a voice. "Why are you doing this?" With the El-cumah gripped firmly in her hand, Ganah marched angrily into the circle of men, her long gray robe swirling about her legs. "You do not know this man," she challenged. "How dare you cut the sacred covenant and join yourself and your family with a stranger."

Momentarily thrown off-guard, Obed faced the aged prophetess. "Be still, old woman. By what right do you challenge me? I do as I please. I am Obed, an elder of the Sethites."

"And I am the Ulah-rah, prophetess of Yah-Adon."

"Yes, but you are old and feeble," retorted Obed, no longer caring if he gave offense. He would not tolerate her humiliating him in the presence of his family and friends.

Ganah's voice abruptly changed, the tones becoming lower but strangely full, as if three or four voices had joined in harmonic unison. "Look at me," she commanded. "Do I look feeble to you, Obed, son of Hamon?"

"It is of no consequence," he replied arrogantly, his words slurring. "I make up my own mind. I do not need the aid of you or Yah-Adon. Now, begone before I show my anger." He spun on his heel, once more facing the imposing stranger.

"Very well," said the Ulah-rah. "Let the consequence of your actions fall upon your head." With eyes flashing, she stalked through the murmuring crowd.

Obed threw back his shoulders and began again. "To all who are present, I proclaim that I am now dead to my own past, and I vow to be dependent upon my new brother."

In his deep, resonant voice, Bel repeated the pronouncement.

There was no need to explain the cutting of covenant since it was an ancient, well-known ceremony even though its origin had been lost in antiquity. Neverless, Obed continued, "By walking between the bloody parts of this bull we wipe out our past lives and now look toward a united future. We pledge before all here that if either breaks this covenant, the life of the covenant breaker will be required, and his blood will be shed just as this bull's has been shed this day."

The two men stood in the midst of the bloody halves. With great arrogance and pride Obed removed his short, outer robe, lifting it high above his head for all to see. Holding it by the shoulders, he offered it to Bel. "Here, brother. Put your arms into my garment."

Slowly, the newcomer lifted his arms, placing them into the sleeves.

Obed removed his wide, leather girdle. He wrapped it around Bel's waist and fastened it securely. "With my robe I give myself to you. All that I possess now belongs also to you. And with this belt I give to you my strength and my aid in time of trouble. If any one comes against you, he must also deal with me."

Obed pulled a treasured bronze knife from a sheath at his waist and drew the sharp blade over his wrist. Blood welled up quickly from the cut and ran down the sides of his arm.

He handed the knife to Bel, who, without emotion repeated the act. As the blood ran from both wounds, the two men clasped each other's hands, pressing their bleeding wrists together.

In the twilight of the evening, the two figures stood silhouetted against the sky as their bloods, one earthly and the other a diabolic imitation, became one.

A hush fell over the assembly.

Without warning, the stillness was broken as a scream erupted from Obed's body, a cry beginning in his belly and gaining intensity until at last ripping itself from his throat. His body convulsed uncontrollably, and he would have fallen had not Bel caught him in his massive arms and held him to his chest. In the fading light it was impossible to tell whether the stranger was protecting him or crushing the life from his body.

In that moment of confusion a look of hatred passed fleetingly over Bel's handsome features. Then his lips formed a mirthless, cruel smile as he whispered to Obed so that only he could hear. "Obed, my brother, you cannot die. Not yet. Breathe! I am not through with you."

Obed's chest heaved as air rushed into his burning lungs. A spasm shook his body. He tried to scream, but there was no sound. His terror-filled eyes stared at the man holding him.

Bel wrapped one arm around Obed's waist and turned to the bewildered crowd. "I am now Obed's blood brother," he shouted. "All that he has or will ever have belongs also to me. A blood covenant has been cut which can never be broken except on penalty of death. Although he can deny me nothing, I claim only one thing from my blood brother. I claim—Utriel."

In the hushed silence, the young woman collapsed into a sea of darkness.

Obed opened his eyes. He was lying on his own pallet. The soft light of morning bathed the interior with a warm glow. His head hurt with an excoriating pain. Never had he experienced such agony. He must remember to drink less wine the next time. Nothing was worth such misery. A dull ache pounded with regularity as brilliant flashes of light pulsed before his eyes. He closed them, squeezing tightly to stop the unwanted display and unrelenting throb.

He raised his hand to massage his aching head. What a strange sensation, almost as if it were no longer attached to his body. He tried again to lift his hand, but it refused to move from the pallet. He wanted to look at it, but his head was like stone. He tried his legs, his feet. Nothing! Panic exploded in his chest.

His eyes searched wildly for Bithra or Utriel. Sweat poured from his body as his mind struggled to will the useless muscles into action. He wanted to thrash on the pallet, but his rebellious frame refused the commands. "Help me! Yah-Adon, help me!" his mind screamed over and over until at last he lay exhausted.

Gradually, recollections of the previous night's festivities returned. He remembered the gaiety, the eating, the drinking, the laughter. He remembered cutting covenant with Bel, the knife slicing across his wrist and the mingling of their blood. And then—he remembered the burning that had begun in his wrist, a burning that engulfed him in a pain so intense that before all consciousness ceased, every part of his body screamed in torment.

He had no knowledge of what happened after that. He knew only that he was no longer master of his body: he was incapable of movement or speech, trapped inside his own flesh and bones. He wanted to scream in horror and frustration, but even that was locked forever within.

A sandal scraped on the floor. Thank God he was not alone. Someone had come to help him. Frantically, he willed his rebellious head to turn, but it stubbornly refused. Sweat poured again from his body, filling the room with the musky scent of fear.

"Good morning, Obed—blood brother. How are you feeling? Your family is gravely concerned. Bithra has been beside your bed all night. It's difficult for her to look after both you and your son."

The voice paused. "Such an unfortunate family. Oh, well," it purred, "such things do happen. I told her to rest, that I'd stay with you for a while. After all, are we not one? Besides, the poor woman is exhausted."

Obed strained to turn his head. He knew it was Bel, but for some reason the voice frightened him.

Two immense hands grabbed each side of Obed's head, twisting it roughly, forcing him to look into the cold, blue eyes of the speaker. As he watched, the eyes blurred, the color fading. Suddenly, they burst like splintering ice into brilliant, yellow-brown orbs, the dark pupils contracting, narrowing, and elongating.

"Look at me, Obed," the counterfeit ordered, holding the man's face in his large hands. "What a fool you are. You should not believe everything that you see." He shook his head slowly. "My poor, foolish blood brother, you thought I had saved Jirad, but it was I who made the lioness attack your son. I directed her claws as she ripped and tore into his flesh. I should have let her kill him, for you would still have honored me if I had brought you only his mangled body." The yellow eyes glowed with a fire of malignant hatred.

"You should thank me, though. I caused his wounds to heal quickly. Don't ask me why. I have an impulsive streak. Who knows, he may still be of service to me."

He leaned his head close to Obed's ear. "And you, you pitiful weakling." He sneered at his victim, letting Obed's head fall heavily onto the pallet. "Your . . . Ulah-rah . . . tried to warn you not to cut covenant, but you could not wait to demonstrate your strength and generosity for all to see.

"And do you know why I have done all of this?" His mouth twisted into a cold, cruel smile. "Because I intend to defile Utriel's body in order to carry out my master's plan. I've been watching her for a long time. She's very beautiful, you know, and—her skin is so smooth." The abomination ran its tongue over full, sensual lips. "I shall enjoy her immensely."

Obed's eyes widened in horror.

"Poor child. She thinks I want her for my wife. Even though she loves another, she finds herself attracted to me. Such struggles you humans endure."

Bel threw back his head, laughing in triumph. "You still don't know who I am, do you?"

Obed's blood pounded, and his heart threatened to burst within his chest.

"I am older than time itself," rasped the horror. "I am one about whom the Old Ones talked. It was my master who embodied himself in the serpent and seduced the Mother of Man. Because of him, Yah-Adon cursed the serpent, that golden-scaled dragon, causing it to fall from the sky and grovel forever in the dirt.

"Some call us the God Haters, others the Shadow Walkers. We dared even to defy Yah-Adon Himself." His voice dropped, piercing Obed's head. "For some reason the Placer of Stars loves you ridiculous creatures. Now, we will block His plan and destroy all He has made."

Anger filled his voice, "Can you believe that He actually wants to restore this rotting dung heap?" The yellow satyric eyes flashed in hatred. "We will never let Him do that. He thinks to use your daughter and Noah, that insignificant, dirt-hoeing farmer. When our dark forces are through polluting the seed of man, Yah-Adon's only choice will be to annihilate all of His precious creation.

"Listen to me, Human," he hissed. I will tell you one last thing. My master's servants have gone out over the world, seducing and corrupting the bodies and souls of men and women to bring about the degradation of your entire race. We turn men's lust to one another while we seduce their women for ourselves. We are raising up a new breed—the spawn of darkness." Leaning over Obed, he looked into his eyes. "I do you an honor, though. I, Asmodeus, have reserved Utriel for myself."

The sinister presence filled the chamber. "You understand now, don't you? Think on these things, old man. Think until you destroy yourself, for no one can stand against us. No one. My lord is he who is feared by all. He is the Destroyer. . . . He is Abaddon."

Cruel, harsh laughter ripped through Obed's soul—then abruptly all was quiet.

The man lay with his eyes closed, not daring to open them.

A hand lightly touched his shoulder.

His eyes snapped open.

"Father. It's Utriel. Did I startle you?"

He looked at his daughter who knelt by his side gently bathing his face with cool water and brushing back the gray, matted hair. Tears welled in his eyes and ran down the sides of his face onto the pallet. What had he done? He was helpless to stop the abomination he had brought into his own household. He had failed to recognize evil, and now it was too late.

Seven

Ephemeral threads spun during the night latticed the countryside and floated lightly in the air, transforming the landscape into an enchanted world of sparkling crystalline evanescence. Wet blades of grass wrapped around Noah's legs and stuck to the bottom of his feet as he shuffled along the edge of the forest. The forlorn bleating of grazing sheep drifted toward him on the morning breezes.

He was angry, wanting to avoid the familiar sounds. Frustration and rage boiled within. He knotted his fists, every muscle in his body tightening. If it had not been for the celebration, he would already have asked Obed for permission to take Utriel to his house—only one more day, and she would have been his. Unable to control his anguish another moment, he threw back his head, all of his rage erupting in a deep, wrenching cry.

He had slept little during the night. He knew he was needed in the fields, but the events of the previous evening were etched indelibly into his mind. If only he could awake and discover it to be only another cruel dream. Never would he accept losing Utriel, but by tribal law Bel could claim her whenever he chose. Blood covenants were binding not only upon the two men who entered into them but also upon their children and their children's children. Obed had sealed Utriel's fate irrevocably with his blood.

Noah had no way of knowing how long he wandered blindly through the underbrush. When consciousness at last penetrated the gray haze clouding his mind and his vision, he looked around, startled to see that he had returned to the sacred grove. It was overgrown with thistles and leafy ferns and smelled of damp soil and fungi.

As torment threatened once again to overwhelm him, Noah lifted his eyes to the vaulted, leafy canopy. "Yah-Adon," he cried, "do You still inhabit this grove? Can You hear me?" He fell to his knees, lifting his hands in despair. "I want only to die. I cannot bear to live without Utriel."

Desolation and loneliness engulfed him. He threw himself before the crumbling altar and lay on the ground, his face pressed into the damp grass. Sobs racked his body.

Although not a breeze stirred the still air, the leaves on overhanging branches trembled, whispering faintly in the stillness. Tiny bits of light danced over the altar, shimmering and sparking. Slowly and mercifully, as oil poured from a vessel, a wave of peace flowed over his body. With a sigh, he closed his eyes and rested in the warm, enveloping folds.

Eight

Noah, confused and exhausted, had returned from the grove sometime late in the evening. He now lay on his pallet in the gray twilight between sleep and consciousness.

At the foot of the mat stood a man in shimmering radiance. Thick, dark hair touched his shoulders, framing a face of enormous strength yet with eyes both gentle and full of compassion. A short, sleeveless white tunic, opened to the waist, revealed arms not only capable of wielding a mighty weapon but, somehow he knew, also of providing immense comfort.

Although the man's lips moved, Noah heard the voice not with his ears but in his mind. "Do not be afraid, Noah. You were chosen before you were born to bring rest to your people. For generations they have waited for a seed through whom they will gain relief from Yah-Adon's curse. You will bring that comfort. Hide these words in your heart and remember them when darkness threatens to overtake you."

As Noah struggled to consciousness, the thought of Utriel flooded his soul. He could not explain what had occurred earlier in the day at the grove or now in his reverie, but the ache in his heart had lessened. His love for her had not diminished, but the burden of loss seemed lighter. A voice spoke to his heart, "It is going to be all right." Yet, hidden in his subconscious, huddled like an unborn infant waiting to be birthed, crouched a deformed chimera called fear.

When Utriel arrived at the well later that morning, Noah was waiting. He lifted the water jar from her arms. She winced at the dark circles under his gentle eyes and the tight lines around his mouth.

He placed his hands on each side of her face and lifted her chin until their eyes met.

She pulled away, took several steps and looked back at him. "This can never be," she said. "Our lives have been changed forever."

"I love you, Utriel."

"And I love you, but that means nothing, now."

Tenderly, he drew her to him, wrapping his arms around her trembling body. "I *will* find a way to free you from your father's covenant."

"It's hopeless. A covenant cannot be broken."

"No! Nothing is impossible. I'll find a way. Trust me."

She pushed away from his chest. "Promise me you won't challenge Bel. You are brave and courageous and a skilled fighter, but you are no match for him."

"I won't let him have you. We'll run away. The caravan is only a few days' travel from here. The traders will take us with them until we can reach another caravan or town."

"Think what you're saying. If we are caught, we will both be killed. To break the covenant means death."

"Once we get across the plains, no one will find us. Not even Bel."

"No," said Utriel, her eyes filling with tears. "It is too dangerous."

Noah pulled her close and touched his lips to hers.

Startled, she drew back, then put her arms around his neck and pressed hungrily against him.

He took her hands and loosened them from his neck. "First, I must free you from the stranger," he murmured.

She leaned weakly on his chest, frightened by the sudden awakening of her body.

Although Obed was an elder of the council, the people adjusted rapidly to the loss of his leadership. As the weeks passed, fewer and fewer friends kept watch by his side. They missed his camaraderie, but their mercurial attention was diverted to the handsome, golden-haired weapon maker.

Gabul, a burly, dark-haired man who lived by himself within the town walls, said to Bel, "You can stay at my house and teach me your skills. I will be a good student. Besides, I have been without a companion for many moons."

"Stay with us as long as you want," urged the townsmen. After all, he was now Obed's blood brother. The least they could do was to show their hospitality.

Nine

Ganah, leaning on the El-cumah, hurried through the town gate. Eliah lumbered after her in the deepening twilight.

Her corpulent guardian had been born with the flat face and slanted eyes that meant he would never understand how to watch the changes of the moon for the birthing of lambs and kids, when to plant for the best crops, or how to increase the family's wealth. Such children were gentle and pleasant, but a male child who used more than he produced was not a luxury many families would tolerate. When Ganah heard that the infant's father intended to leave him in the wilderness for the animals, she was moved with compassion and asked to have the child.

Honored that the prophetess wanted his son, the father presented the baby to the holy woman. "My Ulah-rah," he said. "I have removed the child's buds before giving him to you. If he is to be your servant, then all temptation must be eliminated." The father refused, however, to allow the baby's mother to continue caring for it. "Our child is dead to us," he said. "If it lives, it must be by someone else's hand."

The prophetess had sent messengers into all the streets of Gibaraboni to find a wet nurse for the starving infant. Within hours Paniel appeared at her door. Her own baby had been stillborn, and she was eager not only to relieve her physical discomfort but also to ease the pain of her loss.

The pitiful infant immediately captivated her heart. Within days, though, the two women made a discovery that brought sorrow to their soul—little Eliah was unable to make even the slightest sound. With their love and care, however, he grew into manhood, his strength and girth increasing with each passing year. He became known as the

Tumulac, the Mountain, and zealously served his mistress, seldom letting her out of his sight.

The two unlikely companions, a tall, gaunt old woman and her immense guardian, made their way between the houses and across the fields toward the Great Mound, an imposing tower built of earth and stone by the Old Ones after they inhabited the valley. It had been many years, though, since Ganah had climbed its heights.

The night orb gleamed palely in the purple sky as she made her way along a path, all but obliterated, that wound up the side of the mound. Eliah stomped before her, clearing a way with his huge bulk. A wisp of cloud curtained the moon for a brief moment, then meandered across the dark expanse.

When they reached the top, the prophetess placed her hand on her companion's arm. "Wait here for me," she said, speaking as if to a child. "I wish to study the stars." He sank noiselessly on his haunches into the deep grass.

The Ulah-rah stood before an ancient stone altar, now an amorphous, green mass of overgrown vines and dark, velvety moss. It was here, on the ziggurratus, as the stone and earth towers were called, that the Old Ones had studied the celestial spheres hung in the infinite canopy of space by the Placer of Stars. At some time in the distant past He had taught them to divide the heavens into quadrants for the purpose of telling the time and the seasons. With His guidance, the people had devised a remarkably accurate calendar and had charted the movements of the spheres on cured skins, recording the days, months, and years. They had known, also, the meanings of the constellations that told the wondrous story of the people's promised redemption.

With the passing of the centuries, though, newer generations forgot the purpose of the stars and drifted farther and farther from Yah-Adon, the Great Light and source of all knowledge. In a vain effort to replace the wisdom and guidance from which they had turned, the priests and elders began designing ways to interpret the positions of the Mazzaroth's constellations. With each succeeding generation the beautiful and natural knowledge of Yah-Adon's starry message became twisted into a perverted travesty. The elders added and enlarged upon the mysteries and the promise by developing stories and prophecies from their own imaginations.

Ganah had tried to preserve the truth, but even she had forgotten much of the Promise. It had become so intertwined with the stories of the people that they were sometimes impossible to separate.

She sighed as she ran her hand over the velvety stones. Her ancestors had not only believed the story displayed in the stars, but above all they had believed in the One who had placed the stars.

"There was a time," she said, speaking more to herself than to the Tumulac, "when the people begged me to sing the ancient story of the darkness that hovered over the world while it roamed to and fro seeking an entrance. I sang of the seduction of the first Ulah-rah and of how she wept and mourned when Yah-Adon banished both her and her mate from their beautiful garden.

"The people shed tears to hear how she threw her arms around the animals and cried when she realized she would never again see them. How she begged Yah-Adon to let her take just one creature when she left the garden—the graceful, snow-white unicorn. Through the years, it had been a constant companion, either trotting beside her as they ran through fields of brilliant flowers, its silky mane streaming in the wind, or grazing silently as she and her mate made love under low, heavily laden boughs."

Eliah listened, his dark eyes shining under their ponderous lids.

"The people groaned when I sang of the woman wrapping her arms around the animal's neck, her long, pale hair falling about her delicate, tear-stained face. They cried to hear that Yah-Adon loved the man and woman as only a father could love wayward children, yet he could not let them remain.

"Did you know," asked the prophetess as she rubbed the surface of the staff, now worn to a mellow glow by the many hands that had held it over the centuries, "that Yah-Adon Himself uprooted a straight sapling, stripped its limbs and leaves and made this rod? With His own finger He inscribed upon it His pledge of love—that one day all evil and darkness in the world would be gone. To be certain that neither the man nor woman nor their children nor their children's children would ever forget or doubt His promise, He emblazoned it across the skies for all to see."

Ganah rose and crossed to the edge of the mound. She leaned on the staff as she looked down upon Gibara-boni. "Eliah," she sighed, pressing her forehead against the staff, "I have failed my people. I am too old and too tired to call them back. The tide of unbelief is too strong. And . . . I could not hold it back."

Below, in the valley, the waning fires outside the dwellings glowed like clusters of fireflies. Behind her the slight rising and falling of the Tumulac's massive chest was the only sign of life separating him from the huge stones scattered over the Great Mound.

With a sigh, she turned. Many cycles of the moon had passed since she had last offered a sacrifice. "Help me, Eliah," she said as she pulled at the heavy vines covering the altar. Obediently, the Tumulac rose to aid his mistress.

When the top of the stone slab was clear, she gathered an armful of dry sticks and leaves and piled them on the mossy stones. She reached into the deep leather pouch hanging from her girdle and lifted out a frightened dove, its legs and wings bound against its body. It struggled in her hand. She crooned gently to it and stroked its pale feathers. "Yes, sweet one, you are perfect. You are without spot or blemish."

The small body relaxed to the peaceful voice and the tender caress.

As she held the bird in one hand, she raised her eyes to the heavens. "Yah-Adon, great Placer of Stars, I have come here rather than the grove to present my offering. For here I am closer to your habitation. Have mercy upon your unworthy servant. I have failed in teaching your people. They no longer listen or care, and I am too old and too tired to continue.

"In my dreams you have shown me that a great evil is already in our midst. I want to understand, but your words are clouded in mystery." Her voice faltered, then rose, gaining strength and intensity. "I cannot fight something I cannot see! You must help me! Empower me to carry out your will!"

She drew the obsidian knife from the belt of her tunic. With one swift motion she slit the dove's throat, lifted it high in the air, then laid it gently on the altar. A stain, darker than the night, spattered her hands and ran onto the ancient stones. She wiped her hands on a cloth tucked into her waist. Next, she reached into her pouch and pulled out flints. She struck one against the other until a tiny flame flared under the lifeless body.

She dropped to her knees. "Oh, Great One," she implored. "Help me! I am willing to lay down my life if necessary to stop this evil, but I do not see my way clearly. How will I know what to do? Is there no one to help me?"

Her body trembled in the darkness. The fire flickered and faded on the dark stone. Suddenly, a breeze fanned the meager flames. They flared, growing and leaping, burning brighter and brighter, forming a splendor that glowed with a throbbing luminescence. The prophetess fell prostrate on the ground and covered her face.

Out of the flames, from the long corridor of the ages, spoke a voice, deep and resonant. "Ganah, look at My presence, lest when the days grow dark you forget that I came to you. If I had wanted a mighty warrior to do this deed, I would have chosen one. You are a weak but worthy vessel. Strength cannot win this battle, but I will not leave you helpless. I will be your shield and your protection. Take one step at a time. Put your confidence in no man, only in Me.

"Remember," commanded the voice. "All is not as it appears. That which is beautiful can also be deadly, and the most humble, the most worthy. Listen to the voice that whispers in your heart. Trust, and I will guide you."

The brilliance swirled into a mighty convolution, rising higher and higher until at last fading into the night.

"All right," she whispered. "I will trust You. Show me, step by step, the way." A strange calm came over her, and with it strength flowed into her weary body.

Ten

Utriel's days were consumed with caring for Obed. She chafed at not being able to spend time with her brother. She feared the days were slow and endless for him, but she was pleased that by the end of the third week his wounds had healed, leaving only faint, pink scars. Although he was not yet able to throw a spear or wield a hoe, he was using his arm once again.

Bethuel had been summoned from the wives' quarters to assume the duties of the main house, leaving the two women time to do little more than tend the older man. The girl found it difficult to arise in the morning knowing that everything in her life had changed. Even her visits with Ganah had ceased.

Utriel shifted the heavy basket of wet clothes higher on her shoulder. Her back ached and her knuckles were raw from scrubbing and pounding the laundry at the edge of the river that wound through the valley. If her father were well, he would never allow her to do such a menial chore. Tears welled in her eyes. She rubbed her cheek angrily against her shoulder.

Even worse than the alterations in her life was the torment raging in her mind. Who was this man who had suddenly entered their lives, demanding that she be his wife? Where had he come from? And what about Noah? She loved him with all her heart—but Bel was handsome beyond words. And what of Ganah, who had prepared her to be the next Ulah-rah? Utriel wanted to serve Yah-Adon—or was it only the power of being Ulah-rah that had intrigued her?

Never had she felt so confused. If she dedicated herself to Yah-Adon and chose a life of celibacy, Bel would no longer have a claim on her. Could she choose such a life, though? When she was still a child, the idea of being Ulah-rah had filled her with thoughts of joy. Now that she had become a woman, a passion and desire flared within that often brought fear to her heart. Being a child had been so much easier. Now, when she thought of Noah or of Bel, her heart beat faster, and it became difficult to think.

What if she decided to serve Yah-Adon instead of choosing marriage, and He did not choose to pass the El-cumah on to her? Then she would also have lost both Noah and Bel. A nagging thought gnawed at her consciousness: *Had Yah-Adon sent Bel to punish her for desiring Noah more than wanting to serve Him?*

She climbed the bank of the river, taking care that her bare, wet feet did not slip on the natural rocky steps. Jirad stood at the top of the rise, watching her. A stab of pain pierced her heart at the sight. He had lost so much weight, and his handsome face was drawn and pale.

She dropped her basket and sprinted toward him, the water on her long legs glistening in the sunlight. She wrapped her arms around him.

"Are you all right?" he asked.

"Me?" she retorted, throwing back her head. "Of course. You're the one I worry about." She stepped back and surveyed him. "You look terrible. You're so thin."

"Don't worry about me."

"Why not?" she said, still holding his hands. "You rarely talk to anyone. It's as if you're avoiding even your friends."

"How would you know? You don't even have time for yourself anymore."

She bit her lower lip as another tear threatened to escape. "I hear others talking."

"I'll be fine." Still holding her hand, he pulled her toward the shade of a large, chestnut tree. "Sit here. Bithra won't know you're gone for awhile." He dropped onto the grass, drawing her down beside him.

"I've missed you so," she said.

"I know. And I've missed you."

She dropped her hands into her lap and lowered her head to hide the tears now rolling down her face.

"I'm sorry, Utriel. I'm sorry that things aren't working out as you'd planned."

She wiped her cheeks with the heels of her hands but said nothing for fear of giving way completely.

"I know you and Noah love each other."

She lifted her head and stared at her twin in amazement. "How do you know? I've told no one."

"My sweet sister, it is hardly a secret. Your faces shout the message for all to see."

Once again she felt the hated redness rushing up her neck. "He was going to ask Obed for me as soon as the celebration was over."

Tears welled in Jirad's eyes.

Never had she felt so close to him as she did at that moment. Suddenly, she wanted to tell him of the frightening experience at the lake and in her room. She wanted to tell him of the pain they had shared the morning after his injury. She wanted to cry out her anguish at being torn between wanting to have a husband and to serve Yah-Adon as a successor to Ganah.

"Jirad," she said, "I . . ." But the fear that he would think it only foolish imagination once again loomed in her mind.

"I'm sorry I haven't been able to help you," he continued, his eyes dark and troubled as he massaged the deep ache in his shoulder. "But Utriel, Noah must not challenge the stranger. He is enough in love with you that he might attempt it, but he could never win against such a man."

"I . . . ," she began once again. Couldn't Jirad see how badly she needed him? Didn't they always know each other's thoughts and feelings. Why was he being so insensitive now? With the moment gone, her shoulders sagged, and she lowered her eyes. "Don't worry," she said, fighting the tears. "I've already made him promise."

"Besides," said her brother, snapping off a long blade of grass, "I don't trust Bel. Something is not right about him. I can feel it. He troubles me."

"How can you say such a thing?" said Utriel, her voice rising in astonishment. "He saved your life."

Jirad shrugged and methodically shredded the grassy blade. "I wonder," he muttered. "I know what Bel said, but bits and pieces of the incident keep flashing through my mind. If I could just put them all together so it made sense."

He shut his eyes, squeezing them so that lines formed between his brows. "I remember going to Manua's to purchase a large ram for our flock. When I arrived, one of his sons ran to me screaming that a lioness had carried off a kid from their pasture and had headed toward the Shinar."

Jirad drew up a knee and rested his arm on it. "I should never have followed it by myself, but I was afraid it would get away. I only intended to track it to its den and then come back for help. Besides, I had my knife and sling.

"Utriel," he said, swallowing against the dryness in his throat and pressing his hands against his temples, "the rest is unclear. I remember entering the forest—then a blinding flash of light—then, nothing. But in my head I hear laughter, cruel and malicious. And I feel fear." He raised his head, his pale countenance marked with frustration and dismay. "If I could just put it all together!"

When Utriel entered her father's room, a wave of panic swept over her. "Bithra!" she called, running to the doorway. "Where is he? His bed is empty."

The woman was dropping skeins of recently spun wool into a large pot of bright blue dye. At the sound of Utriel's voice, she paused and wiped her glistening face with the hem of her tunic. "He's gone," she said.

"No!" cried Utriel, alarm putting a frantic edge on her voice.

At the sight of the girl's stricken face, Bithra shook her head, clucking her tongue. "You misunderstand. Bel carried him to the edge of the fields to watch the men."

Utriel felt foolish, but she sighed with relief. "Are you sure it is safe?"

"Why not?" The woman began working a sturdy pole through large holes on each side of the pot to remove it from the fire.

"Father worries me," Utriel said as she hefted the other end of the pole. "Whenever I'm with him, he has such fear in his eyes."

The two women dragged the large vessel to a grassy area, where Bithra stirred the wool again with a long wooden paddle.

"What do you think of him?" ventured Utriel. 'Bel, I mean. Do you like him?"

"Like him? Why shouldn't I like him? He saved your brother, and he is kind to Obed."

Utriel wrinkled her brow. "I know he spends a lot of time with Father, but Jirad doesn't like him."

Bithra grabbed several pieces of wood and tossed them on the fire. "Your brother is behaving like a child." She dusted her hands on her broad hips. "I don't know what I'd do if the man didn't spend time with your father. I'd never get any work done."

"Why don't you let the other wives help you look after him?" asked Utriel.

"What?" the older woman retorted, her voice rising as she stopped her work and stared at the girl. "I am Obed's head wife. I am the one who takes care of him. I would die first before letting any of those women touch him." Shaking her head, she stalked into the shed for more wool.

Bithra was right, reasoned Utriel. Bel was a great comfort to Obed. Jirad should be glad that the man was so kind to their father, for Obed had few pleasures left in life.

There was never any question in Utriel's mind. She loved Noah. Yet the thought of the blond giant desiring her for his wife was unexpectedly intoxicating. Although Bel frequented the compound to visit Obed, he made no reference to his previous demand and never spoke to her. Whenever she thought he was unaware of her presence, she studied his handsome features.

As the weeks passed, troubling thoughts crowded her mind, thoughts of hair the color of ripened wheat and of muscles rippling under sun-bronzed skin. She grew angry with herself, but she could not deny the excitement she experienced in his presence. She felt strangely divided, fragmented almost, and it frightened her. How could she love Noah, she pondered, and still be attracted to Bel, a man who had claimed her weeks ago, but had now seemingly forgotten his demand.

Many of the men, mainly the young and middle-aged, frequented Gabul's house for Bel to repair their tools and blades. They were also intrigued with a weapon he possessed, one they had never before seen—he called it a sword. The long, flat blade was much deadlier than that of a mere knife. Bel spent hours teaching them how to use it.

Even more fascinating than the weapon itself was the strength of the grayish metal from which it was made. Most of the Sethites' knives and spearheads were made of obsidian or bone. A few of the more prosperous men had purchased from passing caravans blades fashioned from bronze, made by the metalworkers of the tribe of Tubal-Cain, many weeks east of the mountains. Never, though, had they seen any blade or head as sharp or as strong as the sword possessed by the newcomer.

When they begged him to teach them how to make such weapons, he selected several men, loaded ten asses and journeyed east four days from the valley to the mountain foothills. Once there, he directed them to collect large piles of a black, volcanic rock.

Next, he instructed them in building a field furnace. First, they gathered huge logs of oak, ash, and acacia, each as tall as a man. With the aid of the asses, the men dragged the logs to the furnace site. They laid the timbers in two layers, one crisscrossing the other. On top they placed a layer of the black rock. They repeated the layers, alternating one on top of the other until the structure was taller than a man and larger than a hut.

Additional logs were gathered and leaned on end against the sides of the mound of wood and black rock. After a day and a half, the task was complete. Then they lighted a fire, allowing it to burn for three days. The men, standing a good distance from the intense heat, continuously fed the blazing inferno.

On the fourth day the fire was allowed to die out and begin to cool. Water was hauled from a nearby stream to quench the glowing coals. When the ashes had turned black, the men raked through the cinders with large branches and collected the irregularly shaped ingots of melted raw iron. After packing the crude metal into heavy leather bags, they loaded their newly found treasure onto the backs of the asses, and the party started the long trek back to Gibara-boni.

After several days of rest, Bel showed the men how to build a furnace out of clay bricks and stone in order to melt the metal. The ingots were placed in the center surrounded by hardwood which burned hot and long, the heat intensified by two men working a large bellows made from the hides of wild boars.

As the ingots melted, the molten iron flowed from a carved stone trough into molds carved out of soapstone and shaped for blades, arrowheads and spearheads.

Finally, Bel taught Gabul how to shape the weapons and produce sharp edges with the massive hammer he had brought with him when he entered the village weeks before with Jirad in his arms.

The furnace and forge quickly became the center of interest for the townsmen. They watched as the giant hammered and shaped the new metal and marveled at its strength.

Gabul was proud that the weapons maker was staying with him and boasted loudly that Bel had chosen him from among all the others to learn the new skill, but he scowled darkly when the man was attentive to others. Lately, his scowls were increasing in intensity.

At the end of a long, hot day at the furnace, Bel would often throw down his mallet and yell loudly to any men within shouting distance, "Enough for now! Let's drink and relax!" Gabul would glower fiercely when Bel, his body glistening with sweat, threw his arm over the shoulder of a townsman and roared, "Let's find a skin of wine and something to eat!" Then, sullen and morose, Gabul would trail behind, grumbling to himself.

When the next morning arrived, the bleary-eyed men who had accompanied Bel invariably watched in amazement as he began his work, alert and unaffected by the nightly carousing. They shook their heads in awe, longing to be like him.

The days slipped by with Noah no closer to finding a solution for freeing Utriel from the covenant. His father, Lamech, provided no consolation. He merely slapped him on the back, saying, "Such is the way with women, my son. But they're like the sheep on the hillsides. You can always find another. They're not worth the loss of a night's sleep. Besides—" he winked—"a woman is good only to give pleasure and to produce sons."

Even Ganah offered no help. She shook her head sadly but reminded him that a blood covenant could not be broken except upon punishment of death. Utriel was counted as one of her father's possessions that would now pass to Bel to be claimed when he desired.

Eleven

Noah worked in the fields all morning, pausing only when his father's servant brought jugs of fresh water and milk and loaves of bread covered with a mixture of rich goat's butter and dark, pungent honey. He poured one of the jugs of water over his head, letting it run down his back and chest. He shook his head like a great hairy dog, slinging spray in all directions.

As he flung back his thick hair, a movement in the distance caught his eye. He squinted. Was that Jirad running toward the Shinar? The glare from the sun made it difficult to be sure. He cupped his hands around his mouth and shouted, "Jirad!"

The runner neither broke stride nor gave evidence of having heard.

Again Noah yelled, "Jirad! Wait!"

When the young man gave no response, he sprinted after him. Why would he enter the forest alone? He had too great a head start, though, and soon outdistanced him, quickly disappearing into the trees.

Noah halted at the edge of the forest, nearly blinded by the sudden absence of light filtering through the leaves. He ran the back of his hand over his perspiring face, leaving a streak of dark soil on his cheek.

Mammoth ferns with long slender fronds arched high above his head. Tall hickories and spreading elms, old and shaggy, stretched their limbs to the sky, branches so close together that small, tree-dwelling animals used the leafy canopy as a thoroughfare above the heads of predators roaming the greenwood. Leaves rustled in the dense, dark undergrowth. Large boulders lay scattered over the neolithic floor as though thoughtlessly tossed by a colossal, petulant child, and numerous caves pocketed the limestone hillsides. Brilliantly colored birds warbled loudly. Others sang sharp staccato notes, their songs blending with the rest into a harmonious cacophony.

Noah advanced into the coolness of the muted light. He paused, listening, but he heard nothing, only the forest.

Jirad was nowhere to be seen.

Noah grabbed a dead branch and snapped it over his knee. He wanted to talk to Jirad without Utriel around, and this would have been a perfect time.

Jirad was intent on only one thing—Bel. He had not seen Noah or heard him call. For weeks he had been watching the weapon maker, determined to learn more about him. On three different occasions over the last two weeks, he had followed the man as far as the Shinar, only to lose him in the dense forest. No matter how carefully he tried to keep him in sight, the enigmatic stranger always eluded him.

The first time he saw Bel heading toward the forest, he followed out of curiosity, for no one ever went beyond the edge of the Shinar. Now it had become an obsession to discover where he went.

Four days earlier, Jirad had trailed the man deeper into the Shinar than he had ever gone before, only to have his quarry seem to disappear before his eyes. Yesterday he had followed him once again to the same area. Again he had vanished. There had to be a cave concealed among the boulders, and this time Jirad did not intend to leave until he found it. So absorbed was he in locating the suspected entrance that even the dangers of the forest no longer disturbed him.

He was convinced that something dark and frightening emanated from the man, a monstrous essence lurking just beyond the bounds of consciousness, but no one else seemed to sense it. He had to prove to himself he was not crazy, yet he feared the unknown. He had told no one of the dreams plaguing him at night or of the faceless horror stalking him in his sleep. Such would be an unmanly thing to do. These things he kept to himself.

Now, as Jirad stood once again within the shadows of the forest trees, he rubbed the aching scars on his shoulder and chest. The softly filtered gold of the early afternoon sun tessellated the forest floor. He saw no evidence of anyone having just made his way through the brush, but he was certain that somewhere among the rock-covered gullies was a cave, and that Bel had entered it.

Agitated insects buzzed and darted around his head as he pushed aside dense, low growing brush, some covered with berries that left dark, wet stains on his hands. He scrambled over large rocks and boulders littering the ground. Something skittered through the leaves at his feet. Harsh thorns raked his hands as he lifted heavy tangled vines. In spite of the coolness in the forest, perspiration soon covered his body.

When he finally paused, wishing he had brought a skin of water, he leaned his back against the rough trunk of a huge sycamore and closed his eyes. He tapped the back of his head against the tree. "I know it's here," he muttered. "It has to be."

A sudden rustling in the leaves caused his eyes to snap open. "Well," whispered Jirad, "look at you!"

A narrow, brown ferret scampered across his foot, arching its long back as it leaped comically over the ground. It stopped, peered at him with bright, black eyes, then wiggled its slender body through a huge cluster of ferns, leaving its musky scent lingering in the air.

In a momentary return to boyhood, Jirad dashed into the ferns, parting them with his arms as he tried to flush out the animal. Suddenly, he halted. Dank, fetid air full of animal smells assaulted his nostrils. "I knew it," he mumbled. Before him yawned a dark recess, large enough for a man to enter if he doubled over.

Although he could see inside only a few feet, he had heard rumors that some of the caves in the forest extended far into the hills, some even deep into the bowels of the earth. He rocked back on his heels and studied the opening. It would be foolish to enter without several pitch torches. The hair on the back of his neck prickled at the thought.

Again he rubbed his shoulder. A dull pain throbbed beneath the scars. Tomorrow he would return with torches, but for now, he pushed the ferns back into place.

Twelve

Ganah rose before dawn. She had wasted too much time already. During the last few weeks, a strength and energy she had not experienced for many cycles of the moon had awakened within her a long-dormant enthusiasm for life.

She sat on a three-legged oak stool and divided her hair into two parts. With fingers long accustomed to this daily routine, she rapidly braided the strands, then intertwined them at the nape of her neck. She prided herself on two things—her thick, gray hair and her strong hands. Unlike most of her peers, her fingers had remained long and tapered, not becoming twisted and gnarled with age.

This morning she had wakened with a compelling desire to go once again to the Mound, but this time she intended to study the ancient stones inscribed by the Old Ones. With the recent influx of strength, she felt an urgency to renew her knowledge of their message. She wrapped a scarf around her shoulders and flung back the door with the end of her staff.

The Tumulac, studiously sharpening a bronze spearhead, sat in a heap beside the entrance. When he saw her, he smiled, adoration spreading over his benign face. She was the only parent he had ever known. Like a huge, hairless bear, he spent his nights outside the door of her dwelling, pulling his outer robe over himself for protection from the cool, evening breeze and early morning dew. No matter how many times she protested his sleeping by her door, he shook his head obstinately, refusing to move. Finally, she let him be.

At her nod, he grasped the spear in one hand and launched himself to his feet. He followed her, lumbering forward with his powerful, lurching gait.

As they made their way through the town gate and into the countryside, Ganah was conscious of the many fires being rekindled in front of the surrounding dwellings. Head wives were barking directions to lesser wives and slaves for the preparation of the morning meals. Squealing and laughing, several half-naked children chased each other around a fire with sticks they had found on the ground.

Once they had crossed the clearing, Eliah went before her, carefully holding aside any branches or brush that might hinder her progress.

The early dew that watered this antediluvian world was thick and heavy under their feet. The bottom of Ganah's dark cloak turned darker as it was dragged through the tall weeds. The grass and foliage glistened, moisture deepening the lush shades of green.

The Mound was as tall as ten men, its base as large as three family tents. A path wound around the sides, leading to a leveled top where several concentric circles of large, flat, carved stones had been positioned centuries before. Now, in the daylight, Ganah was amazed that she and Eliah had been able to make their way up the ziggurat in the darkness, for she saw that the path was covered with weeds and loose rock and completely obliterated in places.

Here the Old Ones had studied the Mazzaroth centuries before, carefully and methodically plotting the path, or "the Way" as they called it, of the progression of the heavenly bodies. Here, they had carved on the stone figures found in the clusters of stars their God had placed in the heavens at the beginning of time.

Ganah wanted to study them once again. The thought nagged at her consciousness that somewhere in their story lay hidden the answer to the fearful evil closing in upon her people.

"Eliah," she said, as she surveyed the overgrown area before her, "help me cut back the weeds and clear the stones."

The gentle giant pulled a large blade from a sheath strapped to the wide girdle encircling his waist. With a single-minded objectiveness, he hacked the larger bushes, then cut and scraped away the growth that had encroached its way across the stone carvings.

As they worked, the sun climbed higher in the sky. Ganah often stopped to stretch her back or rub her neck to relieve the strain, but the

Tumulac never paused. When the last stone was clear, he rocked back on his haunches, looked at his mistress, and smiled broadly.

"Thank you," she said.

The stones were in surprisingly good condition. The overgrowth seemed to have protected them from the wind and moisture. She ran her hand over the exposed stones, then walked to the center and surveyed the ancient circles. It had been so long since she had been here that she needed to reacquaint herself with its layout. The inner circle, consisting of twelve large, flat stones, had been hewn from the lake bed by their ancestors and laboriously hauled to the top of the Mound. Each slab had been carved to depict one of the twelve signs of the Way.

To the right of her foot lay one with the image of a creature having the head of a woman and the body of a lion. It was, she had been taught long ago, a uniting of the beginning of the story, the Virgin, and the ending, the Lion.

She knelt and rubbed the hem of her robe over the surface of the next stone. "Ah," she murmured as she touched the stone with her fingers. The Virgin! Although layers of dirt nearly concealed the branch in her right hand, it was still visible. In her left she held an ear of corn.

Ganah scraped at the next stone. It was the Circular Altar.

"Look, Eliah," she said, pointing to various stones. "Here is the Scorpion, the Archer, the Fish-goat . . . over there the Water Bearer, the Fish, the Lamb, the Bull, the Twins, the Crab and . . ." she said, almost reverentially, "the Lion."

Patiently, as if teaching a child, she continued. The Tumulac studied each stone as she spoke.

"The twelve signs are divided into three sections. Each section contains four of the signs, which are in turn explained by the stone carvings in the larger surrounding circle. There—" she pointed—"in the outer circle, next to each sign is a section divided into three rings. Each ring contains a picture of a different star cluster.

"This is the way the Old Ones recorded the story that Yah-Adon had revealed to our ancestors. It is the same story He wrote in the sky, the story of a coming Redeemer. Never forget, dear friend," she said, pointing with the El-cumah, "that to read the star pictures you must always begin with the inner circle. Start with the Virgin and then proceed to each outer circle for there. . . ."

She cocked her head. "I hear something!" Was that a whispering in the breeze? She strained to catch the words. They were so faint.

Eliah watched, a puzzled expression on his face.

Ganah eyes flashed. "I was right! The Mazzaroth! The answer is here—in the Mazzaroth!"

With great excitement she traced the end of the El-cumah over the stones. "It's here! The answer is here." Her voice was vibrant and alive. "I know the story, but knowing and understanding are not always the same. I have told the tales again and again to the people. They are engraved in my mind, but somewhere I am missing a vital piece."

She turned to the Tumulac. "I must go over and over the story until I find the answer."Grasping the staff in her hand, she turned to the stone of the Virgin. "Eliah, we begin again. Yah-Adon will pull back the veil if we persevere."

The Tumulac plodded to her side, eager to hear the prophetess recite the ancient teachings as she examined each stone.

"The Virgin," she said, pointing with the staff, "is a reminder that her seed holds the hope for all mankind. See, there, in her hand is an ear of corn? In that corn is the brightest of the stars. It is called T*he Branch*, and this other star is *The One Who Shall Have Dominion*. Here are three constellations explaining the Virgin. First is Comah, a woman with a child in her arms. Then, there's Bezeh, half man and half horse. He is also called *The Despised One*, the man with two natures. The third is Bo, a man with a spear in one hand and a sickle in the other. He is *The Coming One*."

Her eyes lingered on Comah as she repeated what she had been taught: "When the time comes for the child to be born, a brilliant star will appear in the sign of the Virgin."

Ganah leaned on her staff. "It just doesn't make sense," she said with a sigh. "I know what it says, but how can a child come from a virgin?"

Deep in thought, she pulled a portion of flat bread from the pouch at her waist. She broke it and handed the larger part to Eliah along with a bit of cheese. "Here, old friend," she said, lowering herself to the ground. "You look hungry. We'll rest for a moment."

A breeze caught the edge of her scarf, lifting it from her body. She grabbed it and flung it around her shoulders.

The Tumulac chewed a mouthful of cheese and waited.

Ganah bit into the bread, then stuck the rest into her pouch. She struggled to her feet and walked to the carving of the Circular Altar. She bent down and touched her fingers to the stone, tracing the outline. "The answer is here," she murmured. "I can feel it. Somewhere in the stones is the key."

In the outside ring above the Circular Altar were three carvings to explain the sign. The first was Adom, or Tau. Four bright stars forming a cross signified a *cutting off* or that *it was finished.* Beside the cross was the star picture of the Victim, a lamb being slain by the half man, half horse. Ganah knelt by the stone, studying the deeply etched lines.

"I have never understood what this picture means. Come here, Eliah." She motioned impatiently with her hand. "Can you see it clearly? It is the man with two natures. He is supposed to slay himself?" Shaking her head, she pondered the strange carving.

"Oh, my friend," she sighed, looking out over the town. "We have forgotten so much. How will we ever recapture what has been lost? It seems to slip like water between my fingers."

Eliah wiped his mouth with the back of his hand.

She brushed the dirt and weeds from the carving of the Crown. "The Old Ones used to say that after the lamb had been killed, it would be given a crown."

She moved to the next stone. "Here is the Scorpion, man's deadly enemy, the opposer of Yah-Adon. If you look up in the darkness of the night sky, you can see in the middle of its body a brilliant star shining with an ominous red glow. This represents the enemy who hates us with an undying passion. It is he who spews forth a darkness that is threatening to engulf everyone and everything that we know and love."

The old woman grabbed the Tumulac's arm. "Look closely. You can still see stains of red on the stone where the Old Ones placed red dye. It has soaked deep into the stone like dried blood.

"And, look—here is the Serpent Treader, a man fighting a mighty serpent while he treads on the Scorpion. Can you see his foot on its head? He must be careful, though, because the serpent is straining to grasp the Crown hanging high above it."

Eliah pointed to another picture.

"That is Bau," explained Ganah. "He is also called the Mighty One. You can see his right heel is lifted. That is because he has been wounded while killing the serpent."

She sighed wearily and threw back her head. "Yah-Adon, I know that You will send a Mighty One to destroy this evil, but what are You trying to tell me now? There is danger in our midst at this moment, and I don't know what You want me to do."

Trembling, she shouted into the air, "Where is the one who will save us? Why has he not come?"

The Tumulac grabbed his spear and jumped to his feet, spinning around to protect his mistress.

Ganah turned to see what had startled him.

Bel strode onto the flat expanse beside the circles of stone.

The Tumulac stepped back but did not lower his spear.

Ganah, squinting in the sunlight, waited for the intruder to speak. His magnificent body towered above her, and she shivered, feeling suddenly very insignificant.

With arms crossed over his massive chest, Bel lowered his head, his eyes locking onto hers.

"It is good to see you, Bel," said Ganah, angry that her voice was too loud and too shrill. "Are you here for a reason?"

"Don't be offended by my intrusion. I saw you leave this morning, and I longed to see the old carvings while in your presence. I had heard about them, and I hoped you would explain them to me."

She nodded. "I have not been here for years, but it's always a joy to tell the story of the stars. The Old Ones loved this place of Yah-Adon's presense." As she talked, her anxiety began to wane. "They spent many hours here, day and night, watching the sun, the moon, and the stars, observing their movements, charting their courses and watching for changes in the sky. I regret, though," she sighed, "that my people have forgotten many of the Old Ways."

"I have no home," said Bel, with a strange look in his eyes. "I'm a wanderer in this country. I know, though, of the ways of the Stargazers.

In my travels I heard that you, Ganah, are one of the few who knows the story well. You have seen many cycles of the moon, and you are wise."

"Ah, they are right when they say I'm very old, but wisdom—no! I'm just an old woman who has lived many years."

"But isn't that the source of wisdom?"

"If that were true, the town would be filled with sages surrounded by those who would learn from them."

"These people are happy in their ignorance," he added. "You said yourself they no longer come to study the stars. Are there not many answers here for those who seek the truth?"

"Well stated. They no longer care. They no longer seek the truth, for they are content in their ignorance." She spread her hands. "I am afraid I have failed them."

"There is nothing you can do," he said, a harshness creeping into his voice. "They were doomed from the beginning. It is only a matter of time before they will be in total darkness. Even humankind itself will be des—" Abruptly, he stopped. His nostrils flared and the veins in his neck distended.

Ganah stared at him in stunned surprise at the venom in his voice.

Attempting to regain his composure, he bowed his head. "Forgive me, Ulah-rah. My nature is a fiery one. I become easily inflamed." He looked at the sky. "I see by the sun that it is time to return to the forge. I will hear the story another time." Turning, he strode rapidly to the path leading down the side of the Mound.

Ganah watched him until he had vanished from her sight. *Why,* she wondered, *do I have such turmoil in my spirit?*

Eliah walked to the edge, waiting for the man to reach the bottom and begin his walk across the field back to the town. He shielded his eyes as he watched for the distinctive figure to appear. He walked around the perimeter of the top of the Mound. He waited. The man had simply vanished from sight.

Thirteen

Bel stood at the edge of Gibara-boni, his chest heaving with the passion of unbridled hatred. His grinding teeth cast white-flecked spittle into the corners of his mouth. His massive hands clenched into white-knuckled fists. His spurious body, struggling to contain the malevolent wrath churning within, blurred and shifted form uncontrollably, threatening to revert to its original state.

"Pathetic old fool," he hissed. "Trying to make sense of idiotic carvings." A growl rumbled deep in his throat.

A large, brown dog trotted across the field with a dead hare hanging from its mouth. It stopped, shifting from one paw to the other. Its senses alert, it dropped its kill and with a frightened whine backed warily from the man. With one swift movement, Bel lunged forward grabbing the hapless animal's head in one powerful hand. The dog uttered one brief, high-pitched yelp before its skull shattered in the viselike grip.

With a roar, the obscenity threw the lifeless body to the ground, then turned toward the town. Eyes red-rimmed and face contorted in fury, he muttered, "I can destroy this town and all its inhabitants if I desire. I can have it in ruin by the day's end and no one can stop me."

His mouth twisted into a brutal sneer. "But," he said, breathing deeply, forcing his body once again to his control, "there is no need to hurry."

He lifted his chin. "These people corrupt easily. I will enjoy myself for a while longer."

He ran his tongue over his full, sensuous lips. "Besides, there is still beautiful Utriel! I can have any woman or man in Gibara-boni, but it is *you,* my little one, that I have come for."

The corners of his mouth turned upward. "You are almost ready. I can see it in your eyes. Soon, my precious. Very soon."

Gabul glanced up from his work when he heard approaching footsteps. "Where have you been?" he complained when he saw Bel crossing the yard. "We have things that need your attention. I'm learning, but I haven't acquired your skill."

Bel grabbed his mallet leaning against the forge. "Give me that blade," he ordered, "before you make a complete mess of it."

He shoved it into the glowing coals.

Neither spoke.

Gabul stood to one side as his mentor hammered and reshaped the red-hot metal, his eyes furtively watching the man's face.

At last Bel broke the silence. "Do you really believe in the one you call Yah-Adon?"

Gabul snickered awkwardly. "Not really. Some of the older ones still hold to the ancient ways, but few believe anymore. They make an occasional sacrifice, but—" he spread his hands—"it never hurts to be careful, does it?" He cleared his throat. "I guess Noah's the only man in Gibara-boni who still truly believes."

When Bel made no response, Gabul continued. "He'll have to find another woman now that you're taking Utriel." He winked conspiratorially. "I guess he just waited too long, eh?"

The only answer was the pounding of the hammer against the iron blade.

Gabul licked his dry lips and swallowed hard. He opened his mouth, hesitated, but blurted, "You're spending too much time away from the forge. I don't like it."

The weapon maker continued working the blade.

"Did you hear me?" Gabul shouted, grabbing the man's arm.

Bel raised his head. "Don't . . . ever . . . do . . . that . . . again. Do you understand?"

Gabul, startled by the unmitigated hatred on the face before him, stepped back, losing his balance and falling against a stack of wood.

Utriel stood by the window of her room, hardly daring to breathe, her senses on edge. Slowly, she let out her breath. She felt no presence in the room. She was alone. How precious that word had become.

She turned to the window. Drops of moisture formed in the cool night air as she watched the brilliant points of light flashing against the dark velvet of the night. If only she could escape into the solitude of its shadows.

Sleep was impossible, for her mind had become a constant battleground. Her recalcitrant thoughts invariably fled to the stranger who had so disrupted her life. Her thoughts were becoming confused. She knew she should seek wisdom from Ganah, but a part of her feared what the prophetess would say.

Sometimes when she tried to imagine what life would be like with Bel, her heart would race and her breath quicken. He could have any woman he desired, but he had claimed her. A perverse sense of pride swelled her heart at the thought. Then anger flared. If he wanted her, why did he not claim her? Had he found someone else?

Only once had Bel actually spoken to her. She had been hurrying to her uncle's house with a basket of freshly baked bread when she saw the weapon maker striding toward her. Her breath caught in her throat.

"That is a heavy basket, Utriel," he said. "Let me carry it for you."

She lowered her eyes.

"Are you afraid of me?"

Her head snapped up defiantly at such an accusation. Then she drew in her breath sharply. A musky, masculine odor emanated from his body and filled her senses. Her head felt light, as if it were spinning, and the street seemed unstable beneath her feet.

Suddenly, Jirad appeared behind her. He wrapped one arm around her waist and placed his other on her shoulder. "I'll take the basket," he said to Bel. "I'm sure you're needed at the forge."

Confused, she looked from one man to the other as if awakening from a trance. Jirad's mouth was firm and his eyes glowered. For a fleeting moment an expression of utter contempt and hatred clouded Bel's face, then vanished before she could be sure.

"How fortunate you are to have such a thoughtful brother," said the man, his voice cold and hard. He smiled, a chilling slash across his face, as slowly he drew his fingers up the side of her cheek. A flush crept over her face, but she shivered at his touch. Then turning, he sauntered toward Gabul's house.

They hurried through the narrow streets until they reached their uncle's house. Utriel handed the bread-filled basket to a young cousin who was cooking over a hot fire. She had planned to visit, but Jirad grabbed her arm, steering her toward the street.

"I'll be back," Utriel exclaimed over her shoulder.

A few steps away Utriel jerked free from her brother. "What are you doing?" she demanded.

"I don't want you within the town walls without me," he said, his voice low and urgent.

"Why? I come here all the time. Why must I now have you with me?"

"Utriel, trust me," he said. The fear and confusion in his voice alarmed her.

"But I don't understand."

"I don't understand it myself, but you're in danger."

"From what?" Her voice was edged with anger.

"I don't know. I just know that Bel is involved."

She jerked free. "Jirad, he saved your life. If it hadn't been for him, you'd have died in the wilderness."

"I know." He ran his fingers through his hair in frustration. "But I don't want him near you, and I don't want him to touch you."

"Don't tell me what to do. I can take care of myself."

"Utriel," he said, "I'm sorry, but I love you, and I'm afraid for you."

At the concern in his voice, her anger quickly died. "It's all right," she said, putting her arm through his. "Come on. Let's walk."

Deep in thought, they had rambled aimlessly through the dusty streets until at last finding themselves by the well outside the town wall.

Jirad ran his hand over the long scars on his shoulder and arm, a gesture that had become habitual.

"You need a drink," said Utriel. "You're sweating as if you've been running."

He wiped his face with the edge of his robe, poured water over his head, shaking the spray in all directions.

Utriel giggled as she grabbed another gourd, filled it with water, and flung the contents at him.

"You're asking for it!" he yelled.

They became like two children, chasing each other around the well, ducking, dodging, and turning to keep from getting soaked.

Jirad lunged, catching Utriel around the waist. He pinned her in his strong arms and dragged her toward the water.

She screamed with laughter.

As he struggled to hold her, he reached for a jug beside the well. Just as his hand touched the vessel, he yelled, releasing her so quickly that she tumbled to the ground.

A viper, coiled around the neck of the jar, undulated its head in the air, a low, deadly hiss escaping its mouth.

"Stand back," Jirad whispered. Slowly, he unsheathed his knife from his belt and drew back the blade. His powerful arm swung it through the air, deftly severing the top of the jar from its base and with it the snake.

"Jirad!" screamed Utriel. "Look out! In the tree!"

He jerked backward and sucked in his breath. Over his head a dark, undulating mass of bodies covered the limbs of the huge sycamore, some coiled around branches, others slithering over limbs, the remainder hanging to drop at any moment.

"Yah-Adon, help us!" whispered Jirad, momentarily immobilized. At that instant, one of the glistening bodies fell from a limb. With a swing of his arm he knocked it aside. His body now alive to the danger, he backed away from the tree, pushing his sister behind him but never taking his eyes from the writhing mass above.

"Run quickly," he ordered, "and get help!"

She gathered her skirt around her thighs, tucked it into her girdle, and raced toward the fields, her long legs flashing in the sunlight.

In a matter of minutes men came running with spears and sticks. Warily, they inched forward. Without warning a loud guffaw sounded, then another. Soon they were laughing and slapping each other on the back, making jokes about being afraid.

Utriel looked around in bewilderment.

Jirad stood under the tree, astonishment on his face.

When the last man had left, she crossed to her brother's side. Nothing. There was nothing in the tree. "It's impossible!" she cried. "Where did they go?"

Jirad put his arm around her shoulder and drew her close.

Utriel turned from the window, her mind returning to the present. The pale linen shift hung loosely about her tall, slender figure. She stood by the sleeping mat and unwound the binding from her hair, letting it fall about her shoulders. She sank onto the mat and drew her legs to her chest. She rested her chin on her knees and stared into the shadows. She felt so alone and afraid.

Fourteen

The fetid smell of souri and sweat filled the front room of Gitel's dwelling. A flat, clay lamp on the squat table between himself and his brother colored their faces a faint, yellow hue. Gitel, partially reclining on a pile of light brown sheepskins, frowned, his gaunt features made thinner and sharper by the shadows from the flickering light. His skin seemed stretched too tightly over his lanky frame, and his brooding eyes stared into the empty cup in his hand.

"More souri!" he shouted, directing his voice toward the next room. "Refill the ewer before you feel the back of my hand across your face!"

A woman threw aside the curtain between the two rooms and scurried to his side. With trembling hands she filled his cup before placing the vessel on the table. With a short, rapid bow, she turned and fled the room.

"See what happens when a man can afford only one wife?" he growled to Benu, his words slurring on his tongue. "She becomes lazy when she does not have to compete for her husband's affections."

Benu laughed, sniffed loudly and wiped his nose on his forearm. Large, square teeth gleamed in his wide mouth. "You just need a fat woman like I have to warm your body."

"It's not my wife I'm worried about, you idiot. It's our father." He filled Benu's cup, then slammed the ewer on the table, sloshing souri over the side and spilling onto the furs.

He raised up on his elbow. "If you weren't so stupid, you'd realize that when Obed dies we could lose our inheritance to Bel. They spend so much time together our father may already have given him leadership of the family to do whatever he wants. Or worse yet—what if he gives it to Jirad?"

"How? Obed can't talk anymore," said Benu dully.

His large, strong body was the antithesis of Gitel's, and he would have been considered handsome except for an unpleasant slackness around his mouth and eyes. Although he was rarely angry, he had few opinions of his own and was frequently a willing pawn to his brother's constant grumbling.

"Maybe he can't talk, but I wouldn't put it past him to somehow give Jirad what should be yours and mine."

"Why? You're the oldest," said Benu, with a loud belch. "What's Obed's should go to you when he dies."

"I know it should, but Jirad is his favorite son. Hasn't Obed rubbed our noses in that fact often enough? Where have you been for the past sixteen years?"

Benu shrugged and scowled. "What can we do about it?"

"Our problem would have been solved," said Gitel as he refilled his cup, "if our little brother had not survived the lion."

"You mean you wanted him to die?" asked Benu, his eyes wide with disbelief. "Obed would have been mad about that."

"Dolt, Obed's not in shape to be mad about anything. In fact," he said, licking his thin lips, "maybe we should just finish what the lioness didn't."

"What do you mean?"

"Now think really hard on that."

Benu wrinkled his forehead. "Kill Jirad?"

"Yes—kill Jirad. Kill him! Kill him! Kill him!"

"But what if the counsel found out?" Benu swallowed a large mouthful of souri. "No," he said, shaking his head, "I don't want to kill him, Gitel. I don't want to do that at all."

"Sometimes I think sheep could outsmart you."

A wounded expression settled on Benu's countenance.

"Look," Gitel continued, trying to placate the big man, "there are other ways to achieve our end than by one of us killing him. We just need to use our heads."

"Maybe we can get someone else to do it."

"We would still have the problem of the stranger. Somehow we must get rid of both Jirad and Bel."

"Maybe we can get them to kill each other," suggested Benu, chuckling to himself.

Gitel's head snapped forward. "Brother, you may be smarter than I thought."

A perplexed gaze clouded Benu's face.

"Next week," continued Gitel, scratching his chin, "is the Harvest Festival. And the Harvest Festival is also a time for contests and feats of skill." He was quiet for a moment as his fingers tapped on the tabletop. "Who knows? We might be able to find a way to eliminate both of our threats." He filled his mouth with souri and swallowed loudly.

Life was more pleasant for Utriel since Bithra had at last taken over most of Obed's care. Now she was once again able to spend time with Jirad. They were careful, though, to avoid the men in the fields as much as possible, for neither wanted to hear the inevitable question, "Seen any snakes lately?" followed by winks and uproarious laughter.

An osprey dived toward the water, skimmed the sparkling surface, then lifted itself into the air. A bass clutched in the bird's strong talons squirmed helplessly beneath the snowy white chest.

"Have you ever seen anything so . . ." Utriel searched for the right word.

"Deadly?" finished Jirad.

"Yes, but also beautiful."

They sat on a large rock at the edge of the lake, dangling their feet in the water, letting its coolness penetrate their skin. Puffs of white clouds drifted across the sky, and the sun's rays touched their skin with a delicious warmth.

Jirad bit into a chunk of yellow cheese that Utriel had brought wrapped in a cloth along with a portion of dark, nutty bread. "Why didn't you tell me sooner what happened here?" When she didn't answer, he tried again. "Why did you keep it a secret?"

"I should have told you, but I was afraid you'd think it was all my imagination." She winced at the hurt in his eyes. "I did tell Ganah," she continued, leaning her chin on her arm, "but she can talk only about some great evil she thinks is threatening the land. Jirad, I love her, but I think her mind is growing feeble. She spends all her days now upon the mound, poring over the ancient stones from early morning until dusk."

He flipped a rock into the water. The ripples fanned outward, expanding over the surface. "She is right, you know. Something evil is in our midst. Can't you feel it?" He wiggled his foot, frightening a tiny blue gill nibbling gently on his toe. "I don't believe Bel is who he says he is. There's something terribly wrong about the man."

He glanced behind himself and lowered his voice. "Can't you feel it when you're around him? Even when he smiles, something dangerous seems to lurk beneath the surface. I've tried telling myself it's my imagination, but my instincts can't be that wrong."

Utriel stared into the water. "How can you speak that way about the man who saved your life?"

He shrugged, rising to his feet and rubbing the dirt from his hands. "I know it doesn't make sense, but—he frightens me. At night, when I'm lying in bed, I relive over and over the lion's attack. And each time I hear Bel laughing while I'm fighting for my life, my arms and legs so heavy I can barely move. And all the while he laughs and watches. The man haunts my dreams."

Utriel pulled her feet from the water and curled one beneath her, resting her chin on the other knee. "Why would such a man desire me for his wife when he could have any woman in Gibara-boni?"

Jirad touched the top of her head, feeling the thick strands of hair under his fingers. "You have no idea how beautiful you are, do you?"

She lifted her head and arched one eyebrow.

He smiled, ruffling her hair. "Stay the way you are, dear one. For if you ever do realize it, you will be impossible to live with."

She smacked his hand away and made a face.

"Who is he?" he asked, kneeling beside her. "Is he a friend or an enemy?"

Utriel shook her head. "I don't know, but he intends to be my husband."

Utriel, clutching a bowl of soup, hurried across the yard toward her father's quarters. Several days had passed since her conversation with Jirad, but she could not rid her mind of his question.

Earlier that morning Bithra had cut her hand while splitting a large melon. Utriel helped stop the bleeding and then wrapped her injured fingers in clean strips of cloth. "Don't worry about feeding Obed today," she said. "I'll do it for you."

Bithra rested the side of her injured hand in the palm of the other. "Thank you."

Utriel touched Obed's shoulder. His eyes snapped open and flicked upward. The veins in his neck and forehead immediately distended in an alarming manner and perspiration broke out on his face. She hated seeing him like this, his once-strong body growing thinner each day. Already his muscles had withered and the skin hung loosely over his large frame. His hair, now dry and brittle, lay matted on the fur beneath his head.

"Father, what is it?" she asked, setting the bowl on a low table beside the mat.

Inarticulate noises erupted from his throat as his eyes jerked wildly in his head. She tried to calm him, but her efforts only increased his agitation.

Finally, unable to soothe him, she dashed from the room. "Bithra!" she yelled. "Hurry! Something's wrong with Obed!"

The woman, still holding her wrapped hand, rushed from the doorway into the yard. "What is it?"

"I don't know. When he saw me, he became wild. Hurry!"

Bithra raced after her, pressing her injured hand to her chest.

Bursting into the room, she dropped to the floor beside the man and placed her arms around his shoulders, cradling his head against her large bosom. "It's all right," she murmured. "Nothing is going to hurt you."

Utriel stood to one side listening to her croon under her breath and rock back and forth as she held his head. As she watched, the panic began to fade from the man's eyes.

"You'd better leave," Bithra whispered to Utriel. "Your presence is upsetting him. It may be best to stay away for a while. I'll manage."

Utriel bit her full, lower lip and wiped her hands down the sides of her tunic. Finally, she walked toward the door, paused, and looked back. "I'm sorry, Father," she whispered.

Fifteen

"No!" rasped Utriel. "You mustn't go back into the Shinar. Not into that cave by yourself." She stood defiantly in front of her brother beneath the large sycamore at the edge of the compound, her legs braced and her hands planted firmly on her hips. "What are you thinking of?"

"I should have gone days ago," Jirad said, his voice a hoarse whisper as he pounded his fist against the rough bark. "I should have returned to the cave as soon as I found it. Instead, I acted like a coward. I must have milk in my veins instead of blood."

"It would be foolishness to enter the Shinar again by yourself."

"I have to. I have to know why Bel goes to that cave in the depths of the forest. I have to find out what's in there."

She stomped her foot and balled her hands into fists. She turned, took several steps and whirled to face her twin. "Then let me go with you."

"No!"

"Why not? I have as much at stake in this as you."

"I know, dear sister, but this is something I have to do on my own."

She started to reply, but he stopped her. "Sh-h-h," he said, holding up his hand. "Try to understand."

She ripped a leaf from a branch above her shoulder, crumpled it, and let it fall from her hand, furrowing her brow as she ground the remains beneath her foot. From the fields and distant hillsides floated the bleating of sheep and the voices of laboring men. She stared at the ground, rubbing her bare toe into the leafy fragments. Finally, she raised her head. "All right. Promise, though, you won't go until after the Harvest Festival."

Jirad made a face.

"Promise!" she said.

"I promise." He sighed, the edges of his wide mouth curling slightly. "I won't go until the festival is over. Now, are you satisfied?"

"No, but I guess it will have to do." She turned to go, then stopped. "You're following Bel because you're worried about me, aren't you?"

"I'm worried about both of us."

She shook her head and hurried toward the cooking area.

"All I need are two good furs," Bethuel said, shaking her finger in front of Gitel's nose. "Your father needs them for his pallet. Surely you can do that, can't you?"

"Nag, nag." He smirked. "If you were my wife, you'd feel the back of my hand."

"Well, praise Yah-Adon—I'm only your mother. Now get out there and find what I need."

When Gitel saw Utriel, he sneered, "Where's Jirad? Let him go hunting and earn his keep for a while. Or is he afraid to get too close to the forest?"

"No, he's not afraid. I just had to make him promise not to go in there."

Gitel's dark eyes grew even darker. "Why would he want to enter the Shinar?" he asked, cocking his head to one side and hitching his thumbs into the belt around his waist.

She reached for the bowl of figs in Bethuel's hands. "He followed Bel to a cave somewhere in the forest, and he wants to go back with torches." She offered the bowl to Gitel, who grabbed a handful of the fruit.

"Why would he follow the weapon maker?"

"Gitel," said Utriel when she saw the interest on his face, "please don't mention to anyone what I just said."

"Oh, of course, little sister. I won't breathe a word." He popped a fig into his mouth. "Who would even be interested?"

Utriel watched him uneasily as he sauntered from the area, still munching on the fruit in his hand.

No sooner was Gitel out of Utriel's sight than he hurried to tell Benu. He found the big man slumped on a large stump, hard at work replacing the cracked crossbar on a plow.

"Well, brother," Gitel said, sidling up to him while making sure no one was around to overhear, "I think I may have something of interest to tell you."

Benu looked up, grinning expectantly.

"I just heard that Jirad has secretly been trailing Bel into the forest."

"Uh-huh?" said Benu, still grinning.

"Don't you see what we can do with this information?" snapped Gitel.

The other man shook his head.

"Tell Bel, you idiot!"

"Why?"

"To make him mad, of course," fumed Gitel. "Mad at Jirad for spying on him. What better way to get them to fight each other."

"Why would Jirad fight Bel?" asked the bewildered man. "Bel saved him from the lion."

"I know that," spat Gitel. "I just want Bel to get angry, that's all. We just need to throw some wood on the fire."

"What fire?"

"There isn't any fire—you—"

With a perplexed expression, Benu set the broken plow on the ground beside the stump. "Don't get mad at me. I can't help it if I don't understand these things like you do."

Gitel rolled his eyes and blew out an explosion of air from his chest. "All right. Just leave your plow alone and let's find Bel. I think he'll be interested in hearing about our little brother."

"No. I don't want to talk to Bel."

"Then don't come," said Gitel, throwing his hands into the air in disgust. "I'll do it myself."

Gitel leaned against the side of Gabul's house, waiting until the man finally set the bellows against the forge and left the yard for the day. The others had already gone to their respective homes for their evening meals. Gitel shifted from one foot to the other, his red-rimmed, watery eyes watching Bel rasp a whetstone along the edge of a large blade.

"What do you want?" asked Bel without raising his head.

"I—uh," stammered Gitel, wondering if he had made a terrible mistake by coming. "I have something to tell you."

When the man did not reply, Gitel wet his lips and tried again. "I thought you should know that Jirad, Obed's son, has been following you."

"So?" answered Bel, still sharpening the blade.

"He followed you into the Shinar and thinks you disappeared into a cave."

The man held the blade at eye level, the sunlight glinting off its honed surface. He ran his thumb over the edge, leaving a bright red line in its wake. Looking up at the man standing before him, he slowly lifted his finger and ran the tip of his tongue over the oozing cut. "When?" he asked.

"What?" responded Gitel, his voice suddenly unnaturally high and thin.

"When did he follow me?"

"I—I don't know. I just know that he did."

"And what did he see?"

Gitel swallowed and shook his head.

Bel rose, locking the man in his mesmerizing gaze.

Gitel edged backward into the wall.

Without a word, Bel grabbed the man's head between his hands and lifted him, his feet flailing the air. "What did he see?" he asked again.

"A cave. He saw you enter a cave."

"What else?"

"I don't know."

"Tell me or I'll crush your head."

"I can't. That's all I know," he wailed, his face dark red and his eyes bulging from their sockets. "Please, if I knew anything more, I'd tell you."

Bel opened his arms, letting the man fall to the ground.

Gitel held his ears and rolled in agony.

"Be grateful, little man, that you're still alive. Now leave before I change my mind."

Whimpering in pain, Gitel scrambled to his feet and scurried from the yard.

Sixteen

Utriel rubbed the polished bronze mirror against her skirt and peered into its surface. She studied her image in the morning light, following the contours of her wide mouth with her fingers and frowning at the reflection of her chin. She tossed the mirror onto her sleeping mat and crossed to the window. "I see only a girl with a jutting chin and a mouth too big for her face," she said, leaning her cheek against the cool wall. "Why would Bel want me? No wonder he has said nothing more about taking me to be his wife. He probably regrets what he said and is hoping others will forget."

She squeezed her eyes shut and whispered under her breath, "Why do I have such thoughts? I should be rejoicing that he doesn't want me."

"Utriel! Hurry!" Jirad's sharp command broke her reverie.

She peered from the window.

He was running across the yard. "Let's go!" he yelled. "The harvest games have started. You don't want to miss seeing me win this year, do you?"

She wiped her eyes, tears deepening the amber flakes that floated in a pool of green. "I'll be right out," she called, forcing a lilt to her voice.

Quickly slipping her feet into her leather sandals, she wrapped the laces around her ankles and tied them above her heels. She grabbed a long, multicolored sash to tie around her waist and dashed outside. She didn't want to miss a single moment of the games.

A slight breeze ruffled the leaves as Utriel and Jirad hurried through the trees to the grazing land on which the contests were held each year. Jirad stopped for a moment and balanced an arrow on his fingertip to read the wind. He hadn't decided if he would participate in archery, but he wanted to be prepared.

The Blessing of the Ground and Offering of the Grain had taken place earlier that morning, a token remnant of worship to Yah-Adon. Now the fun was about to begin.

"You've brought your sling and spear. What other games are you going to enter?" asked Utriel.

"Wrestling. I did all right last year, but now I'm much heavier. I think I can stay in till the last." He slipped his spear from around his shoulder and hefted it in his hand. "I've added more weight to the back of my spear. It's balanced perfectly now. I can hit birds in flight. I can make it fly like an arrow. Remember Jeptha, the man who won last year? He offered me twenty goats for my spear. I just wish," he said, his voice lowering, "that Father were able to see me."

"They're already beginning to line up," cried Utriel. "Hurry!"

Touching the spear to his head in a mock farewell, Jirad sprinted across the ground. "This is one contest I know I'm going to win," he yelled over his shoulder.

Already twenty to thirty men had gathered on the field. While the majority waited impatiently for the contest to start, several paced off the distance to the target. A few even took practice throws at nearby trees.

Squeezing her hands together and biting her knuckles in anticipation, Utriel pushed between the onlookers for a good spot.

"Here comes Jirad," someone behind her muttered. "No one will beat him with that new spear."

She knew he had an excellent chance at winning in spite of his age, for Obed had been a hard but skillful teacher. From the time Jirad had been big enough to walk, his father had taught him to throw a spear, use a sling, fight with a staff, and wrestle. The cuffs around the head and demanding remarks had not fallen on deaf ears, and Obed had never disguised the fact that he loved this youngest son over the others or that he was preparing him to assume leadership of the family.

"Utriel!" squealed Mariah, her uncle's youngest daughter. She threw her arms around her cousin and hugged her. "Is Jirad entering any of the contests?"

Utriel disentangled herself from the girl. "He's on the field now." She pointed to her brother waiting to demonstrate his accuracy and skill.

"This is so exciting," cried Mariah. "They all look so handsome, don't they?" The girl squealed again and clapped her hands. "Look at the one over there stretching his muscles."

As Utriel laughed at Mariah's childish enthusiasm, the laughter stuck in her throat and a chill swept over her. She pressed her hand to the back of her neck and stared straight ahead, determined not to turn. Someone was watching her. She looked at Mariah and forced herself to smile. The girl was speaking. She could see her mouth moving, but the words were making no sense. Even as she willed herself not to turn, she glanced slowly over her shoulder.

Bel's eyes were fixed on her. Their gazes held for a fraction of a second as his pale, blue eyes narrowed. A lock of yellow hair fell over one eye, and he tossed his head like a lion shaking its mane.

Her heart pounded as he strode toward her through the raucous crowd.

In spite of her secret hopes that the blond weapon maker would renew his claim, fears and doubts crowded in upon her as Jirad's words from the previous day echoed in her head. She thought of running, but her feet seemed rooted to the ground. She turned to Mariah, but the girl was yelling and pointing to various participants on the field.

A hand touched her shoulder. She gasped, whirling around.

"I'm sorry," Noah stammered. "Did I startle you?"

She pressed her hand to her chest as she searched the crowd, but Bel had disappeared among the onlookers.

"I saw you with your cousin."

She took a deep breath and tried to smile. Suddenly the fear evaporated, and she felt secure once more as she looked at the dark, curly hair and beard framing the strong but gentle face. He was so unlike Bel, who stirred feelings within her that frightened yet excited her.

"Bithra told me Obed is no better," said Noah.

"He slips farther from us each day."

He moved closer to her. "I still want to take you away from

Gibara-boni if you will let me," he murmured.

Yes, she longed to cry. *Hold me and protect me*. Instead she heard herself say, "No. I could never live with myself if I were the cause of your ruin."

He grabbed her hands and drew them to his chest. "Then I'll challenge Bel for you in the contests."

She pulled her hands from his warm, callused fingers, feeling their roughness rasp lightly across her skin. "Have you lost your mind? You promised you wouldn't fight him."

"She is right, Noah." Ganah had stepped silently between them and laid her hands on their shoulders. "Has Yah-Adon not assured you that all would be well?"

"How . . . ?" Noah began.

Utriel gasped, her eyes staring at the woman before her. "Ganah, what has happened to you? You look so tall and so. . . ."

"Alive?" finished the woman.

Utriel nodded.

Although the ravages of age had not vanished, the Ulah-rah stood tall and straight, the lined, leathery face resolute, strong, and glowing with a long-forgotten radiance. Her thick, gray hair lay beautifully coiled at the base of her neck. A large agate pin, ornately carved, secured the thick strands, and a heavy brass pendant lay on the wrinkled skin of her chest. A scarf of deep azure looped around her neck and hung nearly to the ground. Beneath it, a soft, white, finely spun tunic reached to her ankles. The staff in her hand no longer served merely to support a failing body but to establish an undisputed authority.

"I—I don't understand," said Utriel.

Ganah chuckled, her laugh low and throaty. "Yah-Adon has given me a task to complete. And, since He does not ask what one cannot do, He has renewed my strength to accomplish what is before me. Enough, though. Come with me away from the crowd. I want to speak with both of you."

Utriel looked back at the field, then followed Ganah and Noah to the edge of a clearing beside a copse of trees.

"The shade feels good," the prophetess murmured. "Let's enjoy it a moment while we talk."

"Ganah," began Noah, "I can't stand by and let Utriel be taken from me."

She placed her hand on his arm. "My son, I understand your loss better than you can ever realize, but sometimes we cannot control our lives."

He opened his mouth to speak, but she held up her hand. "Noah, Yah-Adon has revealed to me what He has called you to do. You must be very cautious of the choices that you make. Our people have fallen into great darkness and have turned their backs upon the Placer of Stars. You must keep yourself apart, for He will only use those who walk uprightly before Him. He will guide you, but you must allow Him to do so. And," she said, raising her hand to stop him again, "no matter how it appears, it will be right."

"I do not understand what you are saying, Ulah-rah, and my heart aches at such words. Am I being a man to stand idly by while my world is falling apart?"

"I can give you little comfort," she said. "Except I know that things are not always as they seem to be. Sometimes we must tread one step at a time without knowing what lies ahead. Remember, your faith must lie in the power of Yah-Adon and not in the wisdom of the teachings of men."

"Ganah," whispered Utriel, "tell us what Yah-Adon has told you."

"No, my child. I cannot. He will reveal it to Noah when the proper time has come, but this I will say—you also are a part of His plan if you will yield yourself to Him."

Utriel shivered and her lip trembled. "I am afraid," she said. "I am afraid of the future, and," she hesitated, "I am afraid of myself."

The old woman wrapped one arm around her. "Take heart. Yah-Adon knows the beginning from the end. The important thing, and the hardest, is to stay on the path that He has laid out for you. Too often our own desires lead us astray. "Now, come," she said. "Let's enjoy the contests. There will be enough hard days before us. We should enjoy the fun while we may."

Shafts of afternoon sun slanted through the tall trees ringing the field and fell on both spectators and contestants. Several combatants displayed badges of honor in the forms of bruises, cuts, and abrasions. Jirad had exceeded even his own expectations by winning not only the spear-throwing contest but also the sling. His feats surpassed those of the most experienced men in the town.

Excitement now built steadily as a wide circle in the middle of the field was ringed with glistening white lime for the last and most awaited event of the day—a wrestling free-for-all.

At the hollow trumpeting of the ram's horn, fifty men stepped into the circle. The chief elder moved forward, arms lifted to silence the crowd. "Remember," he shouted when all was quiet. "A man is out of the contest if he is thrown from the ring or if his shoulders are pinned to the ground. Only bare hands are permitted. No weapons. The last man standing inside the ring will be declared the winner. As usual," he continued, "the winner may choose any unwed woman in Gibara-boni to take into his household."

Excited murmurings ran through the crowd.

"What if she's already been spoken for?" shouted a stocky young man near the edge of the circle.

"Even if she's been spoken for," answered the elder. "Our edict supersedes all previous commitments." He paused, turning to Bel, "Including even a blood covenant."

Bel raised his arms above his head as he flexed his enormous muscles.

Gitel huddled with his brother near the edge of the circle. "Remember, Benu," he whispered, "this is our chance to rid ourselves once and for all of Jirad. Accidents happen, and no one could ever hold you responsible."

"I don't know," muttered Benu. "I don't think I should hurt Jirad."

"Shoat of a pig!" Gitel hissed. "If we don't do something, he may get everything that should be ours. Can't you get that through your thick head? If Bel doesn't take him out, you'll have to. Now shut up and get in there!"

Benu shook his head. "I don't like this."

Uzzah nudged Noah as they waited for the second blast of the horn, the signal to begin. "Well, little brother, you'll have your chance to take out your anger on the big man himself." He jerked his head toward Bel, who shifted impatiently from one foot to the other as he stretched his arms behind his head. "I, however," said Uzzah, "intend to stay as far away from him as possible."

"Let Bel take his pick from the women and get it over with," jeered an older man in the crowd.

"No one can beat him!" screamed a woman, lifting her arms above her head and shaking her hips. "Here I am. Take me. I'm yours."

Laughter and shouts filled the air.

Noah moved cautiously with eyes fixed on the source of his frustration. The size of the man was sufficient to raise the gorge in an opponent's throat let alone the sight of his naked, muscular torso glistening in the sun. Attacking the man, though, would not only vent his rage but also presented the possibility of winning back Utriel.

Bel seemed oblivious to Noah's presence, his attention focused instead on someone else among the group of men. Noah shifted several paces to see the object of Bel's interest. He drew in his breath sharply. It was Jirad, his back to them as he adjusted the belt around his swathed loins.

Noah glanced back at Bel. The man's face was hard and his eyes narrowed in a hatred Noah did not comprehend. The hair on the back of his neck bristled. He should warn Jirad.

Before he could put his thought into action, the horn blew, and a pair of strong arms grabbed him around the neck, throwing him to the ground. Instantly, he rolled to one side and sprang to his feet. He couldn't afford to lose his concentration again, or he would be flung over the line and out of the competition.

Bodies slammed onto the ground. Grunts escaped from tortured lungs as adversaries crushed their opponents, pinning them against the flattened grass. Others threw their competitors out of the ring, shouting triumphantly while searching for their next victims.

Soon, only twelve men remained in the circle. The crowd grew quiet, anticipating the strategy of the remaining combatants.

"Give me a hand, little brother," grunted Ephran, struggling to free himself from Lemiel's tight hold around his waist. "He still hasn't forgotten my night with his sister," he sputtered between gasps.

Whirling quickly, Noah grabbed Lemiel's head, jerking it

backward until the man was forced to loosen his hold. Swiftly, Ephran locked his hands around Lemiel's feet and the two men swung him in a high arc over the line where he landed with a groan. "Go find your sister," taunted Ephran.

"Trip Jirad, Benu," rasped Gitel, his hair flying about his face as he raced around the outside of the ring. Twice Benu had grabbed Jirad, but the young man wriggled from his grasp, his skin slippery with sweat and oil.

Utriel watched excitedly.

Ganah's expression gave no hint of her thoughts.

Noah leaned forward beside her, his hands on his knees as he sucked in great gasps of air. He had held his own until Benu swept his legs from under him before pinning him to the ground with his massive body.

Only three men now remained in the ring—Bel, Benu, and Jirad. Already the crowd had begun to cheer for Bel. Benu, they yelled, was too stupid and Jirad too inexperienced.

Slowly the men circled each other, their bodies leaning forward and glistening with sweat, their arms outstretched and ready.

Benu's eyes flicked rapidly between his two opponents.

Jirad paused to wipe perspiration from his forehead, blinking to clear his eyes.

Bel circled, waiting for an opportunity. Then, he lunged for Jirad's legs.

Jirad sidestepped, stumbled, and caught himself.

Bel raked his hand along the churned-up ground, grabbing a handful of dirt and grass. With a flick of his wrist he flung it in Jirad's face.

The young man hollered, clutching at his eyes.

Reacting on instinct, Benu roared. He charged like an enraged bull as Bel approached his disabled victim. "Duck!" Benu screamed to Jirad.

Bel's head snapped around as the big man hurtled forward, head lowered, and arms tucked into his chest.

With a loud thud Benu hit Bel's side, sending the blond giant staggering across the grass.

"Jirad!" yelled Benu. "Get out of the ring! Bel means to kill you!"

"Idiot!" screamed Gitel, jumping with rage on the edge of the circle.

Confused, Benu turned toward his brother's voice. "What?" he mouthed.

Suddenly, two massive, cupped hands smashed against the sides of his head.

Benu groaned and grabbed his ears, collapsing dizzily to his knees. Blood ran from his ears, between his fingers, and dripped from his nose onto his bare chest.

Without a glance at the injured man, Bel turned to Jirad, beckoning him with his fingers. "You couldn't leave well enough alone, could you?" he hissed. "This was not in my plan, but I have no choice. I can't afford to lose Utriel now."

With the speed of a striking serpent, Bel flung Jirad facedown on the ground. Straddling his stunned body, he twisted his hand in Jirad's hair, jerking his head backward. He cupped the young man's chin in his other hand and yanked his body into a bowed position as he tensed, ready to fall onto him with enough force to break his back.

With a yell, Noah dashed into the ring and wrapped his arms around the big man's throat in a death lock like the one used by herdsmen to kill cattle when harvesting hides.

Startled, Bel released his hold on Jirad and pitched across the ring, trying desperately to dislodge his attacker, his arms flailing uselessly at the man fused to his back.

Noah squeezed tighter, shutting off the other's circulation.

Slowly, Bel's face turned blue and his eyes rolled upward.

Noah's breath came in great racking gasps as he held the unconscious man's head still locked in his arms. His mouth twisted and his arms tightened.

"No!" commanded a voice.

Noah tried to focus through the red haze now covering his vision, and his heart thundered in his ears.

"This is not the way. Do not dishonor yourself." Ganah pushed the El-cumah between the back of Bel's head and Noah's chest. "Let him go."

As if emerging from a trance, Noah shook his head and released his hold. Bel slipped from his grasp, slumping to the ground.

"Well done," said the Ulah-rah.

Already Utriel was at her brother's side, helping him to his feet as he massaged the back of his neck.

"Silence," yelled the chief elder, trying to quiet the crowd. "There is no winner. The rules have been broken."

Confused, Utriel turned from Jirad and stepped toward the fallen Bel. Then she whirled on Noah, green fire flashing in her eyes. "What were you doing?" she demanded. "You almost killed him."

Noah started to speak, but the look on Utriel's face cut him like a knife. Ganah squeezed his arm and shook her head.

"Was there need for such violence?" demanded Utriel.

"Don't you realize he was trying to kill your brother?" said Noah, his hands clenched into tight fists.

The girl knelt beside Bel as he raised himself on one arm and shook his head. "Are you all right?" she asked.

He nodded, pushing himself to his feet. "Your friend has quite a temper."

Utriel flushed, but glanced from the corner of her eye at Noah still standing beside Ganah. "He has been our friend for a long time," she said. "I'm afraid he let his loyalty cloud his judgment."

"Come, Noah," said the Ulah-rah. "There will be time to discuss this later when tempers are not running so high."

"Wait!" said Bel, shaking his head as if trying to clear it.

Noah paused.

"I regret," said the weapon maker, out of breath, "that you thought I meant to harm the boy. I often forget my size and strength can be frightening."

Noah's mouth was firm and tension outlined his eyes. "I made no mistake, Bel."

"I am sorry you feel that way."

"Noah!" exclaimed Utriel. "I can't believe you are so pigheaded. Bel has apologized. Can't you just accept it?"

"Don't worry," replied Bel to the trembling young woman. "Soon it will all be taken care of."

Jirad put his arm under Utriel's elbow.

Anger flared in her face, but she clenched her lips and allowed her brother to lead her from the field.

Bel watched them leave, dark anger smoldering in his eyes.

"You stupid pig!" hissed Gitel as he helped Benu to his feet. "How could you have missed such an opportunity to rid ourselves of a certain nuisance? Now you have sealed our fate."

Benu shrugged away from Gitel's hands and trudged wearily across the field, holding his head between his hands.

Gitel ran the palm of his hand over his mouth and turned nervously to Bel. "You fought well," he stammered. "I regret my oaf of a brother interfered. If I can make up for what he did, I am at your service."

Bel turned to leave but paused, then looked at Gitel. "Maybe you can be useful, little man." He walked back and laid his arm over Gitel's shoulder, speaking softly to him as they left the field.

Seventeen

"Utriel! Are you awake?"

Her eyes snapped open. She struggled through the gray fog of sleep. Had someone called her name or was she dreaming? She lay still, listening.

"Utriel," whispered the voice again.

She threw aside the light coverlet, rose from her pallet, and peered through the narrow window into the night shadows. "Who is it?"

"It's me."

"Gitel?" a dark, weasel-like face stared into hers. "You nearly scared the life out of me. What are you doing here at this late hour?"

"Sh-h-h. Keep your voice low. I have a message from Bel."

Her breath caught in her throat.

"Well, do you want to hear it or not?"

"Yes."

"You're to meet him at the lake."

"Now?"

"Yes, now."

"Why not tomorrow when it's light?"

"How do I know," fumed Gitel. "He just said it was important for you to come now."

"I can't meet a man at night by myself."

"Why not? Are you afraid?"

"No, of course not," she flared. "It's just—well, what if someone saw me?"

"What difference would it make? Bel's already claimed you as his."

She hesitated. What Gitel said was true, but there was still Noah, and what of Ganah? She rubbed her bare toes over her instep. "Gitel," she ventured, "will you go with me and wait?"

He twisted his face and chewed thoughtfully on the inside of his mouth. "All right," he said at last. "I'll go, but hurry. We're wasting time."

Silvery light from the full moon dimly illuminated two figures hurrying along the narrow lake path. The early morning mist rose from the warm ground, wetting their feet and penetrating the edges of their garments. Fireflies winked among the tall, moisture-laden weeds while crickets, nestled in tiny crevices, and minuscule tree frogs harmonized in a plaintive, nocturnal melody.

Gitel slapped aside low-hanging limbs that snatched at their faces and hair. Clouds drifted frequently across the moon, forcing them to rely on instinct rather than sight. Once Utriel winced as she stumbled on a sharp rock concealed in the shadows beneath her feet. Dark forms flitted among the trees, but Utriel kept her eyes on the path, refusing to be deterred by fearful imaginings.

Suddenly, Gitel stopped and held up his hand, tilted his head, and listened.

Through the dark silhouettes of the trees she could see silver water shimmering in the moonlight.

He left the path, motioning for her to follow, then plunged silently into the thicket surrounding the lake. At last he paused and pointed.

She peered into the shifting shadows. There, among the trees, his back to her, stood a man. The light filtering through the leaves gave his skin a pale, unearthly luminescence. Thick, ashen hair fell unfettered about his shoulders, and an intoxicating scent filled the air.

"Go back!" screamed a voice in her head. "Escape while you can!" She looked at Gitel, then at the figure.

Slowly, he turned.

In that instant she was lost. She would have yielded her life for only one moment with the man before her.

He extended his arm, his palm outstretched. "I've been waiting for you," he said.

Once more she turned toward Gitel, but he was hidden in the shadows.

Her heart throbbed in her ears. She screamed silently for help and cursed herself for her weakness.

"Come, Utriel," said Bel. "Give in to your emotions. They will not betray you."

She walked toward him, tears welling in her eyes.

He placed his hand under her chin and tilted her head upward.

His face displayed no warmth, no love, no affection, only desire and lust. She shuddered. Tears spilled down her cheeks as she raised her arms. Bel lifted the thin garment over her head. Her body glistened a ghostly paleness in the shadows.

The rising mist swept in from the lake and encircled the two figures. A third skulked silently through the trees, back to the sleeping compound.

Utriel stirred in the early morning light.

"So, you're awake," mumbled Bel, watching her through narrowed eyes, his back against a large willow. Its sweeping branches touched the ground forming a delicate, leafy canopy as if to isolate them from the outside world. "Here," he said, tossing her shift into her lap. "Put this on."

"Why did you summon me?" she asked, pulling the garment over her head. "Why do you risk bringing dishonor upon my name? When you so desire, I will be your wife anyway."

He laughed—harsh, cold, and cruel.

Shame and humiliation overwhelmed her. All of the inner voices she had refused to hear or acknowledge cascaded into her consciousness in a deluge of condemnation. With a cry she scrambled to her feet.

Bel grabbed her shoulder, shoving her to her knees. "Did you really think I would marry you?" He sneered. "Are you that much of a fool?"

She buried her face in her hands.

"Look at me," he ordered, gripping her upper arms. He shook her violently, her head snapping back and forth. "Do you still not know who I am?"

She tried to speak, but only a low moan gurgled in her throat.

"Open your eyes!"

Powerless to resist, she lifted her eyes to his. Her head began to spin as they drew her deeper and deeper into their ice-blue depths. Nausea swept over her, and she felt herself whirling, descending into a vortex rapidly changing into a deep, golden brown, swirling around her, sucking her into its endless abyss. She gasped for air, her hands clawing at her throat as a gray veil closed around her.

"Utriel, look at me!" ordered Bel, shaking her once again.

She blinked, trying to focus her eyes on the ones before her—now dark, elongated, slit-like pupils, the yellow, feral eyes of a serpent.

"What are you?" she gasped.

With a sneer, he flung her from him.

She threw out her arms, but her shoulder struck the ground. Her right cheek grazed against a gnarled root of the willow. Dazed, she shook her head and tried to sit up.

"I am one whom you humans fear." His voice was harsh and deep, as if echoing through a long tunnel. "I am older than your world. I helped bring darkness and death upon this land. I am Asmodeus, chief servant to the lord Abaddon, Prince of the Abyss."

The body towering above her blurred and shifted as the demonic entity struggled to maintain a semblance of its human form.

"We must destroy the plan of our ancient enemy, the one you mortals call Yah-Adon." The creature laughed and spat upon the ground, grinding the spittle beneath its foot.

"He thinks to bring into the world through the bloodline of man a Deliverer for His people. He will never accomplish this feat, for He can use only those humans who are righteous and undefiled." Asmodeus' lips drew back from his teeth like those of a wild animal, and a deep growl rumbled in his throat. "By the time my lord's servants are through with mankind, his seed and bloodline will be so corrupted they will be absolutely worthless."

He glared at the woman cowering before his feet. "Yah-Adon had desired to use you and Noah in His plan of redemption. I have destroyed that possibility." He chuckled to himself.

"Oh," he rasped, "our plan is working perfectly. You should have seen how I directed the lioness to attack your brother. It was magnificent!" He threw back his head, roaring with maniacal glee.

Utriel pressed her hands to her head to obliterate the sound.

"I was tempted to let the beast finish the job, but I knew it would be more interesting if I brought your brother home alive—and I was right."

Suddenly, the laughter ceased.

Utriel shrank back in horror at the malignant hatred darkening the creature's face.

"Your fool of a father actually made me his blood brother. He deserves the living death that has come upon him, for he dared to mingle his blood with mine. I could not have planned it better.

"And," he gloated, "your brother should have been satisfied that I decided to let him live, but no, he had to challenge me." The entity clenched his fists, beating them against his chest. "It was I who filled the tree by the well with snakes. At that moment I could have destroyed you both, but then my master's plan would have been ruined."

Cunning spread over his face. "One thing we have learned. If given enough time, you foolish humans create your own ruin. You are blind to our ways. You are like sheep following wolves to their destruction.

"And you." His lips pulled back from teeth now long and yellowed. "You gave yourself to me because my body was handsome. You ridiculous, stupid woman. You seduced yourself with your vain imaginations."

"Why do you hate me so?" cried Utriel.

"Hate you? I have no feeling for you at all. What I came to do is finished. Go back to your farmer, if he still wants you. I care neither one way nor another. You are no longer of use to Yah-Adon, for now your line can never bring forth the Promised One."

He knelt beside Utriel and leaned close to her face.

She whimpered, cringing in horror.

"No matter what you do, you are mine," he whispered in her ear. "You carry *my* seed. You will bear *my* child, and he will do *my* bidding."

He stood to his feet. "Even as I speak, Abaddon's servants are joining themselves with foolish women such as you all over the earth. Soon this insignificant dung heap will be blotted from existence, and all creation will see that Yah-Adon has failed. It will see that we are the ones who should be ruling this universe."

Utriel clutched her ears to shut out the words that stabbed her heart with hot, savage blows of execration.

With a shout of defiance, Asmodeus stretched his arms above his head. Smoke and flames roiled about his distorted form, and a cacophony of horror thundered through the trees. Then—all was quiet.

Long after the last echo had faded, Utriel remained huddled on the ground, sobbing in terror, her arms covering her head. When she finally struggled to her feet, her body trembling uncontrollably, she steadied herself against a tree. A sullen stillness held the lake like a dark pall. With a cry, she ran, fleeing the demons that now haunted her.

Eighteen

Ganah rose wearily from the Mound's ancient and weathered stones. She brushed dirt from her hands, then wiped them absentmindedly on her skirt. The answer had to be here. She was certain. It had to be part of the story she had repeated to her people for generations. At times she felt the answer within her grasp only to have it slip from her, like oil through her fingers.

She walked to the edge of the Mound, leaned on the El-cumah and stared across the lush valley of the Sethites where the fields of riping grain spread golden.

She sighed with frustration. "Eliah," she said to the mountain of flesh squatting obediently on the grassy plateau, "the days pass so quickly, and I have accomplished so little."

He smiled, thick, dark lashes shielding his gentle eyes.

She stared into the cloud-shrouded distance. "Yah-Adon," she whispered, "why will You not reveal more to me? I cannot stop what I do not understand."

The Tumulac shifted on his haunches.

"Thank you, old friend, for your faithfulness." she said with a deep sigh. "Only Yah-Adon Himself knows what I would do without you."

A breeze stirred the air, ruffling the edges of her robe. She patted his shoulder with her strong, blue-veined hand before returning her attention to the ancient stones of the Mazzaroth.

She gazed at the carvings. "I had almost forgotten," she muttered thoughtfully, running her hand over the chiseled lines of the Scorpion, that Great Deceiver who had brought death and corruption into her world. "The red star in the middle of its body is called the Heart of the Scorpion." Her finger lingered on the faded, dark stain. "It is also called the Wounding. And look," she pointed, "there, in its uplifted tail, poised to sting, is a star named the Perverse."

Deep in study, the old woman walked around the outside of the circles. Then she paused, studying the carved figures of two men, the Serpent Treader and Bau, the Mighty One with the wounded heel. "Many times I have told the people that both of these figures represented the Deliverer promised by Yah-Adon, the one who would bring death to the Destroyer himself."

Ganah turned to Eliah, her voice quivering with emotion. "The people have waited so long for the Deliverer to appear that they no longer believe. It has become only a story to be listened to by the fire at night."

She paced across the top of the Mound. "I have never doubted that the promise is true, but how," she asked, bewilderment in her voice, "how can it be possible for the Promised One to be mortally wounded by the Deceiver and still be victorious?"

She lifted her head to the evening sky. "Yah-Adon," she cried, "why do You refuse to give us the entire picture? You expect us to accept too much on faith."

She closed her eyes. It was late. Below in the valley men were busily gathering their tools and preparing to leave the fields. Head wives had already begun preparations for the evening meals. Sometimes she envied these women for their uncomplicated lives. Most of all, she envied them for their children. A great sadness swept over her. She missed not having children the most, for nothing had ever filled that void or relieved that ache.

Sighing, she signaled to Eliah that it was time to go. With spear in hand, he rose, his mammoth shadow following his Ulah-rah as she descended the winding path.

"Um-m-m-m," Ganah murmured as she entered her house. "That smells delicious." Paniel placed a steaming dish of savory stew on the Ulah-rah's low table. Ganah ate sparingly these days for her mind, desiring much more than food to fill the stomach, was elsewhere, but this evening she relished the thought of eating for she was hungry and her body was tired.

She dropped her brightly colored robe beside the table and dipped water into a heavy, clay basin. She paused, water dripping from her fingers. What was that? A faint mewling, like an injured animal. She peered into the deepening shadows of the room.

She started to call for Eliah but stopped. Instead, she reached for a lamp and lighted it with the attached flint. The pale light spread before her, doing little to dissipate the darkness. Peering into the shadows, she stepped toward a barely discernible darkness huddled in the corner. She reached out her hand. Flesh, cold and damp, trembled beneath her touch.

Ganah set down her lamp and knelt beside the crouched figure. Gently, she lifted the face to the light. "Child," she cried at the despair on her young friend's tear-stained and swollen face. "What has happened?"

A deep sob shook the girl's body.

Ganah put her arm around Utriel's waist and led her to her own pallet. She laid her down, kneeling beside her. Gently, as a mother comforting her child, she held Utriel long into the night, until the last convulsive tremor had left her body. Then she placed pillows under the girl's head and laid a wet cloth across the pallid forehead. Finally, she sank to an animal skin lying on the hard, dirt-packed floor and held Utriel's trembling hand in her own. She waited.

Hours later as the lamp flickered in the room, Ganah asked, "Utriel, can you tell me what happened? I want to help you."

"I am destroyed!" Utriel whispered hoarsely. Her eyes widened in terror, her mouth flew open, and a convulsion seized her.

Ganah threw herself onto the young woman, pressing her firmly to the pallet as tremors racked the slender body beneath her. Not until the last spasm ceased did the Ulah-rah release the girl's shoulders. Then, she raised herself, exhausted, from the limp body. Her arms and back ached. In the dim light she could see that Utriel had passed into a deep sleep.

A hand touched her on the shoulder. She looked up. "It's all right, Eliah," the prophetess said. "She's asleep. She'll not awaken until morning."

Quietly the man slipped from the room to resume his place by the entrance.

The old woman spread a cover on the floor next to the sleeping girl and stretched out beside her, drawing her robe over her own tired body. She slept, but strange dreams, fleeing as quickly as they came, kept her tossing restlessly.

By the early morning light Ganah examined Utriel's pale face. The girl's eyes, ringed with dark circles, were swollen, and bright fever spots dotted her cheeks.

Ganah pushed herself to her feet and walked to the door where the Tumulac sat watching the sunrise. "Eliah, have Paniel start the fire for our morning meal."

Moving slowly, Ganah poured water and washed her hands. She wrung out a cloth and held it to her face to cool her own burning eyes.

A movement on the pallet caught her ear. She dropped the cloth into the basin and hurried to the girl's side. "Utriel," she whispered. "Can you hear me?"

Utriel's eyes opened, blank and staring.

Ganah held her face between her hands. "Can you see me?"

Tears welled in the dark eyes as deep, travailing sobs shook her body.

Unable to help, the Ulah-rah cradled the young woman in her arms.

Paniel prepared the fire and was waiting for instructions, but the Tumulac stood protectively before the doorway, arms crossed and feet wide apart, determined that nothing would disturb his mistress until she gave the command.

When Ganah appeared at last in the entrance, the fire had burned low. "Fix some broth and warm bread, please. And bring it to me as soon as it is ready."

The woman hurried from the room. Utriel lay without moving. Already a pallor had settled over her.

When Paniel brought the broth, Ganah cradled the young woman's head in her arms and placed a sip of the hot liquid to her lips. With each mouthful, color returned to the girl's face.

When the last drop was gone, Ganah laid Utriel's head on the pillows and carried the heavy clay bowl to the doorway. "Eliah, give these to Paniel and then bring Jirad to me. Only Jirad, do you hear? Bring no one else. Now hurry."

The Tumulac hastened to carry out his mistress' command.

Ganah knelt beside Utriel. "Eliah has gone for Jirad. When your brother arrives, you must tell us what happened."

Utriel's eyes stared fixedly before her. Ganah held her hand, occasionally whispering or stroking her arm.

When she heard footsteps outside the door, she called, "Jirad, enter. Your sister is here."

He hesitated before stepping through the doorway. When he saw Utriel's still form, he rushed to her side, falling to his knees. "Is she all right?"

Ganah shook her head. "I have never seen such despair in anyone before. If we don't break through soon, I fear we will lose her."

"Utriel," Jirad cried in desperation, "tell us what happened."

The hours passed slowly as Jirad kept vigil by his sister's side, watching her alternate between convulsive, uncontrollable sobbing and deep, trancelike sleep.

It was well past noon when Ganah touched his arm. "My son, you need to return to your chores. It would be wise to keep Utriel's whereabouts a secret until we know what has happened. Make an excuse to Bithra about her absence. The woman is so busy taking care of

Obed she may not ask many questions. I'll stay here with Utriel."

Jirad shook his head, refusing to move.

The Ulah-rah spoke more firmly, "It is not wise for you to remain here any longer."

"No, I will not leave my sister." Startled at his unaccustomed audacity, he lowered his voice. "Forgive me, Ulah-rah, but I must stay."

"If you and Utriel are both missing, someone is sure to begin searching for you. Until we know what has happened, I beg you to go, for Utriel's sake."

Still, Jirad shook his head.

"I will send for you if there is any change," she promised, "but for now, we must act as if nothing has happened. At least until your sister is able to speak."

"I know you're right," he said, "but my heart breaks at seeing her like this."

"Come," she urged, taking his elbow in her hand.

He rose reluctantly, his eyes never leaving his sister. "Whoever did this," he vowed, "will have to answer to me."

"I'll let nothing happen to her while she is under my roof," assured Ganah as she led him to the doorway. "Now go, but be sure no one sees you leave," she cautioned, patting his arm.

He slipped silently from the house.

"Eliah," said Ganah, after Jirad had left, "see that no one else enters."

The Tumulac bowed his head, his body blocking the entrance.

The prophetess returned to her charge. She knelt by the side of the still figure and whispered, "Sleep, my little one. May the sweet balm of sleep heal your wounds."

Nineteen

Jirad filled a skin with water and shouldered an obsidian-headed hoe. The ground needed tending in the far end of his father's field. It would be good to work the soil, to feel it yield to his hand and to smell its strong, woody scent, for his mind was consumed with concern for his sister.

Ganah had been right, though. Explaining Utriel's absence had not been difficult. Bithra merely nodded when Jirad said his sister was caring for Katha, an old woman within the city walls who had become ill. Now his body was tense, poised to spring into action, but he had promised Ganah he would wait.

When he reached the edge of the field, Gitel was sitting on a large stump, his hoe between his knees and a wineskin in his hand. As Jirad drew closer, the man's furtive eyes darted in all directions.

"Is she all right?" Gitel asked.

"Who?"

"Utriel, of course."

Jirad threw down his hoe and started toward him.

"Benu!" hollered Gitel, leaping to his feet and thrusting the hoe between himself and Jirad. "Come here! Hurry!"

"What do you know about Utriel?" demanded Jirad. "Tell me before I have to choke it from you."

"Nothing," he said, stepping backward. "I—I only delivered a message to her."

"From whom?"

"If I tell you, he'll kill me."

Jirad knocked the hoe from Gitel's hands. "If you don't tell me, I'll save him the trouble."

"Benu!" Gitel screamed again.

The big man had moved in and was standing silently behind his brother, causing Gitel to jump when he felt his presence.

Benu looked at Jirad and shook his head. "Tell him what he wants, Gitel, or I'll pound you into the ground myself."

"All right! All right!" Looking first over his shoulder, he whispered, "It was Bel. He made me take her a message—to meet him at the lake last night."

"What happened?" demanded Jirad.

"I don't know."

Jirad grabbed the man's neck with both hands. "What happened?"

"I don't know!" gasped Gitel. "I just took her there and left."

"Benu, is he telling the truth?" asked Jirad.

"I think so." The man's upper lip curled at the sight of his sniveling brother. "Come on," he said to Jirad, his jaw tightening. "Let's find Bel."

Jirad placed his hand on the coals in the forge. They were cold.

"The house looks empty," said Benu.

"Bel!" Jirad yelled.

"Something's wrong," said Benu. "I can feel it in my gut."

Jirad put his hand on the latch, shoving the heavy door inward. It banged hollowly against the wall.

"Augh—" he gagged, stepping inside. "What is that smell? How could anyone live in such a stench?"

Benu wrinkled his nose.

The empty room showed no sign of life, only an overturned table against one wall and broken pottery littering the floor.

Jirad pulled aside a curtain separating the main room of the house from the sleeping area. He grabbed the edge of the doorway to steady himself as scalding bile rushed up his throat and into his mouth.

"Great Yah-Adon," whispered Benu, surveying the blood-splattered walls. "Who could have done such a thing?"

Jirad stepped into the room, recoiling as he stumbled over a leg bent grotesquely on the floor.

"Whose is it?" Benu asked, swallowing rapidly.

Jirad did not reply but stooped beside the sleeping pallet. He lifted the edge of a pile of blood-soaked covers heaped in the middle of the mat and pulled it back.

Staring at him with unseeing, terror-filled eyes was the disembodied head of Gabul.

Jirad pressed his hand hard against his nose and mouth to staunch the rising flow and fled the house. Leaning against the outside wall, he retched violently.

"What happened?" wheezed an old man hobbling to his side. It was Gamesh, the worker of wood. "I was bringing tools to be repaired," he said, coughing with the effort of running to Jirad's side.

"What's going on?" called Hamel, hurrying into the yard.

Benu emerged from the house, all color drained from his face. "Inside," he said to the two men. "It's Gabul. He's dead."

Hamel started toward the doorway with the old man scurrying behind. Cautiously, the two men entered the house.

"Did Bel do this?" Benu asked when the men were out of earshot, his voice low and hoarse.

"I'm sure of it." He walked to the forge and leaned his arms on its rocky edge, studying the ash and coals. "There is something I must do," he said. "Benu, I need you to look after things for me. Take care of our family, and if anything happens to me, promise you'll look after Utriel."

Benu grabbed Jirad's shoulder. "Let me go with you."

"No. This I must do alone. I have a score to settle."

"You can't go after Bel by yourself. He'll kill you."

"Just do what I ask."

Benu studied the ground for a moment and then placed his large hands on Jirad's shoulders. "I'm not very smart," he said, "but I'll do the best I can."

Jirad turned.

"Wait," yelled Benu.

The young man paused.

Benu enveloped him in his arms. "Take care."

Jirad stood at the edge of town, hands on hips and a perplexed expression on his face. Suddenly, he shouted, "What a fool I am! Why didn't I think of it sooner. The cave!"

Whirling about, he raced back to the compound, chastising himself as he ran.

Bithra was emptying a large basin of water beside the doorway when he dashed into the yard, her eyes narrowing at the sight of his flushed and perspiring face. "What's wrong?"

"Go back to your work," Jirad snapped. "You'll find out soon enough."

"Mind your tongue."

"Be still, old woman," ordered Jirad, cursing himself for his harshness.

Her mouth clamped shut, and she stepped back in surprise.

"Bring me a pouch full of flints. And hurry!"

She rushed from the room.

When she returned, Jirad had already wrapped several of his father's torches in his cloak. The woman handed him a leather pouch. "Look after my father," he said as he tied the bag to his belt. Without another word he strode from the house, leaving Bithra open-mouthed and shaking her head.

This time he would enter the cave, and this time he would find his quarry.

It was well past noon when Jirad entered the forest. The shade was a welcomed relief from the hot sun, but the air felt thick, burning his eyes and making it hard to breathe.

Stories about the terrors of the forest crept into his mind. "I will not think of such things," he said out loud, angry with himself for allowing such thoughts to weaken his resolve. "I must find Bel. The forest is no different now than it was a few days ago."

Forcing the fear from his mind, he dashed into the shadows, darting and dodging the trees that barred his path. As he rushed toward the secret cave, the black twisted branches clutched at his face and pulled at his hair.

Stopping, he listened intently, his eyes straining in the dim, mottled light. The thick, pungent smell of the dank earth and trees stung his nostrils. What had broken his concentration? A twig snapped; he flinched. "May Yah-Adon Himself strike me dead if I don't stop this foolishness," he muttered, lashing at a limb that had broken from its trunk but dangled at a precarious angle, still held to the tree by thin, fibrous strands.

He sniffed and wrinkled his nose at an acrid odor in the air. "What the—" he gasped as a malodorous foulness descended from above and swiftly engulfed him.

Jirad struggled to draw air into his lungs. Coarse, matted hair, reeking with a harsh, caustic fetor filled his mouth and nose. He twisted to see, but a strong grip held him fast. He felt himself swaying rhythmically in a strange lurching, forward motion, each movement accompanied by deep, guttural grunts. Leafy branches brushed and scraped his body with a regular cadence.

Suddenly he understood. He was being carried far above the forest floor while the ground whirled below.

A cold, hard surface lay beneath his prone body. Although Jirad couldn't remember losing consciousness, time and direction blurred and distorted. He drew in great breaths, but the stench still burned in his nostrils. He pushed himself to a sitting position and rubbed his stiff muscles. A soft light began to dispel some of the shadows, enough to see that he was inside a cave. A dark form scuttled toward him, emitting a series of deep grunts. Jirad threw up his hands, but once again the foul odor overwhelmed him as long, powerful, hairy arms encircled his body.

The creature ran, carrying him through winding passageways, some barely wide enough to enter, for stones scraped roughly against his skin. On and on ran his captor in its strange loping gait, never seeming to tire as it carried him deeper into the bowels of the earth.

Jirad fought against the fear threatening to overtake him. Obed had taught him early that fear was man's greatest enemy. If he could overcome his fears, his father had said, the battle was nearly won. Jirad was determined he would not be defeated.

Although he could not see his captor clearly, he knew it to be one of the forest people—large hairy creatures that slipped noiselessly from tree to tree. They walked upright like man but lived deep in the forest. The Old Ones had called them the oranji, but seldom were they seen anymore for they shunned and feared humans.

Jirad groaned and opened his eyes. He rolled over and tried to push himself to his knees. Wincing with pain, he rubbed his arms and legs, attempting to restore life into them.

The oranji stared at him with tiny, close-set eyes. It shifted from one foot to the other, scuttled backward, then squatted on its short, bowed legs, its large jaw working in a slow, grinding motion as it made strange, piglike noises. The bulbous body covered with long, reddish-brown hair rested its strong arms on large, square knuckles.

A dull glow pulsating from a yawning abyss in the center of an immense, vaulted chamber enabled him to view his surroundings. Grotesque shadows danced on the walls, and an unearthly wave of sound rose and fell like breakers crashing against a distant shore.

When Jirad was satisfied that the aberration was not going to attack, he edged toward the light.

The creature grunted, rose, and leaned forward on its knuckles.

Jirad retreated.

Still grunting, the creature sat down.

Jirad stepped forward.

Again, the creature rose, drawing its lips back from large, yellow teeth.

"All right, all right," said Jirad, holding up his hands. Still keeping a wary eye on his captor, he sat down with his back against the rough stone wall.

Without warning, the creature jumped, looking toward the glowing chasm. It shifted anxiously on its haunches.

Jirad felt a pulsation deep beneath the rock. He flattened his hands on the rough surface, feeling the vibration traveling up his arms and into his shoulders. The rocks seemed to grate and crunch, shifting far below. He jerked back, perspiration now running from his body.

The creature began squealing, rocking back and forth on its knuckles and feet. Red-orange coals exploded violently from the chasm, raining down showers of glowing embers, the smell of sulfur heavy in the air. The animal huddled against the cavern wall.

Jirad threw up his arms to shield his head. He gasped in terror.

From the depths of the pit, amid swirling and spiraling vapors, an immense figure rose, hovering in the glowing and flickering light. It stepped onto the edge of the abyss, its powerful arms and hands resting insolently on its hips. "Look at me, Human," commanded a familiar voice. "See me as you know me."

"Bel?" cried Jirad, unable to grasp what his eyes were seeing.

The colossal tossed back its head. "I am Asmodeus. Look upon me and fear." The creature stretched forth its hand.

Instantly, a blinding pain exploded within Jirad's skull. He clutched his head as his back arched in excruciating spasms.

"Mortal," said Asmodeus, lowering his arm. "You are mine to do with as I please."

Abruptly, the searing pain ceased, and Jirad collapsed to his knees, groaning and holding his head. He drew in great breaths, desperately attempting to clear his head.

When he could finally speak, Jirad gasped, "Why did you not kill me when you first had the chance?"

"Because it served my purpose to let you live."

Jirad cringed at the fury in the voice.

"Life means nothing to me," sneered Asmodeus, swinging his arm toward the terrified creature huddled against the wall. With a cry, it threw its long arms into the air as it was lifted and catapulted across the chamber toward the flaming chasm. Squealing in terror, it plummeted into the glowing darkness.

When the last cry had faded, Asmodeus turned his murderous gaze once again toward Jirad. "I will delight in destroying you and all of your kind."

"Why?"

With centuries of smoldering hatred, Asmodeus glared at the man. "Because you are made in Yah-Adon's image. We can't destroy Him, but we can drag those He has made into the mire and filth until we stamp out their insignificant lives."

Caught in a grip of frenzy, Asmodeus screamed, "The enemy has a plan to defeat us, and we cannot see it clearly. You and your people are part of it, for the Sethites are among the last to still believe in the Old Ways." Abruptly, his voice lowered, "It has something to do with your sister and with Noah."

"With Utriel?" Jirad's anger flared, and he struggled to his feet. "What did you do to her?"

The once brilliant eyes darkened, red-rimmed as blazing coals, and the outlines of the abomination distorted, the fury and hatred born from a warped and twisted intellect steadily devouring the deceptive radiance.

Jirad shut his eyes to block the deadly gaze. He felt himself lifted into the air. He tumbled wildly, his arms and legs flailing as he spiraled over the chasm, dangling like an insect over a white-hot flame. He screamed in terror at the roaring inferno below. Tongues of flame leaped high in the air, licking at his body. With the heat scorching his lungs, he writhed to escape the terrible flames.

Fiendish laughter reverberated off the cavern walls and rumbled through the corridors, blending with Jirad's terrified screams into a hideous, chaotic melody. Abruptly, he hit the hard, cavern floor. Rolling in agony, he coughed, struggling to draw air into his seared lungs.

A foot digging into his ribs sent him crashing against a rocky wall. The creature threw back its head and roared, "Welcome, mortal. Welcome to hell!"

Twenty

Noah was confused and worried in his fruitless search for an answer. Not a worry that darts in and out of the consciousness like tiny gnats around a face on a hot day, but the kind that settles deep in the bowels. To make matters worse he had not seen Utriel for two days. Even Bithra had been unable to tell him where she was.

"I'm too busy to notice what Utriel is doing," snorted the woman. "Jirad says she's helping Katha until the old woman feels better. Stop worrying," she chided. "Utriel can take care of herself."

Her expression had softened at the distress on the man's face. "Noah," she said, wiping her coarse, reddened hands on the front of her skirt, "she can never be yours. Why don't you find another woman? There are many who yearn to find favor in your eyes."

"I love her," he replied. "I can't just walk away."

As Noah's hoe dug into the dark earth, images of Utriel flashed through his mind. Last night the dream had occurred again, and again he had awakened, terrified of what it might portend. What disturbed him most was not the snake, but the horror of Utriel opening her arms to its hideous embrace.

He swung the hoe high in the air, sinking it deeply into the soil. He lifted the head, sending clods of dark earth scattering over the ground. Fingers of a strong hand grasped his shoulder. Startled, he spun to face the silent intruder, his hoe cocked over his shoulder. He saw no one, only Uzzah at the far end of the field picking voracious beetles from young plants while Haniah tenaciously turned over the loamy soil. No one else was in the field. Yet still he could feel the pressure on his shoulder.

He wiped his arm across his forehead and surveyed the area while swatting carelessly at a sweat bee alighting on his chest. The sun's rays shimmered hotly on the distant fields.

"Noah," whispered a voice, like the muted sighing of a summer wind. The hair on the back of his neck bristled. "Noah," repeated the voice, "Utriel needs you."

The knuckles on his hands whitened against the handle of the hoe, and his eyes frantically searched the field.

"I have seen that you have a different spirit from your brethren," murmured the whisper. "You have found favor in My eyes. Go to Ganah. She will need you in the days to come."

Noah shook himself as if rousing from a deep reverie. He realized he had been holding his breath. Was it Yah-Adon who had just spoken to him or was he going mad? Either alternative was fearsome to contemplate. Once more he scanned the area. His brothers, still working at the end of the field, gave no evidence that they had seen or heard anything unusual.

With fear for Utriel clutching at his heart, he flung the hoe to the ground, grabbed his tunic and raced across the field, wiping his face and chest as he ran.

As he approached the wall, several town elders stood at the entrance exchanging heated words with a group of traders from Ba-thi. A tall, craggy-faced fellow in their midst lifted dark eyebrows to the others as Noah dashed through the gate. A goat, tethered in front of a house, bleated loudly and bolted out of his way, its back legs kicking over a basket of green squash. A white-bearded man carving a length of wood looked up to watch the vegetables tumble in all directions over the road. He scratched his head, grumbling, "These young people." Still muttering, he rose and hobbled awkwardly to the basket. With a groan, he bent down and began picking up the scattered squash.

When Noah reached Ganah's house, the Tumulac stood in the doorway with arms folded and feet far apart.

"I must see the Ulah-rah," shouted Noah. "Quickly, let me in."

Eliah stood firm, his countenance impassive.

"If she's here, I must see her."

Still, he made no effort to respond.

"Ganah!" Noah yelled in exasperation as he tried to see around the heavy body blocking the entrance. "I must see you."

At that, the Tumulac placed one hand on the man's shoulder and pushed him from the door.

Noah knocked aside his hand, shoving into him with his shoulder.

Instantly, Eliah wrapped his huge arms around Noah and held him.

"That's enough," yelled Ganah, hurrying to the disturbance. "It's all right," she assured Eliah. "Let him in."

The Tumulac released Noah. He stepped to one side, but his eyes never left his mistress's face.

"What do you want?" she asked, a hint of irritation in her voice.

"I must talk to you. Utriel's in great danger."

Ganah's eyes narrowed. "What makes you say such a thing?"

Spreading his hands, Noah shook his head. "I'm not sure," his voice faltered. "A voice told me."

The old woman leaned heavily on the staff, her lips pursed in thoughtful examination of the distraught man. "Come in," she said at last, "but you must remain silent until you have heard what I have to say." She beckoned him to follow.

As he stepped into the large room, he was conscious of the pleasant scent of oleander filling the air. Large bowls of the fragrant, white blossoms sat in the corners, and beautifully woven cloths draped loosely across the walls. An intricately carved wooden chair lined with furs and wools stood in one corner.

Ganah motioned for Noah to sit. She folded her arms and fixed him with a fierce gaze. "Utriel is here, but she is very sick. I've not been able to help her."

"Let me see her, please."

"And so you shall, but first you must listen." As gently as she knew how, Ganah related all that had occurred since finding the girl huddled in the darkness of her room. As the prophetess spoke, the tenderness on Noah's face stirred her heart.

"Utriel has turned within herself," said the old woman. "If we can't bring her back quickly, I fear she'll be lost to us forever."

"I must see her."

"Yes," she said. "Follow me." She pulled aside the heavy curtain into a sleeping room and looped the fabric around an ornate wooden bracket fastened to the side of the wall.

Utriel lay on the pallet, a blanket covering her lean figure. The colorful design of the fabric emphasized the deadly pallor that had settled on the girl's face.

Noah knelt by her side, took her hand between his two work-roughened ones and touched her fingertips tenderly to his lips. "Utriel," he whispered, "can you hear me?"

Her eyelids fluttered. Her lips parted as if to form a word.

He leaned closer, gently pushing the damp auburn strands from her forehead. "It's Noah."

Without warning, her eyes widened in terror and her body stiffened. "Get away from me!" she screamed wildly, jerking her hands free. "Don't touch me!"

"What's wrong?" he cried, turning to Ganah.

"I am destroyed! He mustn't touch me! Keep him away!"

"Go outside! Quickly!" ordered the woman. "I'll try to calm her!"

"What did I do?" asked Noah helplessly as he backed from the room.

Already the Tumulac had lumbered to his side. He touched Noah's arm and gestured toward a large, gray-veined rock under the branches of an enormous oak. Signaling for Noah to sit, he brought him a cup of water and smiled broadly as the man drank, a warm, generous smile marred only by two missing teeth. Then he went back to the door of the house where he sat to wait for his mistress's instructions.

Noah let the cup drop from his fingers, leaned his elbows on his knees and buried his face in his hands. "Yah-Adon," he groaned, "help us."

When Ganah emerged later from the house, she looked tired. Wisps of gray hair had escaped their braids and now hung loosely about her face. She walked laboriously to Noah's side and leaned forward on the staff as if to confide an intimacy. "Utriel has found her way back to us."

Noah leaped to his feet but stopped abruptly at the expression on the woman's face. "Is she going to be all right?"

"Sit down." The prophetess sighed. "Eliah will watch over her." She lowered herself to the rock and pulled him down beside her. She stared at her hands, twisting the fingers together as if seeing them for the first time. "Utriel has told me what happened. You must give me your word that you will listen and not speak until I am through. Then, when you have heard, you must seek counsel before you act."

"But—!"

"You must promise," she insisted, raising her voice.

Realizing that he had no alternative, Noah bowed his head.

Ganah left out nothing, although she knew the pain her words were causing. As she spoke, she realized that the pictures in her head were back once again, pictures of things that had already occurred but that she had never seen. Even as she spoke, she was seeing in her head the insidious betrayal that had taken place shrouded in darkness beneath the willow boughs. Tears welled in her eyes, tears not only for the betrayal of her dear Utriel, but also for the continued return of her powers. "Yah-Adon," she whispered silently, "You have not forgotten me."

She dabbed her eyes with the sleeve of her gown, then looked Noah directly in the eyes. "Utriel is with child."

His face blanched, his features becoming like stone.

"She is lost to you forever. When it is discovered what has happened, our people will take her to the desert and stone her."

"No," he said, his voice devoid of emotion. "We'll leave Gibaraboni and journey to another place. I have flocks and a herd of my own. We'll start a new life."

"You do not understand," she said with great sadness in her voice. "The child she carries is of a demon seed."

Noah's jaw worked as his strong fingers gripped his knees.

"Bel was not what he appeared," she continued. "He was a servant of the Destroyer. What would you do when the child is born? Would you keep it and raise an abomination before your God? "No," she continued, shaking her head. "You cannot run from this trouble. It is far too monstrous."

She rose and paced back and forth, her brow furrowed in thought. "For several cycles of the moon Yah-Adon has spoken to me of a great evil that is upon us, but I did not understand. For many days I have been going over and over the story of the stars written long ago on the Great Mound, trying to understand what the Placer of Stars has been telling me. Perhaps, if I had not been so slow of mind, I could have stopped this poison. Now, it is too late.

"Noah," she said, turning to him, "you must be very important to Yah-Adon. Why else would Abaddon have sent Asmodeus to destroy any hope of you and Utriel being joined together as husband and wife?"

"There must be a way to stop this evil," cried Noah, his head bowed to the ground. "If Yah-Adon has spoken to you, then He will give you power to do what He has asked." He lifted his head, his jaw set. "Help us, Ganah. Abaddon must not win."

"You don't know what you are asking," said the old woman. "How can one man and a worn-out prophetess stand against the powers of the Destroyer and his demon hordes?"

"What choice do we have?"

Throwing her hands into the air, she stared into the deepening twilight. Finally, she closed her eyes. "It will not be easy, and we may not win. Are you prepared for that?"

"My life is nothing if I lose Utriel. I will go to the end of the earth if I must."

She opened her eyes, staring into the distance, her gaze seeing far beyond the present. "You may have to go much farther than that, my friend. Much farther indeed."

Twenty-One

The townspeople organized a search for the crazed animal they were certain had broken into Gabul's house in the dark of night. If it were a beast, they reasoned, it should be tracked down and killed. However, an unnatural fear held sway over the men, making even the boldest hunters hesitant to strike out into the tenebrous depths of the Shinar or even the rugged foothills surrounding Gibaraboni.

Gabul's death became the subject of conversation, each discussion elaborating on the gruesome details. Even Bithra, as she tended Obed, parleyed a running monologue to her captive audience. As she talked, a look of concentration replaced his usual vacuous expression. Then one of frenzy overtook him as his mind struggled vainly for control of his useless body. Great beads of sweat glistened on his thin face, his eyes swollen and red-rimmed.

Bithra, busily chattering to herself, finished her tasks and hurried from the chamber, oblivious to her husband's turmoil.

Obed lay with pillows propped behind his back. Hot tears of rage and frustration streamed down his weathered face. *Yah-Adon,* he screamed silently, *I don't want to live any longer inside this dead body. It is worse than death.*

The high-pitched laughter of children drifting through the window only intensified his anguish. Gradually, in spite of himself, his body began to relax, his breathing slowed and his heart steadied into a more rhythmical pattern.

The voices of the children rose and fell in youthful exuberance. He recognized some of his own. As he listened, he became aware of a different noise, like dry leaves scraping across a barren ground.

Somehow, though, it was different. His skin prickled at the strangeness.

The rasping grew louder and closer. Still out of his line of vision, a sinuous brown and tan body the length of two men writhed across the floor, the sun through the window glistening on its scales. The great serpent raised its snubbed-nosed head, flicked its tongue, then slithered over the foot of Obed's pallet, barely ruffling the cover.

Obed's heart felt as if it would burst.

Methodically, the serpent pushed its head beneath the immobile body and began winding in slow but strong coils around the terrified man. At last, when it lifted its broad head and gazed into the eyes of its victim, a terrible recognition dawned.

Greetings, blood brother, spoke a familiar voice within Obed's mind. *I heard your cry for help.* The triangular head undulated, never shifting its lidless eyes from those of its victim.

Brother, why did you cry to Yah-Adon? You never wanted Him before in your life. Why do you want Him now? The coils tightened imperceptibly, and the dark, forked tongue flicked in and out, the tip lightly brushing Obed's lip.

You belong to me, continued the voice. *Did you forget? You willingly blended your blood with mine. Now, only I can set you free.*

The head of the serpent swayed as cold, dead eyes reflected the image before it. *Rejoice! I have decided to release you from your prison. Today you will be free, free to serve me for eternity.*

Obed gasped for breath as the coils tightened. Voiceless pleas mingling with silent curses filled the victim's head.

Not until the last breath had expired did the serpent relax its hold. As the sightless eyes stared into nothingness, it uncoiled from the lifeless body and slithered unnoticed through the doorway, disappearing into the countryside.

The townsmen continued their halfhearted search for Gabul's killer in every street and house in Gibara-boni, even to the edges of the Shinar although they did not venture into its darkness. By evening, they had discussed the matter so often that no doubt remained that it must had been a large and vicious animal, probably two, that had entered Gabul's house during the night and torn the luckless man to pieces.

The men had begun returning from the search when a scream, followed by a shrill keening, pierced the evening. They found Bithra mourning loudly as she held her outer tunic over her head.

With the death of Obed, Bithra realized that neither Utriel nor Jirad were anywhere to be found. Although normally a source of strength, the poor woman could only stare at the gathering crowd.

Hamel recalled last seeing Jirad soon after the discovery of Gabul's body. "Perhaps Jirad committed the act and fled," he whispered behind cupped hands. "I understand Utriel hasn't been seen for several days."

"Why can't you find her?" cried Bithra to the gathered friends, her agitation increasing. "She's been taking care of Katha for the past few days. Jirad told me so himself."

An old woman stepped forward. "Bithra, I'm not ill, and Utriel has not been taking care of me."

Bewildered, Bithra stared at Katha who stood before her with hands on broad, sturdy hips, very much a picture of health. "I don't understand. Where is she then?"

A murmur rumbled through the growing crowd, voices filled with consternation and fear. "What is going on?" someone asked.

"Could the two of them be involved in Gabul's death?"

"Maybe Bel followed them when they fled," ventured another.

The voices rose, becoming louder, more alarmed. Abruptly, the talk ceased, and the crowd stepped aside.

Ganah, clothed in the sacred blue robe of the Ulah-rah, strode tall and purposeful through the parting crowd. Startled, the Stargazers murmured with excitement to one another, for many years had passed since the Ulah-rah's mere presence had commanded respect from her people. Behind her lumbered the Tumulac, spear in hand.

Bithra uncovered her head and lowered her eyes.

Ganah glanced at the frightened woman, then entered the house of the dead followed by her silent shadow. She stood by the body of the once proud Obed, now ghastly in death, and placed her hand on the cold, blue forehead. A tremor passed through her body. She withdrew her hand. "Eliah, it is as I feared. There is no time to waste."

She turned to the people. "Go," she ordered. "Return to your work. There is nothing further you can do here."

"We must find what killed Gabul," shouted one of the men. "Dangerous animals may enter our town again."

"Listen to me!" she shouted. "An animal did not kill Gabul!"

Dissension rumbled through the crowd.

"Is it impossible for you to believe that the murderer of Gabul could have been one you welcomed into your midst, even one you idolized?"

"What are you talking about?" yelled Uzzah. "It was an animal."

Ganah lifted the El-cumah, a gesture to be still. The people watched her, their eyes puzzled and uncomprehending. "Do you not know," she continued, her voice firm, "that evil can appear disguised as a thing of great beauty? Do you truly think no man could have committed such a deed? Are your souls so withered that you can no longer comprehend evil? Are you afraid you may be forced to acknowledge your own guilt?"

They turned to one another, shaking their heads and shrugging shoulders.

"Can you no longer hear?" she screamed. When they did not respond, the old woman thrust the El-cumah before her. "Go," she commanded. "Return to your homes. It is now in Yah-Adon's hands."

Ganah remained by the door until the room was empty. The flare of anger still in her eyes, she turned to the confused woman, "Bithra, prepare Obed for burial, and do not worry about Utriel."

"But what shall I . . . ?" Seeing the futility of questioning further, Bithra bowed her head in assent.

Grimly, Ganah stalked into the approaching darkness, her staff punctuating each step.

"You maggot from a dung heap!" hissed Benu through clenched teeth. He lifted Gitel by the throat and shook him violently. "You hurt Utriel and almost made me kill Jirad. You're a bad man."

Gitel, his face turning purple, pried at the big man's hands. "Put me down, you fool," he gasped. "I'm your brother."

"I don't care," said Benu, lowering him to the ground. "You're an evil man. You tried to make me do bad things."

"If we do this right," whined Gitel, "we'll end up with all of Obed's possessions. Jirad's gone, Utriel's gone, and now Bel has disappeared from Gibara-boni. You can have anything you want."

"I don't want anything from you," said Benu, slamming his hand into Gitel's chest and knocking him to the ground.

"You're an idiot! A stupid, bumbling idiot!"

"Maybe so, but I don't want to be like you." Benu stood over the cowering man. "Don't even go back to your house. Just leave the valley and never let me see your face here again, or I'll tell everyone what you've done."

"Benu," pleaded Gitel, "you're making a big mistake."

"Get out of here!" Benu pulled back a knotted fist. "If I see you again, I'll kill you."

"All right—all right. Just let me get a few things, and then I'll go."

"No! Leave now." Benu's hand rested on the hilt of his dagger.

Gitel scuttled backward on his hands and heels.

"Now," rasped Benu.

The man scrambled to his feet, keeping an eye on his brother. He brushed himself off. "You'll be sorry," he said, sneering, then turned and headed toward the open plains.

Twenty-Two

Never had Ganah felt such anger toward her people, an anger kindled by the fact they had allowed themselves to be seduced by the world around them, changing their moral standards, their beliefs, their traditions, and above all—turning their backs upon their God. She was angry that they were content in their ignorance of not caring that they had changed, and above all, angry that they would rather believe a lie than face their own failures.

Eliah waited on the grassy mound as his mistress gazed over the distant valley, their figures silhouetted against the velvet darkness of the evening sky. Although she had not moved for a long while, he did not disturb her.

"It is so wonderful," she said, her voice low and husky. "Too awesome to be true, but it must be. Only deity could conceive such a plan. It is beyond a mortal's understanding."

The Tumulac cocked his head, a puzzled expression on his face.

"Eliah," she said, her voice tinged with excitement and awe at the thoughts forming in her head. "At last I see what Yah-Adon has tried over the centuries to tell us in the stars. The story is simple, but we have made it so difficult." She put her hand to her mouth to hold back a sob growing in her throat. "He truly *is* going to send someone to save us from the darkness. All is not lost. The stars tell us that the day will come when a Mighty One will at last defeat the serpent. He is to be like us, and yet—" she shook her head in amazement—"He will be much more. Oh, Eliah, He will be the man with two natures!"

She spun on her heel to face the Tumulac. "Listen carefully," she said. "The stars tell us He will grow like a branch, but—a god does not grow. Do you understand?"

He shook his broad head.

"It can mean only one thing—He must be born into this world as one of us. Of course!" she cried, her hands gesturing with wild excitement. "That's it! First He must be born as a baby and then grow into manhood.

"Do you see, Eliah? That is why the Destroyer has come. He is trying to prevent the birth of this child whom he knows will grow into manhood and will bring about his defeat. He also knows that this child can be conceived only by those who worship Yah-Adon and whose bloodlines remain pure."

Her eyes grew wide with wonderment as she murmured, understanding illuminating her countenance. "If Noah is one of Yah-Adon's chosen, he can never take Utriel to be his wife. She carries Asmodeus's seed. She must never bear Noah's child." Her hands fell to her sides. "Oh, my Lord and God," she moaned. "I understand—if she and Noah were to unite, his line would be forever corrupted."

Even as she spoke, a breeze stirred her hair, lifting the edge of the scarf covering her head. Unnoticed, it slipped to the ground. Quickly, the current increased, whirling madly, round and round, reeling and gyrating, leaves and grass spiraling in a wild vortex.

Ganah and Eliah dropped to their knees.

"Protect My chosen ones," spoke a voice from the whirling mass. "The future of My people lies in their seed."

The night sounds filled the air as the prophetess waited in awed silence.

At last she rose, wrapping her garment around her. "Come, my friend," she whispered. "We have much to do and night is upon us."

Utriel was far from sleep. The dim grayness of the room enveloped her in its shadows. Vaguely aware of her surroundings, she knew that the Ulah-rah had left the house earlier in the evening.

Her mind was healing. She was a survivor, and her will to live would not allow her to stay in the region to which she had nearly escaped. No matter how painful the reality, she could not remain in that dark realm of forgetfulness.

Slowly she surfaced, but one face on the screen of her memory seared her heart—Noah. Although her tears had finally ceased, her remorse was endless.

Even as she placed her hands on her hard, flat stomach, she knew that growing within was a life that had changed her own forever. Bel—Asmodeus—had not lied. This new life had come into being through betrayal and lust. Utriel refused to make excuses for her actions as the imaginary conversations about her defense fled. She, and she alone, had destroyed any hope for a life with Noah, and she despised herself for it.

She clenched her hands into fists, pressing them against her lips until the warm, salty taste of blood filled her mouth. When her people discovered that she was with child, they would stone her. If Noah tried to intervene, they would stone him as well. She was now a pariah to her family.

Utriel did not fear death. On the contrary, it would be a welcome relief. The thought, though, of Noah never understanding why she had turned from him or why she had violated his love and his trust was more than she could bear. How could she face him or, even worst, the possibility that his honor might drive him to seek revenge.

She threw back her cover and sat on the edge of the pallet. Fear and shame engulfed her in an overpowering wave of suffocating guilt. She rose weakly and leaned against the wall to steady herself. She must hurry. Ganah could return at any moment. The girl looked around the room. "I need something of yours to sustain me," she whispered. On the floor by Ganah's pillows lay a skin that she had been studying. Utriel grabbed it, folded and secured it inside the girdle around her waist. She walked unsteadily to the door and stepped into the night air.

Under the pale luminescence of the moon Utriel stumbled from the house, slipping silently through the empty streets. Once through the town gate, she disappeared into the darkness.

Ganah and the Tumulac wound their way down the Mound, past the wall and into the sleeping town. The prophetess's steps were firm and confident. Although she still did not see her way clearly to carry out Yah-Adon's command, at least she had begun to understand, and she was eager to move forward. Now, she could fight the enemy, for at last she understood his objective.

When she reached her house, she threw aside the curtain covering the entrance to where Utriel lay. "Eliah!" she shouted, looking wildly about the room. "She's gone! We must find her. We can't wait until daylight. She's still weak from the illness."

Ganah dashed from the house, hurrying through the dark streets, through the town gate to Obed's compound. "Wake up!" she shouted, pounding on Bithra's door. "Wake up!"

She could hear a grumbling voice as feet shuffled to the entrance. "Who is it?" yawned the woman as she peered out the door. "It's still night."

"I must speak to Jirad immediately."

Recognition dawned through her sleep-clouded mind. "Ganah?" She rubbed her eyes. "What are you doing here?"

"I must speak to Jirad."

"I don't know where he is. He's been gone for two days and doesn't even know his father is dead. No one can find him."

Ganah shook the woman by the shoulders, "Now listen to me. There's much I don't understand, but great evil has come upon us. As your Ulah-rah, I am commanding you to do just as I tell you."

The woman's sleepy eyes opened in awe, a tinge of fear creeping across her broad face.

"Utriel is in grave danger, but it will be even worse if you fail to do as I tell you.

"Prepare Obed and bury him without Jirad and Utriel. There will be talk, but tell no one that you are worried about them. Do you understand?"

"Yes."

"Do you truly understand?" demanded Ganah.

"Yes," Bithra agreed. "I'm to say nothing."

"May Yah-Adon curse you if you fail me." She turned and strode back to her house, the Tumulac following.

"I don't know how long we'll be gone," Ganah said to the Tumulac, "but take only what you will need. Hurry! We have little time."

A figure moved in the shadow of her doorway. She spun, calling out, "Who is there?"

A man stepped out of the darkness.

"Noah?"

"I couldn't sleep."

"Somehow," she sighed, "I'm not surprised you are here." Her face creased into a scowl.

"Where are you going?" he asked.

"Utriel has fled. She is caught up in something beyond our comprehension, but Eliah and I must find her."

"I'm going with you."

Ganah studied him in the dim light. "Yes, it is right that you should go. I believe you are part of the answer, but we must hurry. Utriel's life hangs in the balance."

"I need only to get my weapons."

"Meet us at the tree near the bottom of the mound, and be quiet. No one must see us leave."

Noah was waiting impatiently with spear in hand, a large blade strapped to his waist and a bundle slung over his back when Ganah and

Eliah arrived at the Mound. He wore a short, belted tunic, covered by a dark cloak.

As Ganah approached, she noticed that he was dressed for fighting. "The sun will be rising soon," she said. "We can discuss our plans later. Great evil has been loosed upon the earth, and it will try to stop us if it can."

Under the light of the fading moon, an old woman, a mute giant, and a grief-stricken man began their journey into the unknown.

Twenty-Three

Utriel pressed close to the town wall, crouching in its shadow until clouds, as if willing accomplices to her flight, obscured the pale moon. Then, dashing across the open expanse to the cover of surrounding trees, she paused to catch her breath and listen. She heard nothing except the occasional bleating of sheep and the cry of a restless infant demanding to be fed.

A pain pierced her side. She bent over, biting her lip to stifle a groan as she pressed both hands into the ache. She could not give in to her body. Not now. She must put as much distance as possible between herself and Gibara-boni. With shallow, spasmodic pants, she limped toward the blackness of the Shinar. All fear of the forest faded into insignificance under the unbearable guilt and shame consuming her mind and body.

Her eyes blinded by tears of remorse and loneliness, she stumbled along the periphery of the forest until finally emerging from the trees at the mouth of the valley. The rising sun bathed the mist-shrouded mountains in a coppery brilliance. She raised her hand to her eyes and squinted in the brightness. A wave of nausea washed over her at the sight of the vastness of the plains stretching endlessly before her.

She looked back at her beloved valley, so beautiful with the tall, stone wall encircling the awakening town, the outlying dwellings that dotted the countryside and the dark, fertile fields spread like a motley covering.

A wave of despair swept over her at the thought of her father, of Jirad, Ganah, and—she could barely breathe—of Noah. She was now a thing to be despised. Her life as she had known it was over. "Utriel no longer lives," she whispered, her voice catching in her throat. "I have disgraced my name. From this day forward I will be known as Unah—One Touched by Evil."

She stretched out her arms and lifted her face to the morning sun. "I have nothing," she cried, "except the clothing I wear. No food, no drink, no weapon." She bowed her head. "Yah-Adon, go before me." She laughed bitterly as tears ran down her cheeks. *Why,* she thought, *would He hear me after what I have done? I am unclean.*

With a cry, she fled the valley. Despair, a cruel master, drove her ruthlessly from all that she held dear.

In the light of the full moon, only hours behind the fleeing girl, Ganah, the Tumulac, and Noah left the Mound. Their fear for Utriel's life made them silent companions, each one lost in their private thoughts. They knew full well that the plains were crisscrossed by the paths not only of unscrupulous traders who would rejoice in the discovery of a beautiful, young woman to be traded or kept as a concubine but also savage bandits who lived in the mountains and roamed the plains preying on unwary travelers. It was a common saying that it was better to slit one's own throat than to be captured by the Ur-gatas, the bandits of the hills.

The friends traveled north, circumnavigating the valley, hoping to find Utriel or to pick up her trail. They did not know that her eyes were fixed stubbornly on the far horizon.

Twenty-Four

The Stargazers did not mourn long for their dead, for the Old Ones had taught that death was not the end, although what followed was unclear. Nevertheless, two deaths within two days had created fear and unrest among the townspeople. Now their Ulahrah had vanished, as well as Utriel, Jirad, Noah, and Bel. "Surely," they whispered to one another, "something evil is loose in our midst."

Obed's wives prepared his body for burial. Bithra rubbed the cold flesh with olive oil and cinnamon to retard decay. She prayed silently for Jirad's return, for the boy was Obed's favorite and the one designated to assume leadership of the family. Ganah had instructed her to proceed with burial, and she dared not disobey.

First, the women tore linen strips a hand's breadth wide and soaked them in a boiling solution of tanbark and water. Next, they wound the hot strips around the corpse, inserting between the folds aromatic spices, such as spikenard, cassia, and cinnamon.

"Stop being so careful," snapped Bethuel as she wrung a long strip of cloth. "He no longer knows what you're doing."

"You are disrespectful," said Bithra.

Bethuel wrinkled her nose. "Who cares?"

"I do. He was good to me."

"Good to you!" Kadrah barked. "I don't call his heavy hand good."

"He rarely raised his hand to *me*." Bithra wrapped the cloth tenderly around the dead man's head. "I loved him as much as I could have any man."

Kadrah sniffed. "When Jirad returns, he'll be the master. Just wait until he brings in his own wives. They'll lord it over the three of us. He'll have several, I can assure you, now that his father is dead."

"Stop your chatter," scolded Bithra. "Utriel will still be here. She'll see that he is fair to us."

"Utriel! What good will she be? She gets nothing from Obed. She is fortunate that Jirad, if he ever returns, has to let her continue to live in his house until Bel takes her as his wife."

"Jirad doesn't have to keep her," said Bethuel. "If she offends him, he can cast her outside the town to take care of herself."

"You're cruel and jealous because Obed placed Jirad above your own sons," retorted Bithra. "Jirad would never do such a thing to his sister." She clenched her mouth, fighting to hold back the tears. "If only they would return. I know they had nothing to do with Gabul's death, but it makes me angry to hear such talk." She pulled the linen strip tighter, the furrows deepening across her brow.

When the body was ready for burial, the three women placed it on a wooden litter built earlier in the day by one of Obed's brothers. Above the litter they bent long willow branches, weaving others between them to form a leafy canopy. When finished, they draped a white cloth over the body. Long fringe touched the ground on both sides. On top of the cloth they heaped mounds of fragrant oleander and cassia.

Bithra summoned Benu, who had been waiting stolidly outside the door with three other men. They each lifted a pole extending from the litter. "He is so light," said Benu. "I could carry it myself."

"Never mind," said Kadrah. "Just take your end."

"We should wait for Jirad," said the big man. "He should be here."

"Go," snapped Bithra. "The others are waiting."

"But . . ."

"Go!"

The four men hefted their burden with Benu, still puzzled, then made their way across the yard of the compound.

Friends and family filed behind the litter, over the floor of the valley toward the foothills where centuries before the tomb had been laboriously carved out of the rocky hillside. Huge boulders that long ago had tumbled down the mountainside now lay among the trees and bushes like gargoyles guarding some long-forgotten demigod's domain.

When the men reached their destination, they lowered the litter to the ground.

A large stone covering the opening had already been rolled to one side. A stale, musty aroma, of long-forgotten memories and interrupted dreams assailed their nostrils. Swathed figures in various stages of disintegration lined the sides of the chamber.

As the women carried the body into the sepulcher, a light, powdery fungi rose from the ancient, yellowed burial cloths. The women coughed sharply as their lungs filled with the scent of antiquity. They lowered Obed's body to the floor and leaned it against the cool, rocky wall.

Bethuel and Kadrah covered their noses with their hands and hurried from the tomb.

Bithra laid her hand against the wrapped face, then sniffed loudly, wiping her eyes. As she stepped back into the sunlight, she squinted. The people's heads were lifted, all eyes staring at a rocky protuberance above the tomb. She stepped back to see better the object of their attention. She lifted her hand to her mouth.

Silhouetted by the evening sun on the stones high above the tomb stood the figure of a man, more godlike than human, surrounded by a corona of brilliant gold and apricot. No one spoke. All stared, transfixed by the awesome tableau before them.

"Men of the Valley," shouted the figure. "I am here to mourn for Obed, my blood brother, for my sorrow joins with yours."

A murmur arose among the people as recognition dawned.

"It is Bel!" shouted a large, curley-haired youth, the fuzz of manhood glistening on his upper lip in the dying light. "He's returned!"

"We've been looking for you!" yelled another. "Where have you been?"

"Tracking Gabul's murderer. I saw him run from the house, but by the time I discovered what he had done there was no time to rouse you from bed for fear of losing him."

"Where is he?"

"I lost him in the darkness of the Shinar, but do not worry, we shall find him again. Now we must mourn your friend and my brother who is no longer with us."

Gradually, as the murmuring ceased, all eyes focused again on the unearthly scene before them.

"If you have come to bury your friend and leader," shouted the mesmerizing voice, "why do you not also honor him?"

The people looked at one another, uncertainty in their eyes.

"What do you mean?" shouted Hamesh.

"Are you afraid to show your respect for him?" asked the titan, contempt in his countenance. "Are you afraid to do something that has never before been done?"

"No! No!" yelled several voices.

"Do the rest of you stand there like women? Are you milk drinkers, still at your mothers' breasts?"

"Does he question our manliness?" a voice hollered.

"Does he think we are spineless children?"

The colossus scanned the crowd with his bold, hypnotic gaze. "Why," he asked, "do you send your leader to the land of shadows by himself? Who will tend to his needs?"

Puzzled expressions appeared on the faces before him.

"Why do you send him like the poorest beggar in Gibara-boni?"

"No one takes anything to the place of the dead," retorted a stocky farmer.

"That's right—that's right," ran through the crowd.

"Well spoken," said the taunter. "Then why not send the dead with the dead."

"We don't understand," shouted one of the more daring.

"Send his wives with him!" Bel's words rent the air like sharp spears hurled with unerring accuracy.

"No!" screamed Benu, his face a mask of unbelief and horror.

A large raven, its black feathers glistening in the fading light, lit on a rock above Bel's shoulder. A shower of pebbles scattered down the side of the cliff.

"Send his wives with him!" repeated Bel.

The Stargazers said nothing, but an air of uneasiness permeated the crowd.

"What greater honor could you give Obed than to send his own to look after him in the land of the dead? Does he not deserve such homage?"

"We don't kill our own," yelled a voice. "It's against Yah-Adon's will."

"Yah-Adon?" the enemy sneered. "Since when have you feared Yah-Adon? He has forgotten that you exist much less cares what you do. Besides," he said, lifting his arms into the air, "who are you to fear Him? Stand up and be strong!"

Bithra looked about wildly, her eyes wide with fear. "Surely you would not do such a thing! You would not kill us!"

"Did anyone say you should be killed?" coaxed Bel. "Certainly not I. We'll just seal you in the tomb with Obed, and our hands will be free of blood."

"Be still!" shouted Benu, leaping upon the rocks. "You are an evil man!" His powerful arms and legs propelled him upward as he dug his feet into the loose rocks.

With the setting of the sun behind the mountains, a faint purple descended over the scene as the lone figure held his reign on the cliff above the transfixed crowd.

"Now," urged the voice. "Do it now before Obed begins his journey alone."

No one moved. All eyes remained on Benu who, roaring with fury, scaled the treacherous incline.

Bithra wrapped her arms around Bethuel and Kadrah. The two weeping women clung to her in their terror.

"I'll kill you!" yelled Benu. Lunging forward, he grasped the ledge on which Bel stood. His muscles strained as he pulled himself onto the hard, rocky surface, his once placid face twisted in a snarl of rage.

Bel drew back his leg, swung it fast and hard, his foot striking Benu under the chin. The force of the blow snapped the man's head backward. His hands lost their hold on the rocks.

"Benu!" shrieked Kadrah as her son's hands clawed the air in the fading light. His fingers touched a jutting edge. He clutched it with one hand, digging in his feet. Blood streamed from his nose and mouth.

With a shrill cry, the raven spread its wings and dove at Benu's face, like an arrow sprung from a bow. Its long beak tore at the man's eyes. Benu struck at it with his free hand as he tried to press himself into the cliff. The bird winged upward, turned, and with a shriek plummeted toward the defenseless man.

When the raven struck, Benu, loosening his hold, grabbed it in both hands. An almost human scream escaped the bird, rending the air as man and bird struck the side of the cliff before plunging to the ground.

"Take the women!" yelled Bel to the stunned crowd. "Do it now!"

Several of the men moved toward them. Others held back, uncertain.

Again Bel thundered, "Be men! Do it now . . . now!"

Suddenly gripped in a frenzy, they swarmed toward the helpless victims. "Now!" they shouted as if governed by one mind. "Now! Now!" Lifting the struggling bodies high above their heads, they carried them to the entrance of the tomb, the women's screams echoing across the valley. "Now," chanted the men. "Now . . . now."

With a great shout they flung the women into the dim interior of the sepulcher and rolled the mammoth stone across the entrance, sealing it with a ponderous thud as the boulder fell into place, muffled cries the only sounds.

A chilling wind howled down from the cliffs, ominous in the fast approaching darkness. Shaking their heads as if emerging from a trance, the Stargazers looked once again to the pinnacle. The Inciter was gone. They were alone, dreadfully and agonizingly alone with their deed.

One after another, the people left, slipping into the darkness, a few casting fearful looks at the stone covering the tomb. Soon all were gone, and an unearthly stillness filled the valley.

Utriel fixed her eyes on a large grove of trees visible in the early light. Once she stumbled and fell in the tall grass. She lay still, her breath coming in heavy gasps. Will and determination brought her to her feet and propelled her forward.

Now, a gnawing pain seized her stomach. Her body screamed for rest, and her throat ached with dryness. She must reach the nearest grove and quickly. Trees on the plains always grew near springs. Water should not be hard to find. Step by step, she made her way, not daring to look up for fear she would despair.

At last, pushing aside the heavy branches and thick bushes, she saw water bubbling out of the ground and flowing into a shallow , clear pool. A gazelle lifted its head, droplets falling from its muzzle. Its dark, liquid eyes studied her, its pale brown coat mottled in the early morning light. Nearby a hyrax quivered, then fled on tiny, padded feet.

Weak from fatigue, Utriel held out her hand to the gazelle. It ambled toward her, placing its soft, velvety nose in her palm. She ran her fingers lightly down the side of its neck. The animal trembled, then turned, and darted into the trees. Exhausted, she sank to the ground. She cupped her hands and scooped the cool water into her mouth. When at last her thirst was quenched, she lay back among the tall grass. Her eyes closed, and she fell into a deep sleep.

The sun was slipping toward the horizon when Utriel woke. Deep shadows filled the grove. She splashed her face and drank deeply again from the pool.

If only she could stop the dreams. Whenever she closed her eyes, the face of Asmodeus was before her. At first, he would be smiling, but then his countenance would alter, as if melting and reshaping. The eyes were always the first features to change, the pupils narrowing and elongating, a feral brutishness emanating from their depths, the face contorting as tissue knotted beneath dark, thickened skin, cheekbones rising, jutting outward, the chin widening and enlarging. Erupting from the bulging forehead, two black, gnarled horns pushed violently through the deformed skull. Thick, gray sensuous lips opened, the tongue lolling obscenely from the gaping mouth.

Never could she turn her eyes from the aberration. Knowing that her only hope was to awaken as quickly as possible, she would struggle toward the light of consciousness as the scabrous creature bent over her. Always at this point she would awaken, gasping and shuddering.

Now, as she knelt by the side of the pool, hot, consuming anger rose within. She leaped to her feet, shaking her fists in the air. "You will not possess me, Asmodeus," she screamed. "You invaded my body, but you will not possess me. Hear me now. I will *not* have your child. I will *not* bring such an abomination into this world. I will find a way to defeat you." Her fists tightened, and she said through clenched teeth, "This I swear by Yah-Adon Himself."

As the last word left her white-lipped mouth, a violent wind ripped through the grove, sending leaves and branches wheeling in the air. Utriel tried to shield her face from the flying debris. A nebulous form shimmered in the fading light, and a voice rasped from the shadows, "Never, Utriel. Never will you destroy my child. I shall protect it and keep it safe." Laughter, harsh, cold, and cruel, resounded through the grove. "You are only a mortal. What can you do against me?"

She shivered and wrapped her arms around herself. "I will find a way," she whispered. "I have nothing else to lose. I have already lost it all. You may be watching me, Asmodeus, but my thoughts are my own. These I will keep to myself until I have formed a plan."

Dropping to the ground, she drew her knees to her chest and wrapped her arms around them. Tears came to her eyes. "Jirad," she whimpered, "if only you were here with me."

Jirad had lost all sense of time, no longer sure whether he was asleep or awake, conscious only of cold, smooth rock beneath his body and a muted, wavering glow reflecting off the walls of the vast cavern. A deep depression settled upon him, draining him of the desire or energy to resist. He wanted only to sleep. In this timeless stupor, he found himself longing for the final release of death.

As he drifted deeper and deeper into an endless slumber, a voice called to him, at first so faint that he was barely aware of its presence. Increasing, it swelled in intensity, pushing aside the heavy shroud clouding his consciousness. "Jirad," it implored, drawing him back from the deepening shadows threatening to envelop him. "Jirad, I need you."

He tried to listen—he wanted to listen—but it was so hard to fight through the haze that sealed him from the world.

"Jirad, help me."

Concentrate. Desperately, he fought his way up, out of the darkness, focusing on the voice as it pleaded and called. A light appeared. A tiny, pinpoint of light, expanding and brightening as the beseeching voice pulled him upward.

I'm coming, his mind screamed. Don't leave. *I'm trying to reach you.*

Light flooded his mind. He could see her. Utriel! She was stretching forth her arms. He must reach her, touch her. Then, as if surfacing from the deep, he burst into consciousness. Utriel and the light had vanished.

Jirad groaned in pain and frustration. He was still a prisoner in the mammoth, high-walled cavern. He rolled onto his back and rammed his fist against the rocky wall, welcoming the searing pain that exploded in his hand and shot up his arm. Utriel was in danger, and he could not help her.

From the corner of his eye, he glimpsed a movement in the shadows. "Who's there?" called Jirad. "Come forth and show yourself."

A man-sized creature emerged from the darkness and edged

forward with an awkward, sidling gait.

Jirad pressed against the wall of the cave, his hand closing over a large rock. He winced at the sight of the distorted visage emerging into the pale light, a face seeming to be sculpted from clay but marred before it had had time to dry. Long, matted hair hung from a large, misshapened head. Beneath a broad, protruding forehead, deep-set but intelligent eyes watched him warily. The nose, flattened with one nostril drawn violently to the side, skewed the mouth and caused the lips to twist in a permanent grimace above a prominent but lopsided chin.

Jirad lowered his arm. "Can you speak?"

Making no sign of aggression, the creature nodded.

"Can you help me?" Even as the words left his mouth Jirad realized their foolishness.

It tilted its head and studied the man. Then, turning, it peered around the cavern.

A glimmer of hope brought a surge of renewed strength to Jirad's benumbed body. "Do you have a name?" he asked.

The deformed lips moved, the voice deep and rusty, as though not used for a long time. "Malek," it answered.

Jirad studied the figure before him. At last he asked, "Can you show me the way out of here?"

The creature shook its head and edged closer to Jirad.

"Will you help me?"

"Master kill Malek."

Jirad pushed himself to his feet and pressed his hands against the sides of his head as he wavered unsteadily.

Malek stepped forward.

Jirad threw a hand against the wall and steadied himself, but the marred piece of humanity made no further movement.

"If you help me," said Jirad, "we may both escape. If we stay here, I will die, and you will continue to be his slave."

"You take Malek?" he asked, never taking his eyes off Jirad.

"Yes."

"Not afraid of Malek?"

"Should I be?"

The aberration shook his head and sighed. "Master follow."

"If we can get out of here, we may have a chance."

Malek ran his tongue over his twisted lips and squinted one eye. Then, making up his mind, he beckoned with a crooked but sinewy arm. "Come," he said as he moved cautiously around the side of the chamber, making sure that they kept in the shadows. "Hurry," he whispered, "while Master not here."

"How do you know he is gone?"

"Not feel Master," he said. He grabbed a torch burning in a crevice of the wall and turned into one of many dark passageways, motioning for Jirad to follow.

"Yah-Adon be with us," breathed Jirad as he followed the figure ambling before him.

The tunnel was silent except for occasional movements of large, grayish white beetles in the darkness, their hard shells flashing in the glow of the torch as they skittered from its light.

Jirad followed the awkward figure, not daring to let the man get out of sight, for he knew he could never find his way alone to the surface. He struggled to keep pace, but the effects of the drugged sleep had weakened him, and he had no idea how long it had been since he had eaten.

The creature never hesitated at a passageway but turned right or left without losing stride.

Finally, Jirad called, "Malek, I must rest. I can't go any farther."

"Sh-h-h-h. Master hear us. Walls have ears."

Jirad leaned against the cold stone to catch his breath. "My strength is gone," he whispered. "I need to eat."

"Food?" asked Malek. "Wait." He scurried down the tunnel, the soft padding of his feet soon lost in the distance.

As Jirad leaned against the wall in the darkness, the quiet pressed in upon him. His thoughts returned to Utriel, to the urgency of her call as her soul reached out to his. He must hurry to her before it was too late.

Soon he heard approaching footsteps. Grabbing a rock lying at his foot, he lifted it, poised.

Malek rounded the corner, his face grotesque in the flickering light of the torch.

Jirad lowered his arm, letting the rock drop to the cave's floor.

The man stepped forward, holding out his hand. "Here. Food."

Bile rose to Jirad's mouth as he saw the limp body of a dead rodent. "Man does not eat animals," he said, pressing the offering back into Malek's hand.

Malek's face twisted in puzzlement.

"It's all right," said Jirad. "I can wait. I feel better. Hurry and lead the way."

"Come," said Malek. "Far to go."

Twenty-Five

It was nearing dawn when the three companions reached the open plain. The suffused glow of morning had not yet appeared above the horizon, but the stars had faded and patches of mist still clung to the ground.

Noah lagged behind Ganah, watching for any sign of weakness in the old woman. He was concerned about her undertaking such a trip, but she held the staff firmly in her hand, her back straight, and she had not faltered.

He quickened his pace until he was beside her. "Fear eats at me," he said, "fear that I'll never see Utriel again."

Ganah kept her eyes on the ground.

"She could be lying somewhere in the tall grass," he continued. "She could be ill with no one to help her."

The old woman halted, placing both hands on her staff. "My son, I love her too. The same fears are plaguing me." She laid her hand on his arm. "This I swear to you—we will not go back until we find her. Now, come," she said, striding ahead, a fierce determination in her eyes. "We're wasting time."

In the rear lumbered the Tumulac, a massive club slung over his shoulder and a heavy, bronze-tipped spear clutched in his hand.

Ganah and Noah spoke little, each wrapped in their own thoughts. Although their love for Utriel had pulled in different directions, they were united in their fear for the frightened young woman alone in a hostile world.

Now, seeing the vast plains spread before them in the shadow of morning, their hearts sank. How would they ever find her? Gray clumps of trees dotted the landscape, each a possible haven for the girl.

In the distance loomed a silvery-blue range of tree-covered mountains, its peaks clothed in a gray mist.

Ganah whispered to herself as her eyes surveyed the wide plains, "Yah-Adon, without Your guidance we are helpless." They had brought neither food nor water with them for the land was rich in sustenance. Although aware of the occasional savage animal that might cross their path or the bands of marauding bandits that hid in the hills, their desire to find the girl overshadowed any real or imagined dangers. More frightening to them than the wilds was the unspoken fear that Asmodeus was not yet through with Utriel.

Toward the middle of the day, they rested in a grove of trees surrounding one of the many springs scattered over the area. Sporadic dust clouds churned up by the great herds of roaming animals rose in the distance.

Ganah bathed her face and drank deeply while Noah and the Tumulac cut large, yellow-gold fruit from a nearby tree. Later, as she savored the succulence, she leaned her head against the trunk of a tree. When she became aware of Noah watching her, she said, tossing the rind into the brush, "Stop worrying about me. Yah-Adon has renewed my strength. I am fine. I need no further rest." She stood up and walked to the spring. She knelt beside the pool and washed the sweet juice from her hands, wiping them on the hem of her tunic. "Come, we have rested long enough." Without another word she marched ahead, leaving the two men staring at each other.

Utriel opened her eyes. She could not remember where she was. She had not slept well, for recurring dreams had tormented her during much of the night until she had finally slipped into a much needed deep, dreamless sleep. She yawned and rolled over. Her back ached from the damp ground. She wriggled in the brush to find a more comfortable position. She turned her head, blinking. No more than an arm's length from her face were two dirty, sandaled feet.

Instantly, she twisted, springing into a crouch. A fist knotted in her long hair and yanked her head back. Only a short scream escaped her throat before a blow struck her on the side of her head, slamming her into the ground. Again, fingers twisted in her hair, dragging her from the brush.

She clawed at the hands, relishing the feel of torn skin under her nails. A loud expletive filled the air, and she was again knocked to the ground. Although her head ached from the blows, she could make out the figures of two men standing with feet wide apart, hands on hips, while a third squatted beside her head.

Ur-gatas. Bandits from the hill country. She knew well what they intended to do, for she had heard stories told by the men around the fires at night. A knot tightened in her stomach.

A filthy hand slid down the side of her face. "We've caught a pretty one," snickered the man behind her, showing large discolored teeth in a flat, broad face. Utriel smelled his rancid body odor and the fat rubbed into his skin. "She'll bring a good profit when we sell her to the traders." He leered. "But first, let's see what she's worth."

"Don't touch me," she rasped, her voice tight with fear and her eyes searching for any means of escape.

"Ah, we have a hot-tempered one. Looks like we'll have to tame her." The other men laughed and grunted in agreement.

The broad-faced one grabbed Utriel's ankle and yanked her roughly toward him. He slid his hand up the length of her leg. Without warning, his body arched backward, and his eyes opened wide in surprise. A cry gurgled in his throat as he was hurled across the grove, his body striking a large tree with a sickening thud before falling to the ground in a twisted heap.

The others stared dumbly at the crumpled body. Finally, the older one looked fearfully at Utriel and muttered as he backed away, "Who are you? A sorceress, a worker of magic?"

As frightened as the bandits, she could only stare open-mouthed at the body sprawled obscenely at the foot of the tree.

"Don't hurt us," shouted the other man, his arms stretched out before him, frantically making a sign to ward off evil.

The two men turned to each other, talking too low for Utriel to understand. Blood and the smell of her own fear filled her nostrils.

The older man turned back to her. "Come with us," he said. "We will not hurt you. A magic eye of great power is upon you."

She tried to assess the situation. If she stayed, she might be attacked by someone or something worse then these three. For the moment they feared her, perhaps thinking to make use of what they thought were her powers. She wiped the blood from her nose as she studied the man. Maybe, after all, Yah-Adon was still with her.

She struggled to her feet, wincing at the pain shooting through her head and back. The men made no move to touch her, but moved warily as she stood up, their arms poised at the sides of their bare chests.

"All right," she said, rubbing her neck to ease the ache.

They motioned her to follow to where three, scruffy gray asses were grazing at the edge of the grove. She was unused to riding, but if she intended to survive, it would be best to follow the Ur-gatas' bidding.

"Get on!" ordered the younger man but making no move to come near her.

She swung herself awkwardly onto the animal's back, cringing at the pain in her body. She grasped the rough, woven bridle in her hands and hoped with great fervor that the beast would obey and follow the others.

The men mounted and, with their legs dragging the ground, turned their animals' heads toward the hills. With the broken body of their companion slung in front of the smaller man, they gave the asses stout kicks in the ribs.

The Ur-gatas, silent and sullen, allowed the asses to make their way through the tall grass toward the hills.

"Why did we stop for the woman anyway?" grumbled the younger man. "They are nothing but trouble."

"Shut up, and keep your eye on her. We'll have enough trouble as it is when Hazial hears what happened."

Utriel bit the inside of her lower lip and pressed her arms into her sides to keep them from trembling. Right now the men believed her to possess great powers they were unwilling to challenge, but what would they do when they discovered she possessed none?

Abruptly, the ground sloped upward. Soon, the agile beasts began a more rugged climb, winding their way with care around trees and boulders, their feet, sure and nimble, clicking monotonously over the rocks. The trail seemed to have disappeared. Utriel was grateful that her animal needed no guidance as it carried her into the hills.

When they reached a split in the rocks, the sturdy little beasts wound their way through the defile. The walls rose close about them, leaving a narrow band of blue sky overhead. Wind gusted through the passageway, moaning in its wake.

Utriel found herself dozing intermittently from the rythmic jostling of the animal. The loud caw of a raven jerked her awake. They were now on a narrow path that angled upward. She could hear gruff rumblings as the two bandits talked, their voices too low to make out their words.

"How much farther?" she hollered.

The older man shrugged indifferently.

Shortly afterward, a young, dirty-faced boy swung down from the branches of a tall fir, yelled to the men, and waved them through.

Utriel's back and neck ached and perspiration from the hot, heaving body of her mount ran down her legs as the animal plodded higher into the mountains.

As they progressed, she became aware of new sounds. She looked back at the men who now rode silently on their beasts, their faces immobile as stone. She tried to shift her weight on her animal. The cloth folded over the ass's back did little to cushion the impact of its bony spine.

Finally, they emerged onto a broad plateau that overlooked the plains far below. In spite of the precariousness of her situation, she could not refrain from marveling at the beauty of the breathtaking view that spread before her.

In stark contrast, worn and dirty tents sat squeezed among the trees, and naked children played quietly in the dirt while several women cooked over smoldering fires. Four or five ill-kempt men, squatting on low stools in the doorways, watched with dark, sullen eyes the approach of their comrades in the company of the strange young woman with disheveled hair, dried blood, and bruises on her face and body.

A stocky, middle-aged man, his chest bare and a faded red cloth wrapped around his loins, stood up. He sauntered toward them. His brown hair was long and streaked with gray and bound loosely away from his square face by a strip of greasy leather. He placed his hand on the lead animal and challenged, "Why have you brought this woman?"

"We must speak with you, Hazial—in the tent," said the older rider, as he dismounted, motioning for his comrade to follow.

The man in the red cloth called to two of the women. "Watch her," he ordered, signaling with his hand.

Utriel swung her leg over the back of the ass and slid wearily to the ground. Riding such an animal was only a little better than walking.

An old woman grasped the rope bridle and led the animal away. Her white hair hung in dirty strands, and she studied Utriel with dull, brown eyes.

At a slight touch on her arm, Utriel swung around. She gasped and drew back.

A young girl stood beside her. Thick, dark hair hung in matted locks around her face as if to conceal the dirty, twisted visage beneath. The girl lowered her eyes but not before Utriel drew in a breath at the size and protrusion of them. "Follow me," she said, her voice a whisper as she beckoned with a foreshortened arm. She hurried around the dwellings, glancing back to be sure Utriel was following. When they reached the far side of the village, she held back the door flap of a tent. "Stay here. I'll bring you food." Then, without another word, she slipped from the tent.

Utriel sank onto a worn mat. A clay bowl containing dried-up pieces of fruit lay on its side, and stale, pungent air hung heavily in the tent. She was tired and she ached. The anger fueling her weary body was not enough to continue sustaining her. Once again, she desired only to sleep—to slip into that blessed realm of nothingness. Even that, though, was no longer possible, for now, even her dreams were places of torment. That thing of evil had not only invaded her lake and her body but also her dreams.

She contemplated trying to escape the village before the men returned. But where would she go? Flee farther into the hills to be attacked by wild animals or taken by other bandits. No, it was better to stay where she was, at least for the present.

Approaching footsteps signaled the girl's return. When she slipped through the opening, she carried in one hand a basket with flat, dark bread and a large piece of cheese. In the other was a gourd filled with goat's milk. She approached Utriel hesitantly, still avoiding her gaze but holding the food before her as though presenting an offering.

"Thank you," said Utriel, suddenly so weary that even food did not tempt her.

"Eat," said the girl. "You will feel better."

Too tired to resist, she bit into the bread. It was heavy and chewy, but the nutty flavor was delightful. She took another bite and gulped the milk. The liquid flowing down her throat felt warm and soothing. She drained the gourd, then licked her lips. The strange girl was not watching her, but staring at the floor of the tent.

"What is your name?" Utriel asked.

Without raising her head, the girl replied, "I am Tubila. It means 'Ugly One.'" She peered at Utriel through the matted hair nearly covering her face. "My father gave me to Hazial, the leader of this tribe, as soon as I could walk. He said he might as well throw me to the animals for no man would ever want me."

Too tired to respond, Utriel tried to chew a mouthful of cheese.

"I was too ugly to look upon," the girl continued, "but he thought maybe bandits wouldn't care. Besides, he traded me for the life of my mother."

A shadow fell across the doorway of the tent, and the man in the red cloth entered. "Stupid girl!" he yelled. "You were to feed the witch, not make a friend of her."

With a swift backhand he struck the girl across the face, knocking her to the ground. "Get out of here and finish your duties."

Tubila scrambled to her feet and scurried from the tent, a red welt rising on her cheek.

"So," Hazial said, running his eyes over Utriel, "you are the sorceress who can kill men with a glance."

She felt herself trembling, but she knew it would not do to let him see she was afraid. Steeling her body, she answered, willing her voice not to shake, "I am Utriel, daughter of Obed."

"Ah, I have heard of him." Hazial swayed, his hands on his hips. "He is a hard man. But you—you have killed one of my men."

"He meant to harm me," she said, pleased that her voice did not betray her fear, for this man would not hesitate to kill her and throw her body on the dung heap.

"You are a wild one, aren't you?" chuckled Hazial. "Maybe I'll keep you for myself." As he spoke, he reached for her. A blinding flash of blue-white light arced from her arm to his.

"Aurgh-h-h," he yelled, falling backward and clutching his hand. The smell of seared flesh hung in the air. "What have you done to me?"

Utriel stared in bewilderment at the screaming man.

"You *are* a sorceress," he shouted, backing out of the tent.

Numbly, Utriel sank to the floor. She had seen what had happened, but she had done nothing to cause it. Was she going mad? In spite of the warm tent she shivered, her teeth chattering against each other. It had to be Asmodeus, for she had no powers of her own. Why, though, would he be protecting her?

Outside the tent Hazial cursed and shouted. She could hear scurrying feet as he barked orders to the people.

"Of course!" she whispered as understanding flared in her mind. "He's not protecting me. He's protecting his unborn child." She squeezed her eyelids together, determined not to cry, but a hot tear escaped and trickled down her cheek. Utriel sat in the tent, alone and afraid, her arms wrapped around her knees. She rocked back and forth on her haunches, repeating over and over, "Yah-Adon. Yah-Adon."

Noah, Ganah, and the Tumulac found shelter for the night in a grove of tall, wide-branched elms. Eliah made a fire not only to warm them but also to ward off animals that might stray into their camp. As the sun descended behind the mountains, the group had eaten a meal of fruit and berries. Now they sat around the fire, no one speaking. It had been a long day, one that had produced no results.

Ganah stared into the flames, her mind centered on the dancing light. Gradually, the grove faded from her sight, receding into the shadows. A gray haze rose from the fire and swirled before her, a gentle, warming mist that bathed and caressed her tired body. A voice broke into her consciousness, *Ganah, you must enter the Shinar. From the darkness will come light.*

"No," she murmured, shaking her head. "Utriel would never enter its depths. I will not lead the others there. It is too dangerous."

Remember, whispered the voice, *all is not as it seems. I will be with you even in the midst of darkness.*

"You ask too much," complained the old woman as the mist dissolved into the night air. She rubbed her eyes. Once again the grove surrounded her, but the fire had burned down to glowing coals.

She glanced at her companions. They were both watching her.

Ganah broke the silence, "We must enter the Shinar and look for her there."

"No," countered Noah, pulling his cloak around his shoulders. "What if Utriel's already left the valley and has begun crossing the plains?"

"That is possible, but first we must go into the forest."

He opened his eyes and rolled onto his elbow. "Utriel would never go into its darkness. Why should we do such a foolish thing?"

"You do not have to go with us," she said, "but I must go into its depths."

Eliah sat on his haunches, stirring the coals with a long stick as he laid on long branches.

Noah sighed and sat up. "All right. I can't let you and Eliah go alone. I just pray that you know what you're doing."

"In the morning we will enter the forest," Ganah said. "Now we must rest, for we will need to be strong."

Ganah and the Tumulac soon slept, but Noah sat alone under a tree, staring into the shadows. When he at last lay down again, he closed his eyes, but sleep would not come.

Twenty-Six

"Good morning, friends." Ganah put the last bit of red, juicy fruit into her mouth. "Get something to eat. The sun is up and urges us to move."

Noah yawned, stretched, then shuffled, bleary-eyed, to the spring. He drank deeply from the cool, bubbling water. He dunked his head, lifted it, and spewed water into the air. He shook his wet hair as he pulled several ripe fruit from a low-growing branch. "Eliah," he yelled, tossing one to his companion.

The Tumulac caught it in his huge, pawlike hand and a broad smile spread over his gentle face.

As Noah ate the sweet fruit, the gnawing uneasiness that had been in his stomach increased with each bite. He watched the old woman fold her cloak and secure it in the pouch tied around her waist. He took another bite and wiped his mouth on his shoulder. He had two choices: He could strike out on his own across the plains to find Utriel or he could follow Ganah into the dark interior of the Shinar.

While lying awake under the velvet canopy of night, he had realized that the issue was much deeper. Was he willing to trust her, or more specifically, did he actually believe that Yah-Adon had spoken to her, telling her to lead the party into the unknown dangers of the forest? To follow her meant yielding control of his future to what might be only the whims of an old woman, albeit the Ulah-rah of his people, but an Ulah-rah who had not exhibited signs of power for many years. Yet, as the moon had rolled across the night sky, he knew the question was settled in his mind. He would choose to believe—believe that Ganah had truly heard the voice of their God and that He would lead them to Utriel.

After wiping his hands on the damp grass, he fastened his blade securely around his waist. "Ready?" he asked.

"Yes," said the old woman.

Noah started toward the Shinar, the others close behind. He paused at its edge, looked back at his comrades, then plunged into the cool shadows.

The trio drew their cloaks tighter about themselves to ward off the dampness of the forest. Scampering feet scraped and whisked through the leafy mulch that blanketed the forest floor. Trills and staccatos filled the early morning air.

To avoid walking in circles as they advanced deeper into the woods, Noah attempted to keep three trees continually lined up before him. As he surveyed the shadowy vastness, his heart sank. It was foolishness to think three people could possibly cover it, much less locate one girl who might be lost within its darkness.

Ganah halted, swinging around sharply. "Noah," she said, "nothing is impossible. Yah-Adon is with us, and we must listen for His voice. He will go before us, and He will guide us. He has led us into the Shinar for a reason."

Had she read his thoughts?

"Come," she gestured, muttering under her breath as she pushed through the undergrowth. "We have no time to waste."

Eliah stomped through the brush, cutting through everything with his blade that hindered their progress.

Anger rose in Noah with each step, anger not directed at Ganah, but at himself. Why did he feel so helpless? He was not a weak, timid man. Although he had never provoked a fight, neither had he backed down from one. Yet he was acting like an old woman. At that thought, he smiled as he watched Ganah plodding ahead of him. Well, he mused, like some old women.

The sun was at its zenith, but the farther they went into the forest, the less light filtered onto its floor. Broad, leafy branches intertwined over their heads, blocking out the rays. Here, the trees were older and taller, their limbs lifting and straining to reach the precious light. The shrill songs of birds could no longer be heard, and the sounds of animals had ceased. An oppressive air settled like a pall over the searchers.

As the three friends pushed deeper into the Shinar, one day blended into the next. Their pace became slow and labored, walking more difficult. Vines as thick as a man's wrist hung in great masses blocking their way, clutching at their arms and slithering around their legs. The smaller trees were stunted and gnarled, malformed by their constant fight for survival.

Noah and the Tumulac chopped savagely at the vegetation. Even in the coolness of the forest, they were sweating, cloaks bundled and tied to their waists. Ganah's hair, pulled loose from its bindings, hung in damp disarray around her thin, lined face.

By midafternoon on the third day they halted beneath a rocky ledge to fill their waterskins beside a pool. Water trickled down the sides of mossy stones into a deep basin. A thick carpet of dark, decomposing leaves blanketed the rocky ground. Over the top lay a lighter yellow covering of those more recently fallen. Eliah bent his huge bulk, stooping to move aside the leaves and to scoop up water in his hands.

"Stop!" shouted Ganah. "Don't drink that!" She swept aside the rotting leaves with the tip of her staff. She stirred the water, pushing at a large pile of rocks accumulated on one side until it toppled, scattering over the bottom of the pool. As the water cleared, they saw the rotting remains of what had been a fox or wild dog.

"This is a pool of death," Ganah whispered.

"How did you know?" asked Noah.

"Did I not tell you that Yah-Adon is leading us? Do you still not believe me?" Her gaze shifted beyond him as she murmured, "If I listen closely, I can hear Him, like a voice whispering in the morning breeze. It is only when I stop listening that I cannot hear. He is always willing to speak, but I am not always ready to hear."

She touched Eliah's arm. "We must leave this place of death. We'll rest later." She leaned more heavily, though, on the El-cumah as she walked away.

Tired and thirsty, they spoke little as they pushed through the heavy undergrowth until, finally, Ganah halted. "Here," she said, her breath coming in gasps, "this is where we must make camp for the night."

Noah cleared a small area while Eliah gathered firewood. The mute piled the branches, then lit them from a flint bag concealed in the girdle wrapped around his enormous waist.

Soon the heat from the fire abolished the damp chill penetrating the weary travelers. Fruit and berries cached earlier in their cloaks slaked their thirst temporarily, but the menacing silence of the night only increased the oppression. They pulled their cloaks around their shoulders and sat close to each other as if their unity would provide a shield from the encroaching menace.

Ganah sat very still and listened, concentrating on the fire as it twisted and writhed in monstrous shapes. For some time she had felt that they were being watched, yet she said nothing for she did not want to add to their fears. But she could feel a malignancy emanating from somewhere deep within the heart of the Shinar, and it was steadily gaining strength and power. Already it had devoured Gabul and Obed. It had ensnared Utriel, and it was seeking to engulf them all. It seemed to be sucking the light and life from the forest, feeding on its vitality.

Ganah knew Utriel was not in the forest, but she could not tell Noah, for he would not understand that there were other parts to Yah-Adon's plan that must be played out before the girl could be found. Ganah did not fully understand, but she was struggling to be obedient.

"Why are we always in a hurry?" the old prophetess muttered, breaking the silence. "Why is it so difficult to wait for the workings of Yah-Adon?" She stirred the fire with a long stick. "Because of our haste we ruin much of what the Placer of Stars desires us to do."

Puzzled, Noah tossed a branch into the fire, scattering sparks into the air. "We can never search the entire forest," he said.

Eliah frowned, but Ganah stared into the fire, willing herself to remain calm although every fiber in her body screamed to be free of the Shinar. "This place carries the stench of death," she said, "but this is where we are supposed to be."

Angry with herself because she was afraid, she knew that the fear must be dealt with or it would immobilize each of them. In spite of the chill, a light film of perspiration glistened on Noah's face, and the Tumulac's chest labored with each strenuous breath. Each man in his own way was fighting against the almost palpable fear pulsating around them.

She closed her eyes. What is happening to us? Are we doomed to perish in the Shinar, never to find Utriel? Have I misinterpreted my directions? Waves of doubt cascaded about her. *No*! she screamed silently as the flames dwindled in the darkness. *I know I am right.*

Twenty-Seven

For days Utriel wandered aimlessly through the squalid mountain camp. Her attempts to make friends with the sullen, dull-eyed women or to help with their chores resulted only in clouding their countenances with fear. They made frantic signs to ward off evil, for one man had already died and their leader had tasted the power that surrounded the "witch woman." Her first night in the village someone had smeared blood over the entrance of her tent. Later, fetishes and amulets secretly appeared around her dwelling.

She might be able to walk out of the camp anytime she chose, for who would dare to stop her? But for a while at least she had food and shelter with the Ur-gatas, and she was unsure what lay beyond the camp.

Remembrances of Gibara-boni and Noah flooded her mind. At the thought of him, a tightening seized her chest, and her heart felt as if it were breaking. She longed to see him, to speak to him, to touch him. Then the guilt and shame of what she had done rolled over her again, paralyzing her with remorse. "At least I've hurt no one but myself," she whispered. "Soon my people will forget me, and Noah will find another woman who will make him happy. One day I will be only a memory to him."

She had no plan, just a blind, driving resolve to destroy the child growing within and to seek vengeance upon the fiend who had seduced her. Perhaps he was vulnerable. If not—at least she would die with honor. When the time was right, she would know what to do. Until then, she would take each day as it came.

Tubila hurried toward her with a bowl of steaming stew clutched in her short, stubby fingers. Her mouth twisted in a grotesque caricature of a smile, one side pulling downward. "I've brought you some of Ninunah's stew. I gathered the tubers myself just this morning. It's fresh and tasty."

"Thank you, little friend." Utriel took the hot bowl in her hands. "Sit with me while I eat."

Tubila settled eagerly at the young woman's feet. No longer did she keep her eyes on the floor but now gazed adoringly into the face above her, devouring her every word and expression.

Utriel did not know when it had happened, but the deformed girl had touched her heart. No longer did she see an imperfect creature, for a bond had developed between the young women. Each day Tubila hurried from her servitude among the Ur-gatas to the tent near the edge of the camp. No one tried to stop her because of the aura of fear surrounding the mysterious "sorceress" who had recently entered their camp. No one desired to test her powers again.

As Utriel chewed the spicy vegetables, she stroked Tubila's matted hair and lifted several of the thick strands. She set down her bowl and picked up the girl's hands, turning them over in her own. The nails were ragged with dirt deeply embedded beneath them, the skin red and scarred. "Would you do something for me?" she asked.

"Yes," she replied.

"Go into my tent and wash your face and hands. When you're finished, come back and let me see."

Tubila rose and hurried into the tent. When she returned, her face was clean and glistening, her hands still dripping with water.

"Now, sit down," said Utriel.

The girl squatted at her feet.

Utriel ran her hands over the thick, dark hair. First she rubbed oil into the knotted strands and gently began working through the tangles with a piece of wood from which she had fashioned a makeshift comb for herself. When Tubila winced, Utriel said, "I'm sorry, but it will take us a while to make your hair smooth."

At last, afraid to work any longer for fear of causing Tubila real pain, Utriel untied the thong holding back her own hair, wrapped it around Tubila's and tied it securely.

The girl threw herself into Utriel's arms. "You're so good," she cried with tears filling her eyes. "No one has ever cared for me before. Let me stay with you," she begged. "I'll be your slave forever."

Utriel's eyes clouded with pain. "I am not good," she said, her voice faltering. "Besides, I don't want you to be my slave. I want you to be my friend."

"Friend?" repeated Tubila. "What is a friend?"

Utriel shook her head.

Tubila frowned, and her lip trembled. "Did I say something foolish?"

"No," said Utriel, taking the girl's damp hands in hers. "There is nothing foolish about you."

"What, then, is a friend?" asked the girl, puzzlement in her voice.

"A friend is someone you care about and who cares about you. Someone to share your joys with as well as your hurts. Someone—" her voice caught in her throat"—who won't turn away when you're in need."

"Do you have lots of friends?"

Utriel shrugged. "I'm not sure I even thought about it before."

Tubila clasped her hands together, almost shaking with excitement. "I can do all those things. I will be your friend."

"Thank you," said Utriel, smiling. "I am grateful."

The girl sat back on her haunches, her hands pressed against her chest. "Let me stay with you."

Utriel wrinkled her brow, thinking about the consequences. "Do you think Hazial would allow it?"

"I'd rather die than not be with you," said Tubila, her voice husky with emotion.

"I'm afraid he will take his anger out on you if I ask."

"The Ur-gatas will be glad not to come near you, and if I do everything for you, they won't have to." She grabbed Utriel's hands.

"Please ask him! Please!"

"All right," agreed the young woman, "but you'd better get back before he misses you."

Tubila's eyes once again filled with tears.

Utriel put her arms around the girl's shoulders and pulled her close. "I promise to speak to him right away," she whispered.

Hazial shouted and cursed at Utriel's audacity. He threatened her, even raised his fist, but in the end he relented. "Take her," the Ur-gata chief said at last. "It will be good not to have to look at her ugly face."

Utriel hurried from his presence before he had time to change his mind.

The companionship aided both young women, soothing and mending wounded spirits as well as bodies. With each day, a bond of love knitted together more strongly the lovable and the unlovable. Together they roamed the hills, the tall, slender beauty and the short, distorted hobgoblin whose adoring smile softened her twisted features.

Often, after climbing over the rough terrain until tired and breathless, they pulled themselves onto a large rock to rest and talk while gazing over the wide plains below. Here, Utriel told Tubila about Gibara-boni, about Noah, about her brother Jirad, and about Ganah, her Ulah-rah and friend.

"Noah is gentle and kind," she told the girl as they lay on the warm rock, enjoying an afternoon breeze that gently rustled the leaves of heavy boughs above their heads. "You should see his dark, curly hair. Sometimes it hangs loosely about his face, but when he's working in the fields, he ties it back." She giggled. "When he perspires, it makes tight, little curls, like the tails of tiny piglets. And his smile . . ."

"He sounds so handsome."

"I loved him very much. I—" A hard lump formed in Utriel's throat. "Tell me," she said swallowing quickly, "tell me about your people."

Tubila recounted what little she remembered before coming to live with the hill people and what she had been told by others in the tribe.

Utriel could not, however, bring herself to reveal the terrifying night that had destroyed her life. She longed to share the experience with the girl, but whenever she tried, she was overcome with such guilt that blood rose to her face and a vise tightened in her stomach. Someday she would tell her. Before long she would be forced to. Already her body was changing, and she could feel a thickening in her waist. The infant was growing much too rapidly. For now, though, she would keep the horror to herself.

Although the Ur-gatas continued to avoid Utriel, tolerating her in their midst as they would a dangerous animal, she knew that such an arrangement could not last. Until she had a better plan, she had little choice but to remain.

Twenty-Eight

The Tumulac awakened to the strange silence of the Shinar. It had been weeks since they had entered its depths. A chilling dampness from the moldering leaves now penetrated his thick cloak. A sharp odor hung palpably in the air, filling his nose and lungs.

Gnarled, ropy vines coiled and looped from the skeletal branches of ancient trees nearly engulfed by lacy sleeves of pale, feathery grayness. Multicolored fungi blanketed the ground around the dead and fallen trees, filling the air with pungent, musty aromas. Others multiplied in decaying leaves and branches on the forest floor, some attached to the sides of trunks like tiny, clay steps. The trees and bushes were devoid of fruit, seeming to serve only as hosts for the plethora of fungi in their multitudinous shades and colors. Normally, the three companions would have enjoyed their nutty flavors, but to eat of them now would be to partake of the rotting putrescence pushing relentlessly outward from the heart of the Shinar.

Eliah threw off his cloak, rose from the ground and ran his hands through his long, straight hair, pulling it back and tying it more securely. His mouth was dry, and he grimaced at the discomfort in his throat. Trying not to startle her, he roused his sleeping mistress. Next, he nudged Noah who jerked awake, his hand on his blade. Upon recognizing the huge man bending over him, he licked his cracked lips and sat up. The Tumulac helped Ganah to her feet as if she were a child.

"Thank you, Eliah," she said as she shook the moist leaves from her cloak.

Noah stretched and rubbed his hands vigorously through his hair. "I have seen nothing, but I can't rid myself of the feeling we're being watched."

"We have been since the first day we entered the Shinar."

"Watched?"

She nodded.

"Why didn't you tell us?"

"What good would it have done?" she asked with a shrug. "How can you fight what you can't see?"

"What do we do now?"

"We stay until we discover what our mission is in this abominable place."

"Our mission!" Noah shouted in confusion. "We're here to find Utriel. Why else would we be in this godforsaken place?"

"We don't always do what we think is reasonable," Ganah answered. "Before we find Utriel, we have another task to accomplish."

"What are you saying?" Anger flared in Noah's eyes.

The Tumulac placed his hand on the man's arm, but Noah pushed it aside and spun on him.

The Tumulac was staring into the shadows. He signaled for silence.

"What is—"

"Be quiet," urged Ganah, lifting her hand in warning.

Scarcely breathing, they listened. A tiny, muffled noise, like a twig buried in fallen leaves snapped on the forest floor. Noah's stomach tightened, and his hand gripped the shaft of his spear. Something was moving among the trees. He blinked and looked again. This time he saw nothing. The Tumulac raised his weapon, his body coiled for action.

The hair on the back of Noah's neck prickled. "Steady!" he murmured as he hefted his spear. Ganah gripped her staff with both hands, her lips moving soundlessly as her eyes searched the shadows.

Shifting leaves laid a tessellated pattern over the ground, altering and changing with each movement of a branch. Deep, muffled growls rumbled from shapes now moving stealthily among the trees, shapes darker than the shadows that concealed them, hunters stalking their prey.

Suddenly, primordial animal fury exploded as dark forms catapulted toward them with snarls of rage rending the air.

Noah had time only to be conscious of wicked, yellow-bared teeth before a mass of muscles and gray-black fur crushed down upon him. Instinctively, he raised his spear. The force of the assault impaled the attacker, carrying them both to the ground. Stunned and gasping for breath, he shoved the massive carcass of a wolf from him and scrambled to his feet, his mind trying to comprehend the mayhem around him.

His companions were fighting for their lives. The Tumulac flung aside one beast with his spear, then whirled to fend off yet another. A snarling adversary circled Ganah, warily, its feral, amber eyes burning with an unholy fire.

Without taking his eyes off the animal, Noah advanced cautiously, all the while winding his cloak around his arm.

Sensing Noah's approach, the brute spun, its lips drawn back, revealing long, yellowed teeth. Saliva dripped from the folds of its mouth.

The old woman swung her staff, striking the animal on the side of its head. It yelped sharply and dropped to the ground.

Noah, leaping forward, thrust his spear deep into its chest, pinning it to the forest floor. Its glazed eyes wild with malevolence, the animal convulsed once, trembled, then lay still. Noah yanked his spear from the body and crouched, poised for the next attack.

Gutteral snarls and growls resounded among the trees as the animals melted into the shadows, leaving four of their pack dead on the forest floor.

The three comrades stepped closer to each other, backs together, their faces glistening in the pale light. "How many do you think are out there?" asked Ganah, her breath coming in short, strangled gasps.

Noah ran his tongue over his lips. "More than we can handle if they attack all at once."

"We were not sent here to die," rasped Ganah. "Noah, do as I say. Yell. Shout and scream as loud as you can!"

Puzzled, both men stared at her.

"Do as I say! Our lives depend on it!"

Feeling foolish yet fearing to disobey, Noah yelled, "Eyah-h-h!"

Ganah joined in, shouting and stamping the ground with her feet.

Immediately, the movement in the shadows ceased. The dark forms retreated several paces.

Ganah and Noah shouted until their dry, parched throats rebelled, and they could not utter another cry. They listened to the eerie stillness. They could hear nothing.

"They're still there," warned Noah. He swallowed, forcing back the bitterness of fear rising in his throat.

Eliah's eyes loomed large in his fleshy face.

They watched the shadows, their bodies tense.

"Get ready," Noah rasped. "It won't be long."

"Be strong and have faith," whispered Ganah. Still gripping her staff, she wiped the perspiration from her eyes with one forearm.

Once again the silence was shattered as savage forms hurled themselves from all directions. The three defenders stayed close to one another, each one trying to guard his companions' backs yet keeping out of range of the others' weapons. Both men attempted to shield Ganah. She used the staff with great skill, but she was tiring rapidly.

Eliah speared an animal in midflight then turned to aid her. Blood ran from an open wound on her arm as she swung at two snarling beasts. Eliah struck to distract one of the wolves, but another attacked from the rear, its breath hot upon his neck. With his massive hands he grabbed the animal's head over his shoulder.

Blood roared in Noah's ears.

An unearthly scream echoed above the din of the battle.

One of the wolves howled in pain and rolled into the underbrush.

Noah had time only to see two blurred images dashing into the midst of the onslaught, clubs swinging in fury above their heads.

"Jirad!" shouted Noah, not daring to believe his eyes. Maybe the old woman was right, though—maybe they were not going to die here after all.

With a yell, Jirad placed his foot on the shoulder of the dead wolf and yanked a sharp, wooden lance from its body.

Quickly, the tide of battle turned. The beasts retreated as if pulled back by an unseen hand, their snarls fading into the forest.

Ganah sank to the ground, her body devoid of strength.

Eliah picked her up and, carrying her as a child, rested her against a tree. He examined her wounds with no thought to his own.

Noah threw his arms around Jirad and lifted him off the ground.

"How did you find us?" he breathed, relieved beyond expression.

Jirad laughed. "That, my friend, is a long story, and one I'm not sure you'll believe, but your shoutings could have awakened the dead. When we heard them, we knew someone was in trouble. Little did I know it was you."

Noah surveyed the bloody scene. "I can't believe we're still alive." Turning back to his friend, he drew in his breath sharply.

Jirad, ignoring the expression on Noah's face, said, "This is Malek, my friend. He saved my life."

As the foul smell of death swirled around the band, the dark, contorted visage stared at them, suspicion and apprehension in his eyes, waiting for the expected scorn and revulsion.

Noah held out his hand.

Malek eyed him, unsure what to do.

"Go ahead," motioned Jirad.

Finally, Malek held out his own.

Noah grasped his wrist in a firm grip. "Welcome," he said.

The man nodded, still unsure of his reception by the others.

Jirad poked at one of the dead wolves, ruffling the thick, coarse fur. "Something is wrong with these animals. They are unlike any I have seen before."

"Talk later," said Malek, stooping to pick up the El-cumah lying on the ground by one of the slain animals. As his hand closed over the staff, he screamed in pain and flung his hand to the side. Fastened to his index finger hung a small but deadly viper girdled with ominous red bands.

Noah swung his knife, severing the lethal body with one deft motion.

Without warning, Malek yanked a blade from his belt and sawed frantically at the base of his finger.

"Stop!" screamed Jirad, lunging for his arm.

The man jerked away. "No," he yelled, severing the finger with a final cut. The dismembered digit dropped to the ground and disappeared into a pile of leaves.

Blood spurted from his hand, splattering Noah's cheek and arm as he scooped a handful of moss from the ground and pressed it against the bleeding stub. "Get some more," he yelled. Jirad helped him pack the velvety plant around the wound and bind it tightly with vines. The two men stared at Malek, their faces pale and drawn.

Great beads of perspiration covered Malek's ashen face. "Better lose one finger," he whispered, "than die from poison."

Jirad placed his arm on his friend's shoulder.

"Master send snake to destroy Malek."

"He is not your master any longer," asserted Jirad. "You have left his service. You have renounced him."

He shook his head wearily, "Yes, but Master not let Malek go." He looked at Jirad with sadness in his eyes. "Master not let Jirad go either. Better to stay in cave. Soon all be over."

"Quickly," said Ganah as she struggled to her feet. "We must build a fire to sear the wound. If we don't, the flesh will grow black and bring death to our new friend's body."

Over the succeeding days, Malek's hand began to heal without any evidence of infection. Although they knew his pain was severe, the man never complained. He knew the interior of the Shinar as well as he knew the caves, but the party soon discovered that it had been easier to enter its depths than to leave. Damp, lichen-covered trees barred their progress, and tangled, sinuous vines tugged at their arms and legs, making it difficult for the Tumulac to carry the wounded and exhausted Ulah-rah.

Plodding onward, they fought their way, each one secretly hoping they had not been wrong in trusting the deformed stranger to lead them to safety.

Twenty-Nine

"Enough!" said Noah. "We'll go no farther today. We must rest or none of us will leave this forest alive."

Eliah lowered Ganah to the ground, resting her tenderly against a large, moss-covered rock. He rolled up his cloak and placed it beneath her head.

"Clear an area," Noah ordered, "and we'll make camp for the night."

Eliah scooped out a spot in the moist earth, then gathered dry twigs and branches and piled them in the depression. He removed the flints from the pouch in his belt along with a dry, resin-rich stick of pine. He scraped the stick with his knife until he had a ball of wood shavings among the broken twigs. He squatted in front of the wood and struck the stones together, sending a stream of hot, flying sparks into the ball of pine tinder. The shavings caught fire, and soon a pale, orange glow filled the campsite. Eliah put the stones and resin stick back in his belt and set down heavily beside his mistress, a worried expression on his usually placid face.

Malek untied a waterskin from his belt and handed it to Noah. He dropped wearily beside the fire.

Noah knelt beside Ganah and lifted the skin to her lips. She sipped the water and laid her head against the rock. "My wound is not severe," she said as water trickled from the corner of her mouth. "I'll be all right with food and rest." A musty dampness was already seeping up from the forest floor. Noah tucked Ganah's cloak tighter around her slight body.

Jirad rubbed his hands together and stamped his feet, trying to ward off the chill creeping into his bones. Finally he squatted beside Noah. "Do you think we'll be safe here for the night?"

Noah felt a tug on his tunic. The old woman's fingers were grasping the hem. She whispered, her voice hoarse in the silence, "I told you we will not die here." She motioned with her hand. "The Elcumah," she rasped. "Give it to me."

Eliah picked it up with care and laid it across her chest. As her thin hands grasped it, a smile spread over her gaunt face. She closed her eyes, her lips moving in silent prayer.

Jirad motioned Noah to the other side of the fire where they drew their cloaks about themselves and hunched down by the warm blaze. They talked but kept their voices low. Ganah moaned and held her wounded arm.

"We cannot go on until she is stronger," said Noah. "If we do, we may kill her."

"If we stay in this godforsaken forest we will all surely die," admonished Jirad.

The two men stared into the dying flames that glowed in the darkness, each one grateful for the brightness, a haven within the oppressive heaviness that crushed in upon them. For the moment they were lost in thought.

"Jirad," said Noah, his voice breaking the silence. "Utriel is in danger."

Jirad's head whipped up, a look of fear in his eyes.

As the fire burned low, Noah related to him all that he knew.

The young man listened, his fists clenched and knuckles taut and white. His mouth twisted in rage. "I've failed her," he groaned. "I knew he was evil, and I should have protected her."

"I love her too," Noah said, trying to quiet his friend's anger. "We'll find her, and we'll seek out Bel—or Asmodeus—or whatever he's called. We will avenge her."

Jirad's eyes flashed. "You don't understand, Noah. Asmodeus is not just some wandering weapons maker. He is one of Abaddon's spawns of darkness. How can we fight such evil? We're defeated even before we begin."

"No." Noah's voice rose in anger. "I refuse to accept that. We'll find a way. If we don't," he lowered his voice to a whisper, "then we are all lost."

They talked long into the night, shivering in spite of the warm blaze. The men took turns standing watch. They refused to relax their vigilance until they were out of the foreboding forest.

The next morning Malek was eager to get underway. Although still in pain, much of the color had returned to his face. Ganah was sore and stiff, but she was up and walking. They were all keenly aware that the longer they remained in the forest, the greater their peril.

"Are you able to go on?" Noah asked Ganah.

Dark circles ringed her eyes, but the frailness had vanished and deep lines of determination were etched once again around her mouth. "Yah-Adon and the staff will strengthen me. He has given His promise that none of us will die in this place, and I choose to believe Him."

Noah could feel the power of her faith reaching out to him. Grateful for it, he took hold. "Come," he said, "let's get out of this godforsaken place of death and find Utriel."

Forced to spend several more fearful nights in the Shinar, the small band, with Malek in the lead, fought its way through the tangled forest growth.

On the seventh day after the attack, the weary and bedraggled group broke out of the shadows. Sunlight streamed through the branches of the thinning trees. With a shout Noah and Jirad raced toward the brilliance, the others only a step or two behind. As they emerged onto the plains, they flung their hands and faces toward the warm, life-giving radiance.

Ganah raised the El-cumah high above her head. She turned to the others, their relief mirrored in her eyes. "Gather large rocks," she commanded. "We must build an altar to our God. Through His protection we are alive, and—" she lowered her voice, looking toward Noah—"through His guidance we are now five instead of three."

They gathered stones and stacked them one upon another until the pile reached the Ulah-rah's shoulder. Stepping back, she held forth the staff, the tip touching the top stone. "Great and mighty Giver of Light," she intoned, "Placer of Stars, we build this altar as a memorial to You for delivering us from the death and darkness of the Shinar. May all who see this mound know that it is sacred, and cursed be the one who destroys it."

Lifting her head to the sky, she raised the staff. A harpy eagle circled in the distance, riding the shifting currents of air. No one moved, each held immobile by the sense of an awesome presence. At last, she lowered her arms. "Come," she said. "The plains stretch far. We have many days ahead of us before our task ends."

The five companions stepped resolutely onto the sun-drenched, verdant plains spreading before them.

Thirty

The sun's warmth caressed the bodies of the group, lifting their spirits and their will to continue. The high grass of the plains brushed against their legs like the kisses of a thousand butterflies. Once, they surprised a herd of gazelle. The animals lifted their heads, sniffed the air, then bounded away from the intruders. A cloud of dust near the horizon evidenced the presence of the great lumbering aurochs. Lush watering holes overshadowed by tall trees, acacias, and spreading emerald ferns dotted the land. Lacy white clusters and blue blossoms on tall stalks swayed in the afternoon breeze.

Although the days had slipped by without the discovery of a single clue that could lead them to the object of their search, Ganah infected each of them with her renewed confidence. She had recovered from the encounter with the wolves, and Malek's hand healed rapidly. Each day brought restoration to the once weary sojourners.

One evening after they had eaten and were sitting around the glowing coals, the talk turned to the encounter with the wolves.

Ganah poked at the embers with a long stick. "I knew we were to go to the Shinar, even though I did not believe we would find Utriel there. I must confess, though, that the reason for going eluded me. I know, now, that Yah-Adon intended Jirad and Malek to find us. I suppose, in His wisdom, He knew we would need you both in our quest. And," she continued, "you did save our lives."

"Animals not wolves!" blurted Malek into the conversation with such certainty that all eyes turned toward him, for Jirad's strange companion seldom spoke.

"What do you mean?"

"Not wolves!" repeated Malek, his voice firm with conviction. "Not wolves. Shadow-wolves."

Jirad looked up from the fire. "What is a shadow-wolf?"

Malek glanced nervously over his shoulder. "Shadow-wolves made by master—made by Shadow Walker. Take animal soul and fill body with darkness. When animal become shadow thing—very bad."

"Take an animal's soul?" repeated Noah, looking around at the others. "Surely you don't believe such a thing?"

"Listen to him," urged Jirad. "Would you not agree that strange things are loose in our world?"

"What makes you think those animals were shadow-wolves?" asked Noah.

"No beauty left in animal. Fur old and dry—like fur on animal long dead."

Noah stared into the fire. For several minutes no one spoke. "Can only animals be made into shadow creatures?" he asked, still keeping his eyes on the flames. With the night insects clicking and whirring around them, the others gazed at the nightmarish being crouched in the flickering shadows.

Malek drew a deep breath before exhaling. "Malek not shadow-man." He paused—no one spoke. "Malek ugly, but Malek have soul."

Noah peered at his dour companion. "Forgive me, friend, but I must ask. Why were you serving Abaddon and his dark legions?"

The twisted visage lowered its dark eyes, but not before they saw them full of pain. "Face," he said. "Face—ugly." He stared into the coals. When he continued, his voice faltered and his eyes filled with tears. "When—when Malek little, father full of shame. Take Malek from mother and leave in Shinar for wild animals. Malek find cave and hide. Abaddon's servants find Malek and take deep in cave. There live and serve. Abaddon hate Yah-Adon. Keep ugly things around. Ugly things not remind of lost glory."

The man grunted. "Malek hate Abaddon, but . . ." He paused,

shrugging and staring at his gnarled hands. "No place to go. No one want Malek."

"Why did you help me escape?" asked Jirad.

"Abaddon evil, and—" he lowered his voice—"make Malek do bad things. Worse than death. Malek not want Abaddon kill Jirad."

"What will happen to you now?"

"He find Malek." He shrugged. "Kill Malek, but Malek no longer serve. Now Malek have friends."

In the stillness of the night, no one spoke. Noah stirred the coals and laid wood on the fire as he tried to control his emotions.

At last the old prophetess broke the silence. "Yes, you have friends. When the time comes, I promise we won't desert you."

Malek's mouth contorted into a grotesque smile, forcing one eye to shut in a hideous wink as a tear slid down the side of his cheek.

When the men lay down by the fire for the night and their faint breathing turned into the steady droning of sleep, Ganah rose to her feet. She bent low to rouse one of the sleepers, but before her hand touched his shoulder, his eyes opened.

"What?"

She placed her fingers on his lips. "I must talk to you," she whispered. "Come away from the others."

Malek heaved himself to his feet and followed her to the edge of the grove.

She eased herself to the ground. "You're the only one I know who may be able to give me the answers I need. I must ask you two things."

Once Malek would have turned away from the searching gray eyes that seemed to pierce his soul. Now he merely listened.

"What is in the cave that Jirad described, and why did Asmodeus go there?"

"Cave bring Ganah death," he said, shaking his head.

"That does not matter, my friend. I must know all that you can tell me."

He was silent for so long that Ganah feared he would not answer. Finally, he whispered hoarsely, "Many doors to underworld. Place of darkness and fire. Place of death. From cave Asmodeus and Master's dark servants go to and from man's world." His voice caught in his throat as he struggled to make her understand with his limited vocabulary. "Cave—mouth of hell." He spat on the ground. "Vomit evil into world."

Beads of moisture glistened on the Ulah-rah's face. "Can that mouth be closed?"

Again he gave no answer.

"Malek, can it be closed?"

The man tilted his head and peered at her with his good eye. "Malek not know."

She stared into the darkness, seeing nothing yet seeing more than she desired. "I must find a way to stop the evil that is threatening to overtake us." She sighed deeply. "First, though, I must find Utriel. Come, friend," she said, reaching out her aged but strong hand. "We must go back to the others. Morning will be here soon, and we still have much to do." Her voice trailed off into the night. "Yes, much to do." Turning, she walked back to the still sleeping forms, her figure straight and resolute.

Malek followed like a dark shadow. He did not lie down immediately but sat by the fire.

Ganah eased her tired body onto the ground. She pulled her cloak about her, but she was not ready for sleep. The horror of Malek's revelation was too much to comprehend. Was it possible that somewhere deep in the Shinar was an entrance to the netherworld? She exhaled slowly. No wonder the beautiful forest had become a place of fear and the source of dark, forbidding stories. Did it contain a direct link from the source of all evil to the world of man? How long had the entrance existed? She tried to remember when she had first heard rumors about the forest. A knot of fear tightened in her stomach. How many other entrances linked the two worlds?

As she lay in the still night, she rubbed her eyes. She was tired, but it was not a tiredness that could be remedied by sleep. It was a deep weariness of the soul. "Yah-Adon," she whispered into the darkness, "You promised to help me in my weakness." Again, she pulled her cloak tighter around her thin shoulders.

Thirty-One

"Noah!" shouted Ganah.

He heard her voice but did not turn. They had been gone from Gibara-boni for two cycles of the moon, and they needed skins to make new shoes. Noah crouched lower in the grass. Malek and Jirad had succeeded in separating a young antelope from the rest of its herd, and he had no intention of spooking the animal.

"Noah!" repeated Ganah. "People! To your right!"

Noah remained concealed in the tall grass but lifted his head in the direction indicated.

The cornered animal, sensing the moment of distraction, dashed toward him and leaped over his head, sending him sprawling on the ground.

"Are you all right?" yelled Jirad as he raced toward the stunned man.

"I'm fine," Noah said with disgust as he scrambled to his feet, "but we just lost our shoes."

The landscape shimmered in the brilliant sunlight as Ganah continued to wave, pointing with her staff.

Noah shielded his eyes with his hand and squinted into the brightness. There, a movement, possibly a small caravan. He waved to her in acknowledgment as she and Eliah started running toward him.

"We must talk to them," she exclaimed, nearly out of breath by the time she reached his side. "They're the first people we've seen since leaving Gibara-boni. They may have seen Utriel."

"May be enemy," cautioned Malek. "Many serve Master—many serve Destroyer."

"We must not be afraid," chided Ganah. "Yah-Adon is with us." Without another word, the old woman gripped the staff in her hand. "Follow me," she said and strode toward the approaching band.

Jirad made a movement as though to stop her, but the Tumulac's arm shot forward with lightning speed. The huge man shook his head in silent rebuke.

Noah watched the old woman striding boldly across the plain. "Let her go," he said. "Just pray she knows what she's doing." Placing his hand on his weapon, he struck out after her, the Tumulac only a few steps behind. The remaining two men exchanged glances, then followed, remaining aware of all before them.

As Noah approached the strangers, he counted no more than fifteen men, probably nomads who pursued the herds across the plains. These people lived in tents that could be disassembled, loaded on the backs of donkeys or camels and quickly moved.

The strangers had stopped and were now watching Ganah. Four men who had been carrying an elaborately decorated litter lowered it to the ground and gestured with excitement to a tall, sinewy man, obviously their leader. The man strode toward them, shoulders back and chin high in the air, two of his men following at his heels.

Ganah sucked in her breath sharply. The man walking toward her wore the headdress and bore the marks of the Shulem, a feared tribe of nomadic warriors not seen in the central plains for many cycles of the moon. She had heard of their return but had prayed it was only a rumor. The prophetess could not restrain the tremor that shook her body at the confirmation of their presence. They were cruel, evil people who left terror and destruction in their path. In spite of the fear gripping her stomach, she set her jaw, lifted her head, and breathed a prayer as she stood within arm's reach of the fearsome warrior.

The lofty headpiece worn by the Shulem chief gave the illusion of even greater height than he possessed. Nearly an arm's length tall and fashioned from animal skins and ostrich feathers, the headpiece bore an enormous ornament on the front made of gold that reflected the brilliance of the sun on its shiny yellow surface.

Dark, pigmented circles and lines swirled over the man's bronze cheeks and forehead. Finely tanned skins covered his loins. Others were draped over his shoulders to protect them from the sun. In his hand he held a large wooden spear with a tip made of finely honed bronze. Over one shoulder hung a wooden club with sharp obsidian spikes embedded into its head.

Ganah knew she had to control her emotions. She must show no sign of fear.

The strange, fierce visage gazed down at her until suddenly an incongruous smile spread across the tattooed face and white teeth gleamed in the darkness of his beard. "You have come!" the man exclaimed, his smile growing even wider. "I am Pedrah," he thundered. "Chief of the mighty Shulem nation. You are here as my dream foretold." He grabbed her hand and hurried toward his men, pulling her helplessly behind him.

The Tumulac's hand tightened on his weapon as he lumbered toward her, his three companions close on his heels.

Instantly, six warriors sprang forward, blocking their way.

"She's here," Pedrah shouted, waving his spear high above his head. "Didn't I tell you the holy woman would come. Now my son will be restored to me!"

He dragged Ganah to the covered litter. "My dreams said you would come," he exclaimed. "That you would restore my son."

"I don't understand."

Pedrah's eyes narrowed, "Are you not a holy woman?"

"I am Ganah, Ulah-rah of the Sethites."

"Then," the chief said, the smile once again spreading across his face, "you are the holy woman I have been seeking."

He pulled aside the heavy curtains surrounding the litter and shoved Ganah closer. As he did, the stench of death struck her nose. Before her lay the form of a child, no more than four or five years of age. Dark hair curled in tight ringlets around a face set in a waxy pallor, the body already bloated and swollen.

Waves of nausea swept over her. When she could speak, her voice cracked. "The boy is dead. What do you expect me to do?"

"You will make him live again!"

"I have great skill," said Ganah, "but I cannot do the impossible. I have no power over death."

A dark scowl appeared on the chief's face. "My dreams told me you would heal him. If you refuse, you will all die."

Perspiration had collected on her upper lip, and the palms of her hands were damp. A knot formed in her chest as the fierce warriors closed in around her four companions whose weapons lay uselessly on the ground.

She closed her eyes and focused a plea for help, sending it out to the One who had sent her forth. She turned back to the savage father. "Tell me," she said, with as much calmness as she could sustain, "what happened to your son and what did your dream tell you?"

"He was seized with a burning fever. My shaman made a hole in his head to release the evil spirits trapped within, but two moons ago his spirit left his body. It still hovers over him trying to return. It came to me in my dreams to tell me that a holy woman was coming. It told me to take his body and travel toward the burial ground of my people. There she would find us. "And now," he exclaimed, his voice rising in excitement, "you are here! Restore my son, holy woman. You have the power."

"No," she said, "I do not have the power. The power must come from the Great Light. His name to us is Yah-Adon. He is the source of the power. I can do nothing on my own."

She was silent for a moment. Only the occasional bellow of an auroch could be heard mingled with the scream of an eagle, soaring high in the cerulean sky. When she spoke to the chief, her voice was husky with emotion. "If I fail, you may take my life, but I beg that you spare the lives of those with me."

He shook his head, the huge headpiece swaying and reflecting sunlight with each movement. "No!" he rasped. "If you fail, you will all die!"

She took a deep breath and brushed her hand at the flies buzzing over the eyes and mouth of the child. She tried to think of something to prolong the moment, but Pedrah's fierce gaze never left her face. Willing herself to remain calm, she reached into her belt and pulled out a small knife. She drew the sharp blade over her wrist, leaving a scarlet line that welled up and ran down the sides of her arm. She turned her wrist and held it above the boy. Vermilion drops cascaded onto the body, splattering onto his face and chest, their brightness making the ashen body seem even paler.

Lifting her head to the sky, she said, "As You taught us in ages past, O Giver of Light, the life is in the blood. So, I give to this child the life from my own body. I call upon You, now, to manifest Your power to these unbelievers."

As she grasped the El-cumah with both hands, her heart leaped, for she felt the responding warmth spreading through the staff and into her arms. She raised it to the sky, then rested the tip on the chest of the child.

She waited, not daring to breathe.

A tremor started in the pit of her stomach as a pinpoint of light sparked above the child's head. The light increased in size, the pale yellow bursting into a blue-white brilliance. A power charged the air, prickling her skin. Then—the light was gone and before her lay the healthy body of a child rubbing its eyes as though just awakening from a deep slumber

The Shulem chief stared in disbelief, his spear falling from his hand. With a wild shout he grabbed the boy and hugged him to his chest.

Exhausted, Ganah leaned on the staff, suddenly very weary. Arms encircled her, supporting her slender body. She looked up into Noah's face. "Thank you," she said. "Yah-Adon is merciful."

"How can such a thing be?" Noah asked.

"I cannot say," she replied, keeping her voice low. "Never have I seen the dead come back to life. It is beyond my understanding. I can only say that Yah-Adon, the Great Light and the Placer of Stars, has restored the boy."

Pedrah lifted his son high in the air, shouting over and over, "He's alive! Look! My son's alive!"

In contrast to the jubilant faces surrounding the father, Ganah saw a dark, angry scowl fixed on the heavy-jowled face of one Shulem who was not rejoicing. His fierce eyes caused her to recoil from their fury. She knew instinctively who it was—the tribe's shaman. She knew without doubt that he had tried everything within his knowledge to heal the child and had failed. In his eyes he had not only been humiliated, but worst of all—humiliated by a woman.

"Come!" Pedrah shouted, ignoring the silent rebuke. "We return to our village! We must honor the holy woman and her God with a day of great celebration!"

It was approaching dusk when they arrived the next day at the Shulem village. The Sethites were tired and sore, their shoes by now little more than tattered strips of leather, their feet bruised and bleeding. The sun was dropping toward the top of the mountains. Smoke rose from fires scattered among large, skillfully woven goat-hair tents. Even in the fading light, their ornate decorations and bright colors were evident against the dark and heavy cloth.

Pedrah had sent a runner to alert his people of their return. Friends and family now gathered around them, shouting and laughing at the sight of the child seated astride its father's shoulders. Women beat together long hollow sticks and trilled in wild abandonment as children cavorted around the travelers.

A dark, beautiful woman ran forward, tears streaming down her tattooed face. "Chuzah! My little one!" she cried as she reached to lift the child from Pedrah's arms.

"Be gone, woman!" he shouted, shoving her aside with his foot.

The woman threw out her hands to break her fall but sprawled at Ganah's feet, scraping the side of her face on the ground.

"Because of you," sneered Pedrah, "my son was ill." Then, turning his back on her, he strode into the center of the encampment. None of the Shulem made a move to help her but averted their eyes and stepped aside, holding their garments so nothing would touch her.

Ganah helped the woman to her feet. Already blood coursed from a deep cut on her cheek.

Without looking at the Ulah-rah, the woman muttered, "I will kill him for this. I swear by the gods of my father."

Ganah flinched at the smoldering hatred in her eyes.

The woman looked at Ganah as if seeing her for the first time, then turned and ran into the dusky night.

"My dream was true!" shouted the chief, his voice rising above the cries of the people. "The holy woman met us on the plains and healed Chuzah. The holy woman has great power! Let us rejoice! My son was dead! Now he is alive!"

Thirty-Two

The passing days blurred, one blending into another, but Utriel could not ignore the new life growing within her body at what she knew to be an unusually rapid rate. She had watched her father's women as their stomachs swelled and increased in size with each passing cycle of the moon, and never had they enlarged as quickly as she had.

She lay on a crude, woven straw pallet covered with worn furs. Strong, spastic jabs twisted and knotted within. She clenched her tongue between her teeth. The warm, salty taste of blood filled her mouth. Her body was tall, and her young muscles held the child tightly and high, but the movements that only a short time ago had been gentle flutterings were now vigorous and demanding.

Only two cycles of the moon had passed. A wave of nausea swept over her. "Curse you, Asmodeus," she whispered. "What kind of monstrosity are you trying to bring into this world?" She gasped as a sharp pain pierced her taut abdomen.

"Unah," shouted a voice outside the tent. Tubila burst through the doorway, breathless and laughing, her once dull, lustrous eyes bright with excitement. "Come quickly! I want to show you something!" She grabbed Utriel's hand to pull her to her feet. "Come up to the rocks! Hurry!"

"Not now. I don't feel like it."

The girl's face grew sober. "Are you sick?"

Utriel shook her head and pushed herself to her feet, pressing one hand against her side. "No—I'm all right."

"Are you sure?"

"Yes. I'm fine. What did you want me to see?"

"I can't tell you," cried Tubila, a smile once again spreading across her face. "Just come with me."

Tubila's exuberance was contagious, and Utriel found herself hurrying after the girl as she scurried farther up the mountain, scrambling over rocks and slipping between huge boulders. As the path steepened, they made their way with caution. Pebbles slipped under their feet and tumbled down the cliffs.

"Over there," said Tubila, pointing to a large ledge jutting out from the side of the mountain as if the stone had been chiseled away by ancient promethean hands. The young women pulled themselves over the edge and dropped onto its warm surface.

"What have you found?" asked Utriel, pushing back loose strands of hair from her glistening face.

Tubila placed her finger on her lips. "You will see."

They waited, Tubila giggling in anticipation. Suddenly, the beating of wings broke the stillness, and a shadow descended upon them.

Utriel screamed, leaping to her feet. "Piava," she cried, not daring to believe her eyes. "How did you find me?" The hawk perched on a rock above their heads.

"You know this hawk?" Tubila squealed in delight and amazement.

Utriel laughed at the girl's perplexed expression. "I raised it from a fledgling. How did you know it was mine?"

"I didn't," she said, shaking her head. "I was gathering berries when it began circling and swooping over my head as if it wanted to land. Just when I thought it would, it soared high into the sky again. I wanted you to see it. It is so beautiful."

Utriel held out her arm but quickly drew it back as she remembered the sharp talons. "Give me that bag you were using for the berries."

The girl untied the pouch from her sash and shook the dark, purple fruit onto the ledge.

Utriel wrapped the cloth around her forearm and held it toward the hawk. Blinking its eyes, the bird stepped onto her arm. Gently Utriel stroked the soft breast. "How did you find me, my pretty one?" she crooned as the hawk shifted from one leg to the other. "Oh, if only you would stay with me," she murmured.

She held out her other arm. "Untie the bracelet around my upper arm. Quickly!"

Tubila began unfastening the narrow leather strip holding a delicate green bead laced with streaks of milky white.

"While I hold Piava, wrap the band around her leg. Tie it carefully. I don't want it to fall off."

The hawk watched as Tubila secured the strip. Lowering its head, it pecked lightly at the bead.

"Don't, Piava," whispered Utriel. "Noah gave that to me. I want you to wear it. I want something of mine close to you as you soar high into the heavens. Please," she said, her voice growing desperate, "please don't forget me."

The bird swiveled its head as if in understanding. Then, spreading its wings, it mounted into the sky.

Thirty-Three

"No," said Pedrah, his eyes narrowed into darkened slits. "I have made up my mind. . . . You will not leave. You are a powerful, holy woman, and you will stay here to keep your God in our village."

"We have been with you for many days," said Ganah. "It is time for us to journey on. You have your own gods and your shaman has strong magic. You do not need me."

"May twenty camels run up Danim's back," Pedrah roared.

A slave, little more than a boy, entered the tent, his hands bearing a large platter of dates and ripe pomegranates.

"Get out!" shouted Pedrah.

The boy hesitated, looking for a place to set the fruit.

"I said to get out!" The angry leader lunged toward the slave and struck the platter with his fist, sending the fruit scattering over the floor of the tent.

Frightened, the boy dropped to his knees and began grabbing the pomegranates with trembling hands.

"Leave it, oaf," bellowed Pedrah. He swung his foot, slamming it into the middle of the slave's chest. The boy collapsed to the floor, gasping for breath. "Now, get out of here!"

Pedrah flung himself onto a pile of skins and cushions in the middle of his tent. "Danim could do nothing to heal my son. He called on his gods, but they refused to answer." His face hardened in willful stubbornness. "No," he said, "I will not permit you to leave and take your power with you."

"I have told you," repeated Ganah, "it is not my power. It is Yah-Adon who restored Chuzah. Only He has the power to give back life.

Get rid of the gods you worship and turn to Him, the Placer of Stars. Then you will not need me."

The chief shrugged, then smiled, his eyes widening as if an idea had suddenly come to him. "Why give up our gods? We will just add yours to our own. Are not many better than only one?" He leaned back against the skins and, grinning smugly, laced his fingers behind his head.

"Yah-Adon is the one true God." The Ulah-rah's voice deepened and expanded. "Turn from your worship of demons and prostrate yourself before Him, the Placer of Stars, the God of all Light."

Pedrah's mouth tightened as he pushed himself to a sitting position.

"He is slow to anger," continued the prophetess, "but His wrath is great."

Without warning, a picture filled her head, a picture that caused an icy coldness to clutch her heart. She pressed her hands to her chest and her eyes widened in terror.

"What is it, holy woman? What is the matter?" Pedrah leaned forward as if sensing her fear.

"I—I—" she stammered. How could she tell him? He would think her mad. Never had she seen such things. Water! Water everywhere, even falling from the sky. But that was impossible! Water did not fall from the heavens!

"Speak, old woman," commanded Pedrah. "Why have you turned so pale?"

She held her hands before her. They were trembling. She clasped them together and raised her eyes to the Shulem chief. As she did, words began pouring from her mouth. "A destruction is coming," she cried, "the likes of which no one has ever seen. Yah-Adon will no longer turn His eyes from man's evil ways. His wrath is growing. No longer will He tolerate the wickedness and perversion in the land. I see water everywhere, covering even the highest mountains. I see—"

"Enough," shouted Pedrah, rising to his feet. "I will hear no more of such foolishness. You push me too far, old woman."

The two leaders faced each other, one trembling with dark anger, the other in wonder at the vision in her head and the words that poured from her mouth.

Ganah bowed her head and stepped backward. If she were to save herself and her friends, she must act cautiously, for the tattooed leader placed little value on life. Caught between his refusal to let them leave and the shaman's hatred, it was only a matter of time before disaster would strike herself and her friends. *I must act wisely,* she thought, *and I must ask for understanding of what I have been shown by the Placer of Stars.*

The Shulem were a savage, uncivilized tribe. The fact that the five comrades were still alive was in itself a miracle. So far, only Malek had suffered at their hands. Frightened by his twisted body and believing he was inhabited by an evil spirit, the nomads had refused to allow him in the camp. They would have killed him if it had not been for their awe of "the holy woman with the great power." Truly their shaman could do wondrous things, but never had they seen anyone bring back the dead.

Pedrah had ordered Malek placed in a sturdy pen outside the camp and a strong leather collar fastened around his neck. He was then tied to a large stake driven deeply into the ground. The prisoners each feared that soon Pedrah would tire of keeping him alive. Then not even Ganah's presence could save him.

As the weeks passed, Noah and Jirad watched ceaselessly for a chance to escape, but never were they alone. Even when they slept, guards remained outside their tents. Their weapons had been taken, and they knew it was foolish to attempt an escape unarmed. Each day only increased their frustrations, and the scowl on Danim's face grew darker. Time was rapidly running out.

Holy woman . . . holy woman. Where are you?" Danim bellowed angrily. "Come outside and face me."

The Tumulac sprang to his feet.

Ganah grabbed his arm. "No," she signaled, putting her finger to her lips. Pulling aside the tent flap, she stepped outside, her staff grasped firmly in her hand. "What do you want?" she asked, her chin lifted and her voice bold with authority.

The shaman stood before her, his heavy body weaving in a drunken stupor, his short, bandy legs barely able to support the flabby gut hanging over a long, vermilion skirt fastened about his waist with a wide belt made from the bright, yellow metal the Shulem were so fond of using. Bloodshot eyes glared at her from a bloated face, glowing coals buried in a lump of dark dough. Two warriors flanked his sides.

"I come to challenge you," Danim shouted, his words slurring and spittle drooling from one corner of his mouth. "You cause my people to mock me. I must show them who is greater."

"You have no need to challenge me. Simply convince Pedrah to let us leave. Then I will no longer be a threat to you."

"Threat?" screamed the man insanely. "You are no threat to me, you and your stupid words about water falling from the sky. But," he wobbled, "if you will not meet my challenge, I will kill you."

Eliah stiffened.

"You are drunk," she said with a sweep of her arm. She turned to the two men. "Take your shaman to his tent before he does something foolish." She raised the El-cumah and pointed it toward them. "We are under Pedrah's protection as well as Yah-Adon's."

The two men shrank back, grabbing Danim's arms to pull him away.

"I'm not finished with you," Danim yelled to Ganah as the men struggled to restrain him. "I'll kill you . . . you bag of bones."

Ganah turned and walked into the tent, gesturing for the Tumulac to follow. Eliah, massive fists clenched at his sides, glared at Danim. Reluctantly he turned and followed his mistress.

A crescent shone dimly through the opening in the roof of the tent. Ganah lay still, her eyes fixed on the slender, silver spear of light piercing the darkness of the tent. The Tumulac's deep, muffled snores were strangely comforting as her mind continued searching for a way of escape.

"Yah-Adon," she breathed, closing her eyes. "There is no means of escape without You. The evil closes in upon us with each passing day. I feel the time growing short." She pressed her hands to her chest. "Help us, I pray. We are so close to the end of the task. Don't let us fail."

The old woman's eyes snapped open. She lay still, listening. There. She heard it again, like the claw of an animal raking the side of the tent. She scanned the darkness, straining to see the source of the sound. A pale light flashed through a slit slowly appearing in the thick, woven goat-hair. She watched, barely breathing, as a blade, held by an unseen hand worked through the sturdy fabric. The slit widened and a dark figure wriggled through the opening.

"Holy woman," whispered a voice, "are you awake?"

"Who is there?" she answered.

Only a muffled gasp responded. Eliah, awakened at the first sound, had slipped silently in the darkness along the inside of the tent. His massive arms now held the intruder by the neck.

"Don't scream," Ganah warned, "and he'll not hurt you." She lit the oil lamp kept by the side of her mat and held it high. By the pale, yellow light a frightened face stared at them, dark eyes wide in fear.

"Pedrah's wife," said Ganah, puzzlement in her voice. "What are you doing here?"

"Put out the light before it is seen. Here," said the woman hoarsely, "I have something for you."

"Let her go."

Eliah glanced first at his mistress, then released his hold.

"What do you have?"

The woman turned to Eliah. When he stepped back, she scuttled to the rear of the tent and pulled aside the slashed opening. "I brought you something," she said, moving out of the way.

Eliah peered into the darkness. Something glinted in the soft light. He reached through the opening. His hand closed over an object familiar and welcome to his touch. He turned to Ganah and smiled, then pulled inside his spear, his club, and his knife.

"Here," said the woman. In the palm of her hand lay a slender knife with a fine bone handle carved with intricate, delicate figures.

"It's mine," said the Ulah-rah.

"Yes. Take it. Your friends are waiting for you outside of camp."

"Why are you doing this?"

"If you stay here, you will all die. Danim is making plans to have you killed." Her mouth twisted into a vicious sneer. "Pedrah is too stupid to know what is happening." She grasped Ganah's hands and bowed her head. "You gave my son back his life. I will try to do the same for you."

"Your husband will kill you if he discovers what you have done."

Hatred flashed in the woman's eyes. "Pedrah blames me for the boy's illness. He refuses to let me near my son." Tears rolled down her face, dropping hotly onto Ganah's hands. "I am already dead. I have been cast out of Pedrah's tent. He has taken another in my place." Her face contorted in fury as she spit on the floor. "That is what I care for him. Tonight I drugged his drink before he went to sleep. I did the same to the guards. No one will bother you as you leave."

The Tumulac grabbed his club, slung it over his shoulder, and tucked his knife into his belt.

"Thank you," said Ganah as she squeezed the woman's hands. "Yah-Adon has answered my prayer through you. May He be with you and keep you safe."

The woman's eyes softened, and she held Ganah's hands in her own. "I would like to know this God of yours."

"If that is your desire," replied Ganah, "then you will." The Ulah-rah placed her weathered arms around the woman's shoulders and held her. "Now," she whispered, stepping back, "leave before someone finds you here."

Without a word, the woman melted into the darkness.

Quietly, two figures slipped into the night, picking their way carefully over the sleeping guards sprawled in front of the tent and away from the sleep-filled dwellings. When they reached the edge of camp, they hurried to the wooden pen. It was empty, the collar cut and lying on the hard ground.

Eliah whirled as a pebble landed at his feet. The cry of a night bird trilled. “Hurry,” Ganah whispered. “It came from over there.”

They bent low and, being careful not to make a sound, made their way to a stand of low bushes, little more than a black mass in the darkness. There Noah, Jirad, and Malek waited, crouched in the shadows.

“Be quiet until we are far away,” whispered Jirad.

As one, they vanished onto the vast, spreading plains.

Thirty-Four

They fled, stopping only long enough to rest. Their goal—to distance themselves from the Shulem, for they had no desire to face Pedrah's wrath.

Many days passed before they ceased glancing over their shoulders and surveying the terrain for signs of pursuers. At last, the possibility that they had escaped their captors rested more comfortably in their souls.

Once their paths crossed that of a merchant's caravan as it made its way over the plains. Dust-covered traders with long, sturdy matushas prodded and yelled commands at nearly fifty camels swaying under heavy burdens. Ganah insisted they travel in the safety of the caravan for several days. They must make certain, she said, that Utriel was not being concealed among the huge vats strapped to the camels' sides, or hidden within the curtained litters or bound with the captive humanity soon to be sold in slave markets to the highest bidders. When satisfied that the girl was not there, they slipped away under cover of night, for they did not trust the swarthy old caravan leader even though his boisterous voice and toothy smile assured them of his good nature.

Discouragement once again slithered into the minds and hearts of the group. Even Ganah began to question herself, wondering if she had, after all, mistaken Yah-Adon's voice and heard only what she wanted to hear.

The Ulah-rah opened her eyes to a crystalline landscape sparkling in the early dawn. Light from the morning orb danced with glistening hues off each tiny droplet. She sat up looking around her, ran her fingers through her tangled hair, and pulled back the strands. Shortly after beginning the journey she had given up her accustomed elaborate braiding. Now she simply bound her long hair with dark, leather strips.

The mouth-watering aroma of dark-yellow yams, gathered earlier by Malek and now roasting in the fire, filled the grove. She watched him as he poked the skins with a long stick.

"They smell wonderful."

He grinned and began raking the roasted tubers from the coals.

While the yams cooled, the hungry band broke open bulbous, ruby-red fruit picked from nearby trees. The thick, pulpy flesh was sweet and succulent.

When they had eaten their fill, Ganah tossed the tough end of a yam over her shoulder. The rapid rustling in the leaves signaled its successful acquisition by a small, four-footed creature. "Well," she chuckled, "at least I've made someone happy this morning."

She rose and brushed her hands together. "I think it is time that we go into the hill country."

The men looked at each other, then stared at the ground. Jirad scratched his chin and cleared his throat. Hesitating, Noah asked, "Do you really think Utriel would dared to have gone there?"

The old woman sighed. "If I told you yes, I would be telling an untruth. Just let me say I do not know. But something strong urges me to go in that direction."

Jirad let his head fall backward against the tree behind him. "It will be a hard and dangerous journey," he warned.

Ganah's eyes fastened on the tree-covered mountains still cloaked in the heavy gray mist of early morning. "If we are to find Utriel, we must climb the hills. And," she said as if reading their thoughts, "I must go with you. It is a task I have been given by Yah-Adon. He will give me the strength that I need."

"Ganah," said Jirad, "I know you love Utriel as if she were your daughter, but these last few months have been difficult for you. They have stolen your strength. You have done more than anyone could expect. Let Eliah take you back to Gibara-boni, and we will go on into the hills. There is no need for you to make such a journey."

"Enough," she said sharply. "We will not speak of this again. I will not be a burden. Eliah will be by my side should I need help."

The Tumulac moved closer to his mistress.

"All right," said Noah, realizing the uselessness of further discussion. "Then we start for the hill country."

The wanderers tied their cloaks securely about their waists since they would not be needed again until the sun began its evening fall from the sky. The morning brilliance would soon warm the air and burn off the early morning dew.

Noah fingered his knife as his eyes scanned the foothills. "Ur-gatas can blend easily into the mountainside," he said. "I have heard that travelers seldom venture into these mountains unless heavily armed and many in number. Even traders crossing the plains avoid them." He stepped closer to Jirad, letting the others go ahead. "It will take several days to reach the foothills. I fear it will be another fruitless journey."

Jirad glanced at him, but said nothing.

"I feel hollow inside, and the ache in my heart is more than I can bear," Noah said. "I fear I will never see Utriel again."

"She is alive." Jirad' voice was deep with emotion. "I am sure of it."

Noah halted and swung Jirad to face him. "How do you know—" The words died on his lips at the conviction in the young man's eyes.

"I just know."

He gripped Jirad's arm and nodded.

The plain was changing. The tall, waving grass gave way to thistles, thorn bushes, and dense brush with thickets of trees. The pace of the travelers was now slow and labored. Once again the Tumulac went before the others in an attempt to slash a path with only his huge bulk and the aid of his blade. The five spoke little, each conserving his strength for the climb before them.

Later in the morning Jirad paused by a branch of lethal thorns while he disentangled them from the edge of his cloak. He had swapped one of the traders some newly skinned hides for the garment and a spear, and he desired to keep it in one piece. He was engrossed with extricating himself from the brambles when a chilling scream rent the air, prickling the skin on the back of his neck. He wheeled about, his spear raised in his hand. With the other he ripped the cloak from the thorns. Although he felt more than saw movement, he braced himself. With a loud crack, his weapon shattered in his hands, staggering him backward, the force of the blow nearly knocking him to the ground.

He dropped the splintered shaft and faced his attacker. "Great Yah-Adon!" he gasped. Was it animal or man?

Before him crouched a creature seen only in the twilight of nightmares, a creature standing upright like a man but with the head of a beast, a creature nearly twice his size and covered with thick, gray fur. Its hands wielded a club made from the trunk and roots of a young tree, the natural root system sharpened to lethal spikes. It crouched low, its head moving from side to side like a giant predator readying itself to strike. Slowly, it raised the club high above its demon head.

Jirad tensed for the death blow.

Suddenly, air and blood exploded from the monster's mouth as its body arched violently backward. A growl rumbled in its throat. It reeled about, clutching at its back. With a grunt, it stumbled, falling to its knees, then crashed to the ground at Jirad's feet. Protruding from the middle of its back rose Noah's spear.

Jirad swallowed against the dryness in his throat and put out his hand to steady himself against a tree. He drew in great gulps of air.

Noah smashed through the brush, the others close behind. "When I realized you weren't with us," he gasped, "I came back to find you."

He stopped, staring at the monstrosity on the ground. He shoved one fur-covered leg with the toe of his foot. "What is it?" he breathed, bending closer to stare at the lethal, yellowed teeth bared in the narrow black snout.

"Nephilim," rasped Malek, his voice harsh with loathing.

"Nephilim?" repeated Noah.

Malek grabbed its head and yanked. "Look!" he said as it came off in his hand. "Not real, only wolf skin."

"Why—it's a youth," cried Ganah, kneeling beside it.

The body of a young man, but of such a prodigious size they had never before seen, lay on the ground in an expanding pool of crimson. Blood trickled from the corners of his gaping mouth, matting the light brown hair covering his huge head. Swathed about the young man's loins were wolf skins. Thick hides enveloped his legs and feet, a full pelt draping his arms and chest and down his back.

Malek grabbed the body. "Help," he ordered as he struggled to pull off the fur covering. When he had uncovered one of the giant's arms, he pointed. "Look."

On its shoulder was a dark red stain, the size of a man's thumbnail. Ganah pursed her lips and traced her finger lightly over the mark. "Like a coiled snake ready to strike," she mused.

"Mark of Abaddon," said Malek. "Nephilim bear mark of Master."

"I don't understand," Noah said.

"Nephilim born of servants of darkness and human women."

"Giants," said Noah, understanding awakening in his eyes. "Are these the giants described by the traders from the caravan?" A look of horror twisted his face. "Is this what is growing within Utriel?" With a cry, he threw back his head and, grabbing his hair in his hands, screamed, "No-o-o-o!"

"Hold him!" yelled Ganah. Eliah wrapped his arms around Noah. Screams burst from his throat—screams of anguish and torment. Jirad helped Eliah pin him to the ground and hold him until the wrath and horror were spent from his shuddering body. Then gently, as a mother comforting her child, Jirad cradled his friend in his arms, rocking back and forth as tears ran down both of their faces. Jirad looked up toward Ganah for help, but her head was bowed, and her lips moved silently.

With the approach of evening, Malek circled the camp to gather dry wood for the night. He kept a discrete distance between himself and the area where the giant had been killed, glancing over his shoulder and starting at every rustle. If there were more Nephilim about, he did not want to stumble across one in the dark.

The night seemed to close about him. Images of his life in the cave flashed through his mind. He refused to dwell on such thoughts for terror lurked on the fringes of those memories. He jumped at a sudden rustling in the leaves and cursed himself for being so foolish. There, he heard it again—not only a rustling but also a high-pitched, muffled cry.

He turned to flee the area but stopped. Cocking his head, he listened. It did not seem threatening, more like a small animal caught in the brush. The fading light made it almost impossible to see more than a few feet. He let the gathered wood fall to the ground and moved in the direction of the noise, his knife in his hand. Something dark hung from the branch of a tree. As he drew nearer, he could make out a bag, some kind of skin. He searched the shadows, then lifted the bag from the limb and held it close to his eyes.

It was a large, vented deerskin pouch. He shook it. Something moved inside. Dropping the pouch, he jumped back, crouching in the pale light, his knife poised. Wild, dark eyes peered at him from the brush at the base of the tree.

"Don't hurt me!" whimpered a voice.

"Come out!" yelled Malek.

The eyes drew back within the foliage, and the whimper rose to a loud moan.

Alert to danger, Malek parted the branches with the tip of his blade. Nearly hidden in the shadows crouched a man, his hands tied to the base of the tree. At the sight of Malek, he scuttled backward, an obscene, high-pitched mewing emitting from his throat.

"Malek not hurt you."

The man recoiled, peering through dirty, matted hair that covered sharp, gaunt features.

"Not hurt you," repeated Malek, lowering the knife in his hand.

"Stay away!" the man screeched, cowering and shielding his head with his arms.

"Not hurt you. See," said Malek, motioning with his gnarled hand toward the leather thongs, "cut loose." Being careful not to frighten the man further, Malek sawed through the thick rawhide.

The terrified man inched backward, oblivious of his bleeding wrists, raw from the bindings.

"Come," said Malek. He turned and motioned for him to follow. "Take to friends. Friends help." He picked up the pouch and headed toward camp.

The man stood, hunched in the rapidly falling darkness, his hands drawn to his chest, his eyes darting furtively over the grove. As Malek disappeared among the trees, the man whimpered and skittered after him.

Noah lay on the ground, his breathing ragged, his arm flung over his eyes. Jirad sat beside him with bowed head, his arms resting on his knees. He glanced up at Malek's return.

"Find bag . . . and man," said Malek.

"A man?"

"Come," called Malek as he peered into the shadows. "Come—friends."

As the others waited, a dirty, emaciated figure, naked except for a tattered cloth wound about its loins, staggered into the light of the fire.

Jirad leaped to his feet, staring open-mouthed at the pitiful being before him. "Gitel?" he whispered.

Frenzied, red-rimmed eyes stared back. "No," the creature muttered as recognition penetrated his consciousness. He swung his head frantically from side to side. "No. Don't hurt me. I didn't mean to—" He beat his fists against his forehead. Foamy spittle drooled from his mouth.

"Where did you come from?"

Gitel's eyes flicked over the group. Then, with an unearthly screech, he ran from the light, wailing, "No! No!" as he fled into the night.

"Let him go." Ganah sighed as she grabbed Jirad's arm. "He made his choice long ago. Now he must live with the devils tormenting him."

"But he's my father's son," said Jirad.

"He is also an evil man," the Ulah-rah said. "You can't save him from himself. He must work out his own salvation."

She patted his arm. "Come. Let's see what is in the bag." She picked up the wriggling bundle and severed the tie with her knife. She pulled back the edge and peered inside. "A hawk!" she cried.

Inside the pouch, straining against tight leather thongs binding its wings and legs, a hawk hissed at the sudden assault of light.

Ganah lifted it from the bag, keeping her fingers away from the lethal beak.

"Look," said Malek. "On bird's leg."

"Let me see that." Noah leaned close to get a better view. "Hold its head," he ordered, pulling out his knife.

"Use mine," said Ganah. "It's not as large."

With great care he cut the leather bracelet bound around the hawk's leg. Then, unwinding it, he held it to the light. "It's Utriel's!" he exclaimed.

"How do you know?"

"I gave it to her. I bought the stone from a merchant."

Jirad took the bracelet and turned it over in his hand. "How did it come to be on the hawk?"

A smile was on Ganah's lips. "This must be Piava. That means the girl is nearby, for only she could have placed it around the bird's leg." She took the hawk from Jirad. "It will lead us to her," she whispered. "Piava knows where she is."

"A hawk will lead us to my sister?" scoffed Jirad.

"Yah-Adon has placed this bird in our hands," said Ganah. "It is not an accident that we have found it. And if that be true—it can find Utriel. Here," she said to Noah, "cover my arm."

He wrapped the leather bag around her forearm. She held it to the hawk. It hesitated, shifting from one foot to the other. Again Ganah offered her arm. The bird blinked its eyes and stepped onto it. The old woman stroked its breast with gentle fingers and whispered, "Piava, by the power of Yah-Adon I command you to fly straight to Utriel. Stray not to the left nor to the right. Do not stop until you reach her side."

"Now," she said to Jirad, "cut the bands binding its wings."

When the last strip fell away, the bird stretched its wings, lifted them, caught an air current, and flew through the purple sky toward the dark, brooding mountains.

Thirty-Five

"We should sleep here for the night," suggested Jirad, "and wait for the morning light."

Rugged foothills rose before them, rapidly giving way to the rough, forested mountains. A blast of wind swept down from the heights, moaning through the trees like a demented spirit searching the land for an end to its wanderings.

"Yes," agreed Ganah, rubbing her arms against the sudden chill. "It would be foolish to venture any farther now."

They spread their cloaks in an area sheltered by overhanging trees and huge boulders that had sometime in the past eroded from the towering cliffs. Afraid to build a fire lest it be seen by the Ur-gatas, they ate fruit and berries, then rolled themselves in their cloaks and fell into a restless sleep, each one dreaming his own particular nightmare.

Shortly before dawn, Noah snapped to consciousness as excruciating pain shot through his body. He clutched his chest, sucking air into his tortured lungs. Another vicious blow struck his ribs. He rolled, trying vainly to scramble to his feet. A foot caught the side of his head. Bone cracked, and a flash of light pierced his head. He fell back to the ground, blood streaming from a gash over his eye.

"Be sure the big one is tied tightly," a gruff voice ordered. "We don't want him giving us any trouble."

Noah blinked, trying to clear his vision. He wiped his upper arm across his eye. He could make out the shapes of six men. Ur-gatas. His stomach knotted.

He could see Ganah on the ground clutching her side. Jirad appeared to be unconscious, his hands trussed behind him. Two dark shapes worked feverishly with rope on the Tumulac. But Malek was not among them. "Praise Yah-Adon," muttered Noah. Then his own hands were pulled sharply behind his back. He grimaced as rope bit into his flesh.

A short, stocky man swaggered forward. "Take them back to camp. We'll decide what to do with them later."

"Kill them here and be done with it."

"I said, take them to camp."

Noah twisted to see the speaker, but he was yanked roughly to his feet.

The captives were herded up a trail invisible to their eyes. As the slopes steepened dangerously, they stumbled, struggling to keep their footing. Without the use of their hands, they were soon covered with bruises and cuts from frequent falls accompanied by savage kicks and blows.

Uttering loud curses, the leader grabbed Ganah as if she were a child and flung her across the back of a dark brown ass. A groan escaped her lips as the sharp backbone cut into her stomach.

"Malek," prayed Noah under his breath, "wherever you are, may Yah-Adon protect you."

The bandits forced their captives through a narrow, twisting passageway that cut sharply upward between sheer cliffs. Loose pebbles slipped precariously under their feet. Eliah walked behind the animal bearing Ganah. Pain twisted his face. Fresh blood dripped from Jirad's nose, his lower lip swollen and split.

A peach-hued tint had already colored the sky when the party emerged onto a broad, rugged plateau nearly hidden within rocky walls. Before them spread an array of squalid tents.

Several women, pausing sullenly to watch the procession as it entered the camp, continued building fires in earthen ovens. Others peered from behind tent flaps as the prisoners were herded to the center of the camp.

The stocky leader stopped in front of a large tent. "Put the prisoners in the pen," he shouted to a scraggly bearded young man. "Right now I will eat." He threw back the flap of the tent and disappeared inside.

Dirty, unkempt children gathered like flies around the captives, gazing at them, some even touching them with grimy hands. The Urgatas prodded the prisoners across the compound before shoving them inside a crude but sturdy corral made from saplings bound together. Once inside, the younger bandit cut the captives' ropes. With the release of the bindings, burning pain coursed through their chafed and bloodied arms.

Still rubbing his wrists, the Tumulac knelt beside his mistress. He gently examined her for injuries.

Although sore and bruised from the kicks and the jarring ride across the back of the donkey, Ganah patted his arm, trying to assure him. "I am grateful to be on solid ground once more," she breathed, managing a quick, tight smile as she leaned against the side of the pen and held her side. "I believe, though," she added through clenched lips, "that something is broken inside."

Noah sank to the hard ground, his back against the stout posts. His body ached and his mind was tired, but there was nothing to do now except wait.

Thirty-Six

Tubila burst into the tent. "Unah, come quickly! See what Hazial has brought back!" She grabbed Utriel's hands, dragging her toward the doorway.

"Stop." Utriel planted her feet firmly on the hard-packed dirt floor and pulled her hand from the girl's. "I have no intention of running to see what that barbarian has stolen from a trader or some luckless traveler."

"No." Tubila shook her head. "It's not what he's stolen. He has prisoners. Hurry and see!"

Utriel's smile faded. "What will he do with them?"

"He's put them in the animal pen."

"How many are there?"

"Four! And one is a woman!"

Utriel's lips tensed and her jaw tightened. "He will kill them, won't he?"

The girl cocked her head and squinted one eye.

Revulsion welled up inside Utriel like bile. "We must try to help them."

"No!" cried Tubila, clutching her friend's arm. "He'll kill you if you interfere. He's been waiting for such a chance."

"What? Kill the 'witch woman'?"

"Yes. Even the witch woman."

"He wouldn't dare."

"He would. He is a crazy man!"

Utriel started for the entrance. "You forget," she scoffed, "he's afraid of me. He thinks I have great power."

"Don't go!" screamed Tubila. "He worships demons. He'll call forth

Asmodeus!" The girl flinched and clapped her hand over her mouth.

Utriel's body stiffened. Her breath caught in her throat. Slowly she turned, her eyes narrowing. "What do you know about Asmodeus?"

"Nothing!" cried Tubila, cowering into herself, her face twisted in fear. "Hazial said he'd kill me if I told you about him."

Utriel grabbed the side of the entrance to steady herself, all the terror of that hideous night flooding over her once more. She clutched Tubila's shoulders. "Tell me what you know," she demanded.

The girl began to cry, her thin, stunted body trembling under Utriel's strong hands. "I can't," she cried. "He'll kill me."

Utriel dropped to the floor, pulling Tubila down beside her. She put her arms around the deformed little creature and drew her close. "It's all right," she murmured. "He'll not find out. Now, tell me what you know."

Tubila's terror-filled eyes searched Utriel's face. "The men—" she sniffled—"the men worship Asmodeus. They offer sacrifices to him."

"What kind?"

She lifted her fingers to her mouth. "Their children! They give him their firstborn children."

Horror filled Utriel's eyes. "They give him their babies? Their own children?"

Tubila wiped her face with the backs of her hand. "Yes. They burn them on the Table of the Gods."

Utriel swallowed hard. "Where is that?"

"Farther up the mountain." The girl bowed her head and rubbed her hands on her skirt. "But there is more." She looked over her shoulder before lowering her voice. "They let him have their women."

"They sacrifice their women?"

Tubila lifted fear-clouded eyes. "No. The men let him come to their wives in the night."

"I don't understand," said Utriel.

"Asmodeus lies with them." Tubila ran the heel of her hand under her nose and sniffed loudly. "Haven't you seen how old and tired they look? It's because of him," she whimpered, "of Asmodeus. He drains the life from them."

"Why?" asked Utriel. "Why would their husbands allow such an evil?"

Tubila scratched in the dirt with her fingernail. "In return, he gives the men health and a long life. They are never sick. And—" she lowered her voice—"I have never seen one of them die—except for Dotan, who tasted the power surrounding you."

Utriel was silent for a moment, considering her next words before she opened her mouth. "Listen to me carefully. I must tell you something that I should have told you before."

In the subdued light of the tent, she told Tubila about Asmodeus finding Jirad wounded by the lioness, about Obed making him his blood brother, concluding with the night in the forest, and her fleeing Gibara-boni. She left out nothing. Neither did she try to protect herself or make excuses for her actions. With painful honesty and tears flowing beneath long, dark lashes, she bared her soul.

When she had finished, they sat quietly, neither daring to look at the other. Finally Tubila rose to her knees and wrapped her arms around the one before her. "I love you, Unah. I'll always be your friend."

Utriel rested her tear-stained cheek against the girl's coarse hair. Suddenly, she gasped, clutching her abdomen, her beautiful face contorting in pain as the child within lurched violently. With a groan, she struggled to her feet. "I must never allow this—this thing to be brought into the world. How could I unleash such an abomination upon my people."

"What will you do?"

Utriel ran her tongue over her full, lower lip. "An unborn child cannot live once the mother is dead," she said, holding herself rigid.

"No! You must not do such a thing! You are my friend. I cannot lose you now."

"What else can I do? Each day my stomach grows larger. Soon the baby will come." She shuffled to the entrance of the tent. ""Tubila," she said, wheeling to face her. "I am afraid of the child I carry."

"Why are you so certain that it will be evil?"

Beads of perspiration dotted Utriel's forehead and upper lip. "What else could it be when its father is absolute corruption. Don't you understand?" she cried, pushing her hair back from her face. "He's using me to bring more evil upon my people."

Tubila's eyes filled with tears.

"Asmodeus has destroyed my life," cried Utriel. "I loved Noah, but now I can never be his. Instead, I have brought dishonor to my name." She clutched the top of the entrance and leaned her head against her arm. "Why, Asmodeus," she cried. "Why, you spawn of Abaddon, why did you choose me?" A sob caught in her throat and shook her shoulders.

Tubila laid her head against Utriel's back. She turned and the two young women held each other —one afraid of the past and the other of the future.

The Tumulac sat on the dirt floor of the enclosure trying vainly to shield Ganah from the glare of the sun. Jirad lay with one arm across his eyes. A wiry man with dark, greasy hair stood guard outside the pen, a spear clutched in his hand.

"Bring us water before we die from thirst," called Noah.

"We have better plans for you than dying of thirst," sneered the man. He swaggered to a large jug, dipped a hollowed gourd into the water and sauntered back. "Here."

When Noah reached for the gourd, the man slowly emptied its contents onto the ground.

Noah watched the rivulets of water spider over the hard-packed dirt and vanish into the dry earth.

The bandit laughed, tossed the dipper into the jug, and ambled back to his post.

Noah squatted beside Jirad. "I'm sorry, friend." He sighed. "We may not leave this place alive." When Jirad did not respond, Noah leaned against the roughly hewn posts. He closed his eyes and tried to forget the pain in his head and his burning thirst.

Tubila placed the jug on her narrow shoulder and climbed the path leading to a spring where cold water trickled from the side of the mountain as if the rocks themselves contained the precious life-sustaining fluid.

She longed to flee the village. She hated Hazial, and she hated what he did. One day she and Utriel would leave. They would start a new life for themselves and forget that the squalid village ever existed. "We don't need men," she mumbled to herself. "I'll take care of Utriel."

Tall firs, some with thick, waxy foliage and spreading ferns shaded the shallow pool. Mottled lizards basked contentedly in the sun on the surrounding rocks. Tubila poked a stick at a tiny salamander wriggling beneath a mossy rock. She grabbed its tail, then laughed as the tiny amphibian squirmed through her fingers.

Suddenly, she froze. Two faces stared at her from the pool. She had learned to ignore her reflection over the years, but now, above hers was another like her own. Were the spirits of the hills playing jokes on her? She squinted her eyes and dipped her fingers into the water, stirring the surface. When the ripples disappeared, the images remained.

She turned, scrunching her head between her shoulders. With a scream, she fell backward into the pool, knocking over the water jar. Behind her, gripping a large, carved staff, stood a frightful, misshapen man.

"D-don't scream," he stammered. "Malek not hurt you."

She scooted backward, splashing in the water like a wounded animal.

The man held out his hand, gesturing for her to take it.

She shook her head. He did not act as if he meant to harm her, but never had she seen anyone like him.

Again he gestured.

She pushed back the hair that had fallen over her eyes and studied him. He seemed to be smiling, although the action only contorted his face.

"Come," he said, still holding out his hand.

She lifted hers, hesitated for a moment, then placed it in his dirty, callused one.

"Good," he said as he pulled her from the pool and set her dripping on the grass. "Now, Malek get jar."

"Who—who are you?" she stammered.

"Malek frighten you?"

"No! Of course not! You just—surprised me."

"Malek ugly," he said, averting his head.

She laughed, a silvery, melodic sound. "I thought I was seeing two of me in the pool."

At her laughter, he raised his head. "Not afraid?" he queried.

"Not unless I'm afraid of myself," she said as she wrung out the skirt of her dress. "Who are you?"

"Malek. And you?"

"I am Tubila. My name means—ugly one."

A groan rumbled in his throat. "Bad to be ugly."

"Yes," said Tubila, shrugging, "but my friend says even if I am ugly on the outside, I can be beautiful on the inside. My friend is very wise," she added.

"Tubila live in mountains?" asked Malek.

"Yes. Are you lost? I can show you the way to the plains."

He scanned the area, looking nervously over his shoulder. "Urgatas take friends prisoner. Malek follow."

"I live with the bandits, but they are not my people," said the girl. "My father sold me to the chief of the village. Now, though, I live with Unah. She says that one day we'll both leave here, and we'll never come back. She says we'll live alone where no one can hurt us again."

"Hill people come in night. Malek go make water in bush. When men come, Malek hide in trees. Follow here."

"Then your friends are Hazial's prisoners?" She shook her head. "He is a wicked man. He will kill them."

"Malek must help them. . ." He groaned. "Friends!"

Tubila touched his arm. "Friends are not easy for us to find, are they?"

"No," he said, strangely stirred by the tenderness in the girl's face.

She wrapped her small fingers around his rough hand. "Come," she said. "I'll help you. But you must hide until dark."

She led the lumbering man to a deep indentation in the side of the hill nearly concealed by bushes. "Stay here," she said. "When it is dark, I'll bring my friend to you." Then she hurried back to the village.

Tubila ran cautiously between the tents to the animal pen where the prisoners were being kept. She wanted to see Malek's friends, but she did not want to be seen by Hazial or his men.

"Tie their hands and feet!" ordered Hazial. "And watch the big one!"

Eliah crouched low, his arms holding Ganah as he tried to shield her with his body from the thrusting spearheads.

"Get the dumb one!"

"Put out his eyes!"

Blood streamed down Eliah's arms and back.

"Enough!" shouted Hazial. "We want them alive. What good are dead sacrifices? Only if they're alive will their blood bring blessings from the gods of the hills." He scratched his bare stomach. "We'll put them on the tree," he said.

"Why not burn them at the Table?"

"No. We'll hang them in the tree so that all the gods can feast on them."

"What tree can hold that mountain of flesh?" jeered one of the men.

"We're wasting time," hollered Hazial. "Take the old woman from the mute and tie them up like the others."

The men hesitated.

"Are you afraid of the man mountain?" shouted Hazial. "Are you—women?"

The men grumbled loudly as they tried to get near Eliah while staying out of his reach.

The Tumulac's arm still encircled Ganah as he dodged the spears. He was surprisingly agile for his size.

"Eliah," cried Ganah, "let me go! If you don't, they'll kill you!" She struggled to free herself from his massive arm. "Please," she begged, "let me go!"

Blood pounded in his ears, blurring everything into a meaningless jumble. He held her tightly. Never would he allow them to harm her.

"Eliah," pleaded Ganah, as she writhed in his arms, "you can't save me. Let me go before it's too late."

"Kill him, now!" ordered Hazial. "I'm tired of this. Kill him and get the old woman. You've had enough sport. The gods will have to be satisfied with three offerings instead of four."

The men shouted, relief in their voices that they did not have to take him alive. They swung open the end of the pen and edged inside. One hefted his heavy spear in his hands, marking his sight. Once sure, he threw, sinking the weapon deep into Eliah's back.

The Tumulac stiffened. Ganah slid from his arms. Anger flashing in his eyes, he turned, a trickle of blood seeping from the corner of his mouth. He crossed one arm over his shoulder and grasped the shaft of the spear. He grimaced, then ripped it from his back. Before the bandits could react, he drew back his arm and threw with deadly accuracy, driving the spearhead through the body of the nearest man.

The force of the blow drove the man backward, slamming into the two behind, knocking them to the ground. They pushed the body aside and scrambled to their feet. Armed with clubs and knives, they crouched low, closing in upon Eliah.

With lightning speed the Tumulac lunged forward, his hand encircling the wrist of the closest man. He yanked him forward, grabbed him with both hands, and lifted the screaming man above his head. Then, raising his knee, he smashed him across it, snapping his back with a frightening crack.

"Get him!" roared Hazial.

Eliah dropped the body to the ground and bent low, bracing his mammoth legs for the assault.

"Eliah!" screamed Ganah. "Behind you!"

Before the big man could turn, Hazial rushed forward and with one vicious swing drove his axe deep into the Tumulac's skull.

Eliah opened his mouth as though to speak at last. Instead, blood gushed from his still silent lips. In one final moment of awareness he faced his mistress, then crumpled to the ground.

"No," moaned Ganah, running toward him. She threw herself beside the bloody figure. As tears flowed down her withered cheeks, she ran her hand lovingly over his. "Thank you, my friend," she whispered. "I'll never forget you, never."

"Get her out of there," roared Hazial.

The men dragged her from the lifeless body, threw her to the ground, and bound her hands and feet.

"What shall we do with the dead one?"

Hazial pressed shut one nostril and blew, clearing the other onto the ground. "Take him away from the camp and leave him for the animals."

The men grabbed the body by its legs and began dragging it across the ground.

Tubila shrank back behind a tent. She did not want to be seen by Hazial. It was dangerous to be around when he had drawn blood. She shivered, turned, and hurried to Utriel's tent.

The gods of the hills were ancient spirits, dark servants of the Destroyer. They had entered the land when their master, clothed in a dark mist, first crept into the world to deceive and to corrupt the hearts of the Old Ones. The dark gods had reached out with their tentacles of evil, luring and enslaving all who would listen to their seductive whispers. At first they spun their webs of deceit with caution, covering one area of the land with their darkness and then another. Now, they boldly assaulted all that stood before them.

For centuries they had huddled in the darkness of the underworld, coming to the surface of Yah-Adon's creation to work their wiles and then retreat to the safety of their shadowy abode. Like dark, monstrous moles they had worked a labyrinth of passageways and entrances from their underworld to that of man. From these orifices their malevolence spewed forth, infecting and transforming all it touched.

Recently, a sense of urgency had quickened Abaddon. He knew of Yah-Adon's plan, but the frustration of not being able to understand its scope drove the dark lord into a maniacal frenzy. He was certain of one thing—that the plan involved the bloodline and seed of man. But what man? In desperation he sent forth emissaries in all directions to take human form and to beguile and seduce mortal women in order to corrupt man's seed. With great care, he had narrowed the search to a town called Gibara-boni, and to one man—Noah.

Yet, Abaddon was perplexed. Who was this Noah? The Destroyer could see nothing outstanding about him, yet it was obvious that he was a source of great interest to Yah-Adon. A malevolent glee had filled Abaddon as he commanded Asmodeus, his next in command, to disrupt the enemy's strategy even before it could begin. If Yah-Adon intended to use Noah's progeny to bring forth the Deliverer, then Noah must not be allowed to join himself with the woman he loved.

How simple it had all been. Abaddon still found immense delight in corrupting the frail creatures that were the objects of his enemy's love. And now, even Noah was to be destroyed. Surely, this act would bring Yah-Adon's plan to an end. Abaddon's laughter echoed through the subterranean corridors.

Staring death in the face did nothing to quell Ganah's pain, a deep, gnawing ache that ripped at her entrails. She groaned as the rope pulling her high into the tree cut into her wrists. Surely it would not take long for the weight of her body to separate her arms from her shoulders. She was trussed to a strong limb jutting far over a high ledge. Bile rose in her throat as she swung over the void beneath.

She closed her eyes while first Noah and then Jirad were hauled upward until their bodies swayed beside hers. Already a heavy weight pressed upon her chest. With her arms pulled high above her head, it would become harder and harder to breathe until slowly and inevitably she would suffocate.

How could she have been so wrong? She was sure they would find Utriel, and when they did, they would also find a way to stop the evil corrupting the land. Yah-Adon had sent her on the quest and had promised to help her. Maybe she was, after all, a stupid old woman who had outlived her time. Never had she foreseen that it would end like this.

"You should feel honored!" yelled Hazial. "For now you will be a feast for our gods." The village men lifted their hands high into the air and screamed to the spirits, summoning them to their banquet.

"Soon," Hazial jeered, "the gods will send their birds to gouge out your eyes. When that is done, they will come themselves to dine on your bodies until only white bones are left. Come!" he yelled to his men. "We'll leave them to the gods!"

Amid shouting and laughter, the men started back to the village, leaving the three figures swinging over a vast emptiness.

Tubila slipped quietly through the doorway of their tent. Tears had dried, leaving dirty streaks on her cheeks. She sat down, pulling her knees up to her chin as she watched Utriel trying to force a bodkin through several layers of cloth.

"What happened?" asked Utriel, laying down the bone needle.

"Unah, why are the gods so cruel?"

"What do you mean?"

"Why do they kill us? Do they hate us so?"

Utriel pondered the question for a moment before answering. "There is only one God, Tubila. I have told you about Him, and He does not hate us."

"Then why did He allow Hazial's men to kill the big one? And they've taken the others to the Table of the Gods. Will your God eat the prisoners for His feast as the men say?"

"No! Yah-Adon is awesome and fierce, but He does not eat men."

"Yes He does." The girl sobbed. "They have taken the prisoners to the Table of the Gods. No one comes back from there alive. Only bones are left when the gods are through. I've seen the remains. I know it's true."

"Those spirits are not like Yah-Adon," said Utriel, putting her arm around Tubila. "They are not gods. They serve Abaddon, as Asmodeus does. Ganah told me they are only evil and cruel things not worthy of worship. They are to be hated and despised."

"Unah, if Yah-Adon is so great, then why is He allowing you to bear Asmodeus' child? Why did He let such a terrible thing happen?"

Utriel paused, unconsciously placing her hand on her stomach. "I've wondered that myself, but I believe it happened because I preferred the golden beauty of Asmodeus to following Yah-Adon."

"Do you hate Yah-Adon for not stopping him?"

"At first I did—until I realized that I had wanted to be with Asmodeus. He was so handsome." Utriel stared at her hands as if seeing them for the first time. "You may not understand this—I loved Noah, but I desired to be with Asmodeus. And—I knew it was wrong. Yah-Adon could have stopped me, but secretly I didn't want Him to. No," she said, "I don't hate Yah-Adon, but—" her voice lowered and her eyes darkened—"I hate Asmodeus with all of my being."

"I have something to show you as soon as the sun goes down," said Tubila as she chewed a mouthful of food.

Utriel bit into a dark yellow chunk of cheese. "What did you find this time?"

"I—I met someone like me today."

"Like you? What do you mean?"

"When I went to the spring to fill the water jar, I met a man who's ugly like me."

"Don't speak of yourself like that! To me you are beautiful."

"But I *am* ugly. Everyone says so. It doesn't matter anymore though, since you've become my friend."

Utriel reached for a thick slice of fruit. "Who is he?"

"His name is Malek. I hid him until I could bring you to him." She lowered her voice even more. "The prisoners are his friends. I thought you could help him."

"Help him!" exclaimed Utriel, her voice rising. "How can I help him? You were the one who said Hazial would kill us."

"Please talk to him," Tubila pleaded. "I told him I would bring you."

Utriel shook her head.

"Please," cried the girl, "just let me take you to where he is hidden."

"All right," she said, with a shrug. "But there is nothing I can do. His friends were doomed the moment they were captured."

"As soon as it's dark," said Tubila, "I'll take you to him."

Tubila led Utriel through the thick brush and up the mountainside. Neither spoke as they slipped from the village. When they reached a large clump of bushes, the girl whispered into the darkness, "Malek. It's Tubila. I have brought my friend."

In the pale radiance of the moonlight, the bushes parted and a figure emerged. The shadows cast by the evening light enhanced the distortion of the twisted body and fierce visage.

Utriel's body stiffened at the sight.

"It's all right," said Tubila. "I told you he is like me. This is Malek."

The man lowered his head, turning as if to shield them from its offensiveness.

"Forgive me," said Utriel, ashamed of her reaction.

The man remained silent, but she thought she saw a slight nod.

"Malek must tell you about his friends," said Tubila, "but we must speak softly. It would be dangerous to be found."

Still averting his head, Malek began. "Friends attacked by Ur-gatas. Malek not taken, but friends brought to mountain. Malek follow." He paused, lifting his head until his eyes met hers. "Not tell on Malek?"

"Don't be afraid," Utriel said. "I'm also a captive of Hazial."

Malek's face twisted in thought as he studied her. Even in the darkness it was evident she was with child.

The intensity of his gaze made her want to cover herself, to run, to hide. Instead she tightened her jaw and pushed the urge from her mind. "What was your party doing in the foothills?" she asked. "It's dangerous to travel in this part of the country."

"Friends look for woman," he replied. "Sister. Look for many months—in forest, across plains, in villages. Old woman say Placer of Stars guide. Old woman say search mountains. Make camp in foothills. Wait till morning. Ur-gatas find."

An engulfing wave of fear struck Utriel's heart with such force she had to fight for breath. "Who," she ventured, "are your companions?"

"Old woman, Ganah. Three men, Eliah, Noah, and—" he smiled—"good friend—Jirad."

"Dear Yah-Adon! What have I done?" gasped Utriel, her knees buckling beneath her as the awful truth crashed in upon her. She would have fallen if Malek had not reached to catch her.

Suddenly she stiffened. "We must save them!" she cried. "Hazial means to kill them! We must hurry!"

"We may already be too late," warned Tubila. "They've been taken to the Table." The girl looked around, her eyes wide with fear. "And it's nightfall. What if the gods have already come for their feast?"

"No!" cried Utriel, clutching the girl's shoulders. "It can't be! Can you lead us there in the dark?"

"I don't know," Tubila hesitated. "It's very high and dangerous."

"You must," urged Utriel.

"I can try," said Tubila, near tears. "We must hurry."

The mountain peaks towered above the trees, dark masses of craggy stone jutting skyward. Noises of the night, muted and distant, drifted upward from the plains. The path was steep and difficult as Tubila had said. Sharp rocks scraped their feet and legs, and wispy pockets of mist drifted from the heights. Huge boulders rose out of the descending haze, spectral sentinels guarding the way. The three stayed close together, bumping into one another in the darkness.

Utriel's thoughts wandered. She found herself envisioning her life as it had been in Gibara-boni before that fateful night. It frightened her at the difficulty she was having discerning if what she remembered was real or only as she desired it to be. She had fled, believing that with her removal those left behind would be saved from becoming part of her horror and disgrace, but had she achieved only what might be the destruction of the very ones she had sought most to save?

The air on the mountain was thin, and although Utriel had adjusted to it over the months, she found herself becoming light-headed and her breathing labored. The unborn infant pressed upward beneath her lungs. Several times she was forced to pause for breath.

When she feared she could go no farther, Tubila whispered, "It's just ahead." Malek grabbed her arm to steady her. A prickle of fear touched the nape of her neck.

"Where is Table of Gods?" asked Malek.

"Somewhere ahead," said Tubila, her voice hollow and weak. "I've followed the men before, but I've never been this far. If Hazial knew I followed them, he would have killed me."

"Stay here," ordered Malek.

The two women crouched in the darkness, half expecting the fury of ancient, disturbed spirits to sweep down upon them.

"Something evil is here," whispered Utriel. "I can feel it."

Tubila clutched her hand.

Yah-Adon, begged Utriel silently, *let us not be too late.*

The thick fog fell in silent swirls and eddies as it descended like a capacious shroud shifting over the face of the mountain. She could see Malek inching forward, the clinging moisture threatening to obscure the ground. As she watched, the murkiness closed behind him. She listened, straining to hear anything that could mean her loved ones were alive. The only sound was the heavy breathing of the young woman hunched beside her. They waited in the stillness. Nothing moved. They were alone and adrift in a vast, gray void.

"No-o-o!" A cry broke the silence, a scream from some Caliban of old, erupting from a soul filled with anguish and hatred, "No-o-o-o! Friends!"

Ignoring the dangers, Utriel ran toward the swelling cry, dragging Tubila behind her. Enveloped once more in the gray stillness, she stopped and listened.

Then, she heard a deep, wracking sob.

A gust of wind whipped across her face. She peered into the grayness. It parted as if pulled aside by an unseen hand. She was standing on a bare rock formation, a shelf that overhung the side of the mountain. Below, the ledge fell away to nothingness. The stark outline of a large and twisted tree stood before her. A cry of horror escaped her mouth. Three bodies, like monstrous cocoons, swung, twisting from its branches.

Her hands flew to her mouth. "Are they alive?" she asked, her voice barely a whisper.

Malek shook his head.

"We've got to get them down!" she cried, looking around wildly. "We need a knife."

Malek spread his hands, his chest heaving. "Ur-gatas take weapons."

"I have one," said Tubila. "I stole it from Hazial many moons ago to kill him if he touched me again. I keep it hidden beneath my tunic." She handed the small but deadly blade to Malek.

"How can we reach them?" asked Utriel. "They're too far from the ledge."

"Malek climb tree and pull up from limb. Limb strong enough to hold them—limb strong enough to hold Malek."

A sob caught in Utriel's throat. She wanted to scream, but she was needed. She must not give in to her terror.

Malek reached up, grabbed a branch, and pulled himself into the tree. With his strong, sinewy arms, he swung to the long limb from which the bodies were suspended.

Although the mist threatened to obscure her vision, Utriel could see him inching his way, hand over hand, across the limb. He swung his body forward until his wiry, bowed legs encircled the first figure. With one powerful arm he cut the rope. Still clasping the body between his legs, he worked his way back to the trunk, short grunts escaping his clenched lips. He pulled himself into a fork of the tree and grabbed the body with his arms before lowering it to the ledge.

Utriel and Tubila helped lay the burden on the rocky surface. Malek lifted his head to Utriel, tears streaming down his marred countenance. "Friend," he sobbed as he cut the crude bonds from the bleeding wrists.

A whimper escaped Utriel's mouth. She stretched forth her hand, but quickly withdrew it. Jirad!

Malek laid his ear to the man's chest. "Jirad alive!" he cried, rubbing the cold arms and chest of the unconscious man.

Utriel's lips parted as if searching for speech. She couldn't breathe, and her eyes filled with tears. She threw her arms around her twin's body. "Don't leave me," she cried. "Please don't leave me. I should be lying here, not you."

"Malek," urged Tubila, "get the others down. I'll help Utriel."

He reluctantly rose to pull himself again into the tree.

Utriel lowered her head once more and touched her lips to her brother's. "I love you," she whispered. She laid her cheek against his. "Please, open your eyes."

A groan escaped Jirad's mouth. He coughed, then drew great gulps of air into his chest.

"Help me sit him up!" Utriel cried to Tubila.

Together, trying not to hurt him, they propped him against a large rock.

"Need help," called Malek, who was struggling to lower Noah's body to the ground.

Utriel's jaw tightened and her mouth hardened into a grim line as she and Tubila helped stretch the unconscious form on the ground while Malek cut the rope binding the man's hands and feet. Before returning to the tree, he threw the ropes to the side, blood now glistening darkly on his own lacerated hands.

Utriel turned back to Jirad.

"I'm all right," her brother said, his voice thick and raspy. "Tend to the others. I just need to work my arms and legs."

She lifted Noah's arms and pulled them down beside his body. A groan escaped his lips, and his eyes fluttered. "He's alive," she said.

She leaned close to his face. "Noah, can you hear me?" His eyes opened, and his parched lips moved.

"They need water," said Utriel.

"We have none here," answered Tubila. "We'll have to get down from the mountain quickly. The only spring is the one near the village, and that is too dangerous. If Hazial finds us, death will be a blessing."

"Help!" called Malek. The two women hurried to the tree. He grimaced in pain as he handed down Ganah's body.

Even in the pale light, Utriel could see the gray, waxiness of the aged countenance. The rope had cut deep into the old woman's wrists, and blood had crusted over the rough fibers. Ganah moaned as Tubila severed the rope from her hands.

Malek rubbed Noah's hands and arms. "Noah. Open eyes."

"We've got to leave here now," warned Tubila. "We must get off the mountain before the sun rises."

"Ganah will not be able to walk," said Utriel. "I fear she is near death." She turned to Malek. "Can he walk?" she asked.

Malek shrugged as he continued massaging the man's legs.

"Noah, you must try to move!" she urged. "Please, you must try!"

Noah lifted his arms. A deep cry escaped his lips.

"Keep trying," pleaded Utriel.

"Help," said Malek. "Make Noah stand."

"I can't," he gasped.

"Yes," said Malek, "or all die."

Malek and Utriel put Noah's arms over their shoulders, and, wrapping their own about his waist, pulled him to his feet. He clenched his teeth as blood flowed through his lifeless legs, bringing with it excruciating pain. He tried to stand, but his knees buckled. He would have fallen except for Malek. Once again he put weight on his feet. He winced in agony, but took a step.

"What about Jirad?"

"Just take care of yourself, old man," volunteered Jirad as he pulled himself to his feet, using the rock behind him as leverage. "I'll make it."

Noah twisted his lips in the semblance of a smile. "So will I," he countered.

"Are you sure?" asked Utriel.

He nodded.

She let go of his arm and knelt beside the prophetess. She rubbed the icy fingers. Again, tears welled in her eyes. "You were the mother to me I never had," she murmured. "It's my turn to take care of you now, sweet friend."

Ganah's eyes were closed, and her breath rattled in her chest. "You'll have to carry her," Utriel said to Malek. "Tubila and I will help the others."

Malek gathered the waxen figure in his arms, holding her as he would a child. The Ulah-rah moaned loudly. "Hurry," he said. "Leave mountain before sun come up." He mumbled something, then stepped into the gray mist. The others followed, grateful now for the concealing veil swirling around them.

Thirty-Seven

"She's gone!"

The spearhead Hazial was sharpening fell to the ground. "What do you mean?"

"The witch woman's gone! My wife took cheese to her tent this afternoon, and she's gone." The man fidgeted in fear before the chief. "The ugly one has gone with her."

"Do you realize what this means?" Hazial yelled, anger tinged with fear flared in his dark eyes. He gnawed his lower lip. "He will come soon to demand his sacrifice. What will we do if the woman has escaped?"

"Teza and I checked the lower side of the mountain," whined the informant. "We found nothing."

"Then they're still on the mountain," said Hazial, one side of his mouth curling. "We may still have a chance to find her and her unborn brat." He picked up the spearhead from the dirt, wiped it against his arm and studied it for a moment. "Find four men and meet me at the spring. Now get out of here before I ram this through your heart."

The man backed quickly through the opening of the tent, turned, and broke into a run.

"I have something for you," said a timid voice at Hazial's shoulder. One of his wives handed him a clay cup filled with a sour-smelling amber liquid. "I made it myself."

"I am surrounded by imbeciles!" shouted the man, knocking the cup from her hand. The contents splashed over her face and arm. "If we do not find the woman," he roared, "we will all be destroyed!"

The tent was smaller than the others and older, but it had once been elaborately painted with designs long since faded and now cracked and peeling from the many moves of the tribe. An enormous pile of skins and furs seemed to be thrown carelessly against one side of the tent.

"Wake up, old man!" shouted Hazial as he stepped inside. "I must talk to you."

Two beady dark eyes peered from an ancient face barely discernible among the equally ancient skins. Thin, matted white hair framed sharp, vulturelike features, and a shrill cackle acknowledged the chieftain's presence.

"Sit up," ordered Hazial, "and act like the shaman you are supposed to be."

"Oh-h-h-h," wheezed the old man. "You want Eldobi's help now, do you?" He coughed, spraying sputum in all directions. It ran from the corners of his mouth and dribbled down his beard. "So the satyr is coming for his payment, and you don't have it. Is that it?" He laughed, choking and coughing until his face turned purple and tears ran from his eyes.

"Shut up!" shouted Hazial. "If we do not give Asmodeus the sacrifice he demands, he will destroy all of us, including you, you worthless excuse for a seer."

Eldobi cackled shrilly and pulled himself to a sitting position. "It will be worth it, just to see my prophecy come true. I warned you centuries ago against serving him. Not even prolonged life is worth yielding yourself to that spawn of darkness." He coughed loudly and ran his hand over his drooling mouth. "You have given him your firstborn children," he rasped, "and you have allowed him to ravage your women. My own daughters died by his hands, drained of life until nothing was left, and I was powerless to help."

The old man's face contorted. "What have you gotten in return? Years added to your life? But what kind of life is it when you must run and hide so others will not know what our men have done. So they will not know that you have sold yourselves to Asmodeus, that you worship the dark god Abaddon, that—"

"Silence!" screamed Hazial. "The woman is gone, and with her the child needed for our sacrifice."

"What do you expect me to do?" protested the old man.

"You are a seer," said Hazial. "Tell me where to find her. The night of the full moon is nearly upon us, and Asmodeus will soon be here."

The old man snickered.

"I allowed her to remain in the camp free from harm," continued Hazial, "because she was carrying a child. I even gave her the deformed slave to care for her."

Eldobi shook his head. "You could not have harmed her even if you had tried," he said. "Something protects her. You have already experienced its power."

"She could be killed in her sleep and the child ripped from her belly."

Again Eldobi laughed. "Is that so!" he sneered. "Now you'll never know."

Hazial's face contorted in fury. "I should know better than to come to you. You are worse than useless. You want to see me destroyed."

"Yes," the old shaman hissed. "Your desire to defeat death has destroyed my people. Because of you we are forced to live in the mountains, preying upon any who come near the foothills."

"You fool," said Hazial. "You and I grew up together. You had your chance to remain young. Instead, you refused to bow down to Asmodeus. Now, look at you! You're old and ready for the dung heap."

"Yes," said Eldobi, "but at least I did not sell my soul to the demons of darkness."

"Then I'll send you to them myself," shouted Hazial, his eyes wild with fury. Drawing back his arm, he hurled his spear, piercing Eldobi's chest and pinning the body to the ground.

The old man's eyes opened wide, and his hands gripped the shaft of the spear. His mouth broadened in a toothless grin before his head fell to one side as blood ran from his gaping mouth.

Hazial placed one foot on the old shaman's shoulder and yanked the spear from his chest.

Thirty-Eight

The first rays of dawn spread over the rugged hill country, burning away the heavy fog. Pockets of remaining mist swirled about their legs as the band fled downward, grim-faced but determined. Passage was slow and arduous, their progress impeded by a series of steep and dangerous defiles and cliffs. With the rising of the sun, the group was now vulnerable to the sharp eyes of Hazial's men who would be scouring the mountainsides for them.

Malek, visibly agitated, halted to wait for the others.

"What is it?" asked Utriel. Damp tendrils of hair ringed her flushed face. Her breathing was strong and heavy, and pain radiated across her lower back and down her legs from the additional weight of the child she carried.

"Sun out. Hide till nightfall," he urged. "Need water."

Jirad was walking by himself, but Noah still leaned upon Utriel and Tubila, his arms over their shoulders. In spite of the coolness of the morning, his body was bathed in a sheen of sweat.

"You're right," Utriel said. "They can't keep going without it." Her jaw set rigidly, its squareness emphasizing her own distress despite her efforts to conceal it. Her face was pale and a hint of shadow lay under her eyes, like faint smudges of ash. "Tubila," she asked, having to pause between words to catch her breath, "where can we hide until dark?"

"I know of a place," ventured the girl as she adjusted Noah's arm on her shoulder, "but it is forbidden. I don't want to go there." She shifted from one foot to the other. "I—I'm afraid," she stammered.

"Must go," grunted Malek." Or Ur-gatas find." He shifted Ganah's weight higher on his arm.

Tubila's eyes widened. She hunched her crooked shoulders, her gaze searching around her. "If I take you there, will Yah-Adon protect us?"

Utriel shook her head. "I don't know, but if we stay here, Hazial will find us, and then we will all die."

The girl's brow furrowed over her dark eyes.

"Tubila, we must hurry!"

"All right," she said, her voice rising. "I'll take you there." She sighed, spread her hands and turned toward the western side of the mountain. "Follow me," she said wearily.

Utriel tightened Noah's arm over her shoulder. His skin was clammy to her touch, although color was slowly returning to his face, and his steps were becoming steadier.

Malek followed close behind, carrying Ganah.

"Help me, Yah-Adon," whispered the old woman through clenched teeth as her labored breathing rasped ominously in the early morning air. "My task is not complete. Keep me alive to see it through to the end."

"Ganah," urged Utriel, shifting her grip on Noah's arm, "don't give up. We'll make it." She longed to gather the old prophetess in her arms and bury her face in the gray hair. *Please,* she found herself praying, *don't die.*

The Ulah-rah's parched lips twisted as she grimaced in pain.

"We're almost there," called Tubila, pointing ahead. "The cave is just beyond that precipice."

Utriel's heart sank as her eyes traveled to the top of the sheer wall of rock before her. "We can't climb that."

"We don't have to. There's an opening through it." The girl ran ahead, pushing through the tangle of thorns and brush at the base of the wall. 'See," she said excitedly.

"See what?" asked Utriel, wondering if Tubila was hallucinating from loss of sleep.

"Come closer," urged the girl.

As Utriel stepped forward, a narrow crevice, large enough for a man to slip through, appeared. She blinked and stepped back. When she did, the opening vanished.

"See!" said Tubila. "It plays tricks with your eyes. "Hazial said the gods of the hills made this pass so no one could find it." She dashed through the opening and waved for the others to follow.

Malek pulled Ganah close to his chest to shield her head before he turned sideways and edged between the cleft, wincing as the rough surface scraped against his back.

"There's the cave," said Tubila, her voice quickly falling to a whisper. "The people call it Shugama, the Door of Death."

The entrance yawned before them like a dark, ravenous mouth. Utriel let Noah's arm fall from her shoulder. She took several steps toward the cave, then paused and looked around. Hanging from bushes and rocks were amulets and fetishes fashioned by the hill people and placed there to keep evil spirits from passing beyond the portal and entering their world.

"Malek know this cave!" cried the man.

Utriel jumped at his voice.

"Bad place!" he said, shaking his head. "Evil place!"

"We have no choice," murmured Jirad, although every part of him rebelled at the thought of entering the shadow-filled depths.

"No! Bad place! Malek not go in."

"It's our only chance for survival," said Utriel.

"She's right," agreed Noah. "We've got to find a place to hide and to rest. We can leave as soon as it's dark."

Utriel stepped into the cool, fetid air. She paused, letting her eyes adjust to the lack of light, before walking into the shadows. Her foot, striking something hard, slipped sideways. Strewn over the floor of the cave were the bones of what she hoped had been animals, some yellowed with age, others with bits of flesh still clinging to them. She shivered and fought to keep her imagination in check as she picked her way over the scattered remains.

"Malek not like this," he said, shaking his head. Still mumbling to himself, he found a cleared space and knelt to rest Ganah against the side of the cave.

Noah sank to the floor, letting his head fall forward onto his knees. Jirad leaned wearily against the cool rocks.

Malek headed toward the rear of the cave. "Water in back. Malek fill waterskin."

"Wait," called Tubila. "I'll come with you."

He held out his hand before disappearing into the deepening shadows.

Utriel placed her hands on the small of her back and stretched. The pain was steadily increasing. She crossed to Jirad and wrapped her arms around his waist, resting her head against his. "I never thought I'd see you again."

Gently, he held her close. "We're twins. We're part of each other. Surely you knew I'd find you. Besides," he said, "look at the help I had."

She stepped back and wiped her eyes. Her wide mouth flashed a smile, almost forgotten over the last months.

She looked at Noah, who sat with his eyes closed, rubbing and working his arms and hands. She eased herself clumsily to the floor beside him. If only she could make him understand, but it seemed an impossibility. How could she explain when her own mind was consumed with shame and guilt. What was there to say?

She leaned her head against the wall. "I'm sorry," she murmured. "I'd give my life if I could change what has happened." Again, tears ran down her already tear-stained cheeks.

Without warning, her face blanched and a spasm shook her swollen body. She felt a hot flow down the insides of her legs. "No-o-o-o!" she cried. "Not now, not here!"

"What is it?" Noah asked, scrambling to his knees.

Utriel turned fear-filled eyes toward him. She clutched her stomach. "The baby! It's coming!"

The sun was nearly mid-sky when the infant emerged into its new surroundings. Although early, it was an unusually large baby. The mother lay exhausted, her thick, dark hair hanging in wet strands around her neck and her tunic drenched in perspiration and stained with blood.

Tubila finished cleaning the crying baby with water Malek had brought from the pool. She wrapped it securely in a strip of cloth ripped from the bottom of her own garment. She cradled the little creature, crooning until its crying ceased. Then she laid the swaddled bundle in Utriel's arms.

"I don't want to see it," she said, averting her head. "Take it away."

"Unah," pleaded Tubila, "just look at it. It's a beautiful boy."

"No," she cried, pushing it from her.

Tubila rocked back on her heels. "What do you want me to do? Shall I throw him from the ledge? Or feed him to the wild animals?" Exasperated, she placed the infant once again at Utriel's breast. "Just look at him," she begged, holding Utriel's face between her hands. "Look at him, and then I'll do whatever you want. I promise."

"Don't do this to me," she begged.

"I promise," repeated Tubila.

Utriel choked back a sob and swallowed hard. Against her will, she turned her head toward the infant sleepily nuzzling at her breast.

Light, golden hair covered his head. Tiny, slender fingers opened and closed as his pink mouth searched for nourishment. She ran her forefinger over the soft, ruddy cheek. His seeking mouth tried to grasp her finger. She bent her head and smelled his skin, so new and so fresh. She placed her nipple into the infant's searching mouth. He rooted hungrily, then with wee squeaking noises began his first meal.

Utriel let her head fall back against the rough, cool wall and closed her eyes. "All right, Asmodeus," she murmured, "you have won this battle, but I'll fight you for this child until there is no breath left in my body."

"How is Utriel?" asked Ganah, her voice weak but steady.

"She's fine," answered Tubila. "She's asleep."

"Good." A tired smile formed on the old woman's lips. "That is good." She lifted her hand and motioned for Tubila to draw nearer. "What of the infant?"

"A strong, healthy boy."

"Has she taken it to her breast?"

"Yes," said Tubila, one eye looking askew.

"May Yah-Adon have mercy on her," whispered the old prophetess so low that Tubila was unsure of her response. Lost in thought, Ganah chewed on the inside of her lower lip. She raised her eyes. "I must see Malek," she said, her voice like dry wheat on the threshing floor. "Please get him for me."

Tubila rose to her feet and hurried to the back of the cave, where the three men sat by a shallow pool.

"Malek, Ganah wants you."

The man dipped his hand in the water and ran it over his face. He rose awkwardly and headed toward the front of the cave. Noah and Jirad followed, sore and stiff but functioning once again. They had washed the dried blood from their bodies, and although their injuries were painful, none were life threatening.

Malek walked to Ganah's side and waited. Sensing his presence, she opened her eyes. "Come close," she murmured, gesturing for him to sit. "I must talk with you, and my voice is not strong." She gazed into the distorted face for several minutes as if weighing her words. Finally she asked, "Have you been in this cave before? Tell me truthfully. I must know."

Without answering, Malek put his head in his hands.

"Please, tell me. Our lives may depend on what you say."

He remained silent for many minutes. When he lifted his head, his eyes had become flat and expressionless. "Cave another entrance to world of dead. Must leave soon. If Abaddon come—all die."

"Are you sure this cave is an entrance?" pressed Ganah. "Could you be mistaken?"

"No. Once Malek leave torches and flint in rocks by pool. Still there."

The old prophetess pursed her lips, her gaze fixed on the dark countenance before her. "Can you take me into the depths of the underworld?" she asked.

"Why? Evil spirits kill us."

"You don't understand," sighed the Ulah-rah. "I've gotten this far. I'm so close. I can feel it." She closed her eyes, the lids covering them almost transparent. Her thin fingers picked absently at her torn and stained garment. "If only I had the El-cumah with me," she murmured.

Malek shifted on his heels and scratched at his beard. "Staff here—in cave," he mumbled.

"What?" breathed Ganah, her eyes opening. "How? I thought the hill people took everything."

"Malek find staff in bushes. Too dark. Ur-gatas not see."

Ganah quivered with excitement and swallowed to hold back the tears. "Bring it to me."

He rose, returning a moment later with the staff in his hands. He laid the dark, polished wood across her chest.

Ganah pulled it close. "Ah-h-h, what strength it gives," she murmured. She held out her hand to Malek. "Help me sit up."

He pulled her gently into a sitting position.

"Thank you, friend. Now," she said, "I must be alone for a while."

Ganah closed her eyes. "Yah-Adon, take me to the end of my quest. I am not in Shugama by accident. It must be part of Your plan. My body is dying and my strength has almost gone, but if You'll put Your hand upon me once more, I vow to complete my task."

Her lips continued to move as she clutched the staff. Suddenly her fingers jerked as light flared around the El-cumah and enveloped her hands. The dark wood glowed, growing brighter as light flowed into her arms. Her mouth opened in a soundless scream. She convulsed, her back arching violently as white, translucent flames loosing their unearthly powers ringed her body.

Tubila screamed, leaping to her feet. She backed against the hard rock of the cave, never taking her eyes from the blazing light.

Noah and Malek stood transfixed by the flames until they vanished, as if absorbed into the Ulah-rah's flesh. The staff fell from her hands and rolled onto the floor of the cave.

"What happened?" cried Noah, rushing to her side.

"I'm—I'm all right," she gasped. She rubbed her forehead, her chest heaving with each breath. "I'm all right," she repeated, her eyes no longer dim but glistening with excitement. She looked at first one hand, then the other. "Hand me the staff."

Tubila hesitated. She touched the El-cumah with one finger, then jumped back. Trembling with fear, she reached for it again. When nothing happened, she picked it up, handing it at arm's length to Ganah. She stared at the prophetess. "Look!" she cried.

"Your hair!" Noah said, his voice hushed in awe. "It's white. White as the wool of lambs. And your face glows with an unearthly fire."

"It is Yah-Adon," said Ganah. "He has touched me with His Spirit to allow me to finish my task."

With fingers once again strong, she pushed back her disheveled hair, then turned toward Malek. "You must take me into the depths of the cave—now! Before the fire leaves my body."

"You'll go nowhere without me," interrupted Jirad.

"Nor me," added Noah. "I've come this far, and I've no intention of quitting now."

"Yes," she said, turning toward Noah. "That is as it should be, for you are part of this. Then she shifted her gaze to Jirad. "But you must remain here and guard the women and the child."

"No!" shouted Utriel as she struggled to her feet, swaying slightly with the child clutched to her breast. "This is my fight also! I will not be left behind!"

"You're not strong enough yet," said Noah, reaching for her arm.

Angrily, she pushed his hand aside. "I will be fine." Rancor sparked green fire in her eyes and defiance squared her chin. "My hatred will sustain me."

"You cannot take the child," interrupted Tubila. "Stay here."

"It goes with me. Asmodeus will not harm his own seed."

Jirad moved to her side. "Then I will go with my sister."

Ganah rose, steadying herself with the staff. She closed her eyes and tilted her head as if listening. Finally, she opened her eyes and walked to Utriel's side. "Tubila, bind the infant securely to her chest with the cloth it is wrapped in. Jirad," she said, turning her gaze to the young man, "you are strong and able and would be of great help to us, but Yah-Adon has another plan for you. Stay with Tubila and guard the mouth of the cave. Haziel's men may return. We do not want the enemy at our backs as well as before us. If we are not back by the fifth rising of the sun, the two of you leave the mountain and return to Gibara-boni. Do not come for us. There will be nothing you can do."

"I don't want to leave Utriel," stammered Tubila.

"I pray you will not have to," said Ganah as she grasped her hand.

"Oh!" cried Tubila. A white spark leaped from one hand to the other.

Ganah jerked back her hand. "I'm sorry! Yah-Adon's power is upon me."

Tubila rubbed her fingers against her leg.

Noah's brow knotted. He held out his arms to Utriel and lifted the sleeping infant, holding it before him. Without waking him, he pulled back the cloth from its tiny shoulders and studied the soft skin. Then he placed the child back in his mother's arms.

"Why did you do that?" asked Utriel, puzzlement in her eyes.

Noah said nothing, but his lips tightened. How could he tell her of the tiny red mark on the infant's shoulder?

Ganah grasped the staff in her hand. "Hurry! Wrap the child. We must go. A great task lies ahead of us."

Malek led the way into the interior of the cave. The yellow glow of the pitch-coated torch penetrated the almost palpable darkness as they wound their way deep into the bowels of the earth. Ganah followed with Utriel and Noah a step or two behind as if each feared that to fall outside the sphere of light shed by the torch would mean to be forever lost in the blackness oozing like tar from every crevice of the passageways.

Soon, the party lost track of time, pausing occasionally to drink from the skin of water Malek carried at his side. Only the scraping of their leather sandals over the hard, rocky floor of the narrow passage or the skittering of something unseen in the darkness broke the silence.

Several times they stopped to rest. Although it was impossible to tell whether it was night or day in the outside world, their bodies still dictated their need for rest. They dreaded sitting on the hard-packed floors while they closed their eyes in fitful sleep, but they knew it was necessary. What lay ahead was unknown, and they must be ready. Utriel took these opportunities to nurse the child before binding him once again to her chest where he slept, nestled against her.

From time to time, they passed dark holes in the sides of the passageways, black openings that smelled of putrid flesh and secret horrors. Malek hurried them by the stench-filled maws, his finger pressed to his lips.

A gnawing hunger tore at their entrails, and their arms and legs grew more tired from lack of fresh air. Ganah leaned more heavily on the El-cumah as Malek forged ahead. Although each new corridor seemed identical to the one just traveled, he never paused or retraced his steps.

On what might have been the third day, a pale light pervaded the corridor. Malek found a crevice and hid his remaining torch. "Almost there," he said. He drew his cloak closer around his body although the air was growing warmer. Perspiration coated their skin. His steps were slower now.

Ganah put her hand on his arm as she walked beside him. "Have courage, my friend."

He twisted his head toward her, his eyes clouded with fear.

"We are not by ourselves in this battle," she continued. "The Placer of Stars would not send us to do something He did not equip us for."

"Malek not know Yah-Adon," he said, shaking his head. "Yah-Adon have great magic?"

The lines grew deeper on her face for a moment. "No," she said. "It is power and authority, not magic. He is God over all things—even over Abaddon and Asmodeus."

"Malek not understand."

Her face relaxed. "I pray that one day you shall."

Before Malek could respond, she turned to Noah, her hand on his arm. "I've watched you grow into the man that you are today," she said. "The hand of the Placer of Stars is upon you."

Her eyes moistened as she continued, "I've loved Utriel because I've seen so much of myself in her, and I wanted her to take my place one day. But I've loved you because Yah-Adon has marked you as His own. I don't know what He has called you to do, but be assured, He will reveal it."

Suddenly, her voice changed, shifting into the awesome tone of authority possessed only by the Ulah-rah. "Do not despair, my son. Remain strong and close to Yah-Adon, the Placer of Stars. Keep your mind and your spirit open to hear Him. Obey Him, and He will use you to save the world from a great catastrophe. No matter what happens here, remember what I have said."

As she spoke the last word, she faltered. She grasped the staff with both hands, her strength having drained from her body.

Noah reached to support her, but she waved aside his hand.

"Come," she said, her voice once again her own. "We must continue. There is no time to waste."

The light increased, washing the four with an unearthly glow. Once again Malek took the lead. Ganah leaned heavily on the staff, but she refused to rest. When Noah tried to take her arm, she shook off his hand. "I will finish this task with Yah-Adon's strength," she said.

Sound began replacing the cocoon of silence that had wrapped solidly about them for so long. At first it seemed only a wind sighing through the passageways. Gradually it increased, coalescing into low, moaning cries that blended into an unearthly chorus of sorrow and misery, not cries for help but cries emanating from unmitigated regret and pain so terrible that the four could feel their hearts growing heavy and tears welling in their eyes.

Something cold and rough scraped across Noah's foot. Claws clicked on stones from a small, dark shadow scuttling down the passageway.

Malek held out his hand, a signal to stop. He crouched low, pressing close to the wall. He edged down the corridor until he rounded a corner, disappearing from sight. The others waited, hardly daring to breathe.

In a few minutes he returned. When he emerged from the shadows cast by the unearthly light he seemed a dark creature come to life from stories told beside fires on long nights. Without a word he motioned for them to follow.

Exhaling slowly, they crept after him. As they rounded the bend in the passageway, they drew in their breaths sharply. The cave, rising high above their heads, opened into a vast cavern pulsing with light and reverberations. Even the walls seemed alive, a vast, living organism. Dirt, rocks and boulders mounded high before them as if gigantic hands had scooped out the interior of the cave and ringed the chamber with the rubble.

"Climb," said Malek, motioning upward.

"Can you do this?" Noah whispered to Ganah.

"Be still!" she rasped. "I will do whatever must be done. Soon it will be over." She turned to Malek. "Lead the way."

He glanced at Noah, then began pulling himself up the rise.

Utriel tucked the skirt of her tunic between her legs and fastened it at her waist. Ganah dug her hands and feet into the rocks, clawing and digging for holds. Noah did not touch the Ulah-rah but stayed close behind.

Utriel glanced at him, their eyes meeting for an instant. Even in the pale light bright patches of color glistened on her high cheekbones. She knew he desired to help her, but to give in meant weakness and that was unacceptable to her now.

"Not far," grunted Malek. A stone dislodged by his foot clattered down the side. Ganah ducked, pressing into the rocks as Noah swung aside, the missile bouncing off a boulder near his head.

"I'm caught!" gasped Ganah. "I can't move!"

Noah shifted his hands for a better hold and looked up. The torn and shredded hem of her tunic had looped tautly over a jagged tip of rock, securing her fast. He dug in his toes and stretched upward. His hand searched for a hold. He grunted loudly as one foot slipped beneath him. He pressed close against the rocks and lay still while he shifted his feet for a firmer hold. Once again, he reached toward the garment, stretching until he felt the cloth under his fingers. He yanked. The material ripped free, leaving a thin ribbon dangling loosely on the sharp edge of the rock.

Malek, already on the top and hunching low, grabbed Ganah's hand and pulled her upward. Noah and Utriel scrambled over the edge and crouched by the Ulah-rah.

They stared open-mouthed at what lay below.

"Dear God," muttered the old prophetess. "It is the doorway to Hell!"

Mammoth stalactites hung from the vaulted dome, some meeting their limestone counterparts midway in the air. Crystals glistened on the ceiling, their brilliant facets reflecting the subterranean glow to produce strange and ghastly shapes on the stony walls of the chamber. Water crashed from the jagged rocks above into a raging, white-foamed river on the floor below, then rushed violently along one side of the cavern where it disappeared with a roar among the rocks.

A blood-red, throbbing glow flared from an immense abyss gaping in the center of the cavern floor. The light and noise pressed in upon their senses. Jets of steam hissed upward through fissures in the floor, and the stench of sulfur filled the air. Creatures crawled in and out of the abyss while a cacophony of cries echoed from its depths, a roar of voices rising and falling like a raging ocean in the midst of a roiling tempest.

The four crouched lower among the rocks, the reddish hue flickering across their blanched faces. Without warning an arm emerged from the shadows, whipping around Noah's neck and arching him backward.

"Stand still," hissed a low, sibilant voice.

Ganah and Malek wheeled about with weapons raised. Utriel squeezed herself deeper into the shadows, praying fervently that the infant not cry out. She bit back the moan welling up in her throat. They had come so far. Surely, this was not to be the end. They must not die like this.

A creature stood before them, feet braced, one dark, scaly arm encircling Noah's neck while the other held the side of his head, ready to carry out its threat. Yellow, lidless eyes darted from one to the other.

Ganah gripped her staff, her body coiled to attack.

"Stand still," it ordered, "or I'll break this one's neck."

"Let him go," she shouted.

The dark figure tightened its hold and twisted Noah's head.

"Don't!" yelled Malek to Ganah. "Seti kill Noah."

Ganah heard the fear in Malek's voice and lowered her staff.

"Now," ordered Seti, wrenching his captive's neck even harder, "climb down." Pain flared in Noah's eyes.

Malek started over the other side of the mound. Ganah hesitated, searching the shadows for Utriel, then began easing herself down the treacherous descent. The creature followed, shoving Noah before it. Its rapid breath wheezed loudly, and a heavy, rotting odor emanated from its body. Loose rocks rolled precariously under their feet. Malek clutched Ganah's hand until they reached the chamber floor.

"That way," it yelled, forcing them toward the edge of the glowing abyss. Flames leaped toward the roof of the cavern and molten rock erupted high into the air. Ganah raised her hands to protect her face as glowing embers rained about them.

A wizened, doglike creature leaped over the edge of the fiery chasm and squatted before them on small, humanlike hands and feet. Bulbous, yellow eyes peered up at them. "Yes, Seti," it squealed obsequiously. "What do you want?"

"I have the ones we've been waiting for."

The messenger rocked on its haunches and cocked its broad, flat head to one side, staring at the humans. With a throaty gurgle, it bounded over the side and scurried down unseen steps until disappearing into the glowing depths.

Malek sighed and shook his head from side to side.

"Don't give up," Ganah whispered. "It is not yet over."

"Quiet," Seti ordered and ran its tongue over dry, gray lips. "We have been waiting for you."

The heat was becoming intense, burning their eyes and throats and stifling their breath.

Seti's arm tightened around Noah's neck. "Master!" he shouted. "I have the enemy!"

Ganah's hand tightened on the El-cumah.

"No," cried Malek, his fists clenched at his sides. "Not hurt friends."

Out of the churning midst rose a figure—handsome, majestic, glistening in the light, its golden hair burnished to a deep bronze by the red hue of the flames. Strong hands flanked each hip as the one they had known as Bel threw back its head and laughed, deep, cruel sounds that reverberated throughout the cavern.

The four clasped their hands over their ears and pressed hard, trying to shut out the noise piercing their skulls like searing blades.

"It took you long enough to get here," taunted the golden giant. "I was afraid that Hazial would deprive me of the pleasure of destroying you myself. "It glared at Malek. "And you, stupid servant, did you think you could escape my master? Is this the way you repay his kindness for taking you in and allowing you to serve him, you miserable, deformed bit of human garbage?"

Malek cringed from the malignant fury before him.

"When I am through with you," bellowed Asmodeus, "you will beg for death." He lifted his hand and pointed a forefinger at the frightened man. Black flames shot forth, arcing from the tip of his finger toward the object of his wrath. The force suspended Malek in the air, then hurled him across the chamber. With a groan he crashed against the far rocks and slid to the floor, where he lay in a motionless heap.

"I'll finish with you later, but now," sneered Asmodeus, turning to face Noah and the Ulah-rah, "I have a greater pleasure before me." He folded his arms across his broad chest. "Why are you here, old woman? Why did you not stay with your stones and your stories? You have outlived your time and your usefulness. No one listens to you any longer or believes in your God. Why not lie down and die? You would save me much trouble."

The Ulah-rah raised the staff, gripping it with both hands, and pointed it at the diabolic entity. With a voice of authority and power she spoke, "Where is your master? It is he I have come to face."

Flames spewed higher into the air, burning coals spraying in their wake.

"No," answered Asmodeus. "You are mine. It is not Abaddon you seek, for he has given me authority over this land. I am prince of this realm. I decide your fate, not him."

"So be it," said Ganah, her voice full of anger. "Then it is your time that has come." She shifted her feet farther apart, and the muscles tightened in her arms. "No longer will you pollute the earth with your evil."

Hatred flared from the demon's eyes. "You think you can fight me with that stick of wood? Foolish woman! Who are you to stand against me?" He threw back his head, golden hair flying wilding in the pulsing light. His lips pulled back, baring his teeth as he stretched forth his hand.

The El-cumah quivered, the rod vibrating violently in the Ulah-rah's hands. Her eyes widened in disbelief and horror as she struggled to hold the staff. Suddenly, the wood shattered, sending fragments in all directions.

Asmodeus shook with laughter. "Did you really think that stick could stop me?" he roared. "There is no power on this earth great enough to do that. Do you not know that your world belongs to my master? He owns it! It is his to do with as he pleases. He is the prince of this world—and we intend to destroy it! Nothing can stop us!" He paused and glared at the old woman, a cold, mirthless smile forming on his lips.

Ganah stared at her empty hands.

"Shall I further demonstrate my power for the great Ulah-rah?"

"No!" yelled Noah in spite of the fear gripping his spirit. "Leave her alone!"

"Silence!" growled Asmodeus, never taking his gaze from the old woman who stood defiantly before him. "Do you still think your God will help you?" he mocked, drawing back his lips like a predator before it attacks. "You are a fool." Stretching forth his huge arm, he pointed his forefinger toward her. “I tell your heart to cease beating.”

Ganah staggered, clutching her chest.

“You can’t do that!” yelled Noah.

The fiend whipped around, his maniacal gaze fixed upon the man.

An icy chill ran through Noah’s body. He could both hear and see, but it was impossible to move, as if his body had turned to stone. Unable to help her, he watched Ganah sink to her knees, all the while struggling to draw air into her straining lungs.

Asmodeus turned once again to the Ulah-rah. His eyes narrowed into dark slits. “Your heart is beating slower and slower,” he said. “Soon it will stop altogether.”

Ganah gasped for breath, her hands clutching at her throat, her face mirroring the excruciating pain that ripped through her chest and down her arm.

“Stop fighting me, old woman,” yelled Asmodeus. “It will only take you longer to die.” He turned to Noah, his lips once again curled in a mocking smile. “But you—you are the one we want.”

As if released from a trance at the sound of his name, movement and warmth instantly returned to Noah’s body. “What am I to you?” he cried. “I’m nothing but a farmer.”

“I am not sure,” growled the entity, stamping his foot on the rim of the abyss. The ground shook, sending rocks cascading into the chasm. Even Seti flinched uneasily.

“Our Enemy has conceived a plan,” he continued, “and you are at the center of it. I seduced Utriel because she was to be your wife, but still the plan goes on.” His hands clenched and unclenched, his head twitching as if in spasms. “Insignificant mortal, for some unknown reason you please Yah-Adon. He is determined that through you He will redeem His worthless creation from the death and destruction that we have brought upon it.”

Asmodeus shook with such rage that his massive body shifted and altered, his dark anger breaking the concentration necessary to sustain its human form.

Noah and Ganah recoiled as the monstrous arms and legs twisted and gnarled in the glowing light. The long, golden hair vanished from the magnificent head, leaving in its place a broad, hairless visage. Blue eyes melted into saffron orbs sunk deep within red-rimmed sockets. Thick, sensuous lips drew back revealing yellowed, wolflike fangs. Cloven hooves stamped against the rocky floor of the cavern as the devilish satyr flexed its hairy legs.

Seti cowered in terror, covering his face. "No, master," he screamed as the chimera before them bellowed in fury. The ground trembled and shook under their feet. Rocks shifted, some rolling dangerously toward the chasm. Again Seti shouted, "Master, stop."

The roaring ceased. Gradually the trembling ground quieted as Asmodeus paused, his chest heaving in intense fury. Looking down at the quaking minion before him, he swung one huge taloned hand, tumbling the screaming creature into the flaming abyss. The devilish image shook its head, foaming saliva flying from the obscene lips.

"A-a-a-r-r-g-g-h," he roared as his eyes once again focused on Noah. "You," Asmodeus thundered, "you must die, and our enemy's plan will be ended. I will tear you apart. First a finger, then an ear. . . ."

"Asmodeus!" shouted Utriel.

The hellish visage jerked upward as he whirled toward the voice .

His power over Ganah momentarily broken, the prophetess gasped, drawing precious air into her chest. She pushed herself to her knees and shook her head in a frantic effort to clear her vision.

"Utriel, get back!" yelled Noah.

She had removed the baby from the cloth binding it to her chest and was holding the naked infant before her, his tiny hands and feet flailing the air as he loudly protested the disruption of his snug abode.

Asmodeus stepped forward, then shook his shoulders as if unsure what to do.

"I have your son," cried Utriel, lifting the child into the air, anger and rage flaring in her eyes.

The demon's gaze narrowed. "It's you, my lovely. I had not thought to see you so soon."

Utriel was breathing heavily, the pungent scent of fear emanating from her body, but driven by a strength born of revenge and self-castigation.

"You have lost," she yelled, "you spawn of darkness. You will never use this child for your evil will. You may have seduced me and defiled my body, but neither I nor my son will be pawns for you to use as you please."

"And what will you do?" he sneered, his eyes dark, crimson pools.

"Let my friends go, or I will fling myself and the child into the flames. You have already destroyed my life. I have nothing to lose." In the reddish glow the tears on her face appeared as great drops of blood.

A thought flashed through her mind, causing a stab of fear to pierce her heart: What if the death of the child meant nothing to the creature? And could she truly die for her friends? She felt Noah's presence beside her, and from the corner of her eye she saw Ganah struggling to her feet. A peace descended upon her, washing the rage from her body. She trembled, but she knew beyond a doubt that she could do what she had threatened.

As if reading her thoughts, Asmodeus snarled, his face a mask of rage. "You will die! All of you! But the child is mine to sire a dynasty of adversaries against Yah-Adon. No one will be able to stand against them. As swiftly as a lightning bolt, his gnarled hand snatched the infant from Utriel's grasp. His other arm drew back, whipping across her face and spilling her onto the hard rocks.

She grunted with the force of the blow. Blood ran from her nose and down her chin, dripping onto her chest in great, dark spots.

"Utriel!" cried Noah, falling to his knees beside her and holding her in his arms.

She leaned against him, her head reeling from the impact. Despair rose within her, mixed with bitterness and humiliation. She had failed. All was lost.

Asmodeus threw back his head in laughter as he grasped the child in his hand.

A quick movement caught the corner of Utriel's eye. She was conscious of Ganah crouching low. Before she could react, the Ulah-rah sprang forward like an arrow launched from a bow. With supernatural strength, she struck the monster at its knees, her arms encircling its legs. Knocked off balance by the unexpected force of her attack, he staggered backward, still clutching the infant.

He hung, suspended in space, his arms flailing desperately. Then, slowly, he toppled, plunging into the yawning abyss.

"No!" screamed Utriel, lunging for the crying child still grasped in the hands of the abomination.

Noah grabbed for her, his hands closing on the fabric of her tunic. He twisted sideways, pulling her toward him. With a crash they tumbled to the floor.

Screams of demonic fury shook the cavern and echoed through the passageways.

Utriel's body shook as she buried her face into Noah's chest.

Silence filled the chamber. Almost imperceptibly, the floor of the cavern shuddered beneath them.

Utriel lifted her head and eased herself away from Noah, her senses alarmed by the sudden tremor. The blood had stopped flowing from her nose, but a dark line had risen across its bridge. She pushed herself to her feet, ignoring the pain that throbbed in her body.

A deep rumble shook the ground.

A hand grabbed Noah's shoulder. He whirled about, fist in the air. Malek's battered face stared back at him, blood caked on the side of his head, matting his dark, heavy beard.

Once again the ground trembled and rocks showered from the ceiling of the vast cavern.

"Hurry," Malek shouted above a roar that was rising and swelling in intensity. "Get to tunnel!"

Flames erupted from the deep abyss; coal and sulfurous fumes belched loudly into the air. Rocks and flaming coals rained about them as the ground heaved and groaned.

"Run!" yelled Noah, shoving Utriel before him.

She looked back at the fiery pit, uncertain what to do.

"Run!" Noah shouted again, grabbing her wrist and dragging her toward the rocks.

With each tremor the floor of the cave heaved more violently than before, as if the rock had become fluid. Cracks split the cavern floor, spewing steam upward through yawning fissures. A rock the size of a man's head struck Malek's shoulder. He yelled, stumbled and fell, clutching his arm.

"Go ahead!" screamed Noah, trying to be heard above the din.

Utriel, crouching at his elbow, ran, her long, slender legs dodging the falling rocks and steaming fissures.

Noah wrapped his arm around Malek's waist and dragged him toward the steep slope. The man struggled to get his feet back under himself. Boulders crashed around them, the rocks sliding and buckling beneath their feet.

Ignoring the pain in her body and soul, Utriel jammed her fingers and toes between the rocks and heaved herself up the shifting side of the mound.

With Noah behind her and urging Malek before him, they clawed their way to the top. "Slide!" he yelled.

Utriel clenched her eyes and let go, letting her body drop down the far side of the mound. She groaned as the sharp edges of the rocks dug deeply into her flesh.

In a cloud of dust and rock, the three tumbled onto the hard ground at the base of the encircling mound. Gasping for breath, they lay for a moment, then painfully scrambled to their feet and stumbled up the passageway with Malek still holding Noah's arm but once again leading the way.

Behind them, the gaping maw closed upon itself. The walls of the chasm bulged, then plunged into the fiery inferno. The layers of rock ground loudly as they shifted and groaned in the cataclysmic upheaval. With a thunderous roar, the roof of the cavern collapsed, burying all beneath its rubble.

Thirty-Nine

When Jirad opened his eyes, it was midday. He had remained awake most of the night, listening for Hazial's men. Two days before, he and Tubila had heard muffled voices outside the entrance. He had slipped as close to the mouth of the cave as he dared without being seen. Haziel stood outside the cave, vainly urging several Ur-gatas to search the interior, but they feared the Shugama more than they did him.

As he watched, the ground trembled, sending rocks scattering over the area. The men fled in terror, screaming that the gods were angry. Hazial shouted curses and insults after them, but it did no good. Alone, he edged closer to the entrance and peered into the shadows of the cave, staring so intently that Jirad was certain he had been seen. At last, the Ur-gata leader backed away, making a sign to ward off evil.

Jirad had waited, listening, but when he heard nothing further, he crept to the opening. No one was there.

He and Tubila had then taken turns staying awake, each unwilling to do more than doze intermittently. Jirad slept for a while, but his dreams were full of savage, yellow eyes and writhing serpents. When he woke, his body was wet with perspiration, and his heart drummed in his ears.

Today was the fifth day since the others had disappeared into the depths of the cavern. They would have returned by now if at all possible.

Jirad and Tubila sat near the entrance but out of sight of any who might again be scouting the area. Jirad leaned his head against the cool wall and chewed, thinking, on the end of a short stick.

"Jirad," Tubila said as if reading his thoughts, "I don't want to leave without Malek."

He did not reply but removed the stick from his mouth and scratched idly with it in the dirt.

"Malek is kind," she continued, "and he looks like me." Her voice caught in her throat. "I know he is ashamed of himself."

Jirad sighed and broke the stick in his hands, throwing the pieces to the ground.

"I'll love him, though," she murmured, "if he'll let me." She screwed her face to one side. "Am I foolish to want to be a wife?"

Jirad cleared his throat and spread his hands. "I don't—" he began but paused at the expression of joy on her twisted face. "No," he said, shaking his head. "It is never foolish to love."

One side of Tubila's mouth lifted. "Then I can't leave yet. I know he'll return."

Jirad tried to force a smile, but it was too much of an effort. "We'll wait until nightfall," he conceded. "If they haven't returned by then, we must leave." He rested his hands on his knees, then ran his fingers through his long hair. "I don't want to leave either," he admitted with a sigh, "but we have no choice."

"I want to stay," Tubila said, wiping the corner of her eye, "but you'll never find your way off the mountain without me to guide you, and I promised Ganah to look after you. Besides," she said, "you're my friend's brother." She picked at a torn piece of skin by her fingernail. "I have five friends now," she said, peering at him from beneath her brow. "Before, I had none."

Jirad and Tubila watched the sun fade from the sky. Neither spoke. They sat, neither speaking, awaiting the approaching night, the stillness broken only by the occasional chirping of crickets secluded in tiny crevices of the cave.

When their companions failed to appear, Jirad stood to his feet. "It's time to leave," he said, his voice unnatural in the quietness of the evening.

"Let me walk to the pool and listen one more time," begged the girl, her eyes imploring for what she believed to be the impossible.

He shrugged. "Why not? But come back quickly," he added.

"Thank you," she cried as she threw her arms around his neck and kissed his cheek. Grinning, she leaped to her feet and dashed to the rear of the cave.

When she reached the pool, she peered into the shadows, edging farther into the darkness of the narrowing corridor. In the stillness broken only by her breathing, she whispered into the blackness, "Malek, I don't want to leave without you. I love you."

She listened. Was it only the scratching of a rat or a lizard? There, she heard it again. Louder. She clapped her hands to her mouth to stifle a squeal.

She turned and ran toward the entrance. "Jirad!" she screamed. "I hear them. I hear their footsteps!" She raced back to the passageway.

As she stared into the darkness, Jirad rushed to her side.

"I know it's them," she cried. "Listen! Can't you hear?"

Together they waited in the shadows of the cave, listening to the approaching footsteps. Finally the faint glow of a torch became visible, and at last, three bruised and bloody figures stumbled into the cavern, one leaning heavily upon the other.

Tubila threw her arms around Malek, oblivious of the dirt and blood encrusting his body.

Startled, and unsure what to do, the man looked at the others for help. As Tubila hugged him, he hesitantly wrapped his uninjured arm around the small figure and drew her close.

Utriel clasped her brother around the neck. "Ganah and my baby are dead," she sobbed.

Tubila made Malek lie on the cool, rocky floor while she whispered tenderly to him and cleaned the wound on the side of his head. His arm was cut and bruised but did not appear to be broken.

Noah leaned against the wall of the cave, his eyes never leaving Utriel, who sat with her head bowed and her chest shuddering from tears that no longer flowed. He ached to hold her in his arms, to kiss her lips, her eyes, to comfort her, to reaffirm his love. He longed to soothe the pain that dimmed her eyes, yet he knew she would not receive it.

At last she raised her head. "Noah."

He started at the unexpected sound of his name from her lips.

"Why did they have to die?" she asked. Her eyes lowered once again to the floor before her.

He rubbed his forehead. "I'm not sure. Perhaps it was the only way Ganah could complete her mission."

"But why the baby? I would have raised him to love the Placer of Stars.

Noah shook his head. "No. It would have been impossible." His heart wrenched at the anguish in her eyes, and he found it impossible not to go to her. He dropped onto the rocks beside her and cradled her hands.

"I would have taught him about the Placer of Stars and all that Ganah had revealed to me. I would have been a good mother."

"I know," he said, "but no matter what you did, it would have been for naught." He bit his lip as he studied the contour of her cheek and the golden flakes floating in her green eyes. "Do you not know," he continued, "that the child was one of the Nephilim? Never would he have followed our God."

She removed her hands from his as she shook her head. "How can you be so certain?"

"Because he bore the mark of Abaddon on his shoulder."

She stared at him, not daring a reply.

"The red mark, like a coiled serpent," he said. "Surely you saw it."

"That was just a bruise from birth."

"No," answered Noah. "It was the mark of the Nephilim."

"Why do you say that?" she asked, her jaw squaring as she spoke.

"Utriel," he said, "I have seen it before—on the shoulder of one who tried to kill your brother."

She pressed her hands to her mouth, a sob catching in her throat. All defiance now gone, she let her hands drop into her lap.

Noah sat quietly beside her as she stared at them.

At last she asked, her voice tremulous and husky, "What of Asmodeus? Is he destroyed forever?"

Noah thought for a moment, his lips pursed and lines deepening across his brow. "I don't know," he conceded. "Maybe he can't be destroyed, but at least, that entrance to his world has been closed."

Tubila and Jirad watched the entrance of the cave while the three exhausted and battered companions slept most of the next day. When the sun began disappearing behind the mountains, Jirad awakened his sister and Noah. Then he roused Malek. "My friend, we must leave this cave. Do you feel strong enough to walk?"

The man's face twisted into a tired, lopsided grin. "Malek make it," he said as Tubila helped him to his feet.

The night breeze brushed against their faces. Tubila led the way, trying to choose the easiest yet safest path through the trees. The moon was bright, but the rugged terrain made it difficult to find secure footing and dark, twisted limbs clutched and tugged at their hair and clothing.

Utriel swallowed against the dryness in her throat, and her lips stuck to her teeth. Not even the pain in her head and body could keep the faces of Ganah and the infant from tormenting her mind.

"Are you all right?" asked Jirad from the darkness behind.

"Yes!" she said, breathing deeply to quiet the pounding in her chest. "I'm fine." Her voice was strained and harsh.

Snakelike coils of mist slithered through the branches and spiraled around her feet. Something darted close by her head. She ducked, stifling a cry as its wing brushed her cheek. A wind had come up, gusting in flurries and whipping dark leaves above their heads. She shivered, hugging her arms into herself.

Without warning, Noah stopped in front of her, nearly causing her to stumble. "Wha—" she started. Then, sensing his alarm, her heart jumped. *Please*, she thought, *don't let anything happen. We're almost off the mountain.*

Ahead she could barely make out the dark shapes of Malek and Tubila. The rapidly settling mist was making it increasingly difficult to see.

She drew in her breath. A dark shadow fell upon Malek, crushing him to the ground. At first it appeared that a limb had fallen, but there had been no splintering of wood, only a loud grunt as the man disappeared under its darkness.

"Malek!" she called, starting toward him.

"Sh-h-h-h," warned Noah, grabbing her and holding up a warning hand to Jirad, who was several steps behind him. "Be careful!" he cautioned. "There may be others."

Tubila, ahead of Malek and intent on discerning a path off the mountain, whirled about as two bodies tumbled toward her. Before she could react, she was knocked to the ground. Sprawled on her back, she lay momentarily stunned.

Seeing no other attackers, Noah and Jirad sprinted toward the struggling forms. Malek's hands were locked around the wrist of his assailant, his breath rasping loudly as he held back a large blade poised above his chest.

"No!" screamed Tubila, leaping to her feet, fear and rage welling in her throat. Jerking her knife from her belt, she flung herself upon the Ur-gata's back. With a cry she raised her arms and drove the blade deep into his throat. A gasp burst from the man's mouth, his knife dropping from his clenched hand and clattering onto the rocks. He arched backward, clutching at his throat, then fell, pinning Tubila beneath his weight.

When Noah reached Malek, he fell to the ground and turned him onto his back. "Are you all right?" he asked.

The man groaned and raised one hand to his head. "Tubila," he muttered. "Where Tubila?"

"Help me!" shouted Utriel, tugging at the lifeless body of the Ur-gata. "Get him off her! She may be injured."

As Malek scrambled to his knees, shaking his head to clear it, Noah and Jirad pulled the small, twisted form from beneath the still-warm corpse.

Malek fell to the ground beside the girl and lifted her, cradling her in his arms. "Tubila save Malek's life," he murmured, tears glistening on his cheeks as he rocked her back and forth.

The girl opened her eyes and blinked. Her lips parted. "Are you hurt?" she whispered.

Malek hugged her and buried his face in her hair. "Tubila make good wife!"

Forty

"Before we rest, we must eat," said Noah.

The tired comrades had stumbled into the foothills as the moon still glowed faintly in the pink and gold horizon. Although weak and aching, they dared not stop until they had reached the haven of a large grove of trees beckoning in the light of dawn like a verdant jewel.

Now, all five huddled at the edge of a spring encircled on three sides by the mammoth fronds of variegated ferns. The once long blades of grass lay trampled by the feet of the continuous flux of animals seeking water in the early morning or the dusk of evening.

Jirad rolled over. "Am I dead and don't know it?" he groaned.

Noah rubbed his own throbbing shoulder, rotating it slowly to massage the ache that burned deep within. Sunlight filtered through the trees onto the profusion of wildflowers blanketing the grove. Their fragrance drifted in the fresh, morning air as he examined the nearby trees. "Papayas," he called, yanking a large fruit from a heavily laden limb and tossing it to Jirad.

Utriel, propped against the trunk of a large oak, examined a long cut on the side of her leg. The blood had already formed a rough scab, but it gave her something to do while she sorted out the confusion in her mind. She had made such a mess of everything. She longed to throw herself into Noah's arms, to let his strength sustain her.

He dropped wearily beside her. With a deft twist, he split the papaya, passing half to her.

As she bit into the sweet flesh, her eyes clouded and a tear rolled down her cheek. "I keep thinking about those left in the mountain," she said.

"Eat," he urged. "We have far to go. You must restore your strength."

She closed her eyes, yearning with all of her consciousness to undo the horror of the past. "How can I eat when my heart is so grieved?"

He was silent a moment. A breeze ruffled the silvery, green leaves in a gentle descant as he formed his thoughts. "I wish I could give you peace, but I can't. Only time will lessen your pain."

"But I hurt so now," she said through lips that barely moved. Her tears splashed onto her hand, their saltiness mingling with the sweet juice of the fruit.

After they had eaten, they slept, Tubila curled like a small animal at Malek's side, her head lying on his chest. The others lay in the cool grass, too tired to make a bower of brush to soften the hard ground. Mercifully, their exhausted bodies either refused to dream or forgot the images as quickly as they came.

The sun had passed its zenith, and the hot, still air hung heavily about them. Insects buzzed in the air. Noah roused his sleeping companions. "We mustn't remain here any longer," he said. "We've already stayed too long."

Malek rubbed the sleep from his eyes and sat up. He yawned loudly before shaking Tubila's shoulder.

Jirad stretched and walked to the spring. He knelt, cupping the water in his hands. He drank deeply.

"It's a long journey back to Gibara-boni," said Noah, scanning the horizon for any sign of Hazial's men. "We should get started as soon as possible."

Utriel pushed herself to her feet, her body stiff and tired. As she had slept, a decision had formed in her soul. She knew what had to be done, and she knew she must do it quickly. She touched Noah's shoulder. He turned his warm, brown eyes upon her, searching her face. She drew a deep breath. "Noah, I'm not going back to the valley with you."

His mouth tightened into a dark slash. "What are you saying?"

"I cannot go back to Gibara-boni," she repeated.

"But why?"

"My life is over there."

"But—"

"I cannot return to the life I once knew." Her chin trembled and her eyes filled. "Please, don't make it harder than it is."

His shoulders sagging, he spread his hands. "Is there nothing I can say?"

She shook her head.

He cleared his throat for his voice was husky with emotion. "Utriel, I love you. Come home with me and be my wife."

She closed her eyes, praying for strength. When she opened them, she placed her hand tenderly on the side of his face. "I will always treasure your love in my heart. I'll never forget you, for I can never love another as I have loved you."

"If you won't return to Gibara-boni," he said, "then I'll go with you."

"No!" she whispered fiercely. "You love me now, but how could I bear seeing my shame reflected in your eyes for the rest of my life?"

"That would never—"

"Don't," she interrupted. "Never would you hurt me, but I could not live knowing that I had kept you from being what Yah-Adon has called you to be." Before Noah could speak she placed her finger on his lips. "Please, don't say anything. I don't know what lies before me, but one thing I do know—I must make a new life for myself."

"Utriel." His voice caught in his throat, and his fingers tightened on her arm. "You can't just walk off into the wilderness. Come back with me to Gibara-boni. No one there knows what happened. We have a lifetime before us."

She shook her head, her chest heaving and tears spilling from her eyes. "I have been defiled," she said, her voice rising. "Can you not understand that? No longer can we be together." Bright spots of color flared in her cheeks; her hands clenched at her sides. "Yah-Adon's hand is upon you. He has called you for something that I can no longer be part of."

"I'll go with her," said Jirad.

She wheeled about, unaware he was by her side. "No," she cried. "That is too much to ask. You must not give up your life for me."

Jirad put his arm around her. "Didn't you always say we were two parts of a whole? Besides," he added, "you need me to keep you out of trouble."

Malek, still holding Tubila's hand, stepped forward. "Malek and Tubila go with Utriel."

Tubila's eyes gazed at the dark, brooding man by her side. "We'll stay with Utriel and Jirad, if they will let us."

Noah's eyes searched Utriel's face. "You've made up your mind about this, haven't you?"

"Yes," she said.

His hands dropped to his sides. "Will you send word where you can be found?"

"No," she said. "Noah, you've got to understand that it's not the end, only the beginning. You have a destiny to fulfill, and I—I must find my way back to Yah-Adon."

"You—" his voice broke—"you are my destiny."

"No." She brushed his cheek lightly with her lips. "Yours is with our people. They will need you to teach them of Yah-Adon now that Ganah is gone. If you do not return, there will be no one to call them back from their waywardness." She held Noah's face between her hands as she stared deeply into his eyes. "Return to Gibara-boni, Noah. You are needed. Yah-Adon's mark is upon your soul."

Jirad placed one hand on Utriel's shoulder. "I'll look after her," he said, "and I'll protect her with my life." He held out his other to Noah in farewell.

Noah's jaw tightened as he clasped Jirad's wrist. Then he turned back to Utriel. "May the eyes of Yah-Adon watch over you," he said as he pushed a loose strand of hair from her face.

She smiled, then with Jirad beside her, strode toward the vast plains spreading before them. They were walking toward a new beginning, a life that would be what they made of it with the help of the Placer of Stars.

Malek threw his arms around Noah, nearly lifting him off his feet. "Friend," he said, his voice husky with emotion.

"Friend," replied Noah.

"Malek and Tubila never forget."

Noah nodded without speaking.

Malek threw his waterskin over his shoulder and gripped Tubila's fingers. As they stepped onto the grassy plain, the girl looked back at the solitary figure standing at the edge of the trees. With a cry, she dropped Malek's hand and dashed back. Throwing her arms around Noah's neck, she kissed his cheek. Then, turning, she ran to the side of the waiting man. Hand in hand, they began their trek to an unknown place, but one they would not fear, for they were no longer alone.

Noah did not move until the others had become mere dots in the distance. He closed his eyes against the terrible ache within, Utriel's face etched forever in his memory—hazel eyes, full lips that broke brightly into a smile. A great sob rose in his chest.

He grasped the top of his tunic. With a cry he rent it to his waist. Turning, he looked toward Gibara-boni and toward the work that Yah-Adon had called him to fulfill. Something deep within his soul stirred like a tiny seed sprouting in the warm, moist soil of the earth. He clutched his chest and lifted his face to the sky. He nodded solemnly to the voice whispering to his heart.

I give you hope, it said. *Time heals all wounds, and darkness will be transformed into light. From suffering will come joy. From death will come life.*

Noah threw back his shoulders and stepped toward his destiny.

The Lord was grieved that He had made man on the earth,
and His heart was filled with pain. . . .
But Noah found favor in the eyes of the Lord.
Genesis 6:6-8

Author's Note

Writing about events that occurred before the Great Flood is like walking in a forest at night: Hardly enough can be seen to enable the wanderer to shuffle forward, let alone to walk with confidence, for the actual appearance of the terrain remains a mystery. Little did I realize the difficulty of such an undertaking.

Compounding the problem of understanding this prehistoric period is the assertion put forth by a large segment of academic society that humankind and its culture evolved over millions of years. What would be the outcome, I hypothesized, if I adopted the position that instead of evolving, humankind and its civilizations were in a constant state of devolution, that instead of apelike, ignorant creatures struggling to survive with Stone Age tools, they burst upon the scene with the highest possible intelligence?

Anthropologist Arthur Custance suggests that while early man did not have the technical skills needed to proceed at once to the creation of a high civilization, the Genesis record, one of our earliest accounts, implies that life rapidly developed into a complex culture. Within a short time, city life appeared along with accompanying trades and skills and the division of labor. Could it not be that the remains of many primitive communities discovered in archaeological finds are actually the wreckages of cultures and not the slow, faltering beginnings of a subhuman race?

Intrigued by such an idea, I focused on an ancient character recognized by most Western and Near Eastern cultures, Noah, "a righteous man, blameless among the people of his time" (Gen. 6:5-6).

This story, though, is not about the Flood but about the people caught in the dynamics of a disintegrating world at the center of a cosmic conflict. Therefore, the novel that emerged from my imagination is bittersweet and sometimes dark (it could be no less) because of the circumstances of the time. At the heart of *In the Eyes of the Serpent* is the promise referred to by ancient writings as "the story in the stars" or "the Mazzaroth," the declaration of a Promised One who would come from a virgin.

In writing this story I have told a tale of what might have been. As C.S. Lewis said, "What then is the good of . . . occupying our hearts with stories of what never happened and entering vicariously into feelings which we should try to avoid having in our own person? . . . The nearest I have got yet to an answer is that we seek an enlargement of our being. We want to be more than ourselves. . . . We want to see with other eyes, to imagine with other imaginations, to feel with other hearts as well as our own."

If my use of Noah in this blend of imagination and reality causes some readers to raise an eyebrow, please forgive me. I am merely a spinner of tales frolicking with the age-old question—what if?

C.C.R. 2007

About the Author

Carole Cargal Reeves lives in beautiful South Florida with her husband of forty years and a grown grandson who keeps life interesting. She has two sons and a daughter, as well as loads of grandchildren (sixteen to be exact). Although her passion is writing, she also enjoys painting with watercolors, particularly babies wearing hats.

Brought up on the Bible, Charles Williams, C.S. Lewis, and J.R.R. Tolkien, she has always been intrigued by the creative ways the epic battle between good and evil has been and can be expressed in fiction. "About twenty years ago, while teaching English literature in a Christian academy and upset about the lack of *exciting* Christian novels at that time, I began working on what was to become *In the Eyes of the Serpent,"* Carole says. "During that period I also decided to pursue a doctorate, which meant sporadic abandonment of my novel while it sat on a shelf. However, during that time ideas developed and fomented. At last, when both were completed, I soon learned that it is much easier to get an advanced degree than to get a novel published ... until now! Over the years I've learned much in the practice of patience. However, God is gracious and His timing is perfect." Carole is currently writing the sequels to *In the Eyes of the Serpent.*

Book Two, *From the Ashes,* follows Utriel and her companions as they cross the vast, open plains to the blue sea beyond in their pursuit to fulfill their own destinies.

Book Three will take place during the time of the Crusades.

Book Four, *Deliver Us from Evil,* follows Asmodeus into the twenty-first century to Midwestern Ohio.

Although Carole doesn't enjoy swimming, she does love to sit by the pool with a good book or to chat with friends. She also enjoys hearing from her readers. You may contact her at www.carolecargalreeves.com.

For more information:
www.carolecargalreeves.com
www.capstonefiction.com

Printed in the United States
83524LV00003B/109-120/A

9 781602 900431

開運之前，先開心！

吸引好運上門的快樂秘密

吳若權

目錄 CONTENTS

Part 2

好心，才有好運！

Part 3 轉念，才會轉運！

目錄 CONTENTS

【自序】

給自己多點好運

生日或跨年許願時，我們都會期待「心想事成」，但一年以後，又有多少願望被實現呢？

吳若權

成功的人，一定很努力；但是，努力的人卻不一定成功。從前，我以為問題必定是出在努力的人沒有用對力而已。這些年來，我體驗出另一番道理，同時也驗證了這句話：成功，屬於幸運的人。

當我年紀還小的時候，並不能真切體會這句話的真諦，甚至還會有些反感，而誤解讀為：成功，多少有點僥倖。

這跟我從小認知的成功法則，有很大的不同。成功，不是應該屬於踏實努力的人嗎？人怎麼可以靠一時僥倖而成功呢？

不論是我順利考上大學、退伍後很快找到工作、職場的資歷與薪水步步高升，在親友眼中這些近似平步青雲的過程，都被解讀為：「你的運氣真好！」坦白說，二十幾歲時的我，親耳聽到這樣的評述，內心很不是滋味。

表面上，我會謝謝對方的關心及祝福；內心裡，卻很想頂撞對方：「你懂什麼呀？難道你不知道我很努力嗎？我犧牲多少遊樂及休閒，付出多少血汗，才能朝夢想邁進啊？」

事隔多年以後，至少是過了「而立之年」，到了坐三望四的人生階段，我才有所改觀。記得是在自行創業後不久，一個冬日週末的清晨，我發高燒仍到辦公室加班，路經小公園，獨坐木椅，在冷冽的空氣中仰望藍天，腦海浮現從小到大經歷的很多事情，其中也包括很低潮、很挫折的過往。發現自己經歷過許多曲折的路途，竟然還能獨坐樹下，堅持往目標前行，我突然心存感激地頓悟：

「我的運氣真好！」

努力還不夠，也要好運氣

回首往事，看看未來，若不是那些挫折，怎能讓我學會堅強；若不是那些難堪的遭遇，怎能讓我知道貴人的意義；若不是那些踏實的努力，怎能讓我對成果懂得珍惜；若不是那些因為緣分而碰上的機會，怎能讓我付出的心血沒有白費……認真想來，我的運氣真的很好啊！

一定有人天分比我更高；一定有人比我更努力；一定有人比我更積極；一定有人比我更想堅持到底。但是，如果沒有多點好運氣，即使目標就在眼前，還是無法實現夢想。

終於，我願意徹底承認：如果我過去的努力，能夠得到一點微渺的成果，都要歸功於：我的好運氣！但是，我也要分享另一個觀點：**好運，不等於僥倖！**

「好運」和「僥倖」最大的不同是：**「好運」只會在積極、努力、樂觀的人身上發生，而且可以持續、能夠累積；「僥倖」只是突然冒出極稀有的機率，很難繼續複製、長期擁有。**

舉個最簡單、明顯的實例吧！努力賺錢，持續增加收入、長期累積財富，這是「好運」；好逸惡勞，慵懶度日，卻靠著買彩券中了一次大獎，這是「僥倖」！前者心安理得過了一輩子，還有良好的家教傳世；後者很可能因為天外飛來的這筆橫財，來得快、去得也快，卻沒有得到真正的快樂與幸福。**「僥倖」只能靠極微渺的機率碰到；「好運」卻是可以靠自己的努力創造。**

有了這正確的態度與認知，再回顧過去這些年獲得「好運」的經驗，親友聚會時再有人當面跟我說：「你的運氣真好！」時，我的反應有了一百八十度的改變，不但不覺得生氣或冤枉，反而充滿感恩與理解地向對方鞠躬回應：「你說的對，我的運氣真好！」

因為我終於知道：在一連串的努力過後，若能達成當初預定的目標，真的是有很多貴人相助，冥冥之中也有老天的暗地幫忙，才會水到渠成，有所收穫。

能在「心想事成」之後，承認自己的付出與努力，只占了成就一件事情的過程中很小的部分，其他都要仰仗別人的幫忙及老天的相助，就會打從心底懂得感恩，展現真正的謙卑。

好運，可以靠自己開創

曾經參加好友的慶生會，壽星點燃蛋糕上的蠟燭後，卻沒有許願。壽星老實說出自己的想法：「其實我並不相信許願之後，就能心想事成，所以從不認真許下願望！」

在場的我，聽到壽星本人講出這樣有點洩氣的話，深深替他覺得可惜。一個不相信許願魔力的人，該算是務實、還是無趣呢？

每當生日或跨年，許願的時候，大部分的人都會衷心地期待「心想事成」，但是一年過去以後，又有多少願望真正被實現呢？

經過這麼多年，我才明白：**「心想事成」的關鍵，在於是否擁有好運；而擁有好運的祕密，在於心中是否充滿正向的念頭，以及行動是否也表現正向的態度。**例如：總是體認到自己運氣好，是懂得感恩；不斷歸咎自己運氣不好，是習慣抱怨。而**「感恩」與「抱怨」的一念之間，就是能否擁有好運，並進而「心想事成」的界限。**

親愛的朋友，我知道你真的想努力追求成功，這麼多年來，臨門一腳，你差的只不過是再給自己多點好運！

好運，真的可以靠自己開創！「心想事成」的關鍵及要領雖然很多，但學習起來並不困難。**只要從基本的心態開始調整，想像美好的未來、相信自己做得到、並在日常生活中踏實努力，就可以擁有更多好運。**

為了幫助大家創造好運、擁有好運，我在《開運之前，先開心！》這本書中，彙整了我過去的成長經驗中最靈驗的「開運法則」，並邀請好友Tiffany老師，以專業命理的觀點，提供簡單、實用而有效的開運方法。只要你願意打開心門，以喜悅的態度、快樂的行動去實踐，你也會是全世界運氣最好的人。

你可以不相信我，但你一定要相信自己。

祝福你！

Part 1

開心，才能開運！

想要開運，請先擁抱好心情！
能讓自己開心的說法與做法，才能真正幫你開運。
心念的力量很強大，只要做足準備、敞開心胸，
好運自然會隨著自信降臨。

今日【宜】閱讀一本好書，與好友分享有益的觀點。
今日【忌】找不熟識的命理師批命、問流年、改風水。

開運之前，要先開心！

究竟如何改變運勢、開出好運？
找個厲害的命理師、還是要靠自己呢？

對現代人來說，算命應該可以歸納為最受歡迎的休閒娛樂活動之一。大家都急於想知道自己的運勢，並消災解厄、獲得好運，但究竟要如何算出好運道呢？答案恐怕不在算命師的功力，而是自己面對的態度。

盡量相信算命師預測的好運，心中就會充滿希望，懂得及時把握出現在眼前的機會。有了正面的想法，自然比較容易產生正面的行動。

一則來自《北京晨報》的報導，描述一位就讀中學的女孩，把留了兩年的長髮給剪短了。

原因是她看了剛買的一本星座書，內容提到她所屬的星座，今年留短髮會有好運。雖然我不知道這女孩的運勢是否因此而變好，但我相信「心誠則靈」的說法。只要她堅定地相信自己會有好運，而且心念的力量強烈到足以引導她的情緒和行動，能夠往設定的目標前進，那麼要順利地「心想事成」，指日可待。

其中，有一個很大的關鍵，是要確定她從頭到尾都是開開心心的。假設她是哭哭啼啼去剪掉長髮，回家之後又懊惱悔恨，不用等別的噩運來敲門，自己就先把自己給整垮了。

如果算命的動機，只是覺得運氣背到極點，想藉由法術或佩飾消災解厄，就會掉入負面思考的陷阱——心情不佳，導致諸事不順，影響運勢，而且一不小心，就會受騙上當。因為，這些都不是靠自己內省的力量去改變現狀，而是把改變的契機轉嫁到別人身上。只要被別有用心者看出這個弱點，就會加以利用，有的破財、有的失身。

破財就能消災？

近來心煩意亂的小美，其實好長一段時間沒有算命了，連續幾個月沉溺在徬徨茫然的情緒裡，她開始託人打聽：「哪一家算得比較準？」想找高人指點迷津。

朋友介紹了一個據說很靈驗的命理師給她，而且特別交代：「很準，他讓我發了一筆小財喔！」聽了教她十分心動。

果然很準，她在算命館還沒坐定，留著鬍子的命理師就鐵口直斷，「近來很多事讓妳煩心，愛情有點小波折，老闆對你的工作要求也愈來愈嚴格……」由於句句說中她的要害，加深了他的說服力。雖然只要有點人生閱歷的人，見她額上冒出的痘子，都不難猜出她的心事，但當局者迷的她，還是對他十分佩服。

結束之前，他預告了幾件可能會發生的倒楣事，提醒她特別留意。

被這麼一說，她本來忐忑的心情，就更不安了，於是主動向命理師請教：「有沒有什麼可以消災解厄的方式？」他介紹她買了一串水晶戴在手腕，可以有助於開運，這串水晶手環足足花掉她半個月的薪水，心疼得讓她連續失眠了好幾天。

沒想到，她的運勢並沒有因此而明顯改善，甚至每下愈況。約會時，男友說她心神不寧、疑神疑鬼；她指責男友心猿意馬、不夠體貼。上班時，老闆說她注意力不集中；同事抱怨常因為她工作出錯，害大家必須陪著加班。於是，她又跑去跟介紹她算命的朋友吐苦水，說著說著竟責罵起命理師，口無遮攔之際，也把朋友拖下水：「都是妳啦！介紹我去算那個什麼命，沒消災、還破財……」

算命時，盡量採信好的說法

那位朋友修養到家，並沒有因為她惡言相向而怒目以對，反而等她指天罵地發洩完畢之後，平靜地告訴她：「我覺得妳壓力太大了，心裡面裝了太多委屈，沒有適當的出口，才會影響運氣。」

這番體貼的話，立刻觸動了她心靈深處的憂傷，頓時哭倒在朋友懷裡，「對不起，我錯怪妳了。幫我出個主意吧！我應該回去找那位命理師再問清楚一點，還是請妳介紹另一個命理師給我，我願意再去試試，看會不會有別的轉機？」

老實說，即使完全不具備算命的本事，只要稍微懂得察言觀色，都看得出來她的問題在哪裡——一個看起來沒精打采的年輕女孩，不是感情不如意、就是工作出問題，而這兩個原因都會導致身體覺得不舒服。

朋友勸她，「妳最迫切需要的不是命理師，而是放鬆、休息。如果真有需要，應該找心理諮商師聊聊，請專業人員協助妳紓解壓力。」

她感激地望著這位朋友，但仍然不解地問：「那為什麼算命對妳有效，對我就失靈呢？」朋友笑著說：「因為**我都只採信好的說法，對負面的警告呢，則是小心而不多心**。還有啊，我**絕對不花一毛錢去改運、開運。還沒發財就破財，怎麼行？**我寧願把買水晶手環的錢拿來請妳喝下午茶或SPA，先讓自己開心，運氣才會好起來呀！」

正面想法，帶來正面行動

有一則新聞報導：在台北都會區設立神壇的江姓夫妻，自稱曾到尼泊爾修行密宗，供奉「三寶佛」，法力十分高強，兩人一搭一唱，不但詐騙許多錢財，還假借神明之意，對求助的婦女性侵害得逞。

類似這樣的社會案件，可說是層出不窮。令人費解的是：為什麼在高度開發的現代城市裡，知識水準偏高的國民，還會如此輕易因迷信而受騙？追根究柢來看，還不就是為了開運。

「開運之前，要先開心！」這是說來簡單、但饒富哲理的一句話，值得深思。當然，它也可以是一項判斷的標準，不論你相不相信算命，也不論命理師所說的靈不靈，**只要以「自己是否開心？」作為指標，就可以判斷是否有助於開運。**

簡單地說，能讓你開心的說法與做法，才能真正讓你開運。否則很可能開運不成，還會破財、失身，甚至要了你的命呢！因為，**改變運勢、開出好運，關鍵絕對不在命理師的功力，而是自己面對問題的態度。先讓自己開心，運氣才會好起來。**

開運心咒語　能讓自己開心的說法與做法，才能真正開運！

今日【宜】邀請久違的知己好友喝杯咖啡、談心。
今日【忌】聽信陌生人的話，採用偏方治療病痛。

命運，好好玩？

以輕鬆的心情看待算命這件事，會比用認真的態度去算命更有助於改運。

喜歡算命的民眾，真的為數不少。即使命理師說的不一定準，提供的建議也未必有效，但似乎都可以在當下解除當事人的疑惑，至少是平撫他不安的情緒。長期觀察這些喜歡算命的朋友，我發現一個道理：當人們還不是很習慣透過心理諮商管道來解決問題時，很多命理師在生活中都扮演了心理輔導老師的角色。

朋友阿信離開上一個工作已經半年多了，在他成為「待業族」的這段時間，對星座、命理這些資訊特別感興趣，即使因為沒有固定收入而手頭很緊，他還是忍痛花錢去算了兩次命。

很巧合的是，兩位命理師都說：「你現在的處境是龍困淺灘！」

他繼續追問：「什麼時候才能步上青雲？」

兩位命理師的答案，也都很有想像空間。其中一位說：「春暖花自開；心靜自然涼。」另一位說：「留得青山在；清泉天上來。」意思都是要他稍安勿躁，等待時機。

每次算完命回來，他的心情就平靜多了，隔天又重新開始找工作，變得十分帶勁，不會死氣沉沉。雖然工作的事，並不是很快就有了眉目，他卻跟從前的同事坦承：「不管命理師說的準不準，我都覺得很受用。至少，連個局外人都了解我的狀況。」

算命，的確有這種「感覺自己被了解」的功效。因為，有個客觀的第三者循循善誘地引導當事人說出心中所憂慮、擔心的事，在一來一往的對談中，把思緒整理一遍，既可以獲得心靈的撫慰，也能擁有客觀的建議。

算命成了一種精神寄託

中國科協在北京曾經公布一項有關算命的調查，結果顯示：有超過四分之一的中國人相信算命。這項調查的樣本遍及全中國大陸三十個省、自治區和直轄市，調查對象包括十八歲至六十九歲的成年人，推算出約有三億人口相信算命。

從台灣有線電視頻道的命理節目數量之多，也可以看出算命受歡迎的程度。別以為只有傻哥憨叔、村姑愚婦，才會喜歡聽這些星座專家、算命老師在電視上講得眉飛色舞，其實這些命理節目的忠實觀眾，還是以知識份子居多，尤其女性最愛。

根據AC尼爾森收視調查指出：以命理為主題的談話性節目，是台灣粉領新貴最喜歡的電視節目菜單之一。

儘管有學者專家推測，這個現象和經濟不景氣有關，由於不確定因素太多，使人傾向於「聽天由命」；但事實的觀察卻不盡然，在經濟景氣十分繁榮的時期，命理節目還是有一定程度的賣點。從這裡也可以看出：命理話題，其實已經變成民眾茶餘飯後的娛樂之一。說它妖言惑眾，也許就太沉重了，它只不過是壓力過大的現代人需要的一種精神寄託而已。

如果用輕鬆的角度來看待命理，真的沒有什麼不好，舉凡：星座分析、紫微斗數、手相、面相、塔羅牌……都是有趣的話題，略懂一二，跟陌生人聊天時比較不會言語乏味，的確能增進人際關係。但是，**對命理的解析結果，最好不要太認真。過度言聽計從，恐怕會把自己弄得精疲力竭，也無法美夢成真。**

我有一個男性朋友，結婚三年後，夫妻倆遲遲不能懷孕，他的母親十分著急，於是找人來看風水。不同的命理師給了不同的建議，臥房裡的雙人床換遍不同的方位，幾乎每個星期都在搬移位置。夫妻倆變得比從前還緊張，連做愛做的事時，都覺得壓力很大，懷孕的事就更加遙遙無期了。後來，他們還是乖乖去大型醫院，找專業醫生對症下藥，好不容易才順利「做人」成功。

別把命理師當醫師來治病

生理上有問題，的確不該錯把命理師當成醫生；但若是心理上有障礙，更不能把命理師當成心理諮商師，否則延誤就醫時間，就會造成更大的問題。

董氏基金會曾經發表「民眾憂鬱程度與就醫習慣之相關性」的調查，發現台灣地區民眾，患有嚴重憂鬱症的比例高達十一．七％，有情緒問題者約佔三〇％，但是只有七．六％的患者會尋求專業協助。大部分的人還是對精神方面的症狀諱疾忌醫，害怕別人把他視為「瘋子」或「神經病」，因此有三成的人會採取算命或占卜方式，以求改運。但很顯然的是，**命理師頂多可以安撫人心，卻絕對無法徹底治療身心的疾病。**

對身心健康的人來說，去找命理師多少可以發揮一些「心理諮商」的功能，得到心靈上的安慰；但是對身心有障礙的人而言，若是誤把命理師當作醫師或心理諮商師，勢必延誤病情，既破財、又傷身。

台灣有個很受歡迎的命理節目，名稱就叫做「命運好好玩」。看電視明星和命理專家，在電視上討論星座、血型、紫微斗數……等話題，真的很有趣，我也經常受邀擔任「與談嘉賓」，以專業的觀點提供觀眾在命理之外的建議，作為解決人生問題的參考。

沒事的時候算算命，可以很好玩！但是如果有病不去就醫，而是找命理師解決生理或心理的病症，這玩笑可就開大了。

命理，的確和心理及生理有關，甚至可以說：**命理，就是由心理及生理匯聚而成的動態軌跡**。若是心理及生理出問題，追求再多的感情或錢財，都沒有意義；擁有健康的身心，就是最好命的人！

開運心咒語　擁有健康的身心，就是最好命的人！

幸福開運Q&A

哪些星座愛算命？

Eric

Q 哪些星座的人，特別愛算命？哪些星座，算命只是純粹好玩，增加生活趣味做參考而已？又有哪些星座會對命理師的話言聽計從、奉為圭臬？

Tiffany

A 從太陽星座可以得知你愛算命的程度；也可以數一數盤據在你星盤中，哪種象性的星座最多，來得知自己的鐵齒度喔！

風象星座　迷信度：★★★★　鐵齒度：☆☆☆

風象星座天生是個好奇寶寶，熱愛探究神祕事物，會以科學角度來研究命理方面的事。如果讓風象星座了解到，命理占卜也可以用邏輯來解析，他們就會陷入痴迷啦！

水象星座　迷信度：★★★★★　鐵齒度：☆

直覺過人的水象星座，對「玄祕」向來充滿興趣，不但從小愛算命，對算命結果更是深信不疑，只要知道哪裡有神算就會想去試試。算得多也會成大師，最後還會自己鑽研命理呢！

火象星座　迷信度：★★　鐵齒度：☆☆☆☆☆

相信「創造」的火象星座，堅信人生掌握在自己手中，所以不輕易相信無法證實的事，算命只當參考，甚至是算好玩的。只有當自己因為不信算命而受到教訓，才會對算命深信不疑。

土象星座　迷信度：★★★　鐵齒度：☆☆☆

「算命」對土象星座是個矛盾的存在，他們一方面相信科學，另一方面又相信冥冥中有不可思議的力量，因此對「命理」總保持觀察的態度，遇到不順時就會把算命當心理安慰，而且愈不順就愈相信。

今日【宜】穿著鮮艷明亮的服裝、佩戴閃亮的飾品。
今日【忌】和別人爭論尚未證實的傳言或傳述八卦。

心理會影響命理

為什麼有人不信邪，偏偏卻中邪？
風水，是迷信、還是科學？

儘管近代出現許多稱之為「色彩專家」的人士，建議慎選服裝造型的顏色，以便於增加好運勢，但由於欠缺強而有力的實驗及理論來說服大眾，因此長期以來，都是信者恆信、不信者恆不信。

直到英國出現了新的研究調查結果，顯示：「比賽時，穿著紅色制服的隊伍，獲勝的機率比較高。」色彩與成功之間的關係，又成為熱門話題。

英國德翰大學人類學家希爾和巴頓，針對二〇〇四年雅典奧運中的拳擊、跆拳道、希臘羅馬式摔角及自由式摔角四項運動，進行研究調查，這些參賽者隨機選擇不同顏色的制服，但卻發現在二十一場比賽中，有十六場是由穿紅色制服的選手獲勝，勝出的機率約百分之七十六。他們之前也曾對足球比賽做過分析，同樣發現穿紅色球衣的五個隊伍，比賽時進球數較多，也較常獲勝。

科學家並不清楚在比賽時，紅色對運動選手會造成何種心理效應，但是他們推測，紅色通常與侵略性有關，而且也有警示作用，交通標誌中的禁止標誌也是使用紅色。在運動競賽上，紅色可能會對潛意識產生干擾，穿紅色的衣服有虛張聲勢的效果，當雙方勢均力敵時，會營造勝出的心理優勢。

努力＋實力，好運就會降臨

如果這項調查所言為真，和中國民間傳說農曆年打麻將時，穿紅色內褲會贏錢的道理倒有幾分近似，但也有顯著的差異。賭錢時，穿紅色內褲，對手看不見，純粹只是幫自己壯個聲勢而已。除非把紅色內褲外穿，才能產生威嚇作用，有助於擊敗對手，幫自己贏錢。

不管你相不相信，選擇紅色可以在比賽中產生侵略、警示、干擾……這些元素都是競賽時擊敗對手的致勝關鍵；但不一定非要穿著紅色衣服，才能產生「侵略、警示、干擾」的效果。當你事前準備得很充分，付出足夠的努力，具備旗鼓相當的實力，展現非贏不可的決心，光是眼神就能散發出侵略、警示、干擾的意味，何需紅色的衣服？如果你努力不夠、實力不足、決心不強，就算全身都穿成紅色，也只是讓對手看笑話而已。想像一下那個畫面，應該還滿有喜感的吧！

藉由紅色衣物讓自己更「紅」，雖然是心理作用，但說起來也符合科學原理。就像中國傳統的風水學，其實都有厚實的科學理論隱含其中。**房屋的建築結構，只是硬體的一部分；人與人的關係也是氣場的一部分，卻常被忽略。**如果對風水有足夠了解，就可以住得平安幸福；反倒是堅持不信風水，很可能因為不講究科學，而把一幢好好的房子，住得烏煙瘴氣。

我常說：「心理會影響命理！」以下李桑的實例，就是一個很好的佐證。

錯誤施工，影響居住品質

趕著購買法拍屋的熱潮，李桑以低價搶標到一棟舊公寓五樓的房子，貪圖還有頂樓加蓋了六樓，多出十幾坪，他本只想投資，仔細算算，決定要搬進去住。

李桑請了設計師重新規劃，丈量尺寸時，碰到社區住戶，許多人對他「曉以大義」，說起從前屋主專斷蠻橫的往事，完全不懂敦親睦鄰，而且工作不順，財務狀況不佳，導致房子被法拍。老鄰居勸李桑，若想住進這個社區就要遵守規矩，別搞得天怒人怨。

李桑不是愛惹事的人，但也不是怕事，他對自己的主見，相當有堅持。他決定大興土木、重新裝修，把舊房子所有的牆面都打掉，前後陽台外推，還把本來位於邊間的衛浴改到房屋的正中間，以增加其他房間的採光。

施工期間，很多好事的鄰居前來參觀，七嘴八舌說他的設計有問題，把衛浴放在房屋的正中間，對風水來說是犯了大忌。對於這些意見，李桑泰然處之，覺得是鄰居見識不足，或基於嫉妒心理，才會對他的住宅有些流言蜚語。他甚至告訴裝潢設計師：「風水那一套東西，我才不信哩！」

不料，舊屋裝修完成，李桑住進去以後，才發現問題還真的不少。因為是傳統式公寓，不是先進的智慧型大樓，衛浴改到房舍中間，通風、排氣和水管路線都是不容易克服的挑戰。上完廁所，整個家裡臭氣沖天，根本排不出去；又因管線遷移距離太長，水位高度不夠，馬桶常堵塞不通，而熱水管又在轉角處漏水，四樓的鄰居跑上來抗議，還要求賠償。最糟的是頂樓加蓋，被鄰居檢舉，面臨拆除的命運。

半年後，李桑經診斷得了憂鬱症。

巧用風水裡的科學

朋友跟李桑說：「誰叫你鐵齒不信風水！大家都搶著買衛浴有窗的房子，只有你故意把明明有窗的衛浴給改到房子中間。」聽得李桑更加鬱卒，病情愈見惡化，晚上嚴重失眠，熬到黎明時朦朧睡去，早晨又醒不了，昏昏沉沉，騎車還跌倒。

這會兒，他反倒相信風水了，被介紹到一家廟宇，道士說他中邪，做法事、吞符水，胡搞了一年多，可想而知，憂鬱症愈來愈嚴重，最後連他自己都相信這房子風水真的不好，於是想以低價脫手，交給仲介賣了九個月都還無法成交。因為，社區裡所有的鄰居都跟前來看房子的人說：「這房子喔，風水有問題啦！」

正確的風水理論，都隱藏著很容易了解的科學。我從來不鼓勵迷信風水，卻建議大家理解風水裡的科學，就住家環境而言，採光、通風、排水……都很重要。

偏偏，很多人只相信自己眼睛看到的，卻忽略其他必須用心才能觀察到的。如果只重視採光，忘了通風和排水，整體環境還是不適合居住。人在不適合居住的環境待久了，就很容易生病。這個道理淺顯易懂，卻很容易被忽略。

此外，敦親睦鄰也是居家風水的一部分。**人際關係是無形的氣場，愉悅或憤怒兩種不同的氛圍，形成正向或負面不同的環境，重要性絕不亞於陽光、空氣和水。**

幸福開運Q&A

巧用顏色招好運

Eric

Q 如何運用居家飾品的顏色，調整住家的風水，帶來好心情及好運氣？哪些居家飾品的顏色會讓心情沮喪，連帶影響運氣，應該盡量避免？

Tiffany

A 哈佛大學的研究小組發現：「不同的顏色能刺激人體內的腺體，活化各種內分泌，有效平衡身體的健康和情緒問題。」當身心健康、言行得宜，自然能掌握重點、並開創機會，甚至還能改變他人對你的觀點和感覺。

根據星象的醫療理論，顏色具有影響情緒及平衡心理的作用，經由重複刺激視覺，可以影響內分泌，進而調整情緒與思想失衡的問題，補足體內不足的分泌物質，讓能量得到補充。一旦精神或官能失調，就要從吃、喝、穿、戴，以及藉由視覺和冥想顏色，來達到療癒效果。

根據情緒需求巧用色彩

精神委靡頹喪：在生活中製造一個充滿紅色的環境，不但能振奮心情，還會帶來勇氣與敏捷。

缺乏冷靜情緒：這時需要綠色作為心靈引導。

想法困頓難解：可以運用藍色來加強思考能量。

心中感到寂寞：建議多使用褐色或大地色系。

覺得鬱悶不悅：明亮的白色是很好的選擇。

極度敏感之人：要盡量避免使用陰霾、深沉的黑色。

每種色彩都有神祕力量

自然色：讓內心感到溫暖、有安全感，釋放自信、獨立與冷靜的能量。

藍色：使情緒上的波動得到平衡，帶來理性與思考的能量。

黃橙色：激發熱情與樂觀的想法，帶來表達力、親切、活潑與豁達的能量。

粉色：帶來浪漫幸福的感受，使性格趨於溫柔、包容，獲得愛與純真的能量。

紅色：激發衝勁與勇氣、敢於嘗試創新，帶來活力與希望的能量。

紫色：帶來靈性與超然的思維，能激發靈感，形成敏銳的感知。

綠色：帶來安穩平靜的感受，獲得條理分明、思路清晰的能量。

白色：帶來純粹與自然的能量。

黑色：帶來沉著穩健、富於思考的能量。

灰色：增加哲學性思考，帶來中庸、和平的能量。

駝色：增加機智沉穩的特質，帶來溫和、平靜的能量。

金色：增加高貴雍容的氣質，帶來富貴、大膽的能量。

銀色：增加冷靜與內斂的特質，帶來感性與遠瞻的能量。

色彩運用的不同訣竅

顏色的運用必須寬廣

不僅是「穿著」和「飾物」的顏色要加強，連「生活環境」都要統一用色，才能有效改變磁場喔！

面積愈大，加持愈強

使用的面積愈大，能見度愈高，愈能得到色彩給你的加持力量。

種類不要太多，對比不要太強

將色彩運用在居家空間的時候，所選用的顏色盡量不要超過三種以上，顏色之間的對比也不要太過強烈。

配合每年運勢或個人需求調整

可以配合每年的運勢、或是你特別想增強的部分來改善。例如：想加強讀書運，就要調整書房的裝潢；想加強夫妻運，就要改變臥房的色調……等。

藉由不同環境加強不同運勢

可以個別在工作場所和居家空間，依照不同的運勢進行個別加強。例如：在工作場所加強「事業運」、在居家環境改善「感情運」……等等。

今日【宜】透過禱告、祈福等儀式，虔誠地請求神助。
今日【忌】購買號稱可以改運的水晶、神像或手鍊等。

花錢可以買好運？

不肯相信「心誠則靈」、又不「身體力行」的人，最後淪落到以為「花錢才靈」，卻又破財、傷身。

在我的人生經驗裡，好運，的確可以修得來，但絕對買不到。

在這世界上，沒有人能夠銷售好運給你；強調買賣東西就能好運的人，都是騙子。

《Good Luck!——當幸運來敲門》一書中，也有同樣的提醒：「沒有人能夠販售運氣。因為幸運乃非賣品。切勿輕信那些買賣運氣的人。」

偏偏，這世界上存在非常蓬勃的命理市場，所做的生意就是「幸運」的交易。

而且，愈是經濟不景氣、市場愈低迷，買賣好運的交易就愈欣欣向榮。

我花了很多時間觀察，終於找到命理市場的交易模式，可以說是完全違反商業機制，卻在古今中外實行了幾千年，歷久不衰。其中最大的特色是：沒訂價、不殺價，反而總是成交在最高價。

覺得自己最近很不平順的莉鵑，特別請人介紹，找到一位聽說很權威的命理師算命。對方看來一副為人正直的樣子，而且不明訂收費標準，只要來算命的人「隨意就好」！她因此卸除了心防，竟當場買了一串水晶以求改運，花了將近半個月的薪水。

最令她難過的是：運氣還沒來得及改好，回家就先跟男友崇靖吵了一架。

「心誠則靈」、還是「花錢才靈」？

崇靖向來就討厭莉鵑花錢不知節制的毛病，她常常有衝動性的購買行為，已經揹了一身刷爆信用卡的卡債，幾天之前又負氣辭了工作。兩個人才在規劃未來這幾個月要如何省吃儉用、度過難關，怎曉得她鬼迷心竅，又花了一大筆錢去買水晶，企圖改運。

執迷不悟的莉鵑，為此和崇靖發生強烈爭執。她堅信佩戴水晶會改運，只是需要時間醞釀；他卻認為所謂的「磁場」，應該是「心誠則靈」、而不是「花錢則靈」，並一口咬定她誤信江湖術士，還沒改運就先破財，幸運不成反惹災。

崇靖的說法沒有錯，只是態度錯了。**對於一個覺得自己很倒楣的人而言，需要的是心靈支持的力量，而不是理性的批判。**如果他能忍一兩天，耐住性子，事後好好跟她溝通，用他的愛和包容去「加持」那串「心誠則靈」的水晶，也許就不會落到「花錢還不靈」的地步。

中國江蘇的連雲港，曾傳出一件趣事。一所寺廟會依香客抽到的籤，收取不等的費用——「上上籤」當然是最貴的，約人民幣一千六百元；「中上籤」次之，但也不便宜，要價人民幣八百元。

這些規定引起香客的不滿，後來竟然被拆穿，籤筒中只有「上上籤」和「中上籤」，根本沒有「下下籤」。

花錢，買不到幸運；真正能創造幸運的，只有你自己。

把下下籤當作神明的提醒

我曾和一位經營貿易公司的朋友行經土地公廟，他很虔誠地進去燒香拜拜，自動添了香油錢。臨走前，感覺工作上諸事不順的他，又回頭擲筊求籤，結果竟抽到了中下籤。

他不死心；我不忍心。

於是，我又陪著他重新跪拜，向神明祈求保佑，連續幾次擲筊求籤，卻接二連三抽到中下籤或下下籤。

我趕緊打圓場說：「擲筊求籤，跟心情磁場有關，你心情不好，才會抽到下下籤，就當作是神明的提醒，別太在意。」

這並不是為了鼓勵他才瞎掰出來的，我始終相信：**心念的力量十分強大，絕對**

會影響機運。

沒隔多久，他本來跟我約好談一些公務上的事，卻臨時打電話來跟我延期，理由是：有個朋友向他極力推薦，鄉下有一家神壇，可以請濟公下凡來指點迷津，效果很好。所以他決定取消我們的約會，連夜搭車下鄉造訪神壇，請濟公化解霉運，帶來好運。

握著電話筒，一時之間，我竟說不出話來。都什麼時代了，高級知識份子竟還會信這一套？

我突然感到心疼，不知道他在事業上遭受了多少磨難，才會把自己搞得如此慌張失措、六神無主，每隔一段時間，就要求神問卜，一會兒改名、一會兒搬床位、一會兒改裝潢調整家門的方向……

同時，我也覺得很可惜，如果他願意把這些花費在怪力亂神上的心力，轉而投入學習「時間管理」、「顧客服務」、「提振同仁士氣」、「擬定業務策略」等專業能力，他的機運應該會變得比較好吧。

祈福之前，應該先自求多福

雖然我一直認為：**宗教信仰，是為了給人們帶來內心的平靜，讓我們懂得思考反省，而不是貪婪地向神明乞討好運。**但是，我也不反對透過宗教信仰，向信奉的神明祈福，那也是獲得心靈力量的一種方式。

不過，**向神明祈福之前，應該先自求多福。靠自己的力量，認真做好該做的努力，才有可能改善碰到的問題、度過眼前的難關。**

成功和失敗，都掌握在自己的手中。真正能幫助自己改運的，是「用對方法、使對力」的努力，而不是聽信怪力亂神、甚至大費周章做法事。

有關「神棍性侵害女子」的新聞事件，在媒體報導上似乎從沒斷過。每件案例大都是女性覺得命運不順遂，而求助於神壇，神棍於是以「改運」之名，建議進行「雙修」之實。

通常，性愛儀式結束後，女方立刻後悔，驚覺自己被欺負了，於是提出告訴。

和一般強暴案不同的是，神棍在性侵女子之前，通常都會暗示或告知即將要進行

「雙修」，有些案例之中當事人也同意了，連半推半就的過程都沒有。只不過「雙修」完畢，女方才從沒有如預期改善的人生裡，突然醒悟自己已經受騙上當。

當然，也有些被害人是被神棍下藥，迷昏之後再行性侵。但事後她們對自己主動找上神棍開運的行為，也感到十分懊悔。

還有另一位身世悲慘的女孩，化名曉秋，她求助的對象是有「心靈導師」之稱的專家。她因為在成長的過程中有陰影，經過友人介紹，接受心理輔導，那位來自國外的心靈導師，在「靈修業界」頗負盛名，竟要她進入密室「個別指導」。

她依照指令脫去全身衣物，任由他在她的身上游離進出。翻雲覆雨過後，她才猛然發現這一切都只是騙局，原本想要藉由「靈修」走出成長陰影的她，卻因而陷入更深層的愁雲慘霧。

人性的貪念，魔鬼的交易

從這些被害人的遭遇裡，我看到的是神性裡的魔性。神棍心裡藏著魔鬼，裝扮成為神來加害當事人；而當事人的心裡也有魔鬼，想要快速改變不符理想的人生，卻不願腳踏實地去付出努力，而試圖透過神和另一個魔鬼打交道，才會受騙上當。

神，成為另一個無辜的受害者，為人類的罪愆，背負了沉重的黑鍋。

神棍性侵害女子的事件，之所以會持續上演各種版本，正如同詐騙集團的中獎通知，可以不斷騙取無知百姓的金錢一樣，說穿了，都是利用人性裡的貪念，才能完成魔鬼的交易。

神棍貪色；女子貪運。兩人都有貪念，才能一拍即合。

台灣宜蘭有一座廟宇供奉濟公，信眾把「行動電話」、「太陽眼鏡」、「衝鋒槍」都掛在神像身上，從神並不需要的配備裡，顯現了人性的諂媚與貪欲。

就像生活裡有許多千奇百怪的事，看起來並不合邏輯，卻能不斷重演、複製，有人會評論：「其中必有詐！」或是「這裡頭一定有鬼！」其實，這不是「詐」和「鬼」使壞，而是自己的貪念在作祟。

會被貪念矇蔽，而特別迷信的人，又分為兩種極端：一種是已經功成名就，坐擁權勢及暴利；另一種則是困頓於人生谷底，險些在低迷的運勢中溺斃。

前者，雖然已享受榮華富貴，卻從不知足感恩，對於「權」、「利」的欲求，如同填不滿的無底洞。後者，「缺乏自信」和「諸事不順」形成惡性循環，未曾先「盡人事」，就想「聽天命」，認為自己缺乏好運，而一味地想「改運」。

以上這兩種類型的人，都很容易被神棍或唯利是圖的命理師詐騙，應該特別謹慎小心。

其實，真正通曉命理及心理的專家都知道：不必花錢，就能改運！**只要你相信「心誠則靈」，並且認真往正面的方向努力，就會獲得好運。請隨時提醒自己：不跟魔鬼打交道，好運才會蒞臨。**

開運心咒語　先盡一己之力，認真做好該做的事，才可能改善問題。

幸福開運Q&A

花小錢就能改運

Eric Q 通常很多想賺錢的命理師都會建議失魂落魄、或祈求好運的人買高價水晶、甚至付費綁紅線……如果不想花大錢，只願花小錢，以不超過一百元的花費來說，有沒有什麼隨身配件、家飾品、書桌（辦公桌）小擺飾，可以幫助自己改運？或應該盡量避免佩戴、擺放哪些飾品？

Tiffany A 開運的小方法有很多，這裡特別介紹幾種我嘗試過的給大家。別忘了，開運術是為了增強心願達成率，一定還要配合你的積極行動，才能成功喔！

旺工作

使用時機：工作時常小錯不斷，或總是遇到挫折。

1. 在工作的地方放置跟自己生肖相同的動物擺設，頭部要朝外。

2. 在座位貼上一張畫有六芒星的圖。

增財運

使用時機： 每個月都覺得錢不夠用、想增加賺錢機會的時候。

1. 準備一枚五十元銅板，向你的神明許願。願望一開始不要太大，而且要盡量實際。

2. 找一個陶瓷製的碗（不限大小），將許過願的銅板放在碗中，用布包起來、藏好。之後每個月的月圓，都放入一枚許過願的五十元銅板。

3. 願望達成後，若想再次許願，需將部分銅板拿去行善，留下少數銅板，繼續以先前的方式進行。

擋霉運

使用時機： 犯太歲的年份；或是覺得事事不順、容易傷病的時候。

- 運用「瑜伽」、「打坐」、「氣功」、「芳療按摩」，來調整血氣運行，整頓腦波，凝神聚氣，增進個人磁場與能量。
- 多攝取養生食物來增加靈能，並避開危險——

以能量水調節身上或周遭的氣場：以使陰靈閃避，如電解水、備長炭水……

養肝的食物：可避免被邪物跟隨，如牡蠣、蛇膽、綠豆、檸檬……

養心肺的食物：可避免煞氣衝撞，如西洋參、茄子、大蒜……

今日【宜】請長輩或朋友，給一個自己可以改進的忠告。
今日【忌】向別人抱怨過去所遭受的委屈或不合理對待。

算愈多，命愈薄？

覺得自己好命的人，都很少去算命；
覺得自己歹命的人，才不停地算命！

在變動的時代中，愛算命已然成為重大的流行趨勢！

根據一項調查顯示，愛算命不只是市井小民的全民運動，連企業界的大老闆都深信命理風水之說，甚至把算命當作用人選才的標準。企業老闆迷信的程度，已經成為愛算命排行榜的 Top 1！

從前在唱片界服務時，我就聽說某家唱片公司的老闆，特別喜歡某些星座的人才。那幾年，該唱片公司的經營成績斐然，推出的專輯既有創意、也有口碑，非常受歡迎，利潤可觀。於是，這套「星座管理」之說，雖然不逕而走，但還是以正面的評價居多。

也許，星座真的可以代表某些性格的特質，遴選個性相近的同仁一起工作，比較容易培養團隊的默契，這也無可厚非。但隨著唱片市場的凋零，那家深信星座管理的唱片公司，同樣得面臨殘酷的市場挑戰，特殊的企業文化，是否能再創新猷，就有待時間考驗了。

命理風水，雖非全不可信，但也不可盡信。過度參考，便形成怪力亂神，是對自己不負責任的表現。非但無法藉此提升經營績效，還會讓主管因為迷信而威信蒙羞。

中國南京有一家公司的老闆，竟找了命理師暗地為員工批命，若八字不合，就請他走路。員工仰賴老闆給一口飯吃，敢怒不敢言，只有任憑處置，但不論幸運被留下來的、倒楣被遣送走的，都覺得老闆行事風格不夠理智，企業經營遲早會碰到瓶頸。

過度相信算命，是不負責的表現

不只中國老闆愛算命，美國企業主也不遑多讓。近年來，美國企業界流行「筆跡算命法」。他們認為一個人的筆跡，可以透露性格的特質，並藉此判斷員工的人品。而且筆跡無從造假，比過去幾年來採用的「性格測驗」，更具參考價值。

繼星座、血型、八字、姓名……等算命方法之後，筆跡又變成企業主管遴選人才的指標。有「筆跡專家」美譽之稱的雪拉•柯茲說：「筆跡，是用圖形表現自己的思想型態和行為模式，可以看出一個人的潛意識。」

無論她講的話，是不是有道理，過度依賴算命，絕對不是好事。

我很少聽見成功的人說自己命好，倒是常聽失敗的人說自己時運不濟。若把算命結果作為重要決策的指標，就顯露出「依賴性」的人格特質，不足以為自己的行為負責。可見過度相信命理，失敗的機率也愈高。

幾年前在電視台錄影，我認識了一位擁有高學歷的女性命理師，大學讀心理，研究所念哲學，在科技公司人事部做了三年，決定回家繼承老爸副業，掛牌當起全職命理師。行走江湖七年來，閱人無數的她告訴我：「苦命女最愛算命！」

她倒不認同俗話說的：「命，會愈算愈薄！」反而開玩笑地說：「這些苦命女都巴望著命會愈算愈好，怎麼可能愈算愈薄！她們會想辦法把命變好！」

咦？把命變好？其中的玄機在哪裡？

原來，苦命女若算到不好的命，隔一陣子就會找別的命理師再重新算一次，總之，就是想聽些能讓自己安心的話。

苦命女的命運，很難改變！因為除了換個命理師，她在真實的生活中沒有做出任何改變，所以一路走下去，都差不多是那樣的路徑。不用找命理師，只要稍具人生閱歷的人，大概都能預測苦命女的未來。

男人求事業；女人問婚姻

這幾年她的經驗豐富了，從不鐵口直斷地對來算命的苦命女老實說：「不論過了多少年，妳還是會跟現在一樣，甚至更糟！」而是會語帶玄機地說：「這幾年妳的波折很多喔，會這樣上上下下地震盪，要做點調整、再多些努力，耐心等幾個月會比較平順。」

說完之後，她自己就會替對方感到有些惋惜，只能默默獻上祝福。

近幾年來，社會環境改變很大。從前，來算命的苦命女，面臨的人生困境比較多。有的女人是苦惱生不出孩子、有小孩的女人又擔心小孩不聽話；再不然就是想嫁而嫁不出去的、嫁出去的又嫌自己婚姻不好；其他則是身體不好、久病不癒……但是，現在的問題就簡單很多了，生病的會看醫生、生不出孩子的會做試管嬰兒、小孩不聽話的知道要靠教育，只剩下婚姻狀況不好的會來算命，偏偏這個問題依然無解。

婚姻畢竟是夫妻兩個人的事，不是靠苦命女自己努力就可以解決。而苦命女的丈夫，是永遠不會為了婚姻問題來算命的。

在她的觀察裡，來算命的男性比女性少，通常年輕的男子是問考運、稍有年紀的男人問事業升遷，幾乎沒有男性會來問婚姻。

有趣的是，偶爾有女性來問事業，但這樣的女性多半有個會欺負她的主管或同事。苦命女想知道，何時才會擺脫這些人？命理師實在不知該如何告訴她：「妳眼中的這些壞蛋到處都有，妳可得好自為之啊！」

她做了結論：**愛算命的苦命女，其實本質上命格都還不錯，問題出在她們不夠自信、也不夠努力，遇到不順遂的事，沒有先檢討自己，只會先怪罪別人、或歸咎給環境。**

真正有效的解決之道，還是老生常談的那句話：**要改變命運之前，還是得先改變自己。**

開運心咒語　與其怪罪別人或歸咎環境，更應該先檢討自己。

今日【宜】投遞履歷表、或擬訂向心儀對象告白的計畫。
今日【忌】邀約尚未了解足夠的陌生網友發生親密關係。

緣分豈止天注定！

善緣、孽緣，往往在一念之間。
誰說在錯的時間，就一定遇不到對的人？

撰寫《三個夏天》這部小說時，我安排心碎的女主角將裝了紙條的「瓶中信」投入大海，後來被男主角撿到而重修舊好的情節。身邊很多朋友看了都嘲笑：「你太天真了，竟把小說當童話寫。」他們根本不相信世上會有這樣的事。

相隔不久，美國電影「瓶中信」上映，描述男女主角因為裝在酒瓶中的信件而結緣，我的那些朋友還是沒有對我產生「英雄所見略同」的讚賞，反而又多了一樁嘲笑的話柄：「跟你一樣不切實際的人，還真多！」

大多數的人，都以為所謂的「奇緣」只存在於小說或電影中，而不會在真實的人生出現。直到英國有一對夫妻看到《泰晤士報》徵求瓶中信的故事，於是將四十年前巧遇的經歷公諸於世，終於讓大家見識到：世界上果真有奇緣。

回溯到一九六三年，當時安妮只是個十歲的小女孩，她和家人去法國旅行時，將寫明地址的字條裝在瓶子裡，擲入英吉利海峽，這只瓶子隨後漂流到荷蘭海灘，被另一位同齡男孩艾爾佛斯撿到，雙方開始通信。兩年後，安妮全家前往荷蘭和艾爾佛斯見面，並持續聯絡。多年之後，他們一起結伴去法國旅行而正式墜入情網，在二十五歲那年結婚。這對夫妻育有兩名子女，如今婚齡即將屆滿三十年。

啟動奇緣要用心，更要用力

我在廣播節目裡分享了這樁真人實事，同時開放現場 Call in，百分之百打電話進來的聽眾，都相信「緣分」這回事，並提供自己的經驗作為佐證。

根據這些實際經歷的分享，我發現：**相信緣分還不夠，當緣分來臨時，你必須百般珍惜，並且積極地付出努力，幸福才會真正屬於你。**

如果，安娜當時沒有投擲瓶中信，這一切因緣都不會發生。

如果，艾爾佛斯沒有寫信給她、雙方家長沒有安排會面，或事隔多年後兩人沒有一起出遊，他們還是不可能結婚。

如果，他們婚後不願包容彼此，也不可能把婚姻維持下去。

啟動奇緣，除了用心，還要付諸行動！不必羨慕別人的奇緣，你在茫茫人海中結識朋友或情人，本身就是一段很奇妙的緣分。如果你真的非常嚮往「瓶中信」之類的情節，也不一定要到大海去拋擲訊息，在網路如此發達的年代裡，發布一封電子郵件、或一則留言，就是現代網路版的「瓶中信」，很可能為你創造奇緣。

問題是：你做了嗎？訊息夠清楚嗎？奇緣發生時，你們是否彼此珍惜，而且善待對方？

倘若，**只是一心寄盼奇緣降臨，但始終沒有付出行動，或是雖很努力、卻總是用錯方法，即使奇緣來了，也很容易錯身而過。**

別讓感情不順，造成人財兩失

一位自稱很「衰」的男性朋友，曾經在某年的除夕夜裡，打電話向我訴苦。

過去這一年，他過得很不如意。本想定下心來好好談一場戀愛，但事與願違，他談了不只一場戀愛，結算下來，發展過三段「起初看好，但落荒而逃」的感情，另外還有一段不滿三小時的「一夜情」。總之，人財兩失。

第一段感情，是同事的遠房親戚。彼此說好「以結婚為前提來交往」，他猜想對方應該也是個想安定的女孩。但約會過幾次，親密關係也都發生了，他才發現對方並不單純，不但同時和前幾任已經分手的男友繼續交往，夜裡還活躍在交友網站上。掙扎幾天，他決定當機立斷，同事則向他致歉：「我真的不知道，她竟然是這樣的女孩。」

第二個對象，是他參加交友聯誼活動認識的。對方是個剛從大學畢業不久的單純女生，每天只想著週末可以去哪裡約會，吵著要買東買西，把他當成提款機，不到兩個月，他就決定「止付」，對方失望地主動離去。

第三段感情，來自網路交友。他平常並不很熱衷去別人的網頁「簽名拜訪」或「留言」，但後來碰上了一位女孩，對感情十分認真，從此他的態度也變得比較積極。兩人每天用電子郵件交流往返，熟絡了幾個星期，正當他動了感情，想要正式約對方出來見面，她卻遺憾地說：「晚了一步，我昨天已經接受另一位網友的表白了。」

嚴重失望的情緒，讓他在一時衝動下，刻意去網路聊天室尋找一夜情的對象，見面後才發現對方隱瞞身分，她根本不是「感情受挫的大學生」，而是以「網交」為業的應召女郎。

情場失意的反敗為勝三部曲

時光匆匆，一年下來，他的感情交了白卷，人生閱歷卻豐富了很多。

他感慨萬千地說：「也許我命中注定，去年有許多爛桃花，算是劫數難逃。但希望，『大難不死，必有後福！』」

我卻不以為然。不論為期長短、結局如何，**每一段感情的開始或結束，都是自己的決定，不能全部推給命運**。倒楣的人，別對「大難不死，必有後福！」這個說法過度寄予厚望；生命大難的劫數過去之後，也未必就有後福。如果，不知檢討、沒有智慧、重複錯誤，只會愈來愈糟，怎麼能有好運來報到？

三分天注定；七分靠打拚！無論追求感情或事業，道理都是相通的。情場失意的人，唯有履行下列**「反敗為勝」三部曲**：

1.記取過去的教訓。

2.珍惜當下的相遇。

3.付出未來的行動。

如此，才能擺脫心理的陰影，重見一片天。

開運心咒語　記取教訓，把握機會，即時付出，才能啟動奇緣。

幸福開運Q&A

增加桃花小撇步

Eric

Q 桃花運不只能增加戀愛運勢，也可以有效拓展人際關係。有哪些簡易的方法可以增加桃花運？又有哪些小撇步，可以阻絕爛桃花？

Tiffany

A 覺得自己乏人問津，戀愛的緣分總是遲遲不來嗎？快試試下面的方法，來催動沉睡中的桃花運，同時阻絕耗費你心力的爛桃花吧！快則一個月，慢則三個月，桃花運就會來敲門！

別覺得效果似乎來得太慢，沒有一種風水或魔法是迅速見效的，就像「食療法」一樣，都是逐步提升的，要多點耐心守候喔！

招來好桃花

紫色催情法

- 自古以來，紫色便具有催情、浪漫的神祕魔力，將紫色擺飾放在工作桌、床頭邊或梳妝鏡前，就可以提高自己獨特的美麗氣質。
- 將紫色的卡斯比亞置於浴室與窗台旁，可以增加舉手投足的魅力。
- 生日時，將床單、被褥、枕頭換成紫色綢緞布料，桃花運便會與日俱增，並且覓得良緣。

擺「花瓶陣」

用花瓶來催動桃花運非常有效！以愉悅的心情擺放這個屬於你的桃花陣吧！別忘了每天細心照料鮮花，除了摘除枯枝、也要更換清水。

準備物品：指南針、花瓶、鮮花

做法：

1. 站在客廳中央，面對門口，以指南針找出方位。
2. 依照不同生肖，確認擺放花瓶的方位及顏色，花的數量以雙數為吉（請參照下頁）。

生肖	桃花方位	花瓶適合的桃花色	適合的花種
鼠龍猴	西方	金、白色	香水百合、向日葵、雛菊……
牛蛇雞	南方	紅、紫、橙色	玫瑰、薰衣草、芙蓉、鬱金香……
虎馬狗	東方	青、綠色	野薑花、海芋、茉莉……
兔羊豬	北方	藍、黑色	蓮花、水仙……

運用催情香

古歐洲將玫瑰稱為「催情之后」，稱依蘭為「催情之聖」。你可以挑選其中一種香味的精油製作成噴霧：

1. 將150 cc的礦泉水，加上10滴精油，搖勻。
2. 每天出門前，噴灑在頭髮上或身上。

阻絕爛桃花

桃花運無法篩選，當桃花運降臨，一定會有好的、也有壞的；若想讓目前纏著你的爛桃花離開，不妨試試以下方法。

截桃枝

1. 在花店買一節桃枝，在桃枝的兩端各用黑線綁上死結。
2. 再把對方的照片和桃枝用黑線綁在一起。
3. 盡量避免和對方見面，也不要通電話。當確定這個人已經對你死心，再將綁了照片的桃枝燒掉即可。

帶桃木劍

隨身攜帶小桃木劍，可防止爛桃花引起的災劫。

求助呂洞賓

1. 到廟裡向呂洞賓請求化解你目前的孽緣，並詳細說明對方的姓名、生日。
2. 求一張呂洞賓的圖卡或平安符，並以順時針繞香爐三圈後，隨身攜帶。

今日【宜】健康檢查、汽車保養、或嘗試轉換跑道。
今日【忌】檢討成敗、衡量得失、或精於算計投資。

逆轉厄運變好運

碰到厄運那一刻，蘋果電腦創辦人賈伯斯的口頭禪，竟然是：「這是我最棒的……」

人生中不如意事十之八、九。懂得珍惜幸福快樂的一、二，是很難得的修行。

一般人都難免遇到所謂的「碰壁撞牆」期，這時候很可能有下列四種反應：

第1型：迎面撞上，頭破血流——最常見的反應，因為這是最直覺的動作，表示這個人總是埋頭苦幹，在前進的途中，完全沒有抬頭看看前方可能有什麼阻礙。若暫時放下同情心，客觀地評論，撞到是活該。

第2型：錯愕停留，面壁思過——這種反應其實還不錯，至少在撞壁之前，還懂得煞車。停下來檢討是必要的，但時間不能太久，而且要想出對策，才會有所改進。

第3型：飛簷穿牆，力求突破——選擇這樣因應，表示碰到困難時，有足夠的力量去克服問題，度過難關。碰壁彷彿只是一個簡單的考驗、一次善意的提醒，讓才能具足的人懂得保持謙卑，不至於太驕傲。

第4型：換個方向，重新出發——這個動作看起來簡單，做起來卻不容易，其中有檢討、也有行動，有決心、也有毅力。

能在厄運中轉運，所憑藉的不只是心念的力量而已，更重要的是來自平常的思考、觀察及準備。

換句話說，你必須在遭逢厄運之前，就預知可能會碰到壞的狀況，才不至於事到臨頭手忙腳亂。

而且，平常就要思考人生的「替代方案」，碰壁時才能很快調整到適合自己的新方向，而不是像無頭蒼蠅那樣，拍擊翅膀漫無目的地猛撞亂闖。

「轉運」，是需要練習的

蘋果電腦創辦人史提夫·賈伯斯（Steve Jobs）對美國史丹佛大學畢業生發表演講時，分享了他生命中的三個真實故事。分別是：「從貴族學校自動退學」、「被自己創辦的蘋果電腦開除」、「被醫生診斷罹患胰臟癌」。在很細微的地方，我注意到他的口頭禪，竟是在碰到厄運那一刻說：「這是我最棒的……」

「自動退學」，是他最棒的決定；因為，後來他決定轉學，投入真正有興趣的科系，讓學習變得更快樂而有意義。

「被蘋果開除」，是他最棒的遭遇；因為，後來他重新創業，推出《玩具總動員》，證明自己還是可以做點別的事。

「罹患胰臟癌」，是對他最棒的提醒；因為，後來他手術成功，更了解生命的真諦，從此更懂得珍惜人生。

每次遭逢不如意，他都採用最正面的想法、最積極的行動來回應。他說影響他最深的一句話是：「常保飢渴求知；常存虛懷若谷。」道理大家都懂，但我想借花獻佛所提醒的關鍵字，是「常」這個字。**別以為在厄運時轉運，靠的是臨機應變，其實更重要的是「例常」的準備，它讓你在無意間步入絕境時，有退路、有轉機。**

「轉運」，其實是需要練習的，而且最好培養成習慣，才能在十之八九的不如意事中脫困，不會把自己埋進負面的情緒裡。

有位經常寫信給我的讀者，自認是很努力的上班族，卻未能得到老闆的賞識。有一次他的考績很差，年終獎金幾乎泡湯，感覺諸事不順的他，竟又在深夜回家的路上被警察攔下來開罰單，理由是「左轉車輛行駛直行車道」。自認這根本是微不足道的疏失，警車離去後，他大罵三字經，直呼：「去用搶的比較快啦！」

用相信良善的心，吹滅胸中怒火

難怪他的心情這麼沮喪，雖然罰單金額不高，但確實是雪上加霜。這已經是一個星期以來，他接獲的第二張罰單了。幾天前，他才從信箱裡收到一張，是開車途中無意間壓過雙白線，被埋伏警員拍照舉發。他不禁嘆息連連地對我說：「怎麼這麼倒楣呀？」

我規勸他要多往好處想，把近日來碰到的所有不如意，當作是給自己的提醒：「小小的挫折，換來大大的警覺，是很值得的呀！也許，它們幫你避掉了更大的災禍。」

如果，他能因而更認真做事、更謹慎開車，往後的運勢一定會變得更加平順。可惜，他還繼續沉溺在負面的情緒中，沒有把我的話聽進去。

直到隔天晚上，他在下班回家的路上，又遇上交通警察。

坐在駕駛座的他，用眼睛的餘光感應到有部警車尾隨在後，他根據當時的狀況判斷，自己根本沒有違反交通規則，而且行車速度很緩慢，沒有理由被開罰單，所以看到警車跟上他，警員還搖下車窗，讓他更加生氣，準備跟他對罵。

就在他準備要破口大罵「你想幹嘛？」時，警察搶先對著他大喊：「先生，您忘了將座車的大燈打開，很危險喔，請把車燈打開！」

頃刻間，他愣了一下，胸中的怒火隨即被關心的春風吹熄。事後，他在電話中跟我說：「差點大哭一場。」

別讓噩運追到你

人生難免碰到不如意，此時我們很容易困在負面的情緒裡，埋怨天地無情、時不我予。愈罵愈生氣，愈生氣就愈像一回事，好像全世界都真的對不起自己。直到我們碰到一個好人、聽見一句好話，才恍然大悟，看見自己的脆弱與偏激。

他還算是個幸運的人，在心情的谷底，碰到好心提醒安全的警察，讓他頓時改變觀念，用正向的角度重新看待自己。

不是每個人都有這樣的運氣，**失意時，我們只能勉勵自己，讓頭腦裡正面的想法跑快一點、爬高一點，別留在情緒的谷底，才不會讓噩運追到你。**

天下不會永遠有倒楣事跟定你，除非你自己想要跟負面的情緒混在一起。脫困的關鍵，就在你的一念之間而已。

開運心咒語　正面思考，並準備好替代方案，才會從噩運中脫困再起。

今日【宜】改變造型、換ＭＳＮ暱稱、設定手機答鈴。
今日【忌】固執己見、和朋友相約打賭、借錢給親友。

改名、改運、改風水

姓名、風水，改來改去，究竟要怎麼改才有效？
即便只是想花錢消災，也要問自己：態度改了沒有？

藉由「改名」來「改運」，是近幾年很風行的社會現象。我訪問過身邊為了改運而改名的幾位朋友，大部分都覺得有效，少部分則認為無效。

仔細分析這兩種不同反應的族群，認為改名確實有助於改運的人，在改名的同時，都很配合地做了或多或少的改變，例如：服裝、髮型……等，甚至有人還換了工作。反觀，認為改名無助於改運的人，就真的沒有太大改變，甚至家人都還是用從前的名字叫他，理由是：「叫習慣了，改不過來！」

哦，「習慣了，改不過來！」真是一語驚醒夢中人。原來，**「改名」和「改運」之間，如果要畫上等號，中間還需要很重要的一個動作，叫做「改革」**。

改革，對個人來說，是徹底改掉積習已久的毛病與惰性，清除阻礙溝通的主觀意識，搬移擋住視線的盲點，得到一個全新的自己，重新出發！對企業而言，則是要有無比的魄力和決心，重建願景、再造組織，才能大刀闊斧開闢新里程。

無論是個人或企業，面對需要改革的時候，不忍痛砍掉過去的自己，命運的潮流就會淘汰你。

名字只是符號；性格才是關鍵

聞名台灣健身界的「佳姿」、「亞力山大」先後宣告停業，消費者和員工都受害，險些釀成社會事件。許多媒體又開始充當「事後孔明」，解析這兩家原本聲勢壯大的企業，為何會先後在一夕之間吹了熄燈號？企業負責人的姓名、命格、風水……又被搬上檯面討論。

這些議論也許並非全是空穴來風，但站在企業顧問診斷的立場而言，最主要的原因是：經營團隊中缺乏專業經理人參與決策，而由企業經營者一個人的性格，影響了企業文化、決定了品牌精神，無論是過度保守或太快擴張，都會導致失敗。

至於「姓名學」，也不完全是迷信，企業的名稱是企業識別系統的一環，影響至鉅。我的老友曾是「佳姿」企業旗下的一位幹部，當時我就跟她提過，「佳姿」原是「韻律舞教室」的代表品牌，相對於運動健身這種比較偏向陽剛味的產業，若沿用「佳姿」可能會讓男性消費者望之卻步，連帶影響女性消費者加入的意願。她苦笑說，專業顧問團也曾向老闆提過相同的建議，但老闆沉迷在往日輝煌的品牌印象中，不肯接納意見。

企業可以屹立百年，但品牌形象卻必須隨著經營的階段性使命不同，而有新的溝通或詮釋方式。「佳姿」不一定要隨著市場需求的變化改名，但至少要調整它和市場溝通的調性，若太固執於舊有形式而不思創新，就等於反映出老闆的個性和作風保守，難以適應瞬息萬變的市場環境，很容易會被淘汰。就像那句老話：「性格決定命運！」**如果性格不肯改變，命運的發展就難有重大的突破。**

而「亞力山大」品牌，雖然名字已是陽剛味十足，但因負責人過度擴張事業版圖，透支企業財務及信用，加上經濟不景氣、市場低迷，忽略社區型低價位的「民眾運動中心」興起，會員招收愈來愈困難，終於導致巨大的財務缺口難以填平而關閉。這個相對的案例則顯示：名字對了，性格錯了，同樣難保有好運。

過於迷信「姓名學」的朋友，應該可以從這兩個案例中深思反省。**名字是很重要的符號；但性格才是關鍵。**如果只改名字、不改個性，還是很難改變現狀。

改風水，心理作用牽引實際效果

某大機構連日來頻頻出錯，經高人指點整修門面，花了一筆經費將大門內縮，增加玄關的空間，藉由改變風水來求得好運。

記者敏銳地發現這項事實，徵詢該機構主管未果，於是轉向職員及路人探詢意見：「改變風水，可以帶來好運嗎？」可以想見的是，答案見仁見智，有人斥為無稽之談，有人認為不妨一試。

其實，改變風水是否能帶來好運，並不見得短期內就能立竿見影，而不管是贊成或反對的意見，自然也就很難立刻印證。但是我認為：大興土木改變風水，雖非絕對必要，若順利完工，多少會有些正面的效果。

我的論點絕不是基於迷信的立場，而是從提振士氣的方向來解釋。

主管下令修改大門的位置，形同是決心的宣示，讓同仁們知道管理階層不惜大刀闊斧要進行改革。在大型而散漫的官僚型組織中，這種動作比「喊口號」、「貼標語」、「掛海報」還有效。

同仁們從每天進出的大門，就能感受主管積極的態度，於是更會提醒自己、鞭策自己，進而提升整體的工作效率，減少出錯。

看似沒有科學根據的主張，自然有它邏輯上可以推理成立的意義。但風水之說畢竟只是精神上的激勵，如果主管在改變風水的同時，也能進行其他配套措施的推動，例如：工作規範的教育、工作流程的研議、激勵制度的實施，讓整個系統真正動起來，提升士氣及效率的成果將更為明顯。

別讓命理風水成為推託的藉口

對不相信風水的人而言，需要的是實際的作為。當組織出狀況時，聘請管理顧問公司來做專業的診斷，提出改善效能的具體建議，才能對症下藥，解決問題。可惜，多數主管寧願相信風水命理，用簡化的方式來解決當下的難題，而不願花費心思，聘請專家來鉅細靡遺地檢討改進。除了怕麻煩之外，最主要的心態還是在於他們不敢、也不願負責，於是一味將問題推給命理風水，隱藏自己能力不好、管理不彰的事實。

如果是個人面臨的生命難題，道理也是相通的。**求神問卜、拜佛誦經，給的是心靈的解藥；唯有自我反省、並求助專家，付出努力而且用對力氣，才能真正改善自己，邁向更美好的人生。**

開運心咒語　自我反省與改革，付出努力用對力，就能邁向美好人生！

今日【宜】向貴人表達感恩、或為自己的過失致歉。
今日【忌】為了吸引別人注意自己，講太誇張的話。

最有效的護身符

人生的運勢，總是有起有落，如何掌握穩定的節奏？
能在順境中警戒、逆境中奮鬥，靠的是哪一張護身符？

身處不同國家的兩位優良模範駕駛，竟然都在獲得頒獎表揚之際，出了嚴重的車禍。究竟，他們為什麼會功虧一簣呢？

五十三歲的麥茲，是住在美國愛達荷州的卡車司機。從事這項工作十八年來，駕駛總里程超過一百萬公里，都不曾出過車禍，因此獲頒「安全駕駛獎」。

然而，他卻在開車前往俄亥俄州哥倫布領獎的途中，被另一輛從對面車道越過安全島的車子撞上。他為了閃避對方，讓自己駕駛的卡車衝向路邊，整個人被夾在駕駛座裡，動彈不得。

由於這次車禍的肇事原因，完全是對方的過錯，所以他還是獲頒了「安全駕駛獎」，只不過是在醫院的病床上領獎。

事隔半年多，英國的三十七歲貨車駕駛柯斯，也有類似的遭遇。

他受雇於一家貨運公司，擔任駕駛十二年，從來不曾發生事故，老闆於是頒給他「模範駕駛獎」，並且發出獎金一百英鎊（大約新台幣五千元）。誰知道，才領完獎狀及獎金，還不到兩個小時，他就出了車禍，把小貨車撞得面目全非。

我將上述兩個實例分享給朋友，反應各有不同，有人說他們是緊張過度、有人猜想他們是樂極生悲。

但是，在現實的生活裡，的確有許多類似的經驗。愈接近預定的目標、或剛達成一項難能可貴的成果時，就很容易發生意外。

例如：苦學成功即將畢業、服了多年的兵役剛剛退伍、大半生活都不如意卻突然中獎……經歷這些生命中很重要的里程碑時，心情都會有些變化，太緊張、太開心、太鬆懈，都可能影響了正常的節奏，讓原先行雲流水的生命旋律，瞬間變得荒腔走板。

「平常心」的境界

人生的運勢，也許有起有落，但若要維持恆常的快樂，最重要的祕訣是：掌握穩定的節奏。

凡人一如你我，要做到「不以物喜；不以己悲」，談何容易？但願悲喜之後，沒有動搖自己原來的步伐，只要該做的、該留心的、該付出的、該負責的……秉持所有正面的思考，讓該進行的一切保持該有的行動力，儘管經歷波濤起伏，仍然堅持以平穩的步伐向前走。所謂的「平常心」，大概就是這個境界吧！

前述那兩位駕駛，在領獎的波折過後，只要能保持當初戒慎恐懼的警覺，應該還是可以繼續當個安全駕駛。

我曾在夜間開車行經車禍現場，警察正在對駕駛進行酒測。同行的朋友目睹肇事車輛的後照鏡掛了很多個護身符，應該是車主到不同的民間廟宇求來保平安的，她感嘆地說：「若真要出事，再多的護身符也沒用。」

駕車的我，沒有仔細觀察那部肇事車輛，不過聽到她的評語，我倒是想起曾搭乘一輛剛剛收到違規罰單的計程車，司機索性將違規的相片，貼在擋風玻璃上。他向我坦承，這已經是一個月之內收到的第三張罰單。

原來，是他習慣性開快車，經常超速或闖紅燈，而被自動照相偵測系統拍照罰錢。為了避免再度違規，他故意把照片貼在駕駛座前作為警惕，以隨時提醒自己：「要放慢速度！」

有恃無恐，反易釀成災禍

從廟裡求來的護身符，的確有心理上的安定作用。但是，對於經常開車違規的駕駛而言，在車內貼上違規照片，更有實質的警示效果。

無論從事什麼工作、信奉哪一個宗教，我們常以為只要有護身符，就可以得到神明的保佑，於是便忽略了「自助之後，才能得到天助」的道理。過多的護身符、或過度仰賴護身符，會讓當事人掉以輕心，失去自身該有的警戒，鬆懈下來、有恃無恐，反而容易釀成災禍。

想要藉由護身符來求平安的人，應該轉換另一個角度來看待護身符的意義。**護身符不是一掛上去就能直接發揮保平安的效果，而是當事人必須虔誠地將護身符當作一種提醒，讓自己隨時保持戒慎恐懼的心情，才能降低意外發生的機會，以遠離災禍，常保平安。**

相對地，如果當事人因為相信自己有個法力超強的護身符，而誤以為牛鬼蛇神從此不會入侵，為所欲為、不知節制，反而會惹禍上身。

一位中年朋友的老父親，隨著進香團前往高山中的宗教聖地朝拜，事前他就聽說求得寺廟的護身符可以保平安，但必須連續擲出三個「聖筊」才能得到一個護身符。通常整個團體中能夠求得護身符的人數，不會超過四分之一，更令人深感護身符的寶貴。

經過一個多小時祈禱擲筊，他終於連續擲出三個「聖筊」，獲得一只護身符，但卻在回程途中不慎跌跤，摔斷了腿。

幽默的老人家向兒子自嘲：「不是護身符無效，而是自己樂極生悲！」惜福感恩，不怨天尤人。在他的體驗與告白裡，我看見很難得的人生智慧。

提醒自己隨時保有好ＥＱ，就等於是隨身攜帶最能保平安的無形護身符。即使面對意外、挫折，都能勇敢面對、樂觀處理，就算苦中作樂，也是無比快活。

開運心咒語　惜福感恩、隨時保有好ＥＱ，是最有效的護身符。

幸福開運Q&A

隨身自備幸運物

Eric

Q 除了到廟裡求護身符，還可以隨身攜帶哪些幸運物，用以保平安、也帶來好運呢？

Tiffany

A 以下就提供幾個平常容易遇到的狀況，幫助大家選擇簡單又不貴的幸運物！

香花：驅趕陰氣

有些地方就是會突然讓你背脊發涼，這一定要小心喔！深夜返家，或是上公廁、到醫院探病時……如果怕被「看不見的陰力」跟隨，你可以買一串香花掛在車裡或包包上，香氣的力量就可以驅趕陰氣！

紅色棉線：消災解厄

將紅色棉線拿去過香火或浸沾聖水，然後綁在身上，可消災解厄。洗澡時也不要拿下來喔！

紅色內褲：擋災避禍

覺得自己常常意外受傷、外出不順時，可以穿紅色內褲擋災。價格材質不拘，只要是紅色就可以了。

榕樹葉、茉草葉：帶來好運

覺得窘困而諸事碰壁時，可以將七片榕樹葉或茉草葉，洗淨後放進紅包袋裡，隨身攜帶，可帶來好運。

玉器、磁石：避邪化阻

如果願意花些錢，可以為自己挑一塊玉，或是購買磁石、鈦、鍺做的飾品，不但能避邪、化阻，還能幫你整理磁場。你可以終身使用它，算起來其實也滿實惠的呢！

今日【宜】進廟燒香祈福，到教堂禱告、或真心懺悔。
今日【忌】和朋友相約狂歡、暴飲暴食、或過度消費。

只要相信，就有神力！

泥菩薩過江，並非自身難保，而是要保住蒼生。
信仰，是心靈的修養；迷信，是條件的交換。

出差在飯店吃自助式早餐時，看見一個就讀中學的男孩，正在和他的父親一起享用餐點。

他們父子倆先後拿取餐點回座，男孩並沒有立刻拿起刀叉吃東西，反而靜靜坐在餐桌前，微笑地看著盤裡自己選取的菜餚，然後閉上眼睛，很認真地禱告。

男孩的神情，透露著謙卑與感恩，和時下一般的青少年很不一樣。雖然我不是基督徒，卻對他的儀式充滿尊敬。在這個價值觀多元而混淆的時代，從小就能擁有堅定的信仰，是多麼幸福的事。

從小到大，我信奉過不同的宗教。曾因好奇，參加聖經函授課程，小學五年級就拿到初級班的畢業證書；長大之後，與佛、道教接觸較多；到現在則深深感覺，每個人的心中，都有一位神祇，而宗教是一種儀式，它能幫助你通往內心，和自己的神祇對話。

曾經在青少年時期心靈受困的我，憑藉著宗教的力量，而走出許多難關。當時我怕神明懲罰，不敢做壞事；也靠神明保佑，相信幸運會降臨。消極的和積極的兩種力量，帶著我以穩健的步伐，追尋生命的方向。

泥菩薩過江，並非自身難保

有一位來自印度的女性奇人，被稱為「擁抱聖人」，只要被她擁抱過的人，都有重生的感覺。到目前為止，她已經擁抱過兩千四百萬人，讓他們獲得心靈的力量。緬甸還有一隻小牛，被牠舔過的人，百病全消，有四百多人的疾病，因此而治癒。

以上這兩個案例，強調信仰的神奇功力，可以幫人消災解厄。但是，有時大難臨頭，連神像都遭殃，深信不疑的民眾，又會自圓其說，安頓自己的身心。

幾年前颱風來襲時，台灣一處知名廟宇的神像，因為高度太高而被強風吹倒，附近民宅則無其他災情傳出。

若是用傳統的諺語來嘲諷：「泥菩薩過江，自身難保！」就太尷尬了，所以廟方出面解釋：「這是神蹟，表示菩薩代替信眾受苦受難。」

師父於是為傾倒的神像誦經祈福，並且表示近日內會再重新塑立神像，繼續保佑大家。

以宗教信仰的立場而言，我當然認為廟方解釋得很好，十分正面，道理既說得通，也能安撫人心。同時，也給我們上了一課，改變從前對「泥菩薩過江，自身難保！」這句諺語的負面印象——泥菩薩過江，並非自身難保，而是祂犧牲自己，保住蒼生。

素來嘴巴不饒人的損友阿寬吐槽說：「萬一大災難來了，地震、海嘯……連蒼生都不保的時候，要怎麼辦？」

我笑著模仿起師父的手勢及口氣，對他說：「這表示菩薩和蒼生，受苦受難，同在一起。」他聞言大笑。

表面上看起來，這些強調神蹟的案例好像都很迷信，信仰和迷信之間，的確常被混為一談，而且效果也很相像——都是祈求消災解厄、趨吉避凶。但我認為，**信仰和迷信之間，有個很明顯的差別。**

信仰是靠自己心靈的探索，找到生命的力量，並且有長期的影響；而迷信卻是完全靠別人的力量，解決短期的問題。

前者，是心靈的修養；後者，是條件的交換。

不論是否信奉宗教、或相信某種人生的價值和哲學，我確定：有信仰、而不迷信的人，會比較幸福！

宗教信仰，本來就是要安撫人心，給信眾帶來力量，但若沉迷於這些似是而非、顛三倒四的說法，就是迷信了。

宗教信仰，可以帶來力量

「宗教」和「迷信」之間，看似很難區隔，其中卻有一條若隱若現的界線，值得留意！

1. 宗教，是正向而善意的導引；迷信，則是威脅或利誘的驅策。
2. 宗教，是長期投入之後，循序漸進地改變；迷信，則強調短期的效果。
3. 宗教，所看到的是眾生苦難，解決的是普世問題；迷信，則是針對個人的痛苦，用各種手段解決一己之私。
4. 宗教，鼓勵你愛惜自己、尊重別人，採用好的思考、好的行動，來產生好的力量，改變人生的逆境、往理想的目標發展；而迷信則是要你花錢消災，誆騙你不用付出努力，就可以改變一切。

很顯然地，所有的迷信都是披著宗教外衣進行；而看似正統的宗教，也因為少數人吹捧大師地位，或假借大師之名行騙，而難以與迷信劃清界線，甚至還發動戰爭、恐怖攻擊，以求版圖的安穩或勢力的擴展。

當你分不清自己究竟是「信仰」還是「迷信」時，不妨用上述四個指標檢視一下，以免誤入歧途。

保持對宗教信仰的高度熱忱，可以活出生命的光彩；但若一味地迷信神力、渴求神助，就很容易鬼迷心竅、走火入魔！

開運心咒語 有信仰、而不迷信的人，會比較幸福！

Part 2

好心，才有好運！

以愉悅的神情，表現快樂的行動力，才能輕鬆交好運！
在生活中懂得變通，就不用怕變化；
用想像激發潛力、花心血付出努力，心想事成將指日可待！

今日【宜】確認重大計畫的進度，是否與目標達成度相符。
今日【忌】因為心存僥倖，臨時起意去做些脫軌失序的事。

不是天意，是大意！

在車上嘿咻後就肇事，是因為「車震」辱「車神」？
「天意」和「大意」之間，字形相似，意義有何不同？

遭遇不幸的意外時，人們的反應很兩極。有些人無法接受事實，哭喊：「老天太不公平了！為什麼是我？」另一種人則逆來順受，長聲感嘆：「這是天意！」

針對這兩種截然不同的態度，我沒有對或錯的評論。發生意外的當下，這些反應都是很自然的。

最重要的是：意外發生之後，能懂得平靜自己，並且獲得智慧，把一切的「發

生」，都當成是對自己有意義的學習，這才是關鍵。

住在一流學區的某位親友家裡，有個正在就讀中學的孩子，他的功課向來很優秀，根據平常的在學成績，以及學校的模擬考成績推測，應該可以考上第一志願的高中。

入學測驗結束當天，他自己計算分數，很篤定地認為自己會考上就在住家附近的第一志願，上學只要步行五分鐘。可是，收到成績單時，他發現比預估的成績多錯了兩題，放榜後確定只上了第四志願的高中，距離家裡很遠，卻和父親辦公的地方很近。全家人都不可思議地說：「這是天意！」

朋友的父親患有高血壓，必須按時服用藥物控制病情。幸好，多年來他一直保持運動的習慣，飲食也還算正常，健康狀況維持得不錯。

本來，他們都不擔心了，出乎意料的是，有一天清晨，老人家例行晨泳時，竟在游泳池邊中風，及時送醫後搶回性命，但已不能行動自如，需要旁人協助照料日常生活。仔細一問，才知道當天早上，他出門前忘了服藥。他們全家都同聲感嘆：「這是天意！」

還有一位男性朋友結婚後，和太太取得共識，堅持不生小孩，卻在毫無防備的情況下懷了身孕。由於夫妻倆都是虔誠的基督徒，認為這個孩子是「上帝的恩典、天賜的禮物」，儘管與他們的人生規劃完全背道而馳，還是願意生下小孩，好好扶養。

別把「大意」推託成「天意」

以上發生在我周遭的三個實例，都是在意外狀況下發生事與願違的結果，幸虧當事人的EQ很高，懂得虛心接受既成的事實，把生命中所有好與不好的事，都概括承受。這是很好的修養，但只適用於已經發生的事。

仔細觀察「這是天意」的案例，或多或少，都隱含有「粗心大意」的因素。例如：「忘記按時服藥」、「填答試卷沒有重複檢查」、「做愛做的事不戴保險套」等，其實都可以防患於未然，事先避免遺憾發生。

「天意」與「大意」，兩個「字形」相似的語辭，筆劃只差「一橫」，意義卻相去甚遠。

當意外的不幸已經發生，必須勇敢接受現實，把一切挑戰與磨難當作「這是天意」，去學習、去承擔，不必過度自責，沉溺在無濟於事的悔恨中。但是，面對未來，必須檢討自己曾經犯過的「粗心大意」，避免下一次再有同樣的疏忽。

接受「天意」，別再「大意」，經歷挫折，才會有正面意義。

如果，不回頭深刻地反省，理性地檢討自己，很容易把一切過錯推給「不科學的怪力亂神」或「不知其所以然的神祕原因」，唬騙別人、嚇自己之後，「天意」還是會追隨著「大意」而來，不幸的事件很可能接二連三地發生，覺得自己很倒楣卻又從不檢討的苦主，還會執迷不悟地說「禍不單行」呢！

「車震」辱「車神」？

信彰剛買新車不久就連續肇事，第二次發生車禍時，他和女友都受到擦撞傷，在醫院躺了八天才出院。親友都懷疑他是不是鐵齒沒拜拜，還是車上沒掛平安符？

否則怎麼會這麼倒楣？

直到修車廠技師修理擦撞過後的汽車時，在座椅角落撿到了開封過的保險套包裝盒，真相才漸漸大白，讓他被陪同去修車的同事糗到不行。

他為自己辯解，不是吝嗇到不肯花錢帶女朋友上賓館，而是那個晚上看夜景氣氛太浪漫，以致於情不自禁而慾火焚身，乾脆在車上解決，澆熄熊熊的熾烈。

這則趣聞傳到隔壁部門的主管耳裡，他可擺出一副倚老賣老的架勢，警告辦公室裡的年輕同仁：「每部車子裡，都有一尊車神，如果你們在車上做那件事，就是當面讓車神受辱。這是褻瀆神明啊，所以不久之後就會出車禍！」

瞧他講得口沫橫飛，同仁們也聽得眉飛色舞，幾位看起來很有人生經驗的中年男人，頻頻點頭說：「真的，不要不信邪喔。」

相互印證之下，果然隔壁部門主管所言不假，當場有幾位同事坦承，他們都有相似的經驗，在車震之後不久就發生車禍。

鬼神之說，可以穿鑿附會，卻難有科學證據。但以合理的邏輯推論來看，「在車上發生性關係」和「在路上發生車禍」這兩件事的關連度還滿高的。

想想看，什麼樣的人、在什麼樣的狀況下，會在車上發生性關係？

交叉分析之後，有幾個可能：

大多數是年輕氣盛的小伙子，約會時濃情密意到無法把持的地步，於是就地解決滿腔的慾望。

另一種類型則是偷情的伴侶，礙於顏面或可能東窗事發的壓力，無法找到適當的場所發生親密關係，所以把愛車當作套房，搖搖欲墜地發洩彼此的需要。

還有一種，就是純粹想找刺激，明明有私密而安全的場所可以展開親密關係，卻故意要把車子開到荒郊野外，用不可預期的危險來加強腎上腺素的分泌，讓雙方興奮到差點不能呼吸。

「性」急，才是肇事主因

以上這幾種推理，無論是人物背景、或環境因素，都是容易發生車禍的高危險群。

年輕氣盛，常粗心大意；偷情密會，常緊張兮兮；偏愛刺激，常製造危機。難怪車震之後，肇事的機率高於平常。

此外，在車上發生親密關係之後，駕駛人精神不濟，更是可能的致命要害，即使車神肯原諒，亦擺脫不了魔鬼糾纏上身。

頻繁車震之後，很容易出車禍！除了這些心理和生理層面的推測以外，不妨來聽聽專家說法，居然也有物理的根據。

資深藝人林志穎是賽車好手，愛車如命的他曾在接受媒體採訪時表示：「車震之後，車子的性能一定會受影響，是最大禁忌！」可見激烈的搖晃，也是影響車子性能而肇禍的原因之一。

畢竟，車子是交通工具，還是盡量不要挪作其他用途，比較安全。不論是基於什麼動機或無奈的原因，在房車內「辦事」，總是存在著不可預期的風險，只要避免這些人為的疏失，發生意外的機率就會大幅降低。

行車安全，人人有責。正因為駕駛車輛在馬路上奔馳的變數很多，所以每位駕駛都必須謹慎小心。沒有人想要主動肇事，更不會有人願意開車被撞，所以每次車禍都是「意外」，但是認真想想，事出必有因，哪一次的人為車禍，是完全不可避免的呢？

敬天畏神，是為人處世必須的謙卑。但是把自己一時「大意」所釀成的災禍，說成是「天意」，可就是很明顯的推卸責任囉！

開運心咒語　接受「天意」，不再「大意」，經歷挫折才有正面意義。

幸福開運Q&A

行車平安吉祥物

Eric

Q 自行車、機車、汽車、卡車等，是很普遍的交通工具，對駕駛人來說，「行車平安」是最重要的事。除了掛些「平安符」之外，還有沒有哪些方法可以提升駕駛人的能量，避免車道上的「阿飄」淘氣、搗蛋，以確保行車安全？

Tiffany

A 提供大家幾個簡單又有用的小妙招，確保自己安全上路，平穩駕駛：

擺香花，求保佑

在車上放置具有天然香氣的東西，除了避邪，也可以引來守護的力量，如：檀香木、玉蘭花、茉莉、香水百合……等。不能用加工過的香精取代喔！

灑海鹽，除穢氣

開車前，在四個輪胎上撒一些海鹽或紅胡椒粉；邊撒要邊導唸：「清澈來、污穢去！」也可以在車上放置一包備用，當你莫名其妙覺得煞車怪怪的、或是不停迷路時，就可以中途停車，做這個除穢氣的動作。

放經書，招福運

在駕駛座旁的置物處，放置聖經或佛經，就可以為你帶來福運，甚至連找停車位都會比較順利。但請不要放新的，最好是唸過數次的經文。

貼紅紙，降災禍

在擋風玻璃上貼一張紅色的圓形色紙，可以降災避邪。大小材質不拘，也可以自己剪一張圓形的紅色剪紙喔！

今日【宜】安靜獨處，想像自己的未來，並且許下願望。
今日【忌】光說不練，憑藉魯莽的行動，任性為所欲為。

心想事成的祕密

人生，是一齣持續而即時演出的舞台劇，
不能預演也無法重來，想實現願望，要靠：內心彩排！

全球暢銷書《祕密》講述的道理很簡單，說穿了就是「心想事成」四個字。然而，神奇而有效的座右銘，總是「知易行難」，很容易了解，卻非常難做到。

關於「心想事成」的道理，若要真正實現願望，從「知道」到「做到」之間，需要很強大的右腦思考運作，以「美好而心嚮往之」的畫面不斷激勵自己，才能引導自己向未來可以實踐的夢境走去。

人生如戲，如果你把人生想像成一齣即將上演的舞台劇，就會發現：正式表演前的彩排，不但有助於事先發現可能的問題，也有助於克服恐懼表演的心理。缺乏舞台經驗的人，上場前若在心中多彩排幾次，正式演出就能有超乎水準的表現，得到令人刮目相看的成績。相同的道理，也適合應用在日常生活中。

用「信心」取代「擔心」

例如：要參加一項重大的考試時，不妨先去看看考場的座位，然後努力想像自己考試時鎮定作答的樣子，同時也演練一下發生任何狀況時的處置之道，包括：鉛筆斷掉、試卷編號有誤、忘了帶准考證……針對這些「萬一」的狀況逐一思考解決方法後，就有了「萬全」的準備。

此刻，**你用「信心」取代了「擔心」**，**負面的想法漸漸遠離，正向的思考愈來愈強烈**。你也因而增加了應考的把握，自然會有不錯的成績。

工作生涯中，免不了要參加謀職面談、出席重要會議、或對主管提案，這時可以事先將要進行的程序想像一遍，例如：對方可能提出哪些問題、該如何應對，就像編寫劇本一樣在腦海中排演多次，盡量讓自己所扮演的角色，和其他角色充分互動，面面俱到地設想周全之後，不但可以避免一時緊張而造成失誤，還能讓自己更有信心、表現更加從容。東海大學社工系系主任彭懷真老師指出：「心理學上有所謂的 Pre-activity，意思就是事先假想即將發生的事，在腦海中演練自己和別人的互動關係，既能克服恐懼，也可以增進人際關係的和諧。」

內心彩排，是善用「右腦思考」的一種自我鍛鍊方式，藉由這些積極而正面的影像，刺激內在的潛力，常能讓你在正式上場時，有特別優異的表現。

培養對幸福美好的想像力

我曾受邀參加一家大型直銷商的年度頒獎典禮，為三千多位優秀的直銷從業人員，講解一堂「如何成為銷售高手」的課程。

正式上台講課前的流程，正好是頒發年度最大獎項，首度由本地銷售人員獲得的最高榮譽——粉紅色賓士轎車一輛。主持人宣布得獎人上台領獎，舞台效果十足的會場也飄飛起五彩的泡泡，營造出如夢似幻的情境。

等到熱烈的掌聲稍歇，得獎人開始致詞，麥克風裡傳送出清柔嬌美的語調。她不疾不徐地說：「知道有這項獎勵辦法以後，我就告訴我女兒：『有一天我們家樓下，會出現一台粉紅色賓士轎車。』我也告訴我先生同樣的話。後來，他們常常問我：『粉紅色的賓士轎車什麼時候來啊？』我今天回家，終於可以告訴他們：『打開窗看看，屬於我們的粉紅色賓士轎車已經停在樓下了！』」

短短幾分鐘的致詞，讓我見識了一位超級業務員親自分享美夢成真的過程。她的現身說法，印證了「想像美好畫面」對夢想的實踐，有多麼關鍵性的激勵影響。「有一天我們家樓下，會出現一台粉紅色賓士轎車。」這種描述夢想的方式，非常有畫面感，可以刺激右腦思考，產生行動力！

很特別的是，這位得獎人徹頭徹尾是一名講話客氣、動作婉約的女性，毫無虛假做作的模樣，也沒有咄咄逼人的氣勢，和傳統刻板印象中的「銷售高手」有很大差別。從她身上，我再次印證一個事實：做任何事情，專業的方法與技巧很重要，但更關鍵的是——實現夢想的決心和行動，以及對幸福美好的想像力。這是「心想事成」的過程中不可或缺的成功法則，「剛柔並濟」，缺一不可。

隨心所欲地踏穩生命的節奏

聽她以身作則示範了「心想事成」的成功法則，換我可以上台放心地傳授專業的銷售方法與技巧了。開始問候大家之前，我的腦海仍浮現她剛才幽默的結語。她說：「記得第一次開車上路，我老公坐在我旁邊，一直催我：『開快一點，後面的車都在按妳喇叭了！』後來我很會開車了，我老公則在旁邊說：『開慢一點，後面的警車追上來了！』」

而成為一位「人生高手」，也許就是在實現夢想的過程中，悠遊於快慢的節奏之間，隨心所欲地掌控自己的生命進度，而朝著夢想前進吧！

開運心咒語　用信心取代擔心，用想像刺激潛力，朝夢想勇敢邁進。

幸福開運Q&A

禱告及許願須知

Eric

Q 禱告或許願，不但可以安頓身心，也有助於心想事成，但有些人對上天是「有求必應」，有些人則是「叫天天不靈」，效果相差很多。無論採用何種宗教儀式，禱告或許願時有哪些禁忌？選擇什麼樣的環境或時機來禱告或許願，才會比較靈驗呢？

Tiffany

A 禱告、許願、冥想……都是運用心智力量達到扭轉運氣的目的，或藉此力量讓自己的心念直達天聽，以尋求幫助。

這可不是迷信喔！以科學的角度來分析，祈禱是以「念力」發動成功的。當一個人心無雜念，專注地發出同一頻率時，其念力波是很強大的（當然，每個人的念力強度也各有不同）。若以宗教角度解釋，祈願能讓神靈感受到你的心念和誠心，以施展慈悲，助你達成心願。

不管你相信哪種說法，這的確有效喔！無論你是天主教徒祈求天主、或道教徒祈求菩薩，甚至只是對著滿天星星專心祈願……唯一要注意的是：這些祈禱都只是助你一臂之力，就像是給你一種飛奔的能力，但你若不舉起雙腳跑步，等於還是徒勞無功。所以，自己的基本努力仍然不可少！以下就歸類出最有效的祈願小祕訣，跟大家分享：

保持心誠

東方或西方祈願的共同點，就是「心誠則靈」。這可不是光靠誠意就可以喔！所謂的「心誠」，還包括了專心和信心。

- **專心：**祈願時胡思亂想，就像是講話講不清楚，當然無法心想事成。許多修持者在祈禱前會沐浴更衣，甚至還會在當天斷食。有些密法還規定要穿白色衣服進行……這些都是讓心靈安靜、保持專注的方法。
- **信心：**必須深信祈願是有用的，你的念力才會有效。

清潔更衣

若不方便沐浴更衣，可省略這一步，只要你身上沒有發出擾亂情緒的汗臭味和黏膩感。

輕食減量

祈願前兩小時不要吃太多東西，否則容易有睏意，若是消化不良更糟糕。也不一定要禁食，有些人反而會因為飢餓感而無法專注。

釐清願望

- 將心願單純化，內容要盡量簡潔清楚。不要一次祈求太多事，最好一邊祈願、一邊在腦海中勾勒出願望達成的景象。（想像力若不太好，也可以只在腦海中想像一片光芒。）
- 每天的許願敘述方式與內容，都要相同。

祈願時若容易胡思亂想，可以在祈願前燃燒精油或線香，或是搭配心靈音樂或海潮音效。只要你喜歡，任何時間、任何地點都可以進行祈願。

今日【宜】開始培養長期慢跑、做瑜伽、常閱讀等習慣。
今日【忌】虎頭蛇尾，放棄好不容易下定決心要做的事。

喊出願景，步步為「贏」！

「畫餅充飢」、「望梅止渴」，視覺可以取代知覺嗎？要實現夢想，除了勾勒憧憬的藍圖，還需要什麼條件？

管理學大師們早就主張：「企業長期的發展目標及使命，比短期能賺多少錢更重要！」這幾年來，此番經營理念已被廣為接受。企業要成長茁壯、永續經營，必須有明確而美好的「願景」（Vision），並據此擬定經營策略，統合企業的資源及力量，全力朝此目標邁進。

同樣的道理，也適用於個人生命的經營。每個人的一生，也要有發展的藍圖，全心全意付出努力，才能美夢成真。雖然所謂的「願景」，在描述時比較抽象，也不容易由各種數字堆砌而成，但**「願景」也不是隨便「喊」了就能實現，而是要努力去做、去衝，克服各種困難，才能完成心願。儘管，美好的「願景」具有精神上的激勵作用，但畢竟不是口號，絕非隨便說說就可以！**

正如同一個人的夢想，可以編織得很美、很令人憧憬，甚至從現今來看，可能還有點遙不可及，但至少它不會只是幻覺，只要落實成為計畫，就有可能一步步達成。即使有些目標要達成的時間比較長、中間的變數也比較多，但絕對不能因為這樣，就不肯擬定計畫。

懂得變通，就不怕變化

有些人以「計畫趕不上變化」為由，就懶得做計畫，整個人生東搖西擺，只想仰賴「兵來將擋、水來土掩」的應變能力，卻忽略針對不同變數準備替代方案的重要性，很容易全盤皆輸。

實現願景的道路，是很精密細緻的過程，不能只是走一步、算一步，其間需要邏輯的思考及縝密的推演。只要懂得變通，就不要怕變化。

一家客戶做好年度計畫後，總經理要求我以「顧問」的角色幫他檢視一下。其中，有位業務經理在某個區域預估了很高的年度銷售數字，我問他：「這數字是怎麼推算出來的？有什麼獨特的銷售策略、或是有新產品要上市嗎？否則以現有的市場規模、銷售人力，如何能在同一區域達成比去年的實際銷售數字高出兩倍的目標呢？」他漲紅著臉說：「這是為了配合總經理的期望，自己隨便『喊』出來的。」

我請他回去重新思考這個數字，看是要調整銷售目標、重新擬訂策略、還是增加銷售人力。畢竟，目標和願景一樣，都不是喊得大聲就算數。現在隨便喊，屆時達不到，虛灌的士氣太「膨風」，絕對無法彌補將來更重大的挫折感。

實現夢想，不能只是空想

每個人在實現夢想的路上，都要隨時攤開藍圖，調整步伐、找對路。若只是站在陽光下看著美景發呆，而沒有具體的行動計畫及應變措施，無異只是對自己畫大餅。

「畫餅充飢」就如同「望梅止渴」的效果一樣，用視覺騙知覺，撐不了多久。脫水而死的悲劇，常發生在摘不到梅子的樹下。

想要成就夢想，絕對不能只是空想，要詳細規劃每個步驟，遵循該有的流程。大部分的人，還是要按部就班慢慢來；能夠連著跳過幾個步驟，一蹴可幾的天才，畢竟是少數。沒這個能耐的人，至少要相信「勤能補拙」的道理，該用什麼策略去實現夢想？自己要妥善拿捏，而不是看別人施展什麼高超的手段，就誤以為自己也可以照著做。

按部就班，勢必走得慢；抄捷徑，又有一定程度的風險。這兩種方式，都有可能成功，也有機會失敗，關鍵在於——多一點「量力而為」的自知之明。

我想到一位經常行色匆忙的女同事，她事情很多、心又急，有一天居然在上樓梯時，一個腳步沒踏穩，重重地拐了一跤。當時沒有跌倒，她自己也不以為意，繼續向前走，隔天上班時，看她歪著身體、跛腳走路，非常吃力。

「實在沒想到會這麼嚴重，我只是要去辦一件事，心裡著急，踩樓梯時突然想把兩階併作一階，結果沒踏穩腳踝拐到了，竟然傷得這麼嚴重！」她和大家分享慘痛的遭遇。

在真實的人生中，想必很多人有類似的經驗。我自己也是，跌跤的當時並不覺得痛，可能是為了面子或急著處理更重要的事，忽略了身體的提醒，後來痛到不能正常走路，反而影響了工作進度。

強摘的果子，不會甜

眼睛盯著目標，確定你要的方向，「以終為始」的觀點，的確能避免生命資源的浪費，讓你在勇往直前的路上，掌握正確的目標，不會繞太多冤枉路。但是，按部就班的觀念，同樣值得你提醒自己：踏穩每個腳步。

不必羨慕一步登天的人，得來太容易的成功，常令人不懂得珍惜。就算快速到達目標，也會恐懼自己下一次還有沒有這種運氣。

很多年輕人羨慕某些白手起家的企業主，能夠從臨時工做到總經理，只看到他成功之後的風光，卻不曾用心體會他吃苦努力的過程。這些從基層做起的企業家，之所以有這麼輝煌的成就，都不會是一天兩天的事，而是長期付出與經營的結果。

就像果實的培育與栽植，除了辛勤的耕耘及肥沃的土壤，氣候和季節也是重要的影響因素，「強摘的果子，不會甜。」別著急！如果你持續都在努力，方法也很正確，但還是沒有達成目標，不妨多給自己一點時間，**追尋成功的路上，別忘了要有「耐心」相伴！**

開運心咒語 有計畫按部就班，有耐心量力而為，成功指日可待。

今日【宜】來一趟漫無目的的旅行，放鬆自己的心情。
今日【忌】以作繭自縛的心態，而把自己關在房間裡。

生死由命，富貴在心！

如果自己都放棄了自己，誰又能幫得上你？
與其沮喪地站在原地，不如振奮自己，起來跳支舞吧！

曾有個很熱門的算命網站「預知死亡紀事」，號稱可以幫人推算死因。一位中學女生上網算命，得知自己會「因為求知欲旺盛，自殺而死！」於是拿這個理由，跟媽媽要求不要繼續念書。

青少年不愛讀書的理由，可以無中生有；命運中的死期，是否真的會不幸被猜中呢？

根據科學界的推估，美國每天約有七十七人次在預知的死亡日期中與世長辭。他們並不是找了什麼命理大師，才能準確地預先知道自己的大限，這只是很單純的機率問題而已。這個原理叫做：「大數法則」。當數量樣本較少時，一些偶發性事件發生的機率確實很小；但只要大幅提高樣本數，發生的機率就會變得很高。

但是，人們只會對「命中」的事情，留下深刻的印象。例如：只要有少數幾個人在電視談話節目中陳述自己的奇特經驗，這些故事就會被廣為流傳，而被當作是神蹟的證明。那些口耳相傳有關準確預知死亡的個案，就是在這樣的狀況下，被形容得跟真的一樣。

很多悲劇其實是自尋絕路

中年熟男浩恩，因為生意失敗賠了一大筆錢，太太跟他離婚，在偶然機會下又遇上一個命理師，說他活不過四十五歲。他因而懷憂喪志、鬱鬱寡歡，對一切都很不積極，就此陷入運勢的惡性循環中，不但工作更不順利，健康也愈來愈差。

三年之後，他竟活過了命理師說的大限之期，但也因未能積極突破困境，而活得生不如死。他很感慨地說：「怎麼這麼傻，聽信那老頭的話？」

諾貝爾獎得主馬奎斯的小說作品《預知死亡紀事》中，描述一個男人因為曾經奪去女子貞操，而被她的孿生兄弟追殺，全村都知道此事，只有他自己不曉得，每個人都想盡辦法對他發出預警，但悲劇依舊發生。雖然，這是一個探討人性及貞操的故事，卻也說明了預知死亡其實並沒有意義，很多悲劇看似由天注定，其實是人們一步一步，讓自己走上絕路。

孔子以「未知生；焉知死！」勉勵世人要重視生存的意義，如果現代人道聽途說，相信命理師的「未知生而能知死」，至少也要「置之死地而後生！」，**把握能活著的時候，好好做點有意思的事，總比每天擔心自己會死掉，要來得好過些吧！**

用樂觀的態度面對悲慘的命運

當「置之死地而後生」這句充滿勵志意味的話語，被應用在現實的人生裡，以面對艱難的挑戰、甚至是生死交關的時刻，想要扭轉頹勢，需要的是「意志力」、「努力」，還是「運氣」？

英國一對患有重病的夫妻，以他們的生命經驗，提供了很令人振奮的解答。

一年半以前，妻子身體不適，到醫院檢查，證實罹患乳癌，而她的丈夫，則早就是重度心臟病患者。

各自的醫師分別向他們坦白說明：「來日無多！」

接受近乎死亡的宣判，這對萬念俱灰的夫妻離開醫院，回到家裡，開始詳細列出死亡前要做的五十件事，其中有個共同的願望，就是要一起環遊世界。

幾經考慮，他們決定排除萬難，實現這項願望，啟程去旅行。

一年半以來，他們搭著豪華郵輪，到世界各地去體驗不同國家的風土民情，花費將近四萬英鎊，折合台幣大約兩百萬元。

回到英國之後，他們又進醫院做了健康檢查，結果竟發現丈夫的心臟病病情趨於穩定，而妻子的乳癌則已經痊癒。

他們向醫生表達感激：「若不是被你診斷出絕症，我們不會產生環遊世界的動力；如果我們一直留在家裡，可能早就蒙主寵召了……」

這對夫妻用樂觀的心情面對悲慘的命運，反而替自己帶來莫大的幸運！他們用旅行成功對抗病魔的實例，為「置之死地而後生」做了絕佳的正面示範。

愉悅的心情，有助於身體健康

人愈是到了山窮水盡的時候，愈是要滿懷希望，以正面思考展開積極的行動，為自己開創出柳暗花明的機會。如果自己都放棄了自己，誰又能幫得上你？

喜樂，是最佳良藥。

也許，它不能徹底治療身體的病痛，卻能增進心靈的愉悅。而醫學報告指出：愉悅的心情，的確有助於強化身體的免疫力，即使不能完全打敗體內的毒素，至少可以學會和它們和平相處。

我認識一位資深的護理長，她說：「笑口常開的病人，通常都好得比較快。」

除了心情影響身體的痊癒之外，她還率真地透露一個小祕密：「醫護人員當然比較喜歡跟快樂的病人在一起啊！因此，快樂的病人得到的有形的醫療資源、和無形的關心鼓勵，很自然地也比較多。」

碰到人生的挫折時，可別坐在原地哀聲嘆氣呀！

就像英國歌手羅南（Ronan Keating）唱的〈I hope you dance!〉，與其沮喪地站在原地，不如振奮自己，起來跳支舞吧！

開運心咒語　山窮水盡時，更要正面思考、積極行動，開創柳暗花明的機會。

今日【宜】享受平價美食，吃些新鮮蔬果，犒賞自己。
今日【忌】過度超時工作，導致睡眠不足，掏空自己。

有微笑，財神爺報到！

開店講店格，做人講人氣；
其實，「運氣」和「人氣」一樣，都是經營出來的。

核對完手上的彩券號碼，發現自己又「槓龜」之後，阿德原本深鎖的眉頭更糾結了，連三字經都脫口而出。同事走過他身邊，好心勸告他：「別激動嘛！下次還有機會。」他依然愁眉苦臉。

以上的真實場景，是出現在我負責顧問工作的某大企業辦公室裡。稍長幾歲的我，用不同的方式提醒阿德：有沒有留意到？所有畫像裡的「財神爺」，都面帶微笑！因為，「財神爺」會將樂觀積極的人列為祂優先眷顧的對象；相對地，自怨自艾、牢騷滿腹的人，就比較不容易賺到錢。

我沒有把握，這樣的說法是否能讓他信服，但是，我向來主張、而且深深相信的道理是：**快樂的人，所賺的錢未必輕鬆，但絕對是喜悅的錢；愛抱怨的人，所賺的錢一定都是很辛苦的錢，因為他的財富是用痛苦換來的。**

小至工作發展，大至買彩券中頭獎，道理都是一樣的。很多人以為「運氣」是可遇不可求的；其實「運氣」和「人氣」一樣，都是經營出來的。

一碗拉麵的幸福，從微笑開始

曾經受邀到一位長輩投資的拉麵店做客，享受道地的日式拉麵之餘，也參觀整個作業流程。

長輩十分驕傲地向我展示一貫化的標準作業，從煮水下麵、油炸豬排、到清洗碗筷，都有一套嚴格的規範。

他得意地說：「完全靠機器以及專業的標準化流程，不需要雇用專業的廚師，任何人都可以很快上手。」他講話的時候，一位看起來好像是工讀生的服務人員，正將一塊冷凍麵糰丟進鍋裡。

為克盡做客人的義務，免費被招待吃拉麵，總要講幾句好話，我特別用心地當面讚賞這位同仁：「你看，煮麵還是很講究技巧的，這位服務人員將麵糰放入滾水中，等麵糰一散開就立刻撈起來，難怪你們店裡的拉麵吃起來特別Q！」

原以為這句恭維的話，可以幫助長輩激勵辛苦煮麵的同仁，沒想到這位長輩卻誤會了，他還是一再堅持這種冷凍麵條的煮法非常簡易，再次強調：「哪裡需要什麼技巧，丟下去、撈上來就好！」

瞬間，我觀察到那位本來就沒什麼笑容的年輕服務人員，臉色更難看了。

接著，長輩又開始高談闊論，說要招募加盟店，並且在中央廚房的所在地成立訓練中心，幫助加盟店訓練現場作業人員，以學習操作完整流程的步驟。想到他的偉大計畫，可以造福許多想要創業的青年；想到這些連鎖店賣出的每一碗拉麵，將帶給顧客幸福的感覺；離開現場時，我不得不冒著得罪他的風險，私下對他率性直言：「我認為訓練他們發自內心地微笑，可能和如何煮麵一樣重要！吃一碗拉麵的幸福，應該是從煮拉麵時的微笑開始啊。」

態度誠懇，有效降低負面觀感

表現得很有風度的他，當場愣了一下，隨後就拍拍我的肩膀：「你說的很有道理，我忽略了這些年輕朋友的工作態度，應該好好激勵他們。」

擔任顧問工作這麼多年來，我有下列這幾個很重要的心得，屢試不爽——

如果，你看到笑容滿面的老闆，表示這家公司現在是賺錢的。

如果，你看到笑容滿面的同仁，表示這家公司將來還是會賺錢。

如果，你看到笑容滿面的顧客，表示這家公司不但一直都會賺錢，將來還會是百年老店。

相反地，如果顧客、同仁的臉上都沒有笑容，只有老闆還勉強苦笑著，這家店應該很快就面臨經營危機了。

開店有「店格」，做人講「人氣」。很多人以為「人氣」是可遇不可求的，別人喜不喜歡我？是否看我順眼？好像都不是自己能決定的。我不敢說人緣好壞，百分之一百都操縱在自己手裡，但至少自己應該負起一半以上的責任。

俗語說：「伸手不打笑臉人！」

只要願意表現誠懇和善的態度，就能有效降低別人的負面觀感。這真是很大的學問，我是出了校門才學會的。

剛進入社會工作那幾年，有幸服務於世界一流的電腦公司，見識過很傑出的電腦銷售人員。當時能擔任售價千萬以上電腦的銷售人員，表示學識及能力已受到相當程度的肯定。許多資深的業務經理都很慷慨地與我分享成功的祕訣，包括：積極學習專業知識、把顧客當成最好的朋友、與家人分享生命願景……

這些成功的祕訣，在其他書上也常被提及；但是，有位經理曾告訴我一個很特別的觀念，是我從來沒有聽過的。

他說：「生病時寧願請假，別在上司及客戶面前，露出病懨懨的樣子，以免他們對你產生不信賴的感覺。」

避免露出病懨懨的樣子

身體，難免有生病的時候。通常，為了積極追求成功的目標，很多人會選擇抱病上學或忍痛上班，以表現自己負責、向上的精神。但是，如果身體的狀況已經明顯露出異常的模樣，最好還是留在家裡徹底休養，不要逞強。

在很年輕的時候，聽到這種與一般觀點迥異的指教，我有些驚訝，玩味再三。過了許多年以後，我才體會出這個道理的真諦。

學生或上班族如果掛著一張苦瓜臉，去抱病上學或忍痛上班，頂多會得到一些很浮面的關懷及問候，對病情並沒有什麼實質上的幫助，還可能引來傳播細菌的疑慮。若是經常如此，也容易給人留下身體虛弱、情緒不佳的壞印象，甚至讓人不放心託付重責大任。

要避免經常露出病懨懨的樣子，積極的做法是：平常就多注重養生之道，保持均衡的飲食、充足的睡眠、運動的習慣，盡量不要感冒、生病。萬一，不小心生病了，則要趕緊接受治療，直到看不出「憔悴病容」，才以健康的姿態出現在學校或辦公室。

至於那些經常沒事請病假以逃避責任，或故意誇張病況以博取同情的人，並不是與成功無緣，而是根本就不想成功；講難聽一點，應該好好待在家裡過日子，不要外出影響別人的情緒。

找出正向能量的循環

也許，這種說法有些偏激；但是，卻很實際。主要的用意在於提醒大家：**臉部表情是人生態度的延伸，也是內心想法的投射。**

想要有好運，就要從展現愉悅的表情開始；想要賺高興的錢，也要從快樂的工作態度做起！

即使只是買彩券求財運，也要有積極正面的心態，才有中獎的機會。總沒有人會在買彩券的同時，還詛咒自己不中獎吧？既然如此，又怎能做一行、怨一行呢？

「埋怨別人」和「詛咒自己」，兩者有同等效力，都是負面能量的釋放，「埋

怨別人」就像是在「詛咒自己」。相對地，「感恩別人」和「肯定自己」，兩者也是同等效力，而且都是正向能量的循環。換句話說，「感恩別人」就如同是在「肯定自己」。即使是感恩對方曾帶給你一次很不愉快的經驗，也就是肯定自己在那個不愉快的經驗中有所學習。

若想要擁抱好運，你該選擇的是後者。讓「感恩別人」和「肯定自己」雙效合一，好運就會與你常相左右！

幸福開運Q&A

三個月內有好運

Eric

Q 有時候我們會因為太忙碌、太鬆散或太遲鈍，而忽略身邊可能有好運降臨，進而和好運擦身而過。有沒有什麼簡單的占卜方法，能幫助自己掌握三個月內可能降臨的好運，不讓機會輕易溜走呢？

Tiffany

A 以下有五張塔羅牌，可以用來占卜你在哪方面的運勢最強，希望你好好把握！

現在，請你專注地凝視編號A、B、C、D、E這五張未掀開的牌，接著在心中默唸：「三個月內，我將會遇到哪一種好運呢？」然後選一張牌。

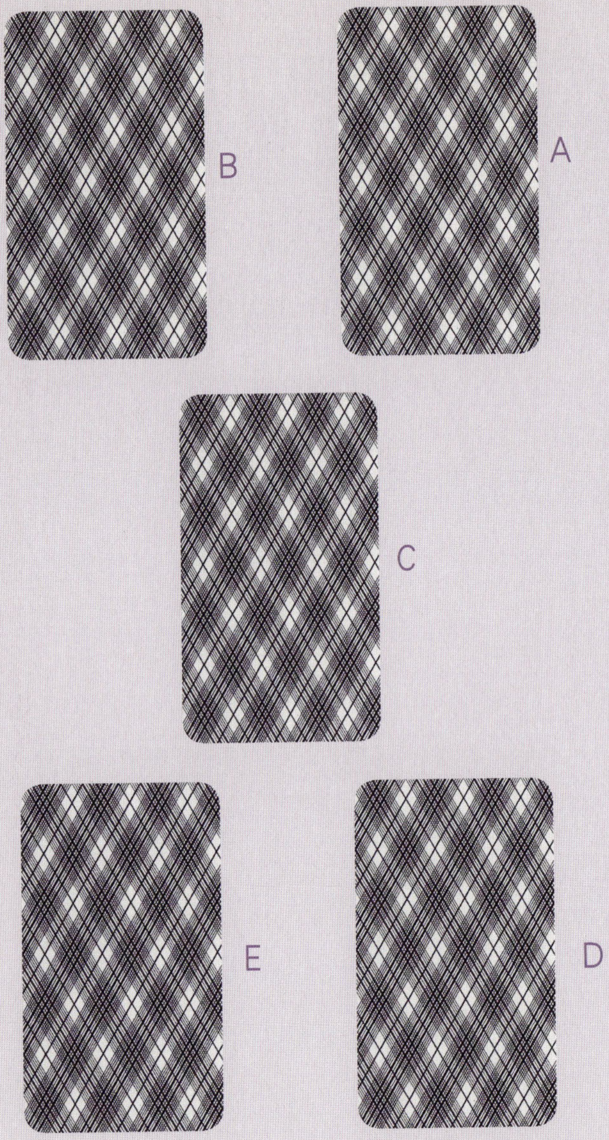
B
A
C
E
D

A戀人：愛情運

恭喜你！桃花舞春風喔！不管到哪裡都人見人愛，還帶動你的桃花朵朵開！不妨對喜歡的異性稍微主動一點，你的「牽緣」成功率會更早達成！

小叮嚀：肉好招蒼蠅，小心爛桃花襲擊！懂得在桃花中挑選適合自己的那一朵，才是聰明人！

B魔術師：學業或工作運

一切將否極泰來，並且能得到各方助力，現在是你發揮實力，得到眾人注目與讚賞的時候了！而且進修、考試、升遷、轉職運都很不錯喔！

小叮嚀：船到橋頭自然直，拚命鑽牛角尖只會讓你白白死掉很多細胞，不妨先抱持平常心，貴人好運自然來。

C女皇：貴人運

人脈越多，貴人運就越旺盛！只要是你在乎的事，冥冥中就會出現各種貴人來相助！即使你不認識對方，他也可能是助你成功的關鍵喔！

小叮嚀：平時若懶於交際，就要多保持親切，否則貴人會少得可憐，除非你倒垃圾時剛好救了大老闆。

D世界：財富運

財運充滿熱能與力量，大膽、革新，就會有好成績！要拿出勇氣往前衝，投資方面要以快、狠、準的方式達成目標，就可以獲得大成功。

小叮嚀：俗話說：「財神送錢給你，總要有管道。」如果你不為自己先鋪出一條路，財神根本找不到你啊！

E太陽：健康運

朝氣煥發、活力充沛，即使在先前有些小病小痛，也可輕鬆消除，就連壓抑的心情也能充分釋放。若好好鍛鍊一番，身體的潛能將更能發揮。

小叮嚀：有健康的身心才能感受到人生的熱情；平常多攝取清淡粗食、釋放壓力，就可以更健康迷人。

今日【宜】接近幸運的親友，向他們賀喜，沾些喜氣。
今日【忌】因為意氣用事，在盛怒中提出分手或辭呈。

做出選擇，轉出好運！

誰說「福無雙至，禍不單行」？
生命中發生的一切，都是被自己吸引過來的。

依照台灣的習俗，大部分的民眾都相信，人生有兩次鴻運當頭的機會，分別是「結婚」及「生子」。

把握這些好運的時機，無論做什麼事都會很得心應手。

這個說法，套用到遠在歐洲的比利時，似乎也行得通。

比利時有一對經濟不是很寬裕的年輕男女，相戀幾年之後，好不容易張羅了一筆錢，其中有大半是借貸來的，很慎重地決定舉辦結婚典禮，兩個人住在一起。結婚，為兩人帶來許多意外的喜氣。

在廣告公司工作多年的男方，他的作品從來沒有得過大獎，卻在休婚假去旅行的期間，傳來喜訊，得到歐洲廣告評選的創意大獎。

女方和一家出版社打著作權官司，纏訟多年之後，也在結婚之際獲得勝訴及賠償。

兩人去蜜月旅行，買了彩券，又中大獎，得到將近台幣三百萬元的獎金。

身邊未婚的朋友們都羨慕地說：「早知道結婚可以交上好運，我就隨便找個人結婚，看看會不會像你們這樣『發』得不像話！」

男主角卻意味深長地警告：「隨便找個人結婚，哪裡會這麼容易走運？必須跟真心相愛的人結婚，才會有好運。」

他說的話，真的很有道理啊！

剛剛結婚的新人，常會有很好的運氣，這倒是司空見慣的情形。但離婚這種俗世歸類為倒楣的事，也能轉成好運道，可就離奇了。

用快樂啟動「幸運的開關」

美國有一位男子佛萊契苦盡甘來，離婚兩天之後中大獎，拿到的獎金大約為台幣九百五十萬元。

據說，佛萊契近來流年不利，數個月前下班回家，發現太太紅杏出牆，接著一九五六年的古董雪佛蘭愛車被鹿撞壞，寵物狼狗毛莉又得了癌症必須安樂死……倒楣事接踵而來，沒想到，辦完離婚手續才兩天，他就中了大獎。

從佛萊契告訴記者「我走運了！」的快樂笑聲中，可以明顯感受到他的好運，其實是來自痛苦的解脫。只要心中快樂，並且相信自己的選擇是對的，不論是結婚或離婚，都會有好運道。

「心中的念頭」永遠比「發生什麼事」，更具有關鍵的影響力。不論遭遇到的是別人眼中的「好事」或「壞事」，只要滿心歡喜地接受，並且認為自己一定會從中得到些好處，「快樂的愉悅感」就會啟動「幸運的開關」。即使是很慘的遭遇，都能因為你的虛心接納與歡喜覺悟，而打開好運的大門。

誰說「福無雙至、禍不單行」？

世間的禍福，都在一念之間，千萬不要忽視自我暗示、自我期許的神奇力量，它可以成就你、也可以摧毀你，就看自己怎麼想囉。

就像《祕密》這本書一再強調的「吸引力」法則：生命中所發生的一切，都是被自己吸引過來的。

你的心就像一塊超級強力磁鐵，將你的念頭與思緒，以及宇宙中頻率相近的元素，瞬間吸引過來，變成眼前的事實。

被拒絕，是重新開始的機會

以下這則真實的愛情故事，來自庭軒的現身說法。花了好多年的時間，他才明瞭：絕處逢生，是多麼可貴的轉機。

庭軒對萍雲愛慕已久，好不容易等到她和交往三年的男友分手，他決定勇敢表白。

在此之前，庭軒也設想過可能被拒絕，或許她會說：「我正處於低潮期，感情的創傷還沒有復原，沒辦法接受你。」最壞的情況，大概就是這樣吧！然後，他會含情脈脈地祝福她：「沒關係，不用那麼著急，我可以等妳！」就算沒有達到立刻可以追求她的目的，至少整個過程是很浪漫的。

但是，完全沒有想到，她竟會那麼斬釘截鐵地說：「我和你並不適合當情人，還是做朋友就好了。」

庭軒當場十分窘迫，他不知哪來的靈感，直接吐出：「難道妳一點機會都不肯給我？」

萍雲很直接了當地搖搖頭回答：「談愛情，沒有機會，我們只能做朋友。」

羞憤大過於傷心的庭軒，忘了當時是如何逃離現場。但事後回想起來，他卻很感謝萍雲，很快地讓他明白，自己連排隊都不必排、等待都不必等，就可以離開，否則將會耽誤更多青春。

一年之後，他出國留學，拿到雙碩士學位，在美國教書、娶妻生子，對這段往事，沒有遺憾，只有祝福。

運氣，是會輪轉的

這裡沒有機會，正是轉往別處發展的好機會。只要能看清事實、認清方向，不要停留在原地踏步，就能更接近目標一些。

在追求成功的路上，最怕的是故步自封，賴在原地怨天尤人，徒然浪費時間而已，到最後一事無成。

庭軒的故事，讓我想起另一位企業界名人李紹唐先生，他曾經在外商電腦公司IBM工作長達十七年，不確定自己是否有升遷的機會，於是主動詢問當時的主管，什麼時候才能爬到總經理的位置？將來是否有接棒的可能？

對方含蓄地回答，在候選補位的隊伍中，他大概位居第十名左右。於是，他做了離開IBM的決定，轉戰甲骨文公司，坐上CEO的位置。

「機會，是給有準備的人！」這是老生常談了，話雖沒錯，但如果做好準備的人數，遠比機會還多，這時就應該仔細評估，機會要等多久才來？如果，不確定的因素大過你所能掌控的前途，不妨勇敢另起爐灶，為自己創造新的機會，而不是苦守寒窯。

我一直相信：運氣，是會輪轉的。但是，轉運的決定權並不是在老天手上，而是在自己的心裡！

你的每一次選擇，都代表一次運氣的輪轉。每一次選擇「向左走」、或是「向右走」，都很可能讓人生從此有了大異其趣的天壤之別。但是，也有可能到最後，其實仍是殊途同歸！

「選擇」的意義與奧妙，就在於你的心是怎麼想的；做出選擇之後，得到的結果好壞，關鍵往往不是選項的內容，而是你的念頭是否足夠正向。

你的樣貌，都是自己的選擇

問自己這個問題：「你滿意自己目前的樣子嗎？」

仔細想想，現在的你有什麼樣貌，其實都是來自你自己的選擇！

同樣的道理，人生的境遇，不論已經壞到什麼地步，你都可以有所選擇！

一位女性朋友平日工作就非常認真、全力以赴。換了一位新主管之後，甚至到了廢寢忘食的地步。

據她說：「忙到連吃中飯、晚飯的時間都沒有！」每天加班到午夜才回家，卸妝、更衣、隨便填飽肚子，已經凌晨三點多，睡不到幾小時，又得準時上班打卡。這樣的日子，已經持續三個多月了。

她曾向新任主管反應過，得到的回答竟是：「我從前也是這樣苦過來的。」

這句聽來似乎很沒人性的話，其實也充滿同理心，必須很內行的人才聽得懂其中的鼓勵意義。翻譯成膚淺的白話文，就是說：「妳若像我這樣拚命，將來也會升遷到我這個位置！」

可惜，她沒聽懂。

既不想辭職、也認為調職無望的她，只會無奈地用勞力與現實的狀況做困獸之鬥。她說：「就看看我做到哪一天倒下了為止！」

她忘了，在倒下去之前，她可以有很多選擇，例如：繼續溝通、爭取將工作外包、甚或越級報告……

「做到哪一天倒下了為止！」其實也是她自己的選擇——一種不想改變現狀的選擇。任憑環境將自己逼上絕路，表面上好像很無辜，卻也是自己做的一種最壞的選擇。

幸運、噩運，一體兩面

每一次選擇，都必須完全負責。即使別無選擇，迫於無奈地接受事實，只要面對及接受，也是一種選擇。

不想對自己所做的選擇負責任的人，常表情無奈地推託：「沒辦法，這不是我要的。」其實是他不肯對自己的選擇負責，表面上好像可以活得輕鬆一點，卻因此付出更大的代價。

某個電影頻道為爭取觀眾，曾推出一系列的電視廣告，大抵是對消費者主張：人生充滿許多選擇，而你可以選擇電影頻道。

說得真好！付費或關機，你永遠可以有所選擇！

付費，要多花些錢，但會得到消磨時間的快樂；關機，要犧牲點娛樂，但也可能改而閱讀，讓內心獲得平靜。

每一種選擇，其實都有得有失。幸運、噩運，其實也可能是一體兩面。幸運到了極致，就可能「樂極生悲」；噩運走到谷底，也可能否極泰來。總歸一句話，無論碰到任何事情，你怎麼想、用什麼態度面對，比較重要！

只要用正向的念頭、做出善意的選擇，都是一次轉好運的機會。往好處想，人生就會往好處走。

開運心咒語　以正向的念頭，為自己的選擇負責，你可以決定人生要怎麼走。

幸福開運Q&A

沾染身邊的喜氣

Eric

Q 聽說多接觸喜事，可以沾染喜氣，碰到親友結婚時，除了給紅包有點「傷財」之外，可以留意哪些事，讓自己沾染更多喜氣、變得更加幸運呢？

Tiffany

A 鴻運當頭的人才會有喜事，這些喜氣是源源不絕，分也分不完的，快跟有喜事的親朋好友們分點喜氣吧！

將喜帖放在枕頭下睡覺

這可是對方寄來的喜氣，別隨手亂丟喔！

和新人擁抱

擁抱、親吻臉頰、握手，都是沾喜氣的方式，別忘了在心中默默祈禱：祝你幸福，多分給我一些喜氣吧！

一定要乾杯

當新人來敬酒，要把握機會跟對方碰一下杯子，然後邊喝邊想著：我要把喜氣喝下去囉！

喜糖不嫌多

這可不是普通糖果，喜糖的蜜運效果，對人氣與桃花最有幫助！喜餅也有這樣的功用。

擁抱有喜事的親朋好友

不只是婚禮，當好朋友買新房子、升職加薪、生寶寶、中獎、考上好學校，都值得你好好跟對方擁抱一下，沾沾對方的喜氣和貴氣呢！

今日【宜】學習新的課程或技能，勇敢跨出第一步。
今日【忌】以「我沒興趣」為藉口，繼續故步自封。

跨越恐懼的柵欄

從「幸好不是我！」到「萬一是我怎麼辦？」，人的心念，會牽引行為的方向及能力的累積。

「心想事成！」這句祝福的話，也是全球暢銷書《祕密》的創作主軸。如果，我們全心全力地禱告，並竭盡所能地付諸行動，卻還是覺得力有未逮，很可能是因為心中有所恐懼。恐懼，是「心想事成」途中最大的障礙。若沒有足夠的信心，夢想怎會實現？

我回想起青少年時期，經常生病、體能很差，一次上體育課時，老師要我們排好隊，短距離助跑之後，依序越過跳箱。還沒有開始助跑，我就暗示自己：「不可能的！」、「絕對跳不過去！」、「會摔斷腿吧！」於是，我始終無法順利跨越跳箱，惹來同學的訕笑。這個心理障礙如影隨形，直到服憲兵役期間，接受軍官訓練時，教官傳授的正確方法，加上必須成為一名優秀軍官的榮譽感，終於讓我能完成艱鉅動作，順利跳箱成功，跨越了心中恐懼的柵欄。

暢銷書《心靈雞湯》作者馬克・韓森曾經說：「恐懼的英文單字是**FEAR**，F代表False，E代表Evidence，A代表Appearing，R代表Real，這四個字合起來，就是False Evidence Appearing Real，正好是『錯誤的證據變成事實』。」所以，他鼓勵所有人在展望未來時，不要恐懼。因為恐懼會限制你的行動，阻礙你鍛鍊實現夢想的勇氣。

恐懼，擺脫噩運的最大障礙

面臨人生的困頓階段、或是遭逢不如意，明明知道該鼓起勇氣重新出發，但依然舉足不前，原因多半是恐懼。

很多人失戀一次之後，就不敢再談戀愛，甚至讓自己深陷在那段未竟愛情的破碎深淵裡。「埋怨過去」和「戀棧往昔」，都會因而走不出全新的自己，其中最大的癥結，就是恐懼的心態——對別人沒信心，對自己沒信心，對老天更沒信心。

我們都以為，落魄到沒什麼好失去的人，應該就沒什麼好恐懼了。但也未必！有些自稱已慘到不能再慘的人，無法從人生谷底爬上來，就是因為他連這種「慘到不能再慘」的狀態都害怕失去，於是持續地顧影自憐，抱著自己可憐的影子，而不願面對它是虛幻的事實，以掩飾對於邁向未來的恐懼。

一位暱稱為「溜滑梯」的讀友，工作上常受挫，在我的部落格留下受傷與失望的訊息。我特地回 e-mail 鼓勵他：「拋開過去，勇敢向前！」但他回信說：「我覺得自己的情況已經糟得不能再糟了，但還是害怕失去最後這方寸間的立足之地。」

困苦的人，有這樣的擔心；長期擁有優異表現的人，到了某個階段之後，同樣會有類似的問題。

守成的心態，若是遠超過接受挑戰的勇氣，贏了太多次以後，就愈來愈經不起輸一次的打擊，出手之前，反而因害怕而再三猶豫。

「幸好不是我！」

從這些現象中，可以發現：**恐懼，是建立自信的大敵**。還沒出師之前，就先自己嚇自己。一旦形成負面的思考，要再翻身就非常不容易。

人的心念，會牽引行為的方向及能力的累積。負面的心念會造成負面的結果；相對的，正面的想法也會帶來成功的希望。**反敗為勝的契機，就在於改變心念，以積極的態度面對事實，才能克服恐懼**。

正如同馬克・韓森所說：「恐懼可以被克服，關鍵在於自己。不要用任何藉口來推卸工作或是該做的事。追求成功並不難，關鍵是克服恐懼，敢於追求目標！」從現在開始，面對你的恐懼吧！了解你的害怕之後，你將發現：沒什麼好怕的，接下來就會變得比較勇敢了！

跟「恐懼」相伴相生的另一個心態是：「僥倖」的心理！對於自己經常擔心發

生的事，不肯面對它可能發生的機率、也不去想萬一發生該怎麼處理，而只是一味逃避，存在著「希望不會輪到我」的妄想，看見別人發生意外或傷害時，還慶幸逃過一劫，出現「幸好不是我！」的念頭，甚至覺得自己真的很幸運呢。

「萬一是我怎麼辦？」

有個長輩很怕得到癌症，偏偏他又經常聽到親友間傳來誰罹患癌症的消息。他盡量要求自己不聽不想，當作沒這些事，連探病都不肯去，怕進出醫院替自己招惹晦氣。

對於上了年紀的老人來說，這也算是人之常情，不能多所苛責。不過讓我比較訝異的是：既然那麼怕得癌症，為什麼不積極地養生保健呢？例如：閱讀防癌抗癌的相關書籍、請教醫生或親友、定期健檢……愈害怕、愈逃避，愈容易誤事啊。

如果，這位長輩除了「幸好不是我！」的念頭之外，能積極地預想：「萬一是我怎麼辦？」整個人的態度與價值，將因此而有一百八十度的大轉變。**在別人經歷**

苦難時，設想「萬一是我怎麼辦？」」，不僅可以產生感同身受的慈悲心，也能培養自己應變的能力，以防止意外之災在自己身上重演。

猶記幾年前，某次颱風在台灣過境期間，桃園機場發生空難，一架某航空公司從台北飛往洛杉磯的班機，起飛失敗墜毀於現場。

時值凌晨零點，電視新聞立刻做了報導，但因SNG採訪車還未抵達現場連線，所以來不及傳送失事現場的畫面。有些民眾可能看到這段消息不久就睡了，在還沒有得到完整資訊之前，坊間透過耳語流傳消息，以訛傳訛到清晨，我在五點多的菜市場裡聽見攤販們說：「C航的班機又出事了！」

勇敢面對災禍，產生智慧與力量

其實，這次出事的飛機，是S航空公司的航班。由於歷年來S航空公司的服務與飛安都頗受各界好評，建立了良好的商譽，反倒是C航的飛機事故頻傳，在民眾的印象中，「C航」與「空難」很容易立刻聯想在一起。

經過我再三澄清說明：「不是C航，是S航。」菜市場的商家才搞清楚是怎麼回事，但仍遲疑地說：「怎麼會呢？S航的飛安不是一直都很值得信賴嗎？」

從這個例子可以看出：聲譽對一個人或一家公司的價值。好的聲譽，總跟好事聯想在一起；不好的名譽，總跟壞事聯想在一起。而一件不好的事，很快地就會摧毀原本的好聲譽；原本的壞聲譽則必須加倍努力、花上很多心血及時間，才能慢慢洗清污名。

後來，我將菜市場的對話轉告一位服務於C航的朋友，他大笑：「這次幸好不是我們公司出事！」我很能理解他語意中的慶幸，對一家急於擺脫污名、建立好形象的公司而言，的確不能再出事。

沒有出事，災難不是發生在自己頭上，固然值得欣慰。但看見別人的悲苦，不妨想想：「萬一是我怎麼辦？」讓自己在悲天憫人的情懷中，生出面對不幸或災難時的智慧與力量。

我很喜歡一句座右銘：**「能解決的事，不用擔心；不能解決的事，擔心也沒有用！」**應用這個道理，也能幫助自己面對內心的恐懼。

沒有人願意碰到災難！正因為如此，所以每個人都應該事先預防災難。

愈是怕事的人，愈要事先訓練自己危機處理的能力，才能在必要時度過難關。就算做了萬全的準備，災難並未發生，至少在「有備無患」的前提下，擁有「高枕無憂」的心安。

這是人生必要的謙卑，幫助自己不淪於傲慢。

開運心咒語 勇敢面對、不存僥倖、有備無患，恐懼就打不倒你。

今日【宜】把夢想告知身邊的人，積極尋求支持。
今日【忌】沒有盡全力溝通說明，只會鑽牛角尖。

開創神奇人生

說出你的渴望，宣揚你的理念。
整個宇宙都會聯合起來幫助你完成。

幾年前，電視購物頻道才剛開始盛行，常出現配音員以誇張的語調說：「喔！傑克，這真是太神奇了。」藉此強調產品難以置信的使用效果，的確能讓消費者憧憬神奇的人生。

據說，這句話的行銷效果出奇地好，除了變成當時的流行語，也幫產品創造了亮眼的好業績。

我常常想著：在這個隨處充斥電腦及網路的世界，究竟是什麼樣的人，可以擁有真正神奇的人生？

有一天，這個問題有了很具體的答案，是來自一位樸實女孩的現身說法。

在健身房運動時，聽見一位窈窕的美女親切地召喚：「吳大哥！」

「喔！這真是太神奇了。」我心中突然浮現這句話，以掩飾內心的尷尬。因為眼前這位身材曼妙的女子，好眼熟啊！

但，她是誰呢？

正當我快要想到答案時，她主動自我介紹：「我是你的忠實聽眾啊！我曾經參加電台舉辦的活動，還拿過你的簽名喔！」

經過她的提示，我的腦袋像是多媒體的放映機，連續快速出現幾個不同場景的畫面，終於找出答案。在一次心靈成長講座中，她勇敢地舉手問主講人一個關於如何讓生命更圓融的問題；另一次參觀及教學的活動，她的作品則展現不凡的創意與精巧的手藝。

親切地打過招呼後，我們各就各位，進行自己的健身運動。

無法被電腦取代的特質

運動期間，遠遠近近聽她的手機多次響起，她總是走到窗邊，細心地接聽，像是在解答學生的問題。

後來還有很多次在健身房碰到她，情況都差不多，比較熟了之後，我好奇地問她：「妳是不是在當老師啊？看你每次來運動時，還要不停接電話，講話的神情都像在幫別人解答問題。」

她笑著說：「是啊！幾年前我的確在當老師，但我已經辭掉教職了。這幾年來是以專職的方式從事直銷工作，我剛剛是在回答下線的問題啦！」

老實說，我對她的答案感到相當意外。從老師的工作轉行到做直銷，是完全不同的跑道。

喔！這真是太神奇了。

後來，想起她細心回答每一通電話的神情，我發現她所創造的神奇人生中，不論是教職或直銷，都有一項最寶貴的共同資產，就是「願意分享」的熱忱與耐性。

而這項成功的要素，也將會是電子商務風行的網路時代中，最無法被取代的人性特質之一。

這位原先是我廣播節目的忠實聽眾，後來變成一起和我在健身房與體能奮戰的好朋友。她有著陽光般的笑容，以及一副熱於助人的好心腸。三年前，她還是一位音樂老師，但因為工作不穩定，勇於轉換跑道之後，從事直銷行業，已經做到主管階級，領導一百多名組員。

有足夠的熱情，就不會被挫折困住

老實說，我曾見識過太多功成名就的直銷從業人員，有些人的直銷事業做得真的很成功，非常了不起，但氣質上卻不免沾染一點「江湖」的氣息。我坦白對她說出我的感受，並且請教她保有天真氣質的祕訣：「該不會是因為妳從前當音樂老師的關係吧？」

「我想，是因為我從來不認為自己在賣東西。」她認真思考後回答：「我不是在推銷產品，而是在宣揚理念。我自己用過了，相信它真的很好，所以我很想告訴我的親朋好友，希望他們不要錯過，如此而已。」

「妳是否也經常碰到挫折呢？譬如妳最好的朋友，並不認同妳所宣揚的理念，拒絕使用你所介紹的產品。」我問。

「這是常有的事，問題可能出在我宣揚的次數還不夠多，或是他沒有類似的經驗，所以很難體會。我會想要知道問題在哪裡，不會把它當成挫折。」她說。

堅持、而且執著，是所有成功業務人員共同的特質。但有人堅持於理想，有人執著於獲利；前者像勇往直前的傳教士，後者只是自營生計的商人。價值觀不同，成就也大異其趣。

讓整個宇宙都知道你要什麼

分享這個經驗、提出這些觀念，並不是要求大家去從事直銷行業，而是邀請你認識自己的理念，然後積極宣揚你的理念，開創不一樣的嶄新人生。

不論在辦公室、在家庭、還是在學校，**能夠宣揚自我理念的人，總是比較清楚自己在做什麼，也比較容易說服別人和自己配合，以便結合這些力量，向人生的目標更邁進一步。**

宣揚理念，並不等於堅持己見；而是積極溝通，共創雙贏。

尤其是轉換人生跑道的時候，即使很清楚自己要的是什麼，還是很可能遭遇親人反對、朋友不看好的處境，簡直就要眾叛親離了。在這個關鍵時刻，別忘了尋求支持的最佳捷徑，就是勇敢告訴別人：

「我需要改變，我想要擁有新的人生！」

愈是碰到別人否定你、不願意幫忙，愈要堅定自己的信念，竭盡所能去溝通。只要是自己想清楚、也必須要去做的事，除了「義無反顧」之外，還要集合群力，即使一時間無法得到實際的幫助，至少要能得到親友的祝福。

我很喜歡、也很經常引用《牧羊少年奇幻之旅》這本書的一句話：「當你真心渴望某樣東西時，整個宇宙都會聯合起來幫助你完成！」

但是實現夢想，除了勇氣、決心、信念、毅力之外，我還想強調的是「溝通」

的重要性！你要「整個宇宙都聯合起來幫助你完成」，總也要讓整個宇宙都知道你要什麼吧！

帶著祝福開創新人生

回顧過往，我曾有兩次轉換工作跑道的經驗。對當時的我來說，都是很重大的決定。一次是離開高科技產業，從HP惠普公司轉職到UFO飛碟唱片；另一次是離開Microsoft微軟公司，自行創業。

剛開始，所有親友都非常訝異。因為，我當時在資訊業界已經累積了相當豐富的專業經驗及人脈資源。以當年的觀點評估，資訊業的前景還相當看好，公司待遇高、福利好、還有完善的教育訓練制度，按照我的年資和績效，職務已經升遷到管理層級……大家都想不通，我為什麼要放棄這麼穩固的基礎，而轉換到全新的跑道工作？

我不否認，親友眼中所認定的這種種職場優勢，的確是令人羨慕的；然而，在我看來，這些都只是既得利益的一部分。我想趁年輕時，還有冒險的機會、還有衝刺的本事、還有承受失敗的能力，勇敢去接受一些自己想嘗試的挑戰。

經過我不斷溝通，他們的態度終於也有了一百八十度的改變，從「你該不會是瘋了吧！」轉變為：「既然你有心想闖一闖，我們替你加油！」

有了這兩次經驗，我終於明白：**啟動新旅程之際，並不是非要「千山我獨行，不必相送！」如此灑脫不可，若能帶著祝福開創新人生，更容易得到貴人相助、有好運相隨，豈不是更好的選擇！**

開運心咒語 表達自我、積極溝通，集結貴人來幫助自己，好運會更快降臨。

幸福開運Q&A

星座開創力評比

Eric

Q 創新，是很重要的習慣、也是很關鍵的能力。紫微斗數中有所謂的「殺破狼」命格，集合「七殺」、「破軍」、「貪狼」三個主星，聽說這樣的人特別有開疆闢土的興趣及能力；而在星座理論中，哪些星座的開創力是最強的呢？他們有哪些特質值得學習？

Tiffany

A 不同星座的人，也具有不同的開創力：

風象星座

滿腦子奇思異想，又熱衷吸收各種知識的風象星座，對稀奇古怪的事特別有興趣。天生愛嘗試，不喜歡被困在既有的想法中，更討厭一成不變；為了設法讓人生更有趣，會將天馬行空的想法組織起來，努力創造出心目中的豐富人生。

火象星座

為了追求最高的成就感，還要致力打造與眾不同的個人國度，火象星座會想盡辦法耕耘出優越的成果。天生不服輸的個性，讓火象星座開創新世界的熱情絕不落人後；因此，雖然本身不是最優秀的創意人，卻是極卓越的開創者。

水象星座

永遠在追求氣氛與美感的水象星座，喜歡一切約定俗成的美麗，因此，只要是關於藝術、美麗、時尚與浪漫情感的事物，都能燃燒起水象星座獨特的創新潛能。雖然平時開創力並不突出，只要埋首於興趣，創造力就會源源不絕！

土象星座

土象星座的創新力好比「石中隱玉」，不慍不火，平時看不出來，但只要獨自待在自己的小世界裡安靜思考，就能出乎意料地迸發出驚人火花。土象星座的創新力永遠來自於人性，充滿了溫馨與感動，而且離現實的生活不會很遠。

Part 3

轉念，才會轉運！

知命而不認命，給自己多點彈性和勇氣，就更有機會轉運！
無需逞強或心急，找對方法走對路，再以微笑的嘴角、
感恩的心情，迎向下一次的柳暗花明！

今日【宜】探索自己的興趣，培養有助於別人的專長。
今日【忌】想盡辦法以公益的美名，包裝私人的野心。

命中注定要承擔？

使命感必須要審慎駕馭、小心運用，以免過度執著於自己的企圖，忽略別人的需求。

朋友看到我的工作既多又忙，常「虧」我是勞碌命！說真的，我從小到大都沒閒過。

學齡前的我，就會幫隔壁開雜貨店的阿婆糊紙袋，賺糖果及零用錢；中學暑假到處打工，連建築工地都去闖蕩過；大學兼差，從家教到廣告公司訪問員，各種工作我都有興趣試試。

其實，我並不覺得自己很辛苦、也不會認為這樣做就是貪財愛錢。我都是抱著「好玩」與「學習」的心情去做這些事，不希望自己虛度此生。曾經不只一次去算命，不同的命理師都跟我講同樣的話：「你這一生會很忙，至少要忙到六十幾歲，為社會人群工作……」聽得我不知道該高興、還是難過。

每當解釋到這裡，朋友又會繼續「虧」我：「你真是很有使命感的人！」這下子，我更緊張了。因為，我實在很不樂意看到「使命感」這三個字，被套用在自己身上。

你有沒有留意到，每次在選舉期間，總會出現一兩位特別有使命感的候選人？有的是名不見經傳的市井小民、有的是赫赫有名的資深政治人物。還沒正式登記，大家就猜想他絕對不可能當選；民調出來了，更加證實他一定會落選。但他還是高喊：「參選到底。」

看不懂的百姓，就會問：「幹嘛啊？難道他以為自己會當選？」老實說，我不知道當事人心裡是怎麼個想法，究竟是神志不清、還是真想壯烈成仁？不過很確定的是：他們都會說自己有崇高的使命感。

為國為民，聽起來真的很了不起。但是他的成功機率和他的使命感比較起來，差距也實在大到不可思議的地步。

開票結果，沒有當選，還算事小；得票數過不了最低門檻，又得賠錢。不過，至少用錢可以解決。

另外有些人的使命感沒這麼偉大，但犧牲卻比這些參選人更慘烈。

我認識很多男性的朋友，出生在一九六〇年代前後，就是台灣地區常說的「五年級生」，受社會環境及家庭價值觀的影響，他們沒有機會選擇自己真正喜歡的行業或工作，不是被迫繼承家裡世代相傳的事業，就是在父母指使下念了當時的「熱門科系」，等到畢業後正式進入社會，才嚐到有志難伸、痛不欲生的滋味。

為了滿足父母的期望，在屈服家族意見時，他們的確體會到「使命感」的重要性；但背負著「使命感」這重大的包袱，走上迢遙人生路，若不是在半路累倒，就是一抓住機會便逃跑。

一位朋友家裡做的是食品加工業生意，長輩要他出國念化工，以便將祖傳的事業發揚光大。

他照著做了，跑到國外之後悄悄改念藝術設計。家長獲悉，大為震怒，經過了很多年才慢慢諒解，親子之間的關係化險為夷，而他也成為設計業界的翹楚，沒有讓父母失望。

「命中注定」我欠你？

除了為國、為民、為家之外，還有些人是為了朋友道義兩肋插刀，不論背負債務、還是尋仇報復，他都答應辦到。

結果朋友落跑，他身陷囹圄，一生都被使命感給害慘了。直到在監牢耗擲多年青春，還說：「這是我命中注定欠他的！」

若不為國為民為家、也不為朋友，這種人的「使命感」多半是為了自己，但一定會包裝成大公無私的樣子，好像真心在為全人類造福。

有一位企業主管因為工作失誤被公司遣散，失意地離開原先的工作崗位。當時他的部門裡有一位交情像「徒弟」般的同仁，跟這件事毫無瓜葛，他卻力勸徒弟提出辭呈，跟他一同進退。

理由可冠冕堂皇了，他說：「你喔，命中注定就是要跟著我走啦！我怕你留在這裡，換了新主管，沒有人像我這樣罩你，出了事會死得比我還慘。」並非他壓根自身難保，而是故意拖人下水。

還有一種企業家是平日不授權、該退位時又捨不得交棒，戀戀不捨的理由，同樣是為了使命感。

我還聽說過一個更駭人聽聞的實例。有一位老母親守寡多年，辛苦獨立撫養兒子長大，好不容易盼到孩子長大、成婚了，她卻不准兒子和媳婦在夜裡睡覺時關上房門。

她振振有詞地說：「我們母子注定要相依為命，我到老死都還要照顧你，不然沒有辦法向你死去的爸爸交代！」

好一個「使命感」，真令人感慨萬千啊！

使命感是相對負責任的表現

有「使命感」並非不好，在能力所及的範圍內適度地承擔「使命感」，會讓一個人擁有值得尊敬的理想色彩。但若是脫離現實太遠、或死抓著「使命感」不放，就會被「使命感」拖著走，甚至以「使命感」為名，操控別人。

在我看來，**「使命感」的確是一種相對負責任的表現，但它必須真的脫除於現實的利益之外，才不會有「假公濟私」的嫌疑。真正的「使命感」，必須是對他人有具體的利益或價值，才有意義。**否則只是一堆很空洞的東西，不見得符合現在或將來的需要。

看過一篇介紹香港知名樂團BEYOND團員之一黃貫中的文章，他曾經表示：「我對社會沒有使命感，因為我不覺得自己有這種能力。對於一個常常躲在家裡彈吉他的人，是沒有使命感這回事的。我唯一的使命感，只會體現在對待BEYOND的樂迷身上。是他們造就BEYOND的，所以我只對他們負有使命感。假若我未能完全滿足給他們的期盼，我便會不快樂，這就是我的使命感。」

他的使命感簡簡單單，而且不會無限上綱。

企業家台積電董事長張忠謀先生，也在一次演講中指出：「願景，我覺得還是很重要。我相信一個企業要的不只是賺錢，但是有很多企業除了獲利以外，就沒別的使命了。我不認為世界級公司最大的使命就是賺錢。我不反對賺錢，但應該還要有使命感，是在錢之外的使命感。」

該下台時，應功成身退

「使命感」必須能和自身名利確實脫鉤，才會被尊重、也才有延續的必要。否則，一切「命中注定」的說法都有點一廂情願，甚至假上天之名，行自私之實。即使真心奉獻，願意承擔艱鉅的任務，在伸張「使命感」的過程中，還是應該有個觀念：「使命感」是可以傳承的，不必一定要「成其在我」！

當一個人在自己的位置上，已經盡了該有的努力、也負過該有的責任，就可以將「使命感」託付給接棒的人，不一定要強佔其位。

如果，捍衛「使命感」的呼聲，超過該有的進退分寸，為自己殘餘價值護航的意圖就太明顯了。

無論是平凡百姓或達官顯要，總要先懂得對自己的生命負責，再用熱忱與理想去照亮別人，這種全心為公眾付出的使命感，才是仰不愧於天、俯不愧於地的生命價值。

開運心咒語 要展現使命感，請先對自己的生命負責，再用熱忱與理想照亮別人。

今日【宜】請教專家、閱讀傳記，向成功的人士學習。
今日【忌】橫衝直撞、胡作非為，矇蔽雙眼誤入歧途。

熱血青年不認命

勇於嘗試，並不是壞事，但必須做好基本的準備。
在嘗試的過程中，必須敏銳地發現問題，隨時做出修正。

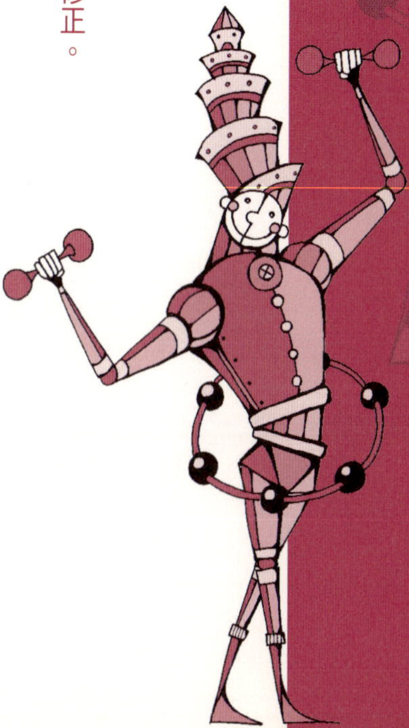

結束下半天的山區旅行，傍晚返程時，決定選擇另一條路，欣賞不同的風光。沿途被一塊廣告招牌所吸引，指向一家位於山麓的音樂咖啡館。基於一時的好奇，同行的四個朋友，都決定前往一探究竟。

座落在眼前的是一片小小的花園，所謂的音樂咖啡館倒也窗明几淨。推開玻璃門，出現了工作人員比顧客還多的情況。

我們主動上前詢問：「現在是營業時間嗎？」服務員才生疏地回應：「昨天開始試吃、今天開始試賣。」

坐進窗邊的位置，服務生送來了一份精緻的菜單，條列十幾項飲料，但都還沒有準備好，只有A、B兩種咖啡可以選用。

服務人員親口報出的價格，比價目表列印的高出二〇%。他說這個時段是下午茶時間，以他口說的為準。

等了幾分鐘，咖啡來了，沒想到種類和數量和我們點用的不同。之前點的是三杯A咖啡、一杯B咖啡；結果服務人員搞錯了，來了一杯A咖啡、三杯B咖啡，而且咖啡居然是涼的。

朋友說：「我剛才看他衝出去買鮮奶，完全沒有加熱，就直接倒進咖啡裡，咖啡當然是涼的。」

一杯半冷不熱的咖啡，幸好有朋友的聊天陪伴，否則真是相當掃興。空盪的咖啡館內，瀰漫著我和朋友的失望。

老闆和工作人員，加起來也有十幾個人，晾在不同的角落瞎扯、閒聊、抽菸、發呆，沒有任何一個人前來問問我們四個傻蛋，有沒有什麼意見可供改善。接受這樣慌亂成軍的試賣品質，無異於自投羅網。

結帳的時候，果然如我所料，不能刷卡、沒有現金找零、缺收據、也沒發票。

有「膽」還要有「識」

試吃、試喝、試賣、試婚……「嘗試」的用意，原本是鼓勵沒有經驗的人，勇敢體驗新的事務，並且在過程中學會解決問題。但若沒有萬全的準備，還是別輕易嘗試。

我鼓勵每個朋友，不要輕易認命，要拿出膽識，積極挑戰自己的潛能，在命運之外闖出更開闊的格局！

但別忘了，**「膽識」這兩個字，有「膽」有「識」，就是要有熱血衝勁、也要有專業知識！不是靠著一股蠻力往前衝就好。**

這家音樂咖啡館，提供服務的每個步驟都有很大問題，就膽敢「試賣」，真是夠勇敢了。更嚴重的是，他們沒有把握顧客可能容許犯錯的試賣機會，誠懇地邀請顧客提供改進的意見，讓他們就這樣帶著不滿意回去，將會告訴更多的朋友，形成不好的口碑。

嘗試新的事物，可以勇敢，但不能沒有智慧；至少要一邊嘗試、一邊努力累積智慧。憑藉一時血氣所做的嘗試，叫做「愚勇」；仰仗一時興起所做的行為，叫做「愚笨」。兩者失敗的機會，都很高。

根據統計：大部分「試婚」的人，最後都沒有和當初同居的對象結婚，即使換了另一個對象結婚，婚姻失敗的比例也高於一般沒有試婚的人。

很多婚姻專家，都把這種現象解釋為：他們把婚姻當兒戲，所以很難維持。但是，在我的觀察裡，試婚者在態度上未必輕率。很多人決定開始試婚的時候，還是很認真地在考慮，要跟對方天長地久走下去，只不過住在一起以後，就發現彼此的變數太多，超過雙方所能掌握。

太快速地做出「可以試婚」的決定；太匆促地下了「彼此不合」的結論。在感情世界裡，這些都是有「膽」無「識」的行為。

真正熱血的人生哲理

沒有準備好，就輕易嘗試，嘗試的過程中，又未能敏銳地發現問題。就這樣，一步一步走向錯誤的路。

但很顯然地，問題不在該不該嘗試，而是該如何去試？試到什麼時候，就應該喊停？

我曾在報上看到一則外電消息：巴西有一名男子，從二十九歲開始，就幫啤酒公司擔任「品酒」工作，嘗試釀酒的味道，長達二十年。

結果，在四十九歲的時候，他發現自己酒精中毒，變成酒鬼，因此被迫離職而失業。雖然他索賠成功，獲得新台幣七千三百萬元，但還是無法順利戒掉酒癮。

錯誤的嘗試，教人上癮，還真是麻煩呢！

這年頭，很流行「熱血」兩個字。的確，做任何事都要很「熱血」，也就是要很熱情地投入。但是，光是「熱血衝勁」還不夠，還必須加上「專業知識」，才能擺脫宿命！

因為，真正的熱血青年，信奉的人生哲理應該是：**知命，而不認命；轉念，就會轉運！**

隨著時代變遷，流行用語也在創新，帶著「復古」感覺的語彙，常常串連著兩個世代的感懷。「熱血」的意義，有青春的衝撞、也有古典的熱情，若能結合「理性」與「智慧」，更能夠發揮真正的影響力，活得更聰明。

開運心咒語 知命而不認命，有熱血也有實力，為人生開拓寬闊格局！

今日【宜】整理舊相本、瀏覽日記，重溫感動，眺望未來。
今日【忌】沉溺舊傷口、抱怨時局，牢騷滿腹，憤恨不平。

跌倒，別急著站起來！

碰到挫折，的確應該力圖振作，但也不要操之過急！心態要堅強，身段必須柔軟。做好準備，等待時機。

一對原本經營旅館的夫婦，幾年前遭歹徒入侵住家，三個幼齡孩子遭到殺害。痛心疾首的他們，哀傷至極後，決定努力生產，把死去的孩子一個一個生回來。

即使太太早已做過輸卵管結紮手術，也算是高齡產婦了，並不非常適合生育，夫妻倆仍排除萬難，透過醫生的幫忙，接回輸卵管，並多次進行人工受孕，終於在惡夢醒後讓美夢成真，又生了三個孩子。

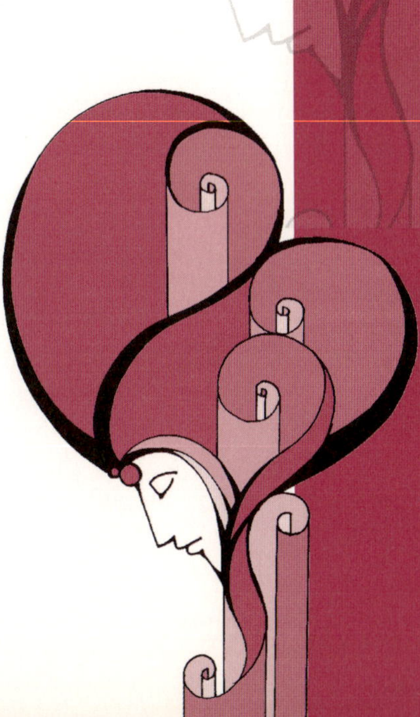

新聞記者前往採訪，性格堅韌的婦人紅著眼眶，對著電視機的鏡頭說：「哪裡跌倒，就從哪裡站起來！」

她度過悲傷的經驗，以及矢志重來的決心，令人十分動容。

類似的境遇，一樣的努力，卻有不同的結果。根據媒體報導透露：電視藝人白冰冰，在愛女白曉燕被歹徒綁架撕票後，經歷了旁人無從體會的傷痛，念女情深，她也下定決心要把白曉燕生回來。同樣歷盡千辛萬苦，甚至遠赴國外求醫，忍受了身心的煎熬，經過很多次的人工受孕，她卻還是沒有如願以償。

兩個案例的結果不一樣，但當事人在面臨人生重大挫敗後，勇敢面對傷痛，決心要「哪裡跌倒，就從哪裡站起來！」的精神，卻同樣都很偉大，教人佩服，堪稱是挑戰逆境的典範。

重新振作是才是唯一的辦法

陸晉德，是另一位傷心的父親。一九八八年，他的孩子陸正被歹徒以擄人勒贖方式撕票，官司纏訟多年，十多年來一直沒有結案，陸先生內心無限感傷。在這悲痛的過程中，他和妻子生育了另一個孩子，但他並不完全認同再次生育，就是所謂的：「哪裡跌倒，就從哪裡站起來！」他覺得兩個孩子有完全不同的性格，在他心中無法相互取代。

聽到這樣的說法，任誰都感到心酸。無論他是否同意「哪裡跌倒，就從哪裡站起來！」的邏輯，但最基本的，至少是他積極面對挫折的態度——跌倒了，就要再站起來！

跌倒，既然是個已經存在的事實；站起來，就是必須接受而且努力的動作。不管用什麼形式、經歷了多久、在哪個地方，最可貴的就是靠自己的力量，重新面對自己的人生。

拉赫曼尼諾夫是十九世紀俄國音樂家，從少年時期就鋒芒畢露，但快速擁有盛名之累，反而成為他前進的包袱。

一八九五年，二十二歲的拉赫曼尼諾夫完成了生平第一首交響曲，竟遭受外界眾多批評，讓他沉寂了三年之久，沒有辦法繼續創作。後來他接受了心理治療，才又找回失落已久的信心。

這些數不盡的實例，都說明了同一件事——面對挫折唯一的辦法，就是重新振作。

賴在原地哭鬧，可以博取一時的同情，卻無法移動生命現場背後那幅不幸的布景，只有找到適合自己的方式、選擇適合出發的跑道，勇敢地站起來，才能重新出發。

年輕而沒有養育經驗的媽媽，看到寶寶跌倒後，為了安撫哭鬧的孩子，常在旁邊叫罵：「馬路凹凸不平不乖，害寶寶跌跤。」事實上，這是危險的教養方式，寶寶長大之後，很可能成為一個不肯為自己錯誤負責的人。人生道路，本就崎嶇，不幸跌倒，別怪路不平，而要警惕自己多加小心。

在「這裡」跌倒，從「那裡」站起來

跌倒之後，必須想盡辦法、用盡努力站起來，但也不必操之過急。曾經轟動華人世界的「偷拍光碟」事件，案發之初女主角努力克制自己的悲傷，很快地重出江湖，面對麥克風與螢光幕，卻惹來很多意想不到的批評。

針對她快速復出的爭議，我個人認為，我們的社會確實還欠缺足夠的包容力；但參考醫學上對「跌倒之後爬起來」的建議，不免也要再三尋思。

在大型教學醫院的牆上，我看到一幅海報，醫生建議跌倒的病人：「不要急著站起來！首先，請務必確定自己有沒有摔傷。看看傷口的情況，再決定用什麼姿勢爬起來。如果傷勢很嚴重，就需要請專業醫護人員前來幫忙。」

我要強調，**爬起來的速度和方式，並不需要顧及旁人的眼光，而是要考慮自己身體和心理所受的傷。**

過度依賴，絕對不值得鼓勵；但一味地逞強，可能會讓自己傷得更重啊！

遭受挫折所獲得的寶貴代價之一，就是了解自己現階段能力的極限。你可以因此而決心開發潛能，但要等傷勢復原了再說！

跌倒之後，到底要用什麼方式、隔了多久，才能站起來重新出發呢？

我的建議是：檢查自己是否準備好了，同時也等待環境轉變和時機成熟。**心態**

上可以很堅強，但身段上不得不柔軟。

「哪裡跌倒，就從哪裡站起來！」這句話最能鼓舞我們的，其實是面對挫折，再站起來的精神，而不是執著於重新出發的地點和未來的方向。

有時候，從「這裡」跌倒，必須要從「那裡」站起來。為什麼？因為跌倒的地方，對你來說可能是個危險的陷阱，必須要爬行到另一個適合你的地方，才能重新站起來。如果你沒有意識到這一點，死心塌地在原處掙扎，結果必然是愈陷愈深而已。

即使跌倒了，也要勇敢站起來！但別忘了，你可能要換個跑道，重新再出發。

開運心咒語　跌倒時不要逞強、也無需心急，找對道路和方法再重新奮起。

幸福開運Q&A

容忍挫折排行榜

Eric Q 容忍挫折，才能虛心檢討，迎接下一次的成功。請問哪些星座對挫折的容忍度最高呢？請列舉前五名，並說明這些星座對於容忍挫折的特質，提供我們學習的榜樣！

Tiffany A 挫折容忍度最高的前五名星座，依序如下：

白羊座

戰鬥感充沛的星座，深信「在哪裡跌倒，就要從哪裡站起來」。雖然火爆的脾氣，讓白羊座看起來似乎無法承受挫折，其實天生好強不服輸的個性，反而會讓他們把挫折當鍛鍊，面對的打擊愈大，愈能激起體內的戰鬥力。

水瓶座

存活本能很強的星座，因此無論是骨子裡樂觀的水瓶座，還是骨髓裡悲觀的水瓶座，都不允許自己不進步，特別能屈能伸、勇敢對抗挫折。他們相信一覺醒來，世界還是要轉動，所以一定會設法鼓勵自己奮發向上。

獅子座

熱血細胞數超高的星座，不管受到多嚴重的打擊，也會給自己千百萬個繼續奮鬥下去的理由，來對抗挫折。即使有時會自欺欺人，假裝一切仍然不壞，但也就是這種阿Q精神，讓獅子座能勇敢接受磨難、再接再厲。

天蠍座

資本嗅覺極強的星座，在內斂的外表下，意外地有種不可思議的樂觀特質。為了享有心中渴望的生活，會不惜一切去爭取幸福，吃苦當吃補，還會以他人奮鬥的歷程鼓舞自己，容忍挫折的胸襟是水象星座之最。

處女座

倔強值無敵高的星座，有種「非得做好」的死硬派特性，對任何事都抱持高度的期望，認真努力。因此，挫折會讓處女座當下像死掉般難受，但不甘認輸的個性仍會讓他們一邊喊痛、一邊爬起來，檢討自己、重新振作。

今日【宜】蒐集資訊，評估自我，釐清未來發展方向。
今日【忌】盲從隨眾，追求熱門，而忽略自己的熱情。

換個跑道，重新出發！

站在人生的分水嶺，究竟該「向左走」、還是「向右走」？
感到迷惘的時候，你會對誰的忠告言聽計從？

一位社會上的知名女性，經歷了一場婚變。丈夫外遇，讓一向以「賢妻良母」自勉的她，感到非常不堪；他背叛婚姻、移情別戀的行為，更令她難以諒解。她出版新書，以小說的形式諷喻前夫，獲得讀者熱烈迴響；她還將前夫告上法庭，最後官司以和解收場，表現夫妻緣盡之後的泱泱大度。

風波平息後，她接受婚紗廠商邀請，走上伸展台，刻意展示曼妙的身材，並談及自己對愛情的憧憬，流露出渴望再談一次戀愛的神情。

有位女性朋友看了這則新聞，感慨萬千地說：「在哪裡跌倒，就從哪裡站起來！」我聽了很緊張，勸她：「若是碰到感情的挫折，不必急著遵循『哪裡跌倒，就從哪裡站起來！』的法則，也許該暫時休息一下，或換個跑道再出發！」

我總覺得，感情的傷口很難復原得那麼快，如果心中還有陰影，雨不過、天怎會青？當然，若是正巧有姻緣來到，可以在感情的苦海中度自己一程，離開憂傷的彼岸，未嘗不是美事。但如果刻意強求，逼自己「哪裡跌倒，就從哪裡站起來」，勢必會掉入另一個悲劇的陷阱。

跌倒之後，站起來！但短暫休息過後，評估一下眼前的狀況，若能換個跑道，再重新出發，也很不錯！

換個跑道，創造不同機遇

美國職棒界名人高登，原本是優秀的終結者，曾在一九九八年替紅襪隊打下漂亮的戰績，以四十六次救援成功拿下當季的「美聯救援王」，但後來因手部受傷，而失去許多發揮的空間。

一九九九年他接受手術治療，休養了一年多之後，在二〇〇〇年十二月以自由球員身分和小熊隊簽約。二〇〇一年，他一度重新展現往日身手，替小熊隊締造不少佳績，最為人稱道的就是：他連續十九場救援成功，寫下隊史紀錄。

然而，因為小熊隊有了新的後援投手，他便轉換跑道，加入太空人隊，在新的環境中又創造了不錯的成績。

碰到發展的瓶頸，自忖已經盡力之後，換個跑道，可以創造不同的機遇，這是美國職棒運動員高登的成功實例。

另一位中國的體操選手奎媛媛，則是在光環未褪之前，因受傷而不得不轉換跑道，為生涯發展開拓全新里程。

奎媛媛曾代表中國獲得體操世界冠軍，後來轉換跑道當起學生，進入北京對外經濟貿易大學，學習法語。

根據中國體育報的報導，她說：「從小練體操，文化學習落後很多。重新當學生學習英語，和其他同學不在同一個水平上，比較吃力。改學法語，大家都是從零開始，應該會好一點。況且法語也是奧運會官方用語，學好了，便能為二〇〇八年北京奧運出更多力呀。」

她的這一席話，充分流露出量力而為的智慧，也對未來的規劃，展現了相當程度的遠見。

多點彈性，會發現更多潛力

談到知名人物成功轉換跑道，美國前副總統高爾也有值得參考的經驗。他離開副總統的職位之後，改行經營家族餐廳。

高爾在美國二〇〇〇年總統大選高票落選之後，在一次公開演說中坦承：「這是段非常不容易的過渡期。」

面對人生的重大轉折，他很努力地想要改變自己的心態。從前所經之處，都有群眾簇擁，到哪兒都有專車專人接送，如今要自己開車，他擔心地說：「已經有好幾年沒開車，對我來說可能會有些危險。」也不諱言：「自從卸下美國副總統職位之後，含飴弄孫，共享天倫，才是『首要任務』！」

我在主持廣播節目時，也曾有聽眾打電話進現場，分享類似的經驗。印象最深的一個聽眾是：他參加國家考試，整整考了八年，都沒能通過，最後他決定放棄考試，回鄉下開民宿，竟開啟人生的另一扇門，終於熬過寒冬，看見春天。

轉換跑道，有時真的事出無奈，但只要自己能以樂觀的心情面對，很可能會找出人生真正的第二個春天。這總比一味地堅持在原本的跑道上做困獸之鬥，要來得有意思。

尤其在全球經濟一片不景氣的浪潮中，很多上班族都被迫轉換工作性質、甚至遭到遣散，必須另起爐灶。在這種情況下，就不必一直死守著「哪裡跌倒，就從哪裡站起來！」的鐵律，應該給自己多一點彈性，試著創造「山窮水盡疑無路；柳暗花明又一村」的奇蹟。

只要你保持良好的體力，帶著勇氣，換一條路走，就會發現自己的潛力。

命理師無法決定命運

矽谷職場網路公司 CareerFables.com 的現任總負責人蘇珊．馬格立，曾經是 AT&T 的職員。她自己轉業成功之後，專門幫助中年轉業的族群，在網站上分享經驗，還提供各種教育訓練與轉業機會。

面對中年轉業的建議，蘇珊提出「五個F」的主張供作參考。分別是：Family（家庭）、Friends（朋友）、Finances（財力）、Fun（趣味）、Fulfillment（滿足感）。

在我看來，與其說是要兼顧這五項，不如說這五項都是機會，可以綜合起來衡量，也可以分開考慮。比如說，失去全薪的工作，改以打工的方式謀生，固然是財力上的損失，但如果因此而獲得更多照顧家庭的機會，也算是有代價了。

跌倒之後，重新站在人生的分水嶺上，究竟該繼續走原有的路途、還是換個跑道再出發？這是很多人都有的疑惑。

事實上，沒有人可以替你解答這個問題。就算是再高明的命理師，也無法決定你的命運。人生之所以好玩，也常是因為有這些結果無法確定的抉擇。

既然，繼續原有的路途、還是換個跑道，都有某種程度的冒險，不如靜下心來傾聽內在的聲音，然後聽著自己心中的鼓聲出發。

至於，將來會不會後悔呢？就留給時間來解答吧。

決定的動機更重要

根據我的經驗，將來回頭看這段路程，會讓你後悔的不是你的決定，而是你為什麼做了這個決定，以及決定之後你如何實踐自己的諾言。

決定的動機，永遠比你決定了什麼更重要！而實踐的態度和方法，則是成敗的關鍵。

堅持，是對成功人生的許諾。但所謂的堅持，並非形式上一成不變。

通往成功，總有不同的道路，你只能選擇當時最適合自己的方式。如果，一時間找不到最篤定的方式，不妨趁著混沌未明的時期，來個不拘形式的小小冒險吧！只要你很認真地摸索一段時間，自然就會通透了。

這也算是正式起跑之前的暖身運動，給自己一段探索學習的時間，做好養成信心的準備，就可以正式重新出發。

正式重新出發之前，難免都有摸索的階段，但不代表就是在「原地打轉」。即使是非常低調的沈潛，只要是擬定策略的思考、系統化的嘗試計畫、確實的累積經驗，都可以歸納為「出發的準備」，對將來的東山再起都有非凡的意義。

開運心咒語　給自己多點彈性，帶著勇氣，換一條路走，創造不同機遇。

今日【宜】對著牆壁練習說「不」，以應將來的不時之需。
今日【忌】面對託付，隨口答應，轉身大罵，再後悔莫及。

向命運說「不」！

別自不量力地掉入「捨我其誰」的陷阱，逞強要當「救世主」，只會累垮自己而已。

為了這次假期出遊，小王安排了很久。他和家人都換好衣服，準備按計畫利用這個難得的假期，到郊外走走，沒想到這時卻來了一位不速之客。

「哇，好久不見！」的確，出現在門口的這位朋友很久沒有聯絡了，「今天正好沒事，來你這裡坐坐！」客人大大方方地進了客廳，往沙發一坐。

客人顯然沒發現他和家人臉色慘白，面對即將泡湯的出遊計畫，全家都憂心忡忡，勉強擠出的笑意背後，都是同樣的禱告：「老天，快把這位客人請走吧！」

但天不從人願，客人坐了一個多小時，還繼續談天說地呢！

如果是你，這時候該怎麼辦？可能的處理方法，不外乎下列幾種：

- 放棄好不容易規劃好的家庭旅行，陪這位久未謀面的不速之客繼續耗下去。
- 既然已略盡地主之誼，坦白告訴對方真相，請他改天再約。
- 雖然不知道家人的意願，仍然硬著頭皮邀請對方一起出遊。（對方可能很不識相，真的跟著去玩、或執意要再多坐一會兒。）

你的選擇是什麼？看對象、看交情、看家人的反應再決定！是的，都有可能，但不論是哪一種決定，都教人左右為難。

為了別人方便，讓自己不便

當我還是一家公司的基層職員時，也曾碰到很類似的情況。當天的工作很忙，上班之前我就告訴家人：「今天會加班到很晚！」一到辦公室時，有位同仁臨時跑來請我幫忙，「這件事一定要靠你啦！否則開了天窗，我恐怕會丟了飯碗。」如果不答應，他可能會誤會我故意藉機整他。

同樣地，我也覺得左右為難。奇怪的是：我們都沒有做錯什麼，卻為了配合別人而痛苦不堪。說穿了，問題就在於我們不懂得拒絕別人。

拒絕，為什麼那麼難？一針見血的答案是：對自己沒有信心！深怕要是向對方說出「不」字，就會得罪他，從此兩人反目成仇。

有個朋友不斷借錢給一個「屢借不還」的人，等對方把錢拿走了，他又十分後悔。每次我都問他，為什麼不當場拒絕，他的回答總是：「不好意思啦！」「說不出口啦！」「不忍心讓對方失望。」表面上，他好像沒有把彼此的關係弄僵；事實上，儘管沒有當場反目，這份友誼早已名存實亡。因為在勉強自己順從對方要求的同時，早已傷害到原先友好的關係了。

所有難以說「不」的案例，最後都回到相同的邏輯——缺乏自信的人，總是為了別人的一時方便，讓自己變得非常不方便。

當場說「不」，又會怎樣呢？其實情況並沒有那麼糟，即時以適當的方式表達拒絕，不僅將彼此可能的傷害降到最低，也可以讓對方有更多時間，去尋覓別的資源、尋找替代方案。

懂得說「不」，拒當「爛好人」

拒絕別人的要求、甚至婉謝別人的好意，時機是最重要的。拖拖拉拉到最後，不是把自己逼上絕路，就是給對方更多耽誤。如果你心中已經決定拒絕，最好不要佯裝成：「好的，我考慮考慮再說。」延遲戰術十分不智，自己熬得痛苦，對方也不會好受。應該拒絕別人的時候，若想要不傷感情地全身而退，關鍵在於要選擇適當的方式表達拒絕，而不是勉強自己答應、或以拖延戰術帶過。

首先，應誠懇說出自己無法配合對方的理由。如果對方真的把你當朋友，一定會諒解你的苦衷；如果對方還故意耍賴，你就應該藉這個機會分辨，他是不是你值得交往的朋友。**友誼中所謂的「道義」，有一定的底限，超過你所能負擔的程度，就是勉強**。一味地勉強，絕對不會有好結果。

不要以為「勉強答應對方的要求」，就會換來長久的友好關係。請記得：「適當地拒絕！」才會贏得真正的尊重。永遠無法說「不」，你只不過是個自身難保的「爛好人」！懂得適時說「不」，才能自由自在地面對友誼。

別陷入「只有你才能幫我忙」的陷阱

當對方已理解你不得不拒絕的立場時，試著幫他想想：有沒有別的替代方案。一定要弄清楚：對方要的是「能夠解決問題的資源」，但他常常包裝成「只有你才能解決我的問題」。千萬不要掉入這個陷阱，否則你常會誤以為自己是救世主。

親子之間的相處，也有類似的困擾。小學二年級的孩子碰到寫作文的瓶頸，一定要爸媽唸給他抄，否則就哭天搶地鬧個沒完。爸媽常因而照辦，讓賴皮的孩子得逞，甚至嘆息地說：「如果你長大了，爸媽不在身邊，可怎麼辦？」

可笑吧！孩子需要的是指導他寫好作文的方法，讓他養成勤於閱讀的習慣、上作文班、請個家庭教師、或買一本寫作參考書給他，都會比爸媽一邊唸、他一邊抄要來得好。給他魚竿、教他釣魚，要比給他一條魚更好，是吧？

感情的習題，道理也是一樣的。如果因為不忍心拒絕對方，就答應和他交往，是很殘忍的事。換到自己頭上時，也該想想：表達愛慕若被拒絕，也是一件好事；至少，無需在不愛你的人身上，繼續浪費時間。

性騷擾，就更別提了。當場正經地拒絕、或禮貌地離開現場，就是說「不」的最佳方法。

我們往往無法在當下說「不」，等到被對方的無理綁架了，還不甘不願地說出喪氣的話，罵自己：「沒辦法，認命吧！你的命就該這麼賤！」

果真命該如此嗎？下次學著拒絕別人，也**練習向命運說「不」吧！別勉強自己順隨你並不想屈服的人與事，活出自己的尊嚴，別人就會懂得尊重你，連「厄運」都會對你敬畏三分！**

開運心咒語 懂得適時拒絕，活出自己的尊嚴，人生才能暢快無礙。

幸福開運Q&A

如何化解下下籤？

Eric Q

心中有疑慮時，想請問神明，如果抽到下下籤，都會有點擔心，甚至情緒受到影響。到日本的某些廟宇拜拜，如果抽到不好的下下籤，可以把籤條綁在樹上，化解心中的疑慮，除了這個方式，有沒有其他方法可以化解呢？

Tiffany A

如果真的抽到下下籤，或是抽到覺得不怎麼滿意的籤，有個最好的化解方法就是：「跟老天打個商量」。

你可以按照以下的步驟來做：

1. 將求到的籤放在神桌上，說明你的心願，祈求神明給你一個好的結果，並且告訴神明，你願意為此做什麼改變，例如：到醫院做義工三個月、吃素一年、捐出每個月薪水的二〇％給慈善機構……等。

2. 詢問神明：「如果您答應我的祈求，請連續給我三個聖筊」。如果第一次求聖筊失敗，可以再向神明請求。（但最多只能跟神明撒嬌五次喔！）

3. 如果求聖筊失敗也別灰心，把籤拿回家後燒成灰，埋在綠葉盆栽裡，植物的生命力會幫你補強運氣喔！

今日【宜】和情人約會，溝通親密關係的界限。
今日【忌】不經思索，就同意讓情人登堂入室。

絕不妥協的「性」格

性與愛，只可騷、不可擾；
一廂情願的熱情，將燃燒出難以收拾的災情。

參加電視台命理節目的錄影，曾經聊到一個話題：「哪種星座或面相的人，比較容易被霸王硬上弓？」為了節目效果，眼前的幾位命理師討論得頭頭是道，不過幾位兩性專家都認為：這是當事人的「性格」問題，關鍵並不在於「命格」。

在兩性交往過程中，懂得互相尊重、適度包容妥協，才能幸福長久，唯有「性愛」這件事，絕不能輕易妥協。尤其是「性騷擾」，若讓對方得寸進尺，一秒鐘的妥協，可能換來一輩子的悔恨。

積極想找到工作的曉卉，根據報紙廣告到了一家旅行社應徵，由男老闆親自面談。他問了一個機智性的問題：「如果妳被男性顧客性騷擾，該如何處理？」接著並要求做現場模擬。

為了趕快就業，讓生活安定下來，曉卉沒有想太多，就照著對方的要求進行模擬。在緊要關頭，曉卉才恍然大悟，趕緊抓住對方漸漸伸進她內褲的手，表情嚴肅地說：「總經理，我們演練到這裡應該夠了。如果對方再有進一步的舉動，我就會大聲呼救，並且報警處理。」

以上的場景，不論是出現在求職面談或真實人生裡，曉卉的應對都算合宜，保有自己不被侵犯的權益，也顧全了大局。

但是，她並沒有因此而獲得那份工作。因為要求她做「狀況處理」的老闆，根本是醉翁之意不在酒，沒有真正錄用職員的打算，只想藉機吃豆腐、揩油！想不到這個毛手毛腳的畫面，被心術不正的老闆偷拍下來自娛。經由別人檢舉之後，事情的真相才曝光。

愈早抽身，愈不會被慾火焚身

事後曉卉告訴朋友這段經歷，大家都稱讚她的機智反應。同性的朋友紛紛貢獻自己被性騷擾的經驗，對象包括：男同學、男同事、甚至剛開始交往沒多久的男朋友。

「我明明就不想，他偏偏要。」這是被騷擾者事後共同的心聲。

無論是誰展開挑逗的行為，當另一方對這個舉止覺得不舒服、不喜悅的時候，當下就構成了「騷擾」！但問題就出在雙方的認知常有誤差。上述的實例中，只要女方沒有立刻拉下臉來嚴詞拒絕，男方就會誤以為她樂於接受他的挑逗、調情，所以「傻呼呼」地繼續冒犯對方，卻還以為自己調情功夫一流！

遺憾的是：通常被騷擾的女性，大部分都不會立刻制止，讓色迷心竅的男性愈陷愈深。

為什麼女性沒有當場明顯地表達抗議呢？大概有下列幾種原因：

- 當場被對方很失禮的舉動嚇壞了，不知道該如何表達心中的不悅。

- 擔心自己反應過度，使得對方惱羞成怒，採取報復行為。
- 總是猜想著：「他應該不敢怎麼樣吧！」「接下來他會停止了吧！」於是給了對方得寸進尺的機會。

由此可見，拒絕性愛的騷擾，應該慎選適當的時機，並且以對方能正確接收訊息的方式說「不」。

男女交往，在正式開始約會之前，就該讓對方知道，交往到什麼程度時，彼此的親密進度可以到哪裡。**如果不想太早讓對方「擊出全壘打」，就不要在私下獨處的時刻頻頻投出好球，給予可以揮棒的機會。**假使對方情不自禁到無法克制，你愈早抽身，愈不會被他的慾火焚身。

如果對方是同事、上司或其他陌生人，在有意或無意間進行騷擾，更應該選擇在第一時間，表達你的拒絕。

一開始的妥協讓步，會讓對方接收到「可以得寸進尺」的錯誤訊息。至於表達拒絕的方式，言語可以直接，但口氣不妨自然大方些，不必刻意選用具有羞辱意味的詞句，以免當場激怒對方，對你不利。

例如：「我很不習慣這樣。」會比「你想要幹嘛?!」多些理性、少點火藥味。「你不小心碰到我不想被碰到的地方。」會比「你這個豬哥、色魔！」多些和氣、少點傷害。

拒絕性騷擾，不分性別

性與愛，必須兩廂情願。只可騷、不可擾！當雙方樂意調情時，儘管使出渾身解數，「騷」到對方癢處；但只要其中有一方不願意接受，任何失禮的舉動都會變成打「擾」。

不只女性要有這樣的自覺，身處多元化的社會，男性也可能被女性騷擾，甚至被另一名男性毛手毛腳。即使是男性，面對性騷擾也會有受侮辱的感覺，而他在當場也一樣會遲疑，事過境遷後，愈想愈不舒服，才忍不住一吐為快。但一吐為快無法真正解決問題，必須學會處理，才能避免事件重演。

曾經，有一位男性民眾向立委陳情申訴，說他大約兩個月前在KTV包廂裡，被一名任職於公家機關的男性主管性騷擾。這個被媒體戲稱為「舔耳案」的事件喧騰一時，甚至還因為指證不確實，張冠李戴，險些引起政治風暴。

在偵查的過程中，很多人都想不透：「他為什麼不當場拒絕，卻在事後才表示不滿？」其實性騷擾案件中，很多受害人都有類似的反應，不分性別。由此可見，拒絕性騷擾這個議題，是兩性都必須面對、學習的功課。

即使是同性相戀的世界，也必須尊重對方的意願。否則，一廂情願的熱情，將燃燒出難以收拾的災情！

開運心咒語 性與愛，必須兩廂情願；學會尊重對方和自己，才能幸福長久。

今日【宜】日行一善，盡力提供協助給需要幫忙的人。
今日【忌】邀功討賞，告訴身邊的人你對他們有多好。

源遠流長的貴人運

對相愛的兩個人來說，彼此都是對方的貴人，
若愛到盡頭，依然把這份好意留在心底，也就留住了幸福。

每當我在主持廣播節目現場的塔羅牌單元時，只要提到「貴人運」，聽眾都特別有興趣，急著想要打聽自己有沒有「貴人運」？什麼時候才會被貴人拉一把？

曾經有位命理師對我說：「你的命盤中有貴人，常能逢凶化吉！」回想起來，我在學校念書時，即使成績很差，老師還是沒有完全放棄我，教過我的恩師，都是我的貴人。步入社會，幾乎每次求職都能順利找到工作，這些願意提供機會給我的

主管，也都是我的貴人。

基於這樣的想法，我特別在意對幫助我的人表達感恩。直到年歲漸漸成熟，我對「感恩」則有了不同的看法，總覺得態度要更謹慎一些，才能讓人與人之間的善意，流傳得更廣更久，所謂的「貴人運」，也會更有意義。

我們從小就被教育：「要飲水思源」、「吃果子，拜樹頭」。心存感恩，適時回饋，固然是美德；但如果表現得太急躁，也可能讓雙方的美意大打折扣。

禮尚往來不見得要交換禮物

幾年前的一個夜晚，突然接到一位久未謀面的朋友來電：「等會兒路過你家，要送個東西過去，請到巷口等候。」好奇的我，當然會事先問清楚，要送什麼禮物給我。對方經不起我的懇求，只好透露口風：「知道你為了工作，經常到處奔波，每天又要花很多時間寫作，我特別選購了一部筆記型電腦，要送給你。」

「啊！這怎麼好意思呢？」萬分驚喜的我，此刻真有「卻之不恭」的壓力。而且對方已經出發了，我也不能招待人家一頓閉門羹。怎麼辦呢？

就年齡和資歷來說，這位朋友算得上是我的前輩，由於過去曾邀他合作一項專案而結識，我非常欣賞他的專業，也感謝他的貢獻，沒想到為人謙和有禮的他，卻常常說：「多虧你邀我加入這個專案，我才有機會發展不同的人生。」

合作很長一段時間，我們彼此鼓勵、相互幫忙。人與人之間的好意，點點滴滴累積在心底，不曾特別去做具體的表達。距離專案結束也已經許多年了，十分意外他會送來這麼一份貴重的禮物。

自作聰明的我，為了表達感激，趁他還沒有抵達之前，搶在商店就快要打烊的三十分鐘，買了幾隻國外進口的泰迪熊，想要在見面時送給他的三個女兒。明明知道不成敬意，卻也有聊勝於無的投機，畢竟，關鍵也不在回送禮物的價值，而是感受「交換禮物」的那種樂趣。

約在巷口，他熱情地遞上筆記型電腦給我，設想非常周到，硬體、軟體和配件一應俱全。我也歡喜地把三隻泰迪熊交給他，請他帶給三個女兒。交流著暖暖的心意，暫時化解了我急於想要「禮尚」往來的尷尬。

直到又隔了很多年以後，有一次我和另一位多年好友，有過類似的互動，他有點生氣，卻也很誠懇地提醒：「你這樣會不會太見外了？」

因為他說這句話的態度一派認真，過濾了嘻笑怒罵的口吻，才讓我覺悟：一直以來，我都**因為很怕虧欠別人、恐懼承擔對方的好意，而在無意間表現了「拒人於千里之外」**的冷漠。

有時候，**太客氣了，反而成為人與人之間的距離**。

我回想起另一次經驗，也很類似。先父往生的第二天，我有一位事業忙碌的長輩，託公司同仁送來一大筆現金，他客氣地說：「為你準備，以應急用。」拆開信封的一剎那，發現金額很大，我心裡的直覺是——數目太大了，不能收，於是我立刻追出去，召回那位已經騎乘機車到巷口的同仁，請他把錢帶回去。對方十分為難，但仍然拗不過我的堅持，平白跑了一趟，非常辛苦。

現在回想起來，我的多禮，反而成為失禮。

也許，那筆錢對我來說，是個了不起的大數目；但是對長輩來說，只是他的一番心意。我可以大方收下，將來有朝一日，再回報他的恩情；我也可以暫時保管一段時間，等喪禮過後，再當面向他致謝，並以「都處理完畢了，沒有機會動用這筆錢」為由，歸還回去。我實在不應該立刻請那位同仁帶回，不近人情地拒絕了對方的好意，反而讓彼此親密的情誼，顯得有些疏遠。

開創不同的貴人運

太過急於表達感謝，就像是打乒乓球，很少有人能遵循著雙方共同的節奏，極有韻律地在你來我往之間，輕輕鬆鬆表達彼此的善意。反而常因為不想欠下人情，急忙推拒對方的好意，竟然把一拍好球變成急殺，留下小小的遺憾。

接受別人的好意，若沒有及時表示感恩，當然令人覺得他的付出有如「石沉大海」一般。但是，真心要對你好的人，並不會很在意你是否立刻道謝。畢竟，人生還長，只要懂得感恩圖報，有的是機會。比較好的做法是，**接受別人好意的當下，要記得表達感謝，但報恩的行動，就不必急於一時了。**

當我們身處人際關係還不夠圓融的階段時，表達感謝最好像是踢足球，穩紮穩打，等待適當的時機、選擇好角度再射門。如果雙方的關係夠熟稔了，這時不妨像是打高爾夫球，老謀深算加上高明技術，才能以最有效的桿數、甚至是一桿進洞，雙方都很窩心。

總之，心存感激、並懂得報答，是很長期的累積，不是短線的操作。如同農人採收葡萄，等到果實成熟才能摘取。未熟的葡萄，釀不出好酒，急不得！

感恩的心意，可以像是葡萄釀成的美酒，愈陳愈香。感恩的行動，可就要慎選時機。能及時說出感謝，固然很好；如果當時沒有機會，也可以把這些好意牢記心底，累積更大的能量，報答對方或回饋社會，會有更大的影響力。

對曾經施恩於我的貴人，表示內心的感激並非只是儀式，除了讓雙方領受好意之外，更要化為更長遠的力量。例如：**牢記這份知遇之恩，讓自己變得更善良、更有用，行有餘力，去幫助更多的人，這樣的感恩會更有力量。**

報答貴人最好的方式；就是成為別人的貴人。所謂的「貴人運」不只是被動等待別人的援助；主動伸手去幫助別人，是更積極、更有開創性的「貴人運」！

至於對相愛的戀人來說，彼此都是對方的貴人。在濃情密意的互動中，讓「貴人運」交流在雙方心底。萬一有天不得不分離，也要用感激貴人的心態彼此祝福，妥善處理分手的局面，將來還有機會真心去愛別人，就不辜負那段以「貴人」相待的美好時光。

開運心咒語 知恩圖報，要慎選時機和形式，你的感恩才會更有力量。

幸福開運Q&A

有效提增貴人運

Eric
Q 追求成功的路上，若有貴人相助，勢必可以事半功倍。有哪些簡單的方法，可以提增貴人運呢？

Tiffany
A 貴人分為「實貴人」與「虛貴人」。不同的貴人運，使用的方法也不同喔！實貴人通常是指在和你結識後，能對你伸出援手的；虛貴人則是你和他並不熟識（甚至不認識），但他會做出對你有益的舉動（好比fans）。

以下就提供幾則不同的魔法，幫助你招來源遠流長的貴人運！

招實貴人

七色繩魔法

準備：七種顏色的線，質料不拘。

做法：

1. 將七種顏色的線編織成一條繩子（編法不拘），總長度不可短於自己的身高。

2. 編好後，分別剪斷，留一段自己繫著（手腕、小指或腳踝都可以），其餘的拿去分送給別人。

招虛貴人

寶石小魔法

準備：絲巾、寶石、孔雀羽毛（花店或藝品店有售）。

做法：

1. 準備一顆你喜歡的真寶石，鑽石、水晶、紅寶石……均可。

2. 月圓時，將寶石和孔雀羽毛放在月光下浸照一小時。

3. 將寶石佩戴在身上，羽毛則以絲巾包好，放在枕頭下。

防小人的叮嚀

人紅遭妒忌，招貴人的同時，也別忘了防小人喔！

1. 避免放置仙人掌或葉緣尖的植物（如鐵樹等）。
2. 衣服要帶有淡淡的清香（也可以是洗衣粉的味道）。
3. 髮型要清爽，原有的髮色可以做些改變。
4. 見討厭的人之前，先吃一塊麥芽糖。

今日【宜】選擇有興趣的運動，享受揮汗如雨的快活。
今日【忌】整天窩在沙發、躺在床上，不斷無病呻吟。

運動，可以帶來好運

在所有的開運魔法中，保持例常運動的好習慣，其實是最有效、也最能維持好運的方式。

你有沒有想過：開運、祈福，到最後求的是什麼呢？大富大貴的享受，還是人在心在的平安？

我不否認剛出社會那幾年，曾經很努力賺錢。但當年賺錢的動機也很簡單，只是想養家活口而已，從來沒有指望自己能發財享福。

養家活口，這麼簡單的動機，在認份上班十幾年後，的確可以安居樂業了。就在人生已經沒有太多牽掛、太多追求的階段，我經歷了母親突然中風、父親接著過世的沉痛，我花了另一個十年，逐漸體會到一個更簡單的道理：

能夠保持身心健康，就是最大的幸運；願意隨時知足感恩，就是最好的福氣。

我還是像從前一樣努力工作，但不會再連續多日熬夜拚命。我照舊把行程排得很滿，但是其中包括陪伴母親聊天的時間，以及例行的運動。

運動，也可以激發出靈感

一位認識不久的朋友，聽說我熱愛運動，幾乎每天清晨起床慢跑四公里，高興地說要邀我去參加馬拉松路跑。

他大概很難想像，少年時期的我十分厭惡運動，只要碰到學校排有體育課的前一天，睡前我都會虔誠地向上天祈禱：「請保佑明天要下大雨喔！」這樣就可以留在教室自習，不必去上那個無聊得要命的體育課。

我從小身體不好，進出急診室的次數，可把爸媽都嚇壞了。對我來說，「體弱多病」，邏輯是倒過來的，因為「多病」所以「體弱」。好不容易成長到青少年階段，我又患了鼻竇炎，每天要帶一大包衛生紙上學，才足以應付不斷從鼻孔流出來的綠色鼻涕。

這個令人有點噁心的症狀，就醫多年，並沒有顯著的好轉。一直到大學畢業入伍服役，抽中憲兵單位，嚴格的體能訓練，竟讓我不藥而癒。

服役兩年期間，每天不分晴雨，清晨五點要帶著排上弟兄跑五千公尺。新竹的微風細雨是出了名的銳利，卻也是鍛鍊強健體魄最好的考驗。

退伍之前，不但我的鼻竇炎痊癒了，整個健康狀況都有顯著的改善。

從此，我愛上運動，也培養了固定運動的習慣。

運動的好處，不只是對健康有幫助，也是很好的情緒管理訓練。我自己開業從事企管顧問的那幾年，每週七天、每天工作超過十二小時，除了例常的顧問工作十分忙碌，清晨五點還起床為報章雜誌的專欄寫稿，壓力非常大，幾乎不是一般人可以承受。

幸好，我加入了公司附近的一家提供溫水游泳池設備的小型健身俱樂部。每天寫完稿子，我就去游泳，從七點到八點的這一個小時，在運動過程中，不但可以沉澱混亂的思緒，也激發出很多新的靈感。

享受一個人運動的快樂

記得有一天，我打算主動提前終止一份商業合約，因為那位客戶很不講理，常讓我和我的同仁感到非常困擾。出發去運動之前，我還忿忿不平地想到他那多麼令人厭惡的嘴臉，沒想到在水池裡五十公尺不斷往返的游泳過程中，慢慢讓我改變了對這件事的想法──「對方沒那麼可恨吧！」「應該要把彼此的期望溝通清楚，然後再做決定吧！」「他也有他的苦衷啊！」……

就這樣，表面上，我原諒了他，其實我很明白：我是在和自己和解。

雖然，運動的好處很多，但要養成運動的習慣並不容易。因為，運動的本身是很枯燥乏味的。為了有點變化，我曾經有系統地規劃運動項目：慢跑、騎自行車、游泳……等，以半年或一年為期，相互輪替，一方面比較不容易有心理上的厭倦，另一方面也可以避免鍛鍊出肌肉的慣性，而抵銷運動的效果。

不論哪一種項目，一個人的運動，總是寂寞的；但也因為如此，讓我更接近真實的人生。

健身房的教練，總是很好奇問我：「你真厲害，有辦法站上跑步機，一跑就是四十分鐘。不會無聊嗎？」我以開玩笑的方式向他透露：把自己鍛鍊成猛男，拍寫真集，是我的人生目標之一。

當然，我是跟他開玩笑的。有人說：「喜歡慢跑和晨泳的人，都是能忍受孤獨的人。」但是，我之所以能忍受別人眼中的孤獨，其實是因為很享受自己一個人運動的快樂。更何況，很多非計畫之內的寫稿題材、或創意靈感，都是在運動時心靈最安定的片刻捕捉到的。

學會讓身體作主！

我骨子裡堅忍的毅力，在運動的時候表露無疑。只要規劃好去運動的時間，絕對不會找藉口拖延或取消。即使失眠、重感冒，身體虛弱得不得了，我還是會說服自己：「去動一動，就沒事了！」

後來，也果真證明——去動一動，就沒事了！但愈接近中年以後，我也愈能體會「讓身體作主！」的道理。

所謂的身心健康，是隨時隨地讓體力和毅力均衡一下。若是過度勉強自己，不論是讓體力領導毅力、還是讓毅力戰勝體力，「人生無常」的感嘆，就會變成「人生無償」的遺憾。

一位非常注重運動養生的長輩，突然生病住進醫院。向來身體健康的他，很不能理解地質問上天：「為什麼會是我？」

在長達三年的治療裡，他有所頓悟地告訴我：「像我們這種個性太積極的人，很容易因為衝得太過頭，忽略了健康所能承受的底線。」

然後，身體就會主動對我們發出警訊——該休息了。如果執意不肯屈服，身體就會讓我們躺在病床上休息，甚至休息得更久。

原來，他也跟我多年前一樣，太刻意「按表操課」，不論「運動」和「工作」

都一絲不苟，偏偏忘了把「放鬆」和「休息」也排進去。

所以說囉！培養運動的習慣，真的很不容易！但是，要讓自己輕輕鬆鬆、快快樂樂地去運動，也要講究方法，不論在哪裡、做什麼運動，適合自己最重要。

身心都快活，運勢動起來

我有一個天生小氣的朋友，為了逼自己去運動，故意參加一個很貴的健康俱樂部，他說：「一天不去，就平白損失數百元。」現在，去運動對他而言，簡直就是去撈本。「運動，兼賺錢！」這是他的邏輯。

另一位更省錢的朋友，建議我不花錢的健身方法是——清晨去公園慢跑。不過這對台北市的人們來說，是個很奢侈的想法。台北盆地清晨的空氣並不好，還有一群野狗跟著你跑。他慢跑時被流浪狗咬了，還得去醫院打針，才算花錢消災。

另一位很有才華的女性朋友更聰明。她索性加入高級健身俱樂部的經營團隊，進駐全世界最高大樓，真正達到「運動兼賺錢！」的境界，十分令我羨慕。

雖然那家公司已經倒閉了，但是當年的廣告詞還是令人印象深刻：「身體決定權力；身體決定位置！」這句針對上班族所訴求的標語，也可以應用在人生上，道理都是一樣的。

我不是要鼓勵功利的思考，也並非是強調健康和權力的關係，但身體健康的確決定了一切。**懂得讓身體作主，心才會快樂！當身心都快活，連帶著整個人的運勢也會被帶動起來。**每天早上運動後沐浴的那段時光，是我一整天最感到平靜、幸福的時刻。我常在窗前對著天地表達感謝，覺得自己非常幸運，能這樣享受人生簡單的幸福。

我知道，隨著生命的四季變化，身體機能總有凋零衰退的一天！正因如此，我更要保持心情的樂觀，即使步調緩慢，幸運依然相隨！

今日【宜】摘錄報章雜誌或網路的笑話，說給別人聽。
今日【忌】列舉親友或同事的缺點，在背後無情批評。

主動向幸福靠近

嘴角的曲線，決定了人生的幸與不幸。
只要自己覺得幸福，就能吸引幸福靠近。

地鐵站出口的左右兩側，各有一個販賣新式吹泡泡玩具槍的人。

他們各自的手裡，都拿著一把塑膠製的玩具槍，扣下扳機，就會發射出很多漂亮的五彩泡泡。

站在左前方那個販賣泡泡玩具槍的人，興高采烈，自己玩得很開心，拿著泡泡玩具槍不斷對空發射，五彩的泡泡飄散在四周，他追逐著飛舞的泡泡，來回奔跑。

每一個泡泡，都像是幸福的夢想，讓路過的人有了捕捉的盼望。許多路過的少女、以及被少婦牽在手上的孩童，都停下來和他一起玩。

最後，大部分的人都向他買了一把泡泡玩具槍。生意愈好，他就愈開心，玩得更起勁了。

位置比較接近地鐵出口廣場的右後方，是另一個販賣泡泡玩具槍的人，選擇獨自坐在花台上，低著頭，將手上的泡泡玩具槍對著地面的水溝蓋發射，五彩的泡泡漸漸堆積在水溝蓋上面，像舊式的洗衣機排放出過多的清潔劑泡泡，堵塞了排水孔的出口。

他面無表情地拿著泡泡玩具槍，繼續朝向地面發射，每一個泡泡就像是傷心人流出的眼淚，不斷墜落，無比淒涼。

可能是受到這樣悲愴的氣氛感染，路過的人很少主動親近他，更別說是掏出錢來向他購買玩具泡泡槍了。

也許是負面循環的影響，生意不好，令他的心情更糟糕，頭垂得愈低，工作就更不起勁了。他的「不快樂」，像磁鐵般吸引更多「不快樂」向他靠近。

幸福不幸福，心態很重要

這是我在地鐵站出口觀察到的實景，也是我們尋常人生的縮影。**自己覺得幸福的人，就像是左前方那個販賣泡泡玩具槍的人，總能吸引更多幸福的人向他靠近，與他互動，交換彼此的幸福。人生，就因此朝往正向發展。**

另一種人，每天自怨自艾、長吁短歎，不知不覺以自我為中心，構成一個十分淒苦的磁場，不但遠離了幸福，也只能吸引悲傷靠近。就像是右後方那個販賣泡泡玩具槍的人，即使有人拿出錢來向他購買，很可能也只是基於一時的同情、貪圖一時的方便，缺少幸福的尊嚴與肯定。

幸與不幸，與實際人生的遭遇並不一定有直接的關連，比較重要的，其實還是心態。

我有一位女性朋友，結婚後辭去工作，一直在家照顧臥病的公公，長達七年。公公過世之後，因為夫妻兩人對這段婚姻關係有不同的期待，彼此協議離婚。

朋友們都為她抱屈，認為她當了七年的看護，竟換來一紙離婚協議書，但她自己卻不這麼認為。

她覺得和公公很有緣分，孝順他也是應該的，而且她對長輩的付出，也感動了兒女，兩個孩子都主動表示，要跟著她這個單親媽媽生活，三個人相處得很貼心，她無怨無悔。

卸下照顧公公的負擔，她懷抱著忐忑的心情，再度踏入職場，工作上雖然有很多挑戰，卻讓她更有機會認識不同領域的人才，和大家一起學習、成長，她覺得很開心。

帶來幸運的嘴角曲線

我知道她在工作上碰到不少挫折，甚至有些難堪的處境，卻都咬著牙撐下去，每天還是發自內心地笑臉迎人。我問她是怎麼做到的，她說：「想到身邊有這麼多好朋友支持我，這點困難實在不算什麼！」

她是個昂起頭、朝向天空吹泡泡的幸福人。

以自信迎接人群、用謙遜面對難關。所以，她總是能夠吸引期待幸福的人們向自己靠近，以相同的信念一起追逐飛舞在空中的夢想。即使現實生活中，依然有許多障礙，也不會輕易被打倒。

就如同《不抱怨的世界》這本書的作者，美國知名牧師威爾．鮑溫說的：

「你發出的抱怨和牢騷越多，你所招惹來的抱怨、牢騷和負面能量，也會愈來也愈多。」

他認為每個人手中都握有翻轉人生、改變世界的祕密，於是發起了一項「不抱怨」運動，試圖幫助大家養成不抱怨的習慣。

他採用的方法是：請參加者戴上一個特製的紫色手環，只要一察覺自己抱怨，就將手環換到另一隻手上，以此類推，直到這個手環能持續戴在同一隻手上二十一天，就已經養成了不抱怨的習慣。

笑臉、哭臉，原來是**嘴角的曲線，決定了人生的幸與不幸。**我們都可能是地鐵站出口的左右兩側，那兩個販賣新式吹泡泡玩具槍的人，站在左邊、還是右邊，並不要緊，比位置更關鍵的是——用什麼態度面對人生。

學習用樂觀的態度，面對不甚完美的人生，這是最能獲得幸運的生活方式，也是最能保有好運的祕訣。不但可為自己創造美好的生活，也會影響周遭的人們，讓活力四射的正面能量，透過互相分享而不斷循環，整個世界就會充滿平靜喜樂，每個人都幸福安康。

開運心咒語　用樂觀的態度、微笑的嘴角，和這個世界分享滿滿的喜樂！

【後記】

你也可以是通靈的幸運星！

幫助自己回到最原始的初心，如嬰兒般天真單純，敏感而不多疑、相信而不恐懼、祈福而不奢求。

很少向別人提及，從小到大，我有過許多次神祕的超能力經驗。包括：清明節上墳祭祖時，眼前冥紙變成現金；在咒語引導下，用一根手指輕輕抬起七十公斤的人；讀高中時，準確預測考上哪所大學；某位親戚重病，感知他的大限之日；以專注的念力，讓陌生路人從口袋掏出十元；登山時，看見古人同行；父親往生前後，我能跟他對話；光碟裡被覆蓋而毀棄的資料，重新出現在電腦硬碟；成績中等的親

戚孩子，我直言她會考進台大，應考前夕去替她加油，結果預言成真……

很多人對幼年的記憶很模糊，我卻能說出四歲前的住家環境及鄰居樣貌，乃至於長大成年後，我能透過敏銳的觀察感應周遭人事的變化。擔任顧問工作的商業談判中，我能在對方發言前猜中他的意圖；在產品正式上市前，預知它的銷售。到法國旅行，我有「他鄉遇故知」的強烈預感，果真在巴黎羅浮宮碰到高中同學……

我發誓，以上所說都是真的！但是，我並不是要藉此說服你相信怪力亂神，而是希望讓你知道：宇宙之間的神祕力量，其實存在於每個人的心底。只要你願意相信，並且努力保持內在自我的純真澄淨，就可以擁有「通靈」的能力。

找到通往自我靈性的道路

關於「通靈」，我的定義是：每個人通往自我內心的靈性道路。它可能是天生的、也可能靠後天的修為而得。我本來以為這些靈通是來自體質或個性，但經過這些年的歷練，我發現**真正能通往內在靈性的主要力量，其實是：安定、專注、單**

純、無私、利他。每當我在閱讀、慢跑、晨泳、靜坐、冥想、禱告時，愈能心無雜念，就發現自己愈往靈性的道路前進一步。而這種「通靈」的能力，讓我更了解自己的本質，更能捨棄不必要的欲望，回到最原始的初心，如嬰兒般天真單純，敏感而不多疑、相信而不恐懼、祈福而不奢求。因此，逐漸學會接受世間所有的好與壞、善與惡，做到「不以物喜、不以己悲」，也可以不再「進亦憂、退亦憂」，**只願珍惜當下，把一切都當作學習的功課，內心就更為清明了，感受恆常的自在快樂。**

分享這些「通靈」的能力，並非要鼓勵每個人都成為命理師，而是希望你也能藉由簡單的練習，恢復內心本來的樣貌，找回通往自我靈性的道路。尤其在這個價值多元發展，導致人心混亂的時代，許多不如意的人都積極向外祈求好運，甚至花了很多錢去改運，卻不知道：唯有轉向內在探索、修行，才是安頓自己的唯一方法。

讓自己快樂，好運就會跟著來

上述許多類似「預知未來」的經驗，只不過是「通靈」能力的印證之一。對於能通往內心靈性道路的人而言，「預知未來」並沒有什麼神奇或太了不起，就像你搭上從台北出發的高鐵直達車，知道一個半小時後會抵達最終站左營，道理就這麼簡單。但是，人生雖能被比喻為列車，事實上卻複雜許多，變數也增加千萬倍，對於大多數不具備「通靈」能力的人而言，很可能連目前所處的位置都不明確，遑論是預知未來了。

問題是，為什麼有人能看清這一切，掌握到自己要的東西、實現夢想，對自己覺得滿意，別人也羨慕他的幸運；但另一些人卻總是把人生搞得一團糟，常常覺得自己很倒楣呢？

在日本有「潛能開發魔術師」之稱的西田文郎說：「『幸運』是巧合！『好運』則是持續發生的幸運！」他認為：成功的人總覺得自己隨時有好運。在《幸運的人想的都一樣》書中，他提出五個問題供讀者測試幸運指數，包括：「認為自己過往的人生都很幸運」、「覺得現在的自己是個幸運的人」、「自己身邊存在幸運的人」、「認為自己能帶給別人幸運」、「自己正在和幸運的人交往」等。

以上五題，我的答案都是「Yes !」，做完問卷的那一刻，我真是惜福感恩！

並非我的人生沒有挫敗與波折，而是我深深相信：**所有的挫敗與波折，都能讓**

我學習成長，獲得寶貴的經驗教訓，帶給我更多幸運，甚至是持續的好運。

所以我提出：「開運之前，要先開心！」的主張。這裡所指的「開心」是雙關語，包括英文的「Open your mind」以及「Be happy」，當然也可以連起來說：**「打開心胸，讓自己快樂，好運就會跟著來！」**我衷心地渴望，能分享自己的「好運」，也把「好運」帶給別人，所以出版了《開運之前，先開心！》。這本書的邏輯架構非常簡單，卻是我累積數十年經驗及觀察而提出的獨創主張。

許多激勵大師都提出「正向思考」的觀念，認為這會帶來成功的力量。道理人人都懂，但很少有人留意到，一般人的思考方式都是被當下的情緒牽著鼻子走。換句話說，情緒不好的時候，就很難正向思考。《開運之前，先開心！》則主張從心靈的運作開始練習，**先學會管理情緒，維持好心情，再接通「正向思考」的電力，持續營造好運的磁場，吸引更多好事靠近。**

站在作者的立場，我當然不希望讀者把它當作「魔法書」，但我卻不能否認它的確具備魔法的力量，只要你相信、並且認真去實行，一定可以改變你的人生，為自己、為家人、甚至為這個亟需平靜的世界，帶來更多好運。

告別不順心，開啟人生新頁

非常感謝我的好友Tiffany老師，發揮俠女精神拔刀相助，在本書中以專業命理觀點，提供讀者簡單、實用的開運方法。她是我在媒體界認識的命理專家，精通星座分析、測字、塔羅牌占卜、紫微命盤、風水等，每週一都會在我主持的廣播節目（中廣流行網「媒事來哈啦」，週一～週六下午四點～五點）擔任固定嘉賓，以心靈導師的角色，輔以她對命理的專長，傾聽聽眾的心聲，並協助分析解答，深受上班族、青少年及其父母信任，也增進了親子關係的互動。

很高興Tiffany老師應允、並在百忙中回答命理問題，讓我的第七十七號作品，有了不同的風貌與內容。也希望翻開這本書的你，就猶如打開內心通往靈性道路的大門，從此告別過去所有的不順心，每翻閱一頁就往前多走一步，永遠都有好運隨行。

吳若權給你的 創作獻禮

幸福主張

《劈腿心理學》《男人心，迴紋針》《每段感情，都是幸福的記號》《懂得付出，才會幸福！》《因為不一樣，愛得更堅強！》《 戀家，才會戀愛！》《愛過流星》《愛情左岸》《選擇幸福，其實你可以》《抓住你要的幸福》（時報）《新 LOVE 學—多點理性，更浪漫》《鰻魚的願望》（圓神）《因為你，幸福近在一釐米》《愛在魚水交歡時》《愛得更簡單！》《你就是我的 100 分》《誰能讓男人付出真心》《愛來愛去》（方智）《哪個男人不偷心》《多情男人愛流浪》《愛要有點乖有點壞》（皇冠）《愛情只是極短篇》（元尊）《愛戀 e 世紀，因為有你》（時報，絕版）

勵志泉源

《開運之前， 先開心！》《從草莓變荔枝》《好人，也該擁有好人生》《培養感性的能力》《幸福月光》《打造自己的幸福》（時報）《遇見你，我更懂自己！》《發現謙卑的力量》《甘露與淨瓶的對話——聖嚴法師開示，吳若權修行筆記》（圓神）《更愛明天的自己》《尋尋 MeMe，贏得自己》《開拓生命的寬度》《創造自己的價值》《站在有光的地方》《栽培自己》《過得好，因為我值得》《明天永遠值得盼望》《上班何必受委屈》（方智）《自己打造金湯匙》《其實，我這麼努力》（天下）《原我》（希代）《媒事來哈啦》（富邦文教）《啟動心靈程式》（時報，絕版）《活出生命能量》（時報，絕版）

心靈點滴

《起飛之前，先學降落》《最簡單的，最難得！》《擁抱幸福的自己》（圓神）

影音饗宴

《3 個夏天》《冬季到台北來看雨》《蛋糕核桃燒》《畢業旅行》《摘星》（圓神）

小說長廊

《下雨天裡的松風聲》（時報）《寧願，愛短短的就好！》《歡唱悲歌》《愛過，總比沒愛好！》（圓神）《你知不知道我好愛你》（方智）《愛情，最幸福的信仰》《好想打開愛情箱子》《愛一次也好》（皇冠）《愛是一生的功課》（希代，絕版）《超人氣戀愛講座》（幼獅）

企管智囊

《衝出人生好業績》（先覺）《你可以賣得更好》《行銷的 20 種玩法》（遠流）《點行銷的燈》《摘行銷的星》《開行銷的窗》（哈佛企管）《管理心主張》《行銷金配方》（商周）《讓你更有 Mail 力》（博碩，與林宏諭博士合著）

音樂映象

「3 個夏天」「戀雨」「幸福相隨」「愛你， 是我的權利！」「來去自如」「冬季到台北來看雨」「愛得越久越寂寞」「久別重逢」「我的心停不下來」「雨過心晴」「聽風的歌」等數十首歌詞寫作；以及「漂浮咖啡館」專輯

吳若權與你的 幸福交集

專業的交集

畢業於政大企管系的吳若權，曾經任職於 IBM、HP（惠普）、UFO、Microsoft（台灣微軟）等公司，是資訊界極受信賴的資深行銷企劃主管，曾負責HP電腦工作站、Microsoft Windows及Microsoft Office電腦軟體等行銷專案，為台灣資訊科技業提出許多創新的行銷企劃構想，成為業界標竿。

創作的交集

吳若權多年來積極投入各種形式的文字創作，包括歌詞、散文、小說及行銷管理書籍，已經出版七十七本著作，經常榮登各大暢銷書店排行榜，更連續十年被金石堂書店評選為台灣最暢銷作家之一。小說作品《摘星》除改編為網路動畫影片，更改拍成電視連續劇。

媒體的交集

吳若權曾主持許多廣播〈中廣、飛碟、台北之音〉與電視節目〈中視衛星、三立都會台、中天娛樂台等〉，目前則應富邦文教基金會之邀，主持中廣流行網「媒事來哈啦」節目，樂於與聽眾、觀眾分享人生不同階段的心靈成長，成為大家眼中的生活導師。他同時也是商業機構及公益團體的最佳代言人，拍過「預防老人失智症」「陽光基金會關懷顏面傷殘」「門諾醫院長青社區」「Daikin日本大金空調冷氣」「寶島眼鏡」等廣告。

網路的交集

在網路上，你也可以遇見吳若權：

吳若權時報出版官方網站「若是有緣」
http://www.readingtimes.com.tw/TimesHtml/authors/ericwu/

個人網誌「吳若權@若有所思」：
http://www.wretch.cc/blog/eric599

吳若權的開運心魔法

Book Collection of Eric

【抓住你要的幸福】定價◎二二〇元

幸福是一顆夢想的種子，需要用生命的熱情去灌溉。幸福不是靠別人給的，而是要認真抓住，用心選擇。看吳若權以成長角度剖析男人與女人、愛與性、婚姻與外遇、生活與事業，告訴你如何「用心生活認真愛」，創造自己的幸福。

【下雨天裡的松風聲】定價◎二二〇元

榮獲中興文藝獎章小說獎

在愛情旅程中，我們會以優美的姿勢滑翔，通往幸福的方向。聽吳若權訴說十個都會男女的愛戀故事，品味記憶中最美好的重逢，詠嘆縈縈不忘的戀情。

【選擇幸福，其實你可以】定價◎二二〇元

幸福，是一種理性的選擇，而不全然是感性的追求。選擇幸福，需要溫柔的智慧，更需要積極的勇氣與行動力。走進吳若權為你搭建的幸福轉運站，選擇實現幸福的出口，為自己的愛情選擇題圈選最美麗的答案。

【打造自己的幸福】定價◎二三〇元

成就自己的關鍵，取決於你和別人相處的方式；擁有均衡的人際關係，才能和幸福的自己相遇。吳若權邀你重新學習成就自己的祕訣、和別人相處的方法，讓自己成為懂得幸福的人，再邀請有共同理想的人一起打造美麗人生。

【愛情左岸】定價◎二二〇元

愛情，是兩個人之間最深奧的相對論。愛情，不是單純讓對方屬於自己的過程，我們必須在這個過程中，發現自己。吳若權的叮嚀與祝福，將引領你隔著合適的距離，用著寬容的心情，找到向真愛靠近的方法，學習與幸福溝通的言語。

【愛過流星】定價◎二二〇元

愛像流星，每一個愛過的人，每一段付出過的感情，都是生命夜空中耀眼的流星，劃下你曾用心尋覓幸福的軌跡。吳若權帶領你在別人的經驗中、在自己的體悟裡，培養幸福的習慣，在愛情星圖上找到最明亮的方向。

【幸福月光】定價◎二二〇元

人生有許多缺口，並不減損幸福。只要懂得用愛填補，日子依然圓滿。吳若權以纖細柔軟的創作情懷，訴說自己面對的成長與挫折、感傷與喜慰、相聚與離別，與你分享在人世流轉間探索幸福真相的知遇感受。

【戀家，才會戀愛！】定價◎二二〇元

戀家的人，懂得以幸福相待，談好戀愛。能享受於對家負責的愉快，才會陶醉於為愛付出的慷慨。吳若權從真愛滋養、自我成長、親情互動到生命課題，與你激盪幸福的靈感，守護戀家的溫柔情懷、累積戀愛的厚實能量。

【因為不一樣，愛得更堅強！】定價◎二三〇元

瞭解你，讓我開闊了自己；接納彼此的不同，拓展幸福的交集。吳若權解析兩性思緒和互動的差異、傳遞男人和女人對彼此的期望，願每對戀侶都能透過溝通協調，獲得圓滿的聯集，讓愛情的視野更遼闊，讓一生的幸福更堅定。

【培養感性的能力】定價◎二三〇元

「知識就是力量」還不夠，感性，才能為你提升競爭力！善用感性的力量，可以豐富人生，讓你活出獨特的自己，也樂於把幸福分享出去。吳若權透過生活中的體悟，陪你展開心靈練習，以激發感性的潛能、拓展幸福的空間。

【懂得付出，才會幸福！】定價◎二三〇元

施比受更有福？付出的過程就是享受？你願意給的，必須正好是對方需要的，在付出與獲得之間永遠保持動態的平衡，相愛的兩人才能航向幸福的遠方。吳若權陪你鍛鍊感情的品質，把握相愛的時機、學習對等的付出。

【每段感情，都是幸福的記號】定價◎二三〇元

收藏感情中留下的各種記號，戀情濃烈時，可以和所愛分享彼此的真誠；揮手道別後也能心存感謝，將相愛的記憶化為智慧。吳若權引領你辨識幸福的指標，成為自己生命的嚮導，懷抱著愛人如己的真心，朝恆久的美好邁進。

【好人，也該擁有好人生】定價◎二三〇元

小人常得意；好人難出頭？只要把握原則、充滿自信，懂得對別人付出、也知道成就自我，就能開心自在地做好人。吳若權傳授你「做好人；防小人」的撇步，提點你不景氣時代的成功妙招，幫助善良的好人一吐怨氣！

【男人心，迴紋針】定價◎二三〇元

男人心是迴紋針。看似迂迴，打直了就是一根腸子通到底。了解它的基本功能，能折成一顆愛心；善用它的附加價值，可以創造一輩子的幸福。吳若權解析看似迂迴剛強、實則坦率柔軟的男人心，讓女人與男人以愛彼此激勵。

【從草莓變荔枝】定價◎二五〇元

【真誠推薦】曲家瑞・邱文仁・李偉文・周行一・徐璐・劉鳳珍・鄭家鐘

吳若權結合企管顧問的專業經驗，以及與年輕朋友的互動體會，提出懇切而具前瞻性的工作建議與生涯指引，鼓勵你鎖定夢想的方向，在職場上從起步就領先！

【劈腿心理學】定價◎二五〇元

只想專注一份愛？請先學會洞悉人性的祕密……史上最精闢的劈腿學說，吳若權藉由理性分析、敏銳觀察和感性的愛情故事，精準解析劈腿與外遇的成因、預防、處理與療癒，幫助你改善相愛的品質，學會捍衛自己的幸福主權！

吳若權作品集⑳

開運之前，先開心！——吸引好運上門的快樂秘密

作　者—吳若權
主　編—郭玢玢
編輯協力—鍾孟育
插　畫—JUN
美術編輯—優秀視覺設計、周家瑤
專案企劃—艾青荷
校　對—吳若權、郭玢玢、鍾孟育
董事長
發行人—孫思照
總經理—莫昭平
總編輯—林馨琴
出版者—時報文化出版企業股份有限公司
台北市10803和平西路三段二四〇號三樓
發行專線—（〇二）二三〇六—六八四二
讀者服務專線—〇八〇〇—二三一—七〇五・（〇二）二三〇四—七一〇三
讀者服務傳眞—（〇二）二三〇四—六八五八
郵撥—一九三四四七二四　時報文化出版公司
信箱—台北郵政七九～九九信箱
時報悅讀網—http://www.readingtimes.com.tw
電子郵件信箱—ctliving@readingtimes.com.tw
法律顧問—理律法律事務所　陳長文、李念祖律師
印　刷—盈昌印刷有限公司
初版一刷—二〇〇八年十二月一日
定　價—新台幣二六〇元
⊙行政院新聞局局版北市業字第八〇號

國家圖書館出版品預行編目資料

開運之前，先開心！/ 吳若權著. -- 初版. --
臺北市：時報文化, 2008.12
面；公分. -- (吳若權作品集；20)

ISBN 978-957-13-4956-5(平裝)

855　97021330

ISBN：978-957-13-4956-5
Printed in Taiwan

編號：CR0020	書名：開運之前，先開心！
姓名：	性別：____ 1.男 2.女
出生日期： 年 月 日	連絡電話：

____ 學歷：1.小學 2.國中 3.高中 4.大專 5.研究所（含以上）

____ 職業：1.學生 2.公務（含軍警） 3.家管 4.服務 5.金融 6.製造 7.資訊 8.大眾傳播 9.自由業 10.農漁牧 11.退休 12.其他

通訊地址：□□□ ____ 縣（市）____ 鄉鎮區 ____ 村 ____ 里

____ 鄰 ____ 路（街）____ 段 ____ 巷 ____ 弄 ____ 號 ____ 樓

E-mail address：____

（下列資料請以數字填在每題前之空格處）

____ 購書地點
1.書店 2.書展 3.書報攤 4.郵購 5.網路 6.直銷 7.贈閱 8.其他 ____

____ 您從哪裡得知本書
1.書店 2.報紙廣告 3.報紙專欄 4.雜誌廣告 5.網路資訊
6.親友介紹 7.DM廣告傳單 8.其他 ____

____ 您希望我們為您出版哪一類的作品
1.心理 2.勵志 3.成長 4.潛能 5.知識 6.其他 ____

您對本書的意見
____ 內容 1.滿意 2.尚可 3.應改進
____ 編輯 1.滿意 2.尚可 3.應改進
____ 封面設計 1.滿意 2.尚可 3.應改進
____ 校對 1.滿意 2.尚可 3.應改進
____ 定價 1.偏低 2.適中 3.偏高

您的建議

請沿虛線撕下後對折裝訂寄回，謝謝！

請沿虛線摺下裝訂，謝謝！

廣告回郵
北區郵政管理局登記證北台字2218號
免貼郵票

時報出版
CHINA TIMES PUBLISHING COMPANY
尊重智慧與創意的文化事業

地址：台北市108和平西路三段240號2F
電話：（0800）231-705（讀者免費服務專線）
（02）2306-6842·2304-7103（讀者服務中心）
郵撥：19344724時報出版公司

請寄回這張服務卡（免貼郵票） 您可以——
- ●隨時收到最新消息。
- ●參加專為您設計的各項回饋優惠活動 。

我們非常重視您對本書的意見，
請踴躍寄回本卡，將可獲得吳若權的最新出版訊息。

吳若權 作品集

讓吳若權的文字，
陪你品嚐幸福的滋味，發現生命的光華。

Eric Wu